TO THE LOR███████N I TU████

When the Esse███ ████ms from the heavens, this strangely-fo███ will be many feastings for me. Safety and assured essence are mine. O boon at last granted! To the Lord of the Heaven I turn all thought! Lad-nar's essence is yours at ending!

The thing rose nine feet on powerfully-muscled legs; it had a sheened, glistening fur. It resembled a gorilla and a Brahma bull and a Kodiak bear and a number of other Terran animals, but it was none of them. . . . Kettridge half-turned. He saw one of the thing's huge paws crashing toward him. The brief moment ended and Kettridge lay unconscious. . . .

Lad-nar looked over one massive shoulder at the sky.

Even as he watched, the roiling dark clouds split and a forked brilliance stabbed down at the jungle. Lad-nar squinted his eyes, unconsciously lowering the thin secondary lids over them, filtering out the worst of the light.

He shivered as the roar screamed across the sky.

He shoved the man under one furry arm, clasping his unconscious burden tightly. Lad-nar's eyes were frightened. He knew the time of death and forbidden walking was at hand.

—From BLIND LIGHTNING
by Harlan Ellison

STARHUNTERS: VOL. II

created by

DAVID DRAKE

THINGS HUNTING MEN

BAEN BOOKS

THINGS HUNTING MEN

This is a work of fiction. All the characters and events portrayed
in this book are fictional, and any resemblance to real people
or incidents is purely coincidental.

A Baen Books Original

Baen Publishing Enterprises
260 Fifth Avenue
New York, N.Y. 10001

First printing, June 1988

ISBN: 0-671-65412-8

Cover art by Pat Ortega

Printed in the United States of America

Distributed by
SIMON & SCHUSTER
1230 Avenue of the Americas
New York, N.Y. 10020

DEDICATION

To Dan Breen
Because he's a helpful friend
And because it's nice to know
somebody who's able to run
a bookstore as a business.

CONTENTS

             Introductions by David Drake

Acknowledgments

Among the people whose help was crucial on this one are Jim Baen; Jerry Page; the Miesel clan; the Coulsons; Richard Minter; Forry Ackerman; Harlan Ellison; Marcia Decker; Charles Waugh; Marty Greenberg; and with particular emphasis, Karl Wagner.

I was thirteen when I read my first Theodore Sturgeon story: "Thunder and Roses." It scared the hell out of me.

Twenty-five years later, I had occasion to reread "Thunder and Roses." It still scared the hell out of me.

Sturgeon had a remarkable talent for turning a standard SF situation into something unique—and uniquely memorable—through the depth of his characterizations. He must have cared very deeply about his characters in order to sketch them so believably, lovable for their faults as surely as for their skills and excellence.

That's why it was so shocking when Sturgeon brought his characters to horrible ends, as he often did.

Permitted them to come to horrible ends, I should rather say, because the tragedy is never gratuitous. It flows from the events of the story. It stays in memory because, when you think back on it, that's the only way the particular set of events could be expected to turn out.

"It" was the second Sturgeon story I read. I cared as much about the plight of a little farming family as I had for the doomed half-world of "Thunder and Roses."

And "It" scared the hell out of me, too.

IT

Theodore Sturgeon

It walked in the woods.

It was never born. It existed. Under the pine needles the fires burn, deep and smokeless in the mold. In heat and in darkness and decay there is growth. There is life and there is growth. It grew, but it was not alive. It walked unbreathing through the woods, and thought and saw and was hideous and strong, and it was not born and it did not live. It grew and moved about without living.

It crawled out of the darkness and hot damp mold into the cool of a morning. It was huge. It was lumped and crusted with its own hateful substances, and pieces of it dropped off as it went its way, dropped off and lay writhing, and stilled, and sank putrescent into the forest loam.

It had no mercy, no laughter, no beauty. It had strength and great intelligence. And—perhaps it could not be destroyed. It crawled out of its mound in the wood and lay pulsing in the sunlight for a long moment. Patches of it shone wetly in the golden glow, parts of it

were nubbled and flaked. And whose dead bones had
given it the form of a man?

It scrabbled painfully with its half-formed hands, beat-
ing the ground and the bole of a tree. It rolled and
lifted itself up on its crumbling elbows, and it tore up a
great handful of herbs and shredded them against its
chest, and it paused and gazed at the gray-green juices
with intelligent calm. It wavered to its feet, and seized
a young sapling and destroyed it, folding the slender
trunk back on itself again and again, watching atten-
tively the useless, fibered splinters. And it snatched up
a fear-frozen field-creature, crushing it slowly, letting
blood and pulpy flesh and fur ooze from between its
fingers, run down and rot on the forearms.

It began searching.

Kimbo drifted through the tall grasses like a puff of
dust, his bushy tail curled tightly over his back and his
long jaws agape. He ran with an easy lope, loving his
freedom and the power of his flanks and furry shoulders. His tongue lolled listlessly over his lips. His lips
were black and serrated, and each tiny pointed liplet
swayed with his doggy gallop. Kimbo was all dog, all
healthy animal.

He leaped high over a boulder and landed with a
startled yelp as a longeared cony shot from its hiding
place under the rock. Kimbo hurtled after it, grunting
with each great thrust of his legs. The rabbit bounced
just ahead of him, keeping its distance, its ears flattened on its curving back and its little legs nibbling
away at distance hungrily. It stopped, and Kimbo
pounced, and the rabbit shot away at a tangent and
popped into a hollow log. Kimbo yelped again and
rushed snuffling at the log, and knowing his failure,
curvetted but once around the stump and ran on into
the forest. The thing that watched from the wood raised
its crusted arms and waited for Kimbo.

Kimbo sensed it there, standing dead-still by the

path. To him it was a bulk which smelled of carrion not fit to roll in, and he snuffled distastefully and ran to pass it.

The thing let him come abreast and dropped a heavy twisted fist on him. Kimbo saw it coming and curled up tight as he ran, and the hand clipped stunningly on his rump, sending him rolling and yipping down the slope. Kimbo straddled to his feet, shook his head, shook his body with a deep growl, came back to the silent thing with green murder in his eyes. He walked stiffly, straight-legged, his tail as low as his lowered head and a ruff of fury round his neck. The thing raised its arms again, waited.

Kimbo slowed, then flipped himself through the air at the monster's throat. His jaws closed on it; his teeth clicked together through a mass of filth, and he fell choking and snarling at its feet. The thing leaned down and struck twice, and after the dog's back was broken, it sat beside him and began to tear him apart.

"Be back in an hour or so," said Alton Drew, picking up his rifle from the corner behind the wood box. His brother laughed.

"Old Kimbo 'bout runs your life, Alton," he said.

"Ah, I know the ol' devil," said Alton. "When I whistle for him for half an hour and he don't show up, he's in a jam or he's treed something wuth shootin' at. The ol' son of a gun calls me by not answerin'."

Cory Drew shoved a full glass of milk over to his nine-year-old daughter and smiled. "You think as much o' that houn' dog o' yours as I do of Babe here."

Babe slid off her chair and ran to her uncle. "Gonna catch me the bad fella, Uncle Alton?" she shrilled. The "bad fella" was Cory's invention—the one who lurked in corners ready to pounce on little girls who chased the chickens and played around mowing machines and hurled green apples with a powerful young arm at the sides of the hogs, to hear the synchronized thud and grunt;

little girls who swore with an Austrian accent like an ex-hired man they had had; who dug caves in haystacks till they tipped over, and kept pet crawfish in tomorrow's milk cans, and rode work horses to a lather in the night pasture.

"Get back here and keep away from Uncle Alton's gun!" said Cory. "If you see the bad fella, Alton, chase him back here. He has a date with Babe here for that stunt of hers last night." The preceding evening, Babe had kind-heartedly poured pepper on the cows' salt block.

"Don't worry, kiddo," grinned her uncle, "I'll bring you the bad fella's hide if he don't get me first."

Alton Drew walked up the path toward the wood, thinking about Babe. She was a phenomenon—a pampered farm child. Ah well—she had to be. They'd both loved Clissa Drew, and she'd married Cory, and they had to love Clissa's child. Funny thing, love. Alton was a man's man, and thought things out that way; and his reaction to love was a strong and frightened one. He knew what love was because he felt it still for his brother's wife and would feel it as long as he lived for Babe. It led him through his life, and yet he embarrassed himself by thinking of it. Loving a dog was an easy thing, because you and the old devil could love one another completely without talking about it. The smell of gun smoke and wet fur in the rain were perfume enough for Alton Drew, a grunt of satisfaction and the scream of something hunted and hit were poetry enough. They weren't like love for a human, that choked his throat so he could not say words he could not have thought of anyway. So Alton loved his dog Kimbo and his Winchester for all to see, and let his love for his brother's women, Clissa and Babe, eat at him quietly and unmentioned.

His quick eyes saw the flesh indentations in the soft earth behind the boulder, which showed where Kimbo had turned and leaped with a single surge, chasing the rabbit. Ignoring the tracks, he looked for the nearest place where a rabbit might hide, and strolled over to the stump. Kimbo had been there, he saw, and had been there too late. "You're an ol' fool," muttered Alton. "Y' can't catch a cony by chasin' it. You want to cross him up some way." He gave a peculiar trilling whistle, sure that Kimbo was digging frantically under some nearby stump for a rabbit that was three counties away by now. No answer. A little puzzled, Alton went back to the path. "He never done this before," he said softly.

He cocked his .32-40 and cradled it. At the county fair someone had once said of Alton Drew that he could shoot at a handful of corn and peas thrown in the air and hit only the corn. Once he split a bullet on the blade of a knife and put two candles out. He had no need to fear anything that could be shot at. That's what he believed.

The thing in the woods looked curiously down at what it had done to Kimbo, and tried to moan the way Kimbo had before he died. It stood a minute storing away facts in its foul, unemotional mind. Blood was warm. The sunlight was warm. Things that moved and bore fur had a muscle to force the thick liquid through tiny tubes in their bodies. The liquid coagulated after a time. The liquid on rooted green things was thinner and the loss of a limb did not mean loss of life. It was very interesting, but the thing, the mold with a mind, was not pleased. Neither was it displeased. Its accidental urge was a thirst for knowledge, and it was only— interested.

It was growing late, and the sun reddened and rested awhile on the hilly horizon, teaching the clouds to be inverted flames. The thing threw up its head suddenly, noticing the dusk. Night was ever a strange thing, even for those of us who have known it in life. It would have

been frightening for the monster had it been capable of
fright, but it could only be curious; it could only reason
from what it had observed.

What was happening? It was getting harder to see.
Why? It threw its shapeless head from side to side. It
was true—things were dim, and growing dimmer. Things
were changing shape, taking on a new and darker color.
What did the creatures it had crushed and torn apart
see? How did they see? The larger one, the one that
had attacked, had used two organs in its head. That
must have been it, because after the thing had torn off
two of the dog's legs it had struck at the hairy muzzle;
and the dog, seeing the blow coming, had dropped
folds of skin over the organs—closed its eyes. Ergo,
the dog saw with its eyes. But then after the dog was
dead, and its body still, repeated blows had had no
effect on the eyes. They remained open and staring.
The logical conclusion was, then, that a being that had
ceased to live and breathe and move about lost the use
of its eyes. It must be that to lose sight was, conversely,
to die. Dead things did not walk about. They lay down
and did not move. Therefore the thing in the wood
concluded that it must be dead, and so it lay down by
the path, not far away from Kimbo's scattered body,
lay down and believed itself dead.

Alton Drew came up through the dusk to the wood.
He was frankly worried. He whistled again, and then
called, and there was still no response, and he said
again, "The ol' flea-bus never done this before," and
shook his heavy head. It was past milking time, and
Cory would need him. "Kimbo!" he roared. The cry
echoed through the shadows, and Alton flipped on the
safety catch of his rifle and put the butt on the ground
beside the path. Leaning on it, he took off his cap and
scratched the back of his head, wondering. The rifle
butt sank into what he thought was soft earth; he staggered and stepped into the chest of the thing that lay

beside the path. His foot went up to the ankle in its yielding rottenness, and he swore and jumped back.

"*Whew!* Somp'n sure dead as hell there! Ugh!" He swabbed at his boot with a handful of leaves while the monster lay in the growing blackness with the edges of the deep footprint in its chest sliding into it, filling it up. It lay there regarding him dimly out of its muddy eyes, thinking it was dead because of the darkness, watching the articulation of Alton Drew's joints, wondering at this new uncautious creature.

Alton cleaned the butt of his gun with more leaves and went on up the path, whistling anxiously for Kimbo.

Clissa Drew stood in the door of the milk shed, very lovely in red-checkered gingham and a blue apron. Her hair was a clean yellow, parted in the middle and stretched tautly back to a heavy braided knot. "Cory! Alton!" she called a little sharply.

"Well?" Cory responded gruffly from the barn, where he was stripping off the Ayrshire. The dwindling streams of milk plopped pleasantly into the froth of a full pail.

"I've called and called," said Clissa. "Supper's cold, and Babe won't eat until you come. Why—where's Alton?"

Cory grunted, heaved the stool out of the way, threw over the stanchion lock and slapped the Ayrshire on the rump. The cow backed and filled like a towboat, clattered down the line and out into the barn-yard. "Ain't back yet."

"Not back?" Clissa came in and stood beside him as he sat by the next cow, put his forehead against the warm flank. "But, Cory, he said he'd—"

"Yeh, yeh, I know. He said he'd be back fer the milkin'. I heard him. Well, he ain't."

"And you have to— Oh, Cory, I'll help you finish up. Alton would be back if he could. Maybe he's—"

"Maybe he's treed a blue jay," snapped her husband. "Him an' that damn dog." He gestured hugely with one hand while the other went on milking. "I got twenty-six head o' cows to milk. I got pigs to feed an' chickens to put to bed, I got to toss hay for the mare and turn the team out. I got harness to mend and a wire down in the night pasture. I got wood to split an' carry." He milked for a moment in silence, chewing on his lip. Clissa stood twisting her hands together, trying to think of something to stem the tide. It wasn't the first time Alton's hunting had interfered with the chores. "So I got to go ahead with it. I can't interfere with Alton's spoorin'. Every damn time that hound o' his smells out a squirrel I go without my supper. I'm gettin' sick and—"

"Oh, I'll help you!" said Clissa. She was thinking of the spring, when Kimbo had held four hundred pounds of raging black bear at bay until Alton could put a bullet in its brain, the time Babe had found a bearcub and started to carry it home, and had fallen into a freshet, cutting her head. You can't hate a dog that has saved your child for you, she thought.

"You'll do nothin' of the kind!" Cory growled. "Get back to the house. You'll find work enough there. I'll be along when I can. Dammit, Clissa, don't cry! I didn't mean to—Oh, shucks!" He got up and put his arms around her. "I'm wrought up," he said. "Go on now. I'd no call to speak that way to you. I'm sorry. Go back to Babe. I'll put a stop to this for good tonight. I've had enough. There's work here for four farmers an' all we've got is me an' that . . . that huntsman.

"Go on now, Clissa."

"All right," she said into his shoulder. "But, Cory, hear him out first when he comes back. He might be unable to come back. He might be unable to come back this time. Maybe he . . . he—"

"Ain't nothin' kin hurt my brother that a bullet will hit. He can take care of himself. He's got no excuse good enough this time. Go on, now. Make the kid eat."

Clissa went back to the house, her young face furrowed. If Cory quarreled with Alton now and drove him away, what with the drought and the creamery about to close and all, they just couldn't manage. Hiring a man was out of the question. Cory'd have to work himself to death, and he just wouldn't be able to make it. No one man could. She sighed and went into the house. It was seven o'clock, and the milking not done yet. Oh, why did Alton have to—

Babe was in bed at nine when Clissa heard Cory in the shed, slinging the wire cutters into a corner. "Alton back yet?" they both said at once as Cory stepped into the kitchen; and as she shook her head he clumped over to the stove, and lifting a lid, spat into the coals. "Come to bed," he said.

She laid down her stitching and looked at his broad back. He was twenty-eight, and he walked and acted like a man ten years older, and looked like a man five years younger. "I'll be up in a while," Clissa said.

Cory glanced at the corner behind the wood box where Alton's rifle usually stood, then made an unspellable, disgusted sound and sat down to take off his heavy muddy shoes.

"It's after nine," Clissa volunteered timidly. Cory said nothing, reaching for house slippers.

"Cory, you're not going to—"

"Not going to what?"

"Oh, nothing. I just thought that maybe Alton—"

"Alton," Cory flared. "The dog goes hunting field mice. Alton goes hunting the dog. Now you want me to go hunting Alton. That's what you want?"

"I just—He was never this late before."

"I won't do it! Go out lookin' for him at nine o'clock in the night? I'll be damned! He has no call to use us so, Clissa."

Clissa said nothing. She went to the stove, peered into the wash boiler, set aside at the back of the range. When she turned around, Cory had his shoes and coat on again.

"I knew you'd go," she said. Her voice smiled though she did not.

"I'll be back durned soon," said Cory. "I don't reckon he's strayed far. It is late. I ain't feared for him, but—" He broke his 12-gauge shotgun, looked through the barrels, slipped two shells in the breech and a box of them into his pocket. "Don't wait up," he said over his shoulder as he went out.

"I won't," Clissa replied to the closed door, and went back to her stitching by the lamp.

The path up the slope to the wood was very dark when Cory went up it, peering and calling. The air was chill and quiet, and a fetid odor of mold hung in it. Cory blew the taste of it out through impatient nostrils, drew it in again with the next breath, and swore. "Nonsense," he muttered. "Houn' dawg. Huntin', at ten in th' night, too. Alton!" he bellowed. "Alton Drew!" Echoes answered him, and he entered the wood. The huddled thing he passed in the dark heard him and felt the vibrations of his footsteps and did not move because it thought it was dead.

Cory strode on, looking around and ahead and not down since his feet knew the path.

"Alton!"

"That you, Cory?"

Cory Drew froze. That corner of the wood was thickly set and as dark as a burial vault. The voice he heard was choked, quiet, penetrating.

"Alton?"

"I found Kimbo, Cory."

"Where the hell have you been?" shouted Cory furiously. He disliked this pitch-darkness; he was afraid at the tense hopelessness of Alton's voice, and he mistrusted his ability to stay angry at his brother.

"I called him, Cory. I whistled at him, an' the ol' devil didn't answer."

"I can say the same for you, you . . . you louse. Why

weren't you to milkin'? Where are you? You caught in a trap?"

"The houn' never missed answerin' me before, you know," said the tight, monotonous voice from the darkness.

"Alton! What the devil's the matter with you? What do I care if your mutt didn't answer? Where—"

"I guess because he ain't never died before," said Alton, refusing to be interrupted.

"You *what*?" Cory clicked his lips together twice and then said, "Alton, you turned crazy? What's that you say?"

"Kimbo's dead."

"Kim . . . oh! Oh!" Cory was seeing that picture again in his mind— Babe sprawled unconscious in the fresh-et, and Kimbo raging and snapping against a monster bear, holding her back until Alton could get there, "What happened, Alton?" he asked more quietly.

"I aim to find out. Someone tore him up."

"*Tore him up?*"

"There ain't a bit of him left tacked together, Cory. Every damn joint in his body tore apart. Guts out of him."

"Good God! Bear, you reckon?"

"No bear, nor nothin' on four legs. He's all here. None of him's been et. Whoever done it just killed him an'—tore him up."

"'Good God!" Cory said again. "Who could've—" There was a long silence, then. "Come 'long home," he said almost gently. "There's no call for you to set up by him all night."

"I'll set. I aim to be here at sunup, an' I'm going to start trackin', an' I'm goin' to keep trackin' till I find the one done this job on Kimbo."

"You're drunk or crazy, Alton."

"I ain't drunk. You can think what you like about the rest of it. I'm stickin' here."

"We got a farm back yonder. Remember? I ain't

going to milk twenty-six head o' cows again in the mornin' like I did jest now, Alton."

"Somebody's got to. I can't be there. I guess you'll just have to, Cory."

"You dirty scum!" Cory screamed. "You'll come back with me now or I'll know why!"

Alton's voice was still tight, half-sleepy. "Don't you come no nearer, bud."

Cory kept moving toward Alton's voice.

"I said"—the voice was very quiet now—"*stop where you are.*" Cory kept coming. A sharp click told of the release of the .32-40's safety. Cory stopped.

"You got your gun on me, Alton?" Cory whispered.

"Thass right, bud. You ain't a-trompin' up these tracks for me. I need 'em at sunup."

A full minute passed, and the only sound in the blackness was that of Cory's pained breathing. Finally:

"I got my gun, too, Alton. Come home."

"You can't see to shoot me."

"We've even on that."

"We ain't. I know just where you stand, Cory. I been here four hours."

"My gun scatters."

"My gun kills."

Without another word Cory Drew turned on his heel and stamped back to the farm.

Black and liquidescent it lay in the blackness, not alive, not understanding death, believing itself dead. Things that were alive saw and moved about. Things that were not alive could do neither. It rested its muddy gaze on the line of trees at the crest of the rise, and deep within it thoughts trickled wetly. It lay huddled, dividing its newfound facts, dissecting them as it had dissected live things when there was light, comparing, concluding, pigeonholing.

The trees at the top of the slope could just be seen, as their trunks were a fraction of a shade lighter than the dark sky behind them. At length they, too, disappeared, and for a moment sky and trees were a monotone. The thing knew it was dead now, and like many a being before it, it wondered how long it must stay like this. And then the sky beyond the trees grew a little lighter. That was a manifestly impossible occurrence, thought the thing, but it could see it and it must be so. Did dead things live again? That was curious. What about dismembered dead things? It would wait and see.

The sun came hand over hand up a beam of light. A bird somewhere made a high yawning peep, and as an owl killed a shrew, a skunk pounced on another, so that the night shift deaths and those of the day could go on without cessation. Two flowers nodded archly to each other, comparing their pretty clothes. A dragonfly nymph decided it was tired of looking serious and cracked its back open, to crawl out and dry gauzily. The first golden ray sheared down between the trees, through the grasses, passed over the mass in the shadowed bushes. "I am alive again," thought the thing that could not possibly live. "I am alive, for I see clearly." It stood up on its thick legs, up into the golden glow. In a little while the wet flakes that had grown during the night dried in the sun, and when it took its first steps, they cracked off and a small shower of them fell away. It walked up the slope to find Kimbo, to see if he, too, were alive again.

Babe let the sun come into her room by opening her eyes. Uncle Alton was gone—that was the first thing that ran through her head. Dad had come home last night and had shouted at mother for an hour. Alton was plumb crazy. He'd turned a gun on his own brother. If Alton ever came ten feet into Cory's land, Cory would fill him so full of holes, he'd look like a tumbleweed. Alton was lazy, shiftless, selfish, and one or two other things of questionable taste but undoubted vividness.

Babe knew her father. Uncle Alton would never be safe in this county.

She bounced out of bed in the enviable way of the very young, and ran to the window. Cory was trudging down to the night pasture with two bridles over his arm, to get the team. There were kitchen noises from downstairs.

Babe ducked her head in the washbowl and shook off the water like a terrier before she toweled. Trailing clean shirt and dungarees, she went to the head of the stairs, slid into the shirt, and began her morning ritual with the trousers. One step down was a step through the right leg. One more, and she was into the left. Then bouncing step by step on both feet, buttoning one button per step, she reached the bottom fully dressed and ran into the kitchen.

"Didn't Uncle Alton come back a-tall, Mum?"

"Morning, Babe. No, dear." Clissa was too quiet, smiling too much, Babe thought shrewdly. Wasn't happy.

"Where'd he go, Mum?"

"We don't know, Babe. Sit down and eat your breakfast."

"What's a misbegotten, Mum?" Babe asked suddenly. Her mother nearly dropped the dish she was drying. "Babe! You must never say that again!"

"Oh. Well, why is Uncle Alton, then?"

"Why is he what?"

Babe's mouth muscled around an outsize spoonful of oatmeal. "A misbe—"

"Babe!"

"All right, Mum," said Babe with her mouth full. "Well, why?"

"I told Cory not to shout last night," Clissa said half to herself.

"Well, whatever it means, he isn't," said Babe with finality. "Did he go hunting again?"

"He went to look for Kimbo, darling."

"Kimbo? Oh Mummy, is Kimbo gone, too? Didn't he come back either?"

"No dear. Oh, please, Babe, stop asking questions!"

"All right. Where do you think they went?"

"Into the north woods. Be quiet."

Babe gulped away at her breakfast. An idea struck her; and as she thought of it she ate slower and slower, and cast more and more glances at her mother from under the lashes of her tilted eyes. It would be awful if daddy did anything to Uncle Alton. Someone ought to warn him.

Babe was halfway to the woods when Alton's .32-40 sent echoes giggling up and down the valley.

Cory was in the south thirty, riding a cultivator and cussing at the team of grays when he heard the gun. "Hoa," he called to the horses, and sat a moment to listen to the sound. "One-two-three. Four," he counted. "Saw someone, blasted away at him. Had a chance to take aim and give him another, careful. My God!" He threw up the cultivator points and steered the team into the shade of three oaks. He hobbled the gelding with swift tosses of a spare strap, and headed for the woods. "Alton a killer," he murmured, and doubled back to the house for his gun. Clissa was standing just outside the door.

"Get shells!" he snapped and flung into the house. Clissa followed him. He was strapping his hunting knife on before she could get a box off the shelf. "Cory—"

"Hear that gun, did you? Alton's off his nut. He don't waste lead. He shot at someone just then, and he wasn't fixin' to shoot pa'tridges when I saw him last. He was out to get a man. Gimme my gun."

"Cory, Babe—"

"You keep her here. Oh, God, this is a helluva mess. I can't stand much more." Cory ran out the door.

Clissa caught his arm: "Cory I'm trying to tell you. Babe isn't here. I've called, and she isn't here."

Cory's heavy young-old face tautened. "Babe— Where did you last see her?"

"Breakfast." Clissa was crying now.

"She say where she was going?"

"No. She asked a lot of questions about Alton and where he'd gone."

"Did you say?"

Clissa's eyes widened, and she nodded, biting the back of her hand.

"You shouldn't ha' done that, Clissa," he gritted, and ran toward the woods, Clissa looking after him, and in that moment she could have killed herself.

Cory ran with his head up, straining with his legs and lungs and eyes at the long path. He puffed up the slope to the woods, agonized for breath after the forty-five minutes' heavy going. He couldn't even notice the damp smell of mold in the air.

He caught a movement in a thicket to his right, and dropped. Struggling to keep his breath, he crept forward until he could see clearly. There was something in there, all right. Something black, keeping still. Cory relaxed his legs and torso completely to make it easier for his heart to pump some strength back into them, and slowly raised the 12-gauge until it bore on the thing hidden in the thicket.

"Come out!" Cory said when he could speak.

Nothing happened.

"Come out or by God I'll shoot!" rasped Cory.

There was a long moment of silence, and his finger tightened on the trigger.

"You asked for it," he said, and as he fired, the thing leaped sideways into the open, screaming.

It was a thin little man dressed in sepulchral black, and bearing the rosiest baby-face Cory had ever seen. The face was twisted with fright and pain. The man scrambled to his feet and hopped up and down saying over and over, "Oh, my hand. Don't shoot again! Oh, my hand. Don't shoot again!" He stopped after a bit, when Cory had climbed to his feet, and he regarded the farmer out of sad china-blue eyes. "You shot me," he said reproachfully, holding up a little bloody hand. "Oh, my goodness."

Cory said, "Now, who the hell are you?"

The man immediately became hysterical, mouthing such a flood of broken sentences that Cory stepped back a pace and half-raised his gun in self-defense. It seemed to consist mostly of "I lost my papers," and "I didn't do it," and "It was horrible. Horrible. Horrible," and "The dead man," and "Oh, don't shoot again."

Cory tried twice to ask him a question, and then he stepped over and knocked the man down. He lay on the ground writhing and moaning and blubbering and putting his bloody hand to his mouth where Cory had hit him.

"Now what's going on around here?"

The man rolled over and sat up. "I didn't do it!" he sobbed. "I didn't. I was walking along and I heard the gun and I heard some swearing and an awful scream and I went over there and peeped and I saw the dead man and I ran away and you came and I hid and you shot me and—"

"*Shut up!*" The man did, as if a switch had been thrown. "Now," said Cory, pointing along the path, "you say there's a dead man up there?"

The man nodded and began crying in earnest. Cory helped him up. "Follow this path back to my farm-house," he said. "Tell my wife to fix up your hand. *Don't* tell her anything else. And wait there until I come. Hear?"

"Yes. Thank you. Oh, thank you. *Snff.*"

"Go on now." Cory gave him a gentle shove in the right direction and went alone, in cold fear, up the path to the spot where he had found Alton the night before.

He found him here now, too, and Kimbo. Kimbo and Alton had spent several years together in the deepest friendship; they had hunted and fought and slept to-

gether, and the lives they owed each other were finished now. They were dead together.

It was terrible that they died the same way. Cory
Drew was a strong man, but he gasped and fainted
dead away when he saw what the thing of the mold had
done to his brother and his brother's dog.

The little man in black hurried down the path, whim-
pering and holding his injured hand as if he rather
wished he could limp with it. After a while the whimper faded away, and the hurried stride changed to a
walk as the gibbering terror of the last hour receded.
He drew two deep breaths, said: "My goodness!" and
felt almost normal. He bound a linen handkerchief around
his wrist, but the hand kept bleeding. He tried the
elbow, and that made it hurt. So he stuffed the handkerchief back in his pocket and simply waved the hand
stupidly in the air until the blood clotted. He did not
see the great moist horror that clumped along behind
him, although his nostrils crinkled with its foulness.

The monster had three holes close together on his
chest, and one hole in the middle of its slimy forehead.
It had three close-set pits in its back and one on the
back of its head. These marks were where Alton Drew's
bullets had struck and passed through. Half of the
monster's shapeless face was sloughed away, and there
was a deep indentation on its shoulder. This was what
Alton Drew's gun butt had done after he clubbed it and
struck at the thing that would not lie down after he put
his four bullets through it. When these things happened the monster was not hurt or angry. It only wondered why Alton Drew acted that way. Now it followed
the little man without hurrying at all, matching his
stride step by step and dropping little particles of muck
behind it.

The little man went on out of the wood and stood
with his back against a big tree at the forest's edge, and
he thought. Enough had happened to him here. What

good would it do to stay and face a horrible murder inquest, just to continue this silly, vague search? There was supposed to be the ruin of an old, old hunting lodge deep in this wood somewhere, and perhaps it would hold the evidence he wanted. But it was a vague report—vague enough to be forgotten without regret. It would be the height of foolishness to stay for all the hick-town red tape that would follow that ghastly affair back in the wood. Ergo, it would be ridiculous to follow that farmer's advice, to go to his house and wait for him. He would go back to town.

The monster was leaning against the other side of the big tree.

The little man snuffled disgustedly at a sudden over-powering odor of rot. He reached for his handkerchief, fumbled and dropped it. As he bent to pick it up, the monster's arm *whuffed* heavily in the air where his head had been—a blow that would certainly have removed that baby-face protuberance. The man stood up and would have put the handkerchief to his nose had it not been so bloody. The creature behind the tree lifted his arm again just as the little man tossed the handkerchief away and stepped out into the field, heading across country to the distant highway that would take him back to town. The monster pounced on the handkerchief, picked it up, studied it, tore it across several times and inspected the tattered edges. Then it gazed vacantly at the disappearing figure of the little man, and finding him no longer interesting, turned back into the woods.

Babe broke into a trot at the sound of the shots. It was important to warn Uncle Alton about what her father had said, but it was more interesting to find out what he had bagged. Oh, he'd bagged it, all right. Uncle Alton never fired without killing. This was about the first time she had ever heard him blast away like that. Must be a bear, she thought excitedly, tripping over a root, sprawling, rolling to her feet again, without noticing the tumble. She'd love to have another bearskin in her room. Where would she put it? Maybe they could line it and she could have it for a blanket. Uncle Alton could sit on it and read to her in the evening— Oh, no. No. Not with this trouble between him and dad. Oh, if she could only do something! She tried to run faster, worried and anticipating, but she was out of breath and went more slowly instead.

At the top of the rise by the edge of the woods she stopped and looked back. Far down in the valley lay the south thirty. She scanned it carefully, looking for her father. The new furrows and the old were sharply defined, and her keen eyes saw immediately that Cory had left the line with the cultivator and had angled the team over to the shade trees without finishing his row. That wasn't like him. She could see the team now, and Cory's pale-blue denim was nowhere in sight. She giggled lightly to herself as she thought of the way she would fool her father. And the little sound of laughter drowned out, for her, the sound of Alton's hoarse dying scream.

She reached and crossed the path and slid through the brush beside it. The shots came from up around here somewhere. She stopped and listened several times, and then suddenly heard something coming toward her, fast. She ducked under cover, terrified, and a little baby-faced man in black, his blue eyes wide with horror, crashed blindly past her, the leather case he carried catching on the branches. It spun a moment and then fell right in front of her. The man never missed it.

Babe lay there for a long moment and then picked up the case and faded into the woods. Things were happening too fast for her. She wanted Uncle Alton, but she dared not call. She stopped again and strained her ears. Back toward the edge of the wood she heard her father's voice, and another's—probably the man who had dropped the brief case. She dared not go over there. Filled with enjoyable terror, she thought hard, then snapped her fingers in triumph. She and Alton had played Injun many times up here; they had a whole repertoire of secret signals. She had practiced birdcalls until she knew them better than the birds themselves. What would it be? Ah—blue jay. She threw back her head and by some youthful alchemy produced a nerve-shattering screech that would have done justice to any jay that ever flew. She repeated it, and then twice more.

The response was immediate—the call of a blue jay, four times, spaced two and two. Babe nodded to herself happily. That was the signal that they were to meet immediately at The Place. The Place was a hide-out that he had discovered and shared with her, and not another soul knew of it; an angle of rock beside a stream not far away. It wasn't exactly a cave, but almost. Enough so to be entrancing. Babe trotted happily away toward the brook. She had just known that Uncle Alton would remember the call of the blue jay, and what it meant.

In the tree that arched over Alton's scattered body perched a large jay bird, preening itself and shining in the sun. Quite unconscious of the presence of death, hardly noticing the Babe's realistic cry, it screamed again four times, two and two.

It took Cory more than a moment to recover himself from what he had seen. He turned away from it and leaned weakly against a pine, panting. Alton. That was Alton lying there, in—parts.

"God! God, God, God—"

Gradually his strength returned, and he forced himself to turn again. Stepping carefully, he bent and picked up the .32-40. Its barrel was bright and clean, but the butt and stock were smeared with some kind of stinking rottenness. Where had he seen the stuff before? Somewhere—no matter. He cleaned it off absently, throwing the befouled bandana away afterward. Through his mind ran Alton's words—was that only last night?—

*"I'm goin' start trackin'. An' I'm goin' to keep trackin'
till I find the one done this job on Kimbo."*

Cory searched shrinkingly until he found Alton's box
of shells. The box was wet and sticky. That made it—
better, somehow. A bullet wet with Alton's blood was
the right thing to use. He went away a short distance,
circled around till he found heavy footprints, then came
back.

"I'm a-trackin' for you, bud," he whispered thickly,
and began. Through the brush he followed its wavering
spoor, amazed at the amount of filthy mold about,
gradually associating it with the thing that had killed his
brother. There was nothing in the world for him anymore but hate and doggedness. Cursing himself for not
getting Alton home last night, he followed the tracks to
the edge of the woods. They led him to a big tree
there, and there he saw something else—the footprints
of the little city man. Nearby lay some tattered scraps
of linen, and—what was what?

Another set of prints—small ones. Small, stub-toed
ones.

"Babe!"

No answer. The wind sighed. Somewhere a blue jay
called.

Babe stopped and turned when she heard her father's
voice, faint with distance, piercing.

"Listen at him holler," she crooned delightedly. "Gee,
he sounds mad." She sent a jay bird's call disrespect-
fully back to him and hurried to The Place.

It consisted of a mammoth boulder beside the brook.
Some upheaval in the glacial age had cleft it, cutting out
a huge V-shaped chunk. The widest part of the cleft
was at the water's edge, and the narrowest was hidden
by bushes. It made a little ceilingless room, rough and
uneven and full of pot-holes and cavelets inside, and
yet with quite a level floor. The open end was at the
water's edge.

Babe parted the bushes and peered down the cleft. "Uncle Alton!" she called softly. There was no answer. Oh, well, he'd be along. She scrambled in and slid down to the floor.

She loved it here. It was shaded and cool, and the chattering stream filled it with shifting golden lights and laughing gurgles. She called again, on principle, and then perched on an outcropping to wait. It was only then she realized that she still carried the little man's brief case.

She turned it over a couple of times and then opened it. It was divided in the middle by a leather wall. On one side were a few papers in a large yellow envelope, and on the other some sandwiches, a candy bar, and an apple. With a youngster's complacent acceptance of manna from heaven, Babe fell to. She saved one sandwich for Alton, mainly because she didn't like its highly spiced bologna. The rest made quite a feast.

She was a little worried when Alton hadn't arrived, even after she had consumed the apple core. She got up and tried to skim some flat pebbles across the roiling brook, and she stood on her hands, and she tried to think of a story to tell herself, and she tried just waiting. Finally, in desperation, she turned again to the brief case, took out the papers, curled up by the rocky wall and began to read them. It was something to do, anyway.

There was an old newspaper clipping that told about strange wills that people had left. An old lady had once left a lot of money to whoever would make the trip from the Earth to the Moon and back. Another had financed a home for cats whose masters and mistresses had died. A man left thousands of dollars to the first person who could solve a certain mathematical problem and prove his solution. But one item was blue-penciled. It was:

One of the strangest of wills still in force is that of Thaddeus M. Kirk, who died in 1920. It appears that he built an elaborate mausoleum with burial vaults for all the remains of his family. He collected and removed caskets from all over the country to fill the designated niches. Kirk was the last of his line; there were no relatives when he died. His will stated that the mausoleum was to be kept in repair permanently, and that a certain sum set aside as a reward for whoever could produce the body of his grandfather, Roger Kirk, whose niche is still empty. Anyone finding this body is eligible to receive a substantial fortune.

Babe yawned vaguely over this, but kept on reading because there was nothing else to do. Next was a thick sheet of business correspondence, bearing the letterhead of a firm of lawyers. The body of it ran:

In regard to your query regarding the will of Thaddeus Kirk, we are authorized to state that his grandfather was a man about five feet, five inches, whose left arm had been broken and who had a triangular silver plate set into his skull. There is no information as to the whereabouts of his death. He disappeared and was declared legally dead after the lapse of fourteen years.

The amount of the reward as stated in the will, plus accrued interest, now amounts to a fraction over sixty-two thousand dollars. This will be paid to anyone who produces the remains, providing that said remains answer descriptions kept in our private files.

There was more, but Babe was bored. She went on into the little black notebook. There was nothing in it but penciled and highly abbreviated records of visits to libraries; quotations from books with titles like "History of Angelina and Tyler Counties" and "Kirk Family History." Babe threw that aside, too. Where could Uncle Alton be?

She began to sing tunelessly. "Tumalumalum tum, ta ta ta," pretending to dance a minuet with flowing skirts like a girl she had seen in the movies. A rustle of the bushes at the entrance to The Place stopped her. She peeped upward, saw them being thrust aside. Quickly she ran to a tiny cul-de-sac in the rock wall, just big enough for her to hide in. She giggled at the thought of how surprised Uncle Alton would be when she jumped out at him.

She heard the newcomer come shuffling down the steep slope of the crevice and land heavily on the floor. There was something about the sound—What was it? It occurred to her that though it was a hard job for a big man like Uncle Alton to get through the little opening in the bushes, she could hear no heavy breathing. She heard no breathing at all!

Babe peeped out into the main cave and squealed in utmost horror. Standing there was, not Uncle Alton, but a massive caricature of a man: a huge thing like an irregular mud doll, clumsily made. It quivered and parts of it glistened and parts of it were dried and crumbly. Half of the lower part of its face was gone, giving it a lopsided look. It had no perceptible mouth or nose, and its eyes were crooked, one higher than the other, both a dingy brown with no whites at all. It stood quite still looking at her, its only movement a steady unalive quivering.

It wondered about the queer little noise Babe had made.

Babe crept far back against a little pocket of stone, her brain running round and round in tiny circles of agony. She opened her mouth to cry out, and could not. Her eyes bulged and her face flamed with the strangling effort, and the two golden ropes of her braided hair twitched and twitched as she hunted hopelessly for a way out. If only she were out in the open—or in the wedge-shaped half-cave where the thing was—or home in bed!

The thing clumped toward her, expressionless, moving with a slow inevitability that was the sheer crux of horror. Babe lay wide-eyed and frozen, mounting pressure of terror stilling her lungs, making her heart shake the whole world. The monster came to the mouth of the little pocket, tried to walk to her and was stopped by the sides. It was such a narrow little fissure, and it was all Babe could do to get in. The thing from the wood stood straining against the rock at its shoulders, pressing harder and harder to get to Babe. She sat up slowly, so near to the thing that its odor was almost thick enough to see, and a wild hope burst through her voiceless fear. It couldn't get in! It couldn't get in because it was too big!

The substance of its feet spread slowly under the tremendous strain and at its shoulder appeared a slight crack. It widened as the monster unfeelingly crushed itself against the rock, and suddenly a large piece of the shoulder came away and the being twisted slushily three feet farther in. It lay quietly with its muddy eyes fixed on her, and then brought one thick arm up over its head and reached.

Babe scrambled in the inch farther she had believed impossible, and the filthy clubbed hand stroked down her back, leaving a trail of muck on the blue denim of the shirt she wore. The monster surged suddenly and, lying full length now, gained that last precious inch. A black hand seized one of her braids, and for Babe the lights went out.

When she came to, she was dangling by her hair from that same crusted paw. The thing held her high, so that her face and its featureless head were not more than a foot apart. It gazed at her with a mild curiosity in its eyes, and it swung her slowly back and forth. The agony of her pulled hair did what fear could not do— gave her a voice. She screamed. She opened her mouth and puffed up her powerful young lungs, and she sounded off. She held her throat in the position of the first scream, and her chest labored and pumped more air through her frozen throat. Shrill and monotonous and infinitely piercing, her screams.

The thing did not mind. It held her as she was, and watched. When it had learned all it could from this phenomenon, it dropped her jarringly, and looked around the half-cave, ignoring the stunned and huddled Babe. It reached over and picked up the leather brief case and tore it twice across as if it were tissue. It saw the sandwich Babe had left, picked it up, crushed it, dropped it.

Babe opened her eyes, saw that she was free, and just as the thing turned back to her she dove between its legs and out into the shallow pool in front of the rock, paddled across and hit the other bank screaming. A vicious little light of fury burned in her; she picked up a grapefruit-sized stone and hurled it with all her frenzied might. It flew low and fast, and struck squashily on the monster's ankle. The thing was just taking a step toward the water; the stone caught it off balance, and its unpracticed equilibrium could not save it. It tottered for a long, silent moment at the edge and then splashed into the stream. Without a second look Babe ran shrieking away.

Cory Drew was following the little gobs of mold that somehow indicated the path of the murderer, and he was nearby when he first heard her scream. He broke into a run, dropping his shotgun and holding the .32-40 ready to fire. He ran with such deadly panic in his heart that he ran right past the huge cleft rock and was a hundred yards past it before she burst out through the pool and ran up the bank. He had to run hard and fast to catch her, because anything behind her was that faceless horror in the cave, and she was living for the one idea of getting away from there. He caught her in his arms and swung her to him and she screamed on and on and on.

Babe didn't see Cory at all, even when he held her and quieted her.

The monster lay in the water. It neither liked nor disliked this new element. It rested on the bottom, its massive head a foot beneath the surface, and it curiously considered the facts that it had garnered. There was the little humming noise of Babe's voice that sent the monster questing into the cave. There was the black material of the brief case that resisted so much more than green things when he tore it. There was the little two-legged one who sang and brought him near, and who screamed when he came. There was this new cold moving thing he had fallen into. It was washing his body away. That had never happened before. That was interesting. The monster decided to stay and observe this new thing. It felt no urge to save itself; it could only be curious.

The brook came laughing down out of its spring, ran down from its source beckoning to the sunbeams and embracing freshets and helpful brooklets. It shouted and played with streaming little roots, and nudged the minnows and pollywogs about in its tiny backwaters. It was a happy brook. When it came to the pool by the cloven rock it found the monster there, and plucked at it. It soaked the foul substances and smoothed and melted the molds, and the waters below the thing eddied darkly with its diluted matter. It was a thorough brook. It washed all it touched, persistently. Where it found filth, it removed filth; and if there were layer on layer of foulness, than layer by foul layer it was removed. It was a good brook. It did not mind the poison of the monster, but took it up and thinned it and spread it in little rings round rocks downstream, and let it drift to the rootlets of water plants, that they might grow greener and lovelier. And the monster melted.

"I am smaller," the thing thought. "That is interesting. I could not move now. And now this part of me which thinks is going, too. It will stop in just a moment, and drift away with the rest of the body. It will stop thinking and I will stop being, and that, too, is a very interesting thing."

So the monster melted and dirtied the water, and the water was clean again, washing and washing the skeleton that the monster had left. It was not very big, and there was a badly-healed knot on the left arm. The sunlight flickered on the triangular plate set into the pale skull, and the skeleton was very clean now. The brook laughed about it for an age.

They found the skeleton, six grimlipped men who came to find a killer. No one had believed Babe, when she told her story days later. It had to be days later because Babe had screamed for seven hours without stopping, and had lain like a dead child for a day. No one believed her at all, because her story was all about the bad fella, and they knew that the bad fella was simply a thing that her father had made up to frighten her with. But it was through her that the skeleton was found, and so the men at the bank sent a check to the Drews for more money than they had ever dreamed about. It was old Roger Kirk, sure enough, that skeleton, though it was found five miles from where he had died and sank into the forest floor where the hot molds builded around his skeleton and emerged—a monster.

So the Drews had a new barn and fine new livestock and they hired four men. But they didn't have Alton. And they didn't have Kimbo. And Babe screams at night and has grown very thin.

The theme of Arthur Porges' seventy short, meticulously-crafted stories was frequently that of a man (very infrequently a woman or child) faced with a seemingly insoluble problem.

More often than not, the problem is going to kill the main protagonist if he doesn't solve it in time.

Well, that situation's a staple not only of adventure fiction but quite a lot of horror writing as well. What sets some of Porges' stories off from most adventure—bringing them closer to horror stories which use similar themes—is that occasionally the problem the protagonist faces really is insoluble. Absolutely nothing he does will permit him to survive.

I have a personal bias against the usual sort of horror story in which evil (or retribution, if the victim is an evil-doer to be punished) closes inexorably around the protagonist who cowers in the growing realization of inevitable doom.

I don't mean that these are bad stories or that those who write them are bad people: friends and friendly acquaintances of mine are extremely good in this subgenre, blackening the mood expertly until it doesn't matter what physical result obtains at the conclusion. The protagonist has been spiritually destroyed. In a purely SF context, Harry Harrison's Make Room! Make Room! shows how well-written and hideously depressing a work based on insoluble problems can be.

I'm biased against that treatment because I was raised in the notion that giving up was never a virtue; that you can't always win, but you sure can keep on trying if it's something important to you. I don't offer this as "the right way to be"; it's a bias and by definition irrational.

But it's how I am, and it's one of the reasons that I take such delight in Arthur Porges' work. His protagonists keep on trying, bringing all their physical and mental skills to bear on the problem—right up to the very end.

The only thing is: sometimes the problem really is insoluble.

THE RUUM

Arthur Porges

The cruiser *Ilkor* had just gone into her interstellar overdrive beyond the orbit of Pluto when a worried officer reported to the Commander.

"Excellency," he said uneasily, "I regret to inform you that because of a technician's carelessness, a Type H-9 Ruum has been left behind on the third planet, together with anything it may have collected."

The Commander's triangular eyes hooded momentarily, but when he spoke his voice was level.

"How was the ruum set?"

"For a maximum radius of 30 miles, and 160 pounds plus or minus fifteen."

There was silence for several seconds, then the Commander said: "We can't reverse course now. In a few weeks we'll be returning, and can pick up the ruum then. I do not care to have one of those costly, self-energizing models charged against my ship. You will see," he ordered coldly, "that the individual responsible is severely punished."

But at the end of its run, in the neighborhood of

35

Rigel, the cruiser met a flat, ring-shaped raider; and when the inevitable fire-fight was over, both ships, semi-molten, radioactive, and laden with dead, were starting a billion year orbit around the star.

And on the earth, it was the age of reptiles.

When the two men had unloaded the last of the supplies, Jim Irwin watched his partner climb into the little seaplane. He waved at Walt.

"Don't forget to mail that letter to my wife," Jim shouted.

"The minute I land," Walt Leonard called back, starting to rev the engine. "And you find us some uranium—a strike is just what Cele needs. A fortune for your son and her, hey?" His white teeth flashed in a grin. "Don't rub noses with any grizzlies—shoot 'em, but don't scare 'em to death!"

Jim thumbed his nose as the seaplane speeded up, leaving a frothy wake. He felt a queer chill as the amphibian took off. For three weeks he would be isolated in this remote valley of the Canadian Rockies. If for any reason the plane failed to return to the icy blue lake, he would surely die. Even with enough food, no man could surmount the frozen peaks and make his way on foot over hundreds of miles of almost virgin wilderness. But of course Walt Leonard would return on schedule, and it was up to Jim whether or not they lost their stake. If there was any uranium in the valley, he had twenty-one days to find it. To work then, and no gloomy forebodings.

Moving with the unhurried precision of an experienced woodsman, he built a lean-to in the shelter of a rocky overhang. For this three weeks of summer, nothing more permanent was needed. Perspiring in the strong morning sun, he piled his supplies back under the ledge, well covered by a waterproof tarpaulin, and protected from the larger animal prowlers. All but the dynamite; that he cached, also carefully wrapped against moisture, 200 yards away. Only a fool shares his quarters with a box of high explosives.

The first two weeks went by all too swiftly, without any encouraging finds. There was only one good possibility left, and just enough time to explore it. So early one morning towards the end of his third week, Jim Irwin prepared for a last-ditch foray into the northeast part of the valley, a region he had not yet visited.

He took the Geiger counter, slipping on the earphones reversed, to keep the normal rattle from dulling his hearing, and reaching for the rifle, set out, telling himself it was now or never so far as this particular expedition was concerned. The bulky .30-06 was a nuisance and he had no enthusiasm for its weight, but the huge grizzlies of Canada are not intruded upon with impunity, and take a lot of killing. He'd already had to dispose of two, a hateful chore, since the big bears were vanishing all too fast. And the rifle had proved a great comfort on several ticklish occasions when actual firing had been avoided. The .22 pistol he left in its sheepskin holster in the lean-to.

He was whistling at the start, for the clear, frosty air, the bright sun on blue-white ice fields, and the heady smell of summer, all delighted his heart despite his bad luck as a prospector. He planned to go one day's journey to the new region, spend about 36 hours exploring it intensively, and be back in time to meet the plane at noon. Except for his emergency packet, he took no food or water. It would be easy enough to knock over a rabbit, and the streams were alive with firm-fleshed rainbow trout of the kind no longer common in the States.

All morning Jim walked, feeling an occasional surge of hope as the counter chattered. But its clatter always died down. The valley had nothing radioactive of value, only traces. Apparently they'd made a bad choice. His cheerfulness faded. They needed a strike badly, especially Walt. And his own wife, Cele, with a kid on the

way. But there was still a chance. These last 36 hours—
he'd snoop at night, if necessary—might be the pay-off.
He reflected a little bitterly that it would help quite a
bit if some of those birds he'd staked would make a
strike and return his dough. Right this minute there
was close to 8,000 bucks owing to him.

A wry smile touched his lips, and he abandoned
unprofitable speculations for plans about lunch. The
sun, as well as his stomach, said it was time. He had
just decided to take out his line and fish a foaming
brook, when he rounded a grassy knoll to come upon a
sight that made him stiffen to a halt, his jaw dropping.

It was like some enterprising giant's outdoor butcher
shop: a great assortment of animal bodies, neatly lined
up in triple row that extended almost as far as the eye
could see. And what animals! To be sure, those nearest
him were ordinary deer, bear, cougars, and mountain
sheep—one of each, apparently—but down the line
were strange, uncouth, half-formed, hairy beasts; and
beyond them a nightmare conglomeration of reptiles.
One of the latter, at the extreme end of the remarkable
display, he recognized at once. There had been a
much larger specimen fabricated about an incomplete
skeleton, of course, in the museum at home.

No doubt about it—it was a small stegosaur, no bigger than a pony!

Fascinated, Jim walked down the line, glancing back
over the immense array. Peering more closely at one
scaly, dirty-yellow lizard, he saw an eyelid tremble.
Then he realized the truth. The animals were not dead,
but paralyzed and miraculously preserved. Perspiration
prickled his forehead. How long since stegosaurs had
roamed this valley?

All at once he noticed another curious circumstance:
the victims were roughly of a size. Nowhere, for example, was there a really large saurian. No tyrannosaurus.
For that matter, no mammoth. Each specimen was
about the size of a large sheep. He was pondering this

odd fact, when the underbrush rustled a warning behind him.

Jim Irwin had once worked with mercury, and for a second it seemed to him that a half-filled leather sack of the liquid metal had rolled into the clearing. For the quasi-spherical object moved with just such a weighty, fluid motion. But it was not leather; and what appeared at first a disgusting wartiness, turned out on closer scrutiny to be more like the functional projections of some outlandish mechanism. Whatever the thing was, he had little time to study it, for after the spheroid had whipped out and retraced a number of metal rods with bulbous, lens-like structures at their tips, it rolled towards him at a speed of about five miles an hour. And from its purposeful advance, the man had no doubt that it meant to add him to the pathetic heap of living-dead specimens.

Uttering an incoherent exclamation, Jim sprang back a number of paces, unslinging his rifle. The ruum that had been left behind was still some 30 yards off, approaching at that moderate but invariable velocity, an advance more terrifying in its regularity than the headlong charge of a mere brute beast.

Jim's hand flew to the bolt, and with practiced deftness he slammed a cartridge into the chamber. He snuggled the battered stock against his cheek, and using the peep sight, aimed squarely at the leathery bulk—a perfect target in the bright afternoon sun. A grim little smile touched his lips as he squeezed the trigger. He knew what one of those 180-grain, metal-jacketed, boat-tail slugs could do at 2700 feet per second. Probably at this close range it would keyhole and blow the foul thing into a mush, by God!

Wham! The familiar kick against his shoulder. E-e-e-e-! The whining screech of a ricochet. He sucked in his breath. There could be no doubt whatever. At a mere twenty yards, a bullet from this hard-hitting rifle had glanced from the ruum's surface.

Frantically Jim worked the bolt. He blasted two more

rounds, then realized the utter futility of such tactics. When the ruum was six feet away, he saw gleaming finger-hooks flick from warty knobs, and a hollow, stinglike probe, dripping greenish liquid, poised snakily between them. The man turned and fled.

Jim Irwin weighed exactly 149 pounds.

It was easy enough to pull ahead. The ruum seemed incapable of increasing its speed. But Jim had no illusions on that score. The steady five-mile-an-hour pace was something no organism on earth could maintain for more than a few hours. Before long, Jim guessed, the hunted animal had either turned on its implacable pursuer or, in the case of more timid creatures, ran itself to exhaustion in a circle out of sheer panic. Only the winged were safe. But for anything on the ground the result was inevitable: another specimen for the awesome array. And for whom the whole collection? Why? Why?

Coolly, as he ran, Jim began to shed all surplus weight. He glanced at the reddening sun, wondering about the coming night. He hesitated over the rifle; it had proved useless against the ruum, but his military training impelled him to keep the weapon to the last. Still, every pound raised the odds against him in the gruelling race he foresaw clearly. Logic told him that military reasoning did not apply to a contest like this; there would be no disgrace in abandoning a worthless rifle. And when weight became really vital, the .30-06 would go. But meanwhile he slung it over one shoulder. The Geiger counter he placed as gently as possible on a flat rock, hardly breaking his stride.

One thing was damned certain. This would be no rabbit run, a blind, panicky flight until exhausted, ending in squealing submission. This would be a fighting retreat, and he'd use every trick of survival he'd learned in his hazard-filled lifetime.

Taking deep, measured breaths, he loped along, watching with shrewd eyes for anything that might be used for his advantage in the weird contest. Luckily the valley was sparsely wooded; in brush or forest his straight-away speed would be almost useless.

Suddenly he came upon a sight that made him pause. It was a point where a huge boulder overhung the trail, and Jim saw possibilities in the situation. He grinned as he remembered a Malay mantrap that had once saved his life. Springing to a hillock, he looked back over the grassy plain. The afternoon sun cast long shadows, but it was easy enough to spot the pursuing ruum, still oozing along on Jim's trail. He watched the thing with painful anxiety. Everything hinged upon this brief survey. He was right! Yes, although at most places the man's trail was neither the only route nor the best one, the ruum dogged the footsteps of his prey. The significance of that fact was immense, but Irwin had no more than twelve minutes to implement the knowledge.

Deliberately dragging his feet, Irwin made a clear trail directly under the boulder. After going past it for about ten yards, he walked backwards in his own prints until just short of the overhang, and then jumped up clear of the track to a point behind the balanced rock.

Whipping out his heavy-duty belt knife, he began to dig, scientifically, but with furious haste, about the base of the boulder. Every few moments, sweating with apprehension and effort, he rammed it with one shoulder. At last, it teetered a little. He had just jammed the knife back into its sheath, and was crouching there, panting, when the ruum rolled into sight over a small ridge on his back trail.

He watched the gray spheroid moving towards him and fought to quiet his sobbing breath. There was no telling what other senses it might bring into play, even though the ruum seemed to prefer just to follow in his prints. But it certainly had a whole battery of instruments at its disposal. He crouched low behind the rock, every nerve a charged wire.

But there was no change of technique by the ruum;

seemingly intent on the footprints of its prey, the strange sphere rippled along, passing directly under the great boulder. As it did so, Irwin gave a savage yell, and thrusting his whole muscular weight against the balanced mass, toppled it squarely on the ruum. Five tons of stone fell from a height of twelve feet.

Jim scrambled down. He stood there, staring at the huge lump and shaking his head dazedly. "Fixed that son of a bitch!" he said in a thick voice. He gave the boulder a kick. "Hah! Walt and I might clear a buck or two yet from your little meat market. Maybe this expedition won't be a total loss. Enjoy yourself in hell where you came from!"

Then he leaped back, his eyes wild. The giant rock was shifting! Slowly its five-ton bulk was sliding off the trail, raising a ridge of soil as it grated along. Even as he stared, the boulder tilted, and a gray protuberance appeared under the nearest edge. With a choked cry, Jim Irwin broke into a lurching run.

He ran a full mile down the trail. Then, finally, he stopped and looked back. He could just make out a dark dot moving away from the fallen rock. It progressed as slowly and as regularly and as inexorably as before, and in his direction. Jim sat down heavily, putting his head in his scratched, grimy hands.

But that despairing mood did not last. After all, he had gained a twenty minute respite. Lying down, trying to relax as much as possible, he took the flat packet of emergency rations from his jacket, and eating quickly but without bolting, disposed of some pemmican, biscuit, and chocolate. A few sips of icy water from a streamlet, and he was almost ready to continue his fantastic struggle. But first he swallowed one of the three benzedrine pills he carried for physical crises. When the ruum was still an estimated ten minutes away, Jim Irwin trotted off, much of his wiry strength back, and fresh courage to counter bone-deep weariness.

After running for fifteen minutes, he came to a sheer

face of rock about 30 feet high. The terrain on either side was barely passable, consisting of choked gullies, spiky brush, and knife-edged rocks. If Jim could make the top of this little cliff, the ruum surely would have to detour, a circumstance that might put it many minutes behind him.

He looked up at the sun. Huge and crimson, it was almost touching the horizon. He would have to move fast. Irwin was no rock climber but he did know the fundamentals. Using every crevice, roughness, and minute ledge, he fought his way up the cliff. Somehow—unconsciously—he used that flowing climb of a natural mountaineer, which takes each foothold very briefly as an unstressed pivot point in a series of rhythmic advances.

He had just reached the top when the ruum rolled up to the base of the cliff.

Jim knew very well that he ought to leave at once, taking advantage of the few precious remaining moments of daylight. Every second gained was of tremendous value; but curiosity and hope made him wait. He told himself that the instant his pursuer detoured he would get out of there all the faster. Besides, the thing might even give up and he could sleep right here.

Sleep! His body lusted for it.

But the ruum would not detour. It hesitated only a few seconds at the foot of the barrier. Then a number of knobs opened to extrude metallic wands. One of these, topped with lenses, waved in the air. Jim drew back too late—their uncanny gaze had found him as he lay atop the cliff, peering down. He cursed his idiocy.

Immediately all the wands retracted, and from a different knob a slender rod, blood-red in the setting sun, began to shoot straight up to the man. As he watched, frozen in place, its barbed tip gripped the cliff's edge almost under his nose.

Jim leaped to his feet. Already the rod was shortening as the ruum reabsorbed its shining length. And the leathery sphere was rising off the ground. Swearing loudly, Jim fixed his eyes on the tenacious hook, drawing back one heavy boot.

But experience restrained him. The mighty kick was never launched. He had seen too many rough-and-tumbles lost by an injudicious attempt at the boot. It wouldn't do at all to let any part of his body get within reach of the ruum's superb tools. Instead he seized a length of dry branch, and inserting one end under the metal hook, began to pry.

There was a sputtering flash, white and lacy, and even through the dry wood, he felt the potent surge of power that splintered the end. He dropped the smoldering stick with a gasp of pain, and wringing his numb fingers, backed off several steps, full of impotent rage. For a moment he paused, half inclined to run again, but then his upper lip drew back and snarling, he unslung his rifle. By God! He knew he had been right to lug the damned thing all this way—even if it had beat a tattoo on his ribs. Now he had the ruum right where he wanted it!

Kneeling to steady his arm in the failing light, Jim sighted at the hook and fired. There was a soggy thud as the ruum fell. Jim shouted. The heavy slug had done a lot more than he expected. Not only had it blasted the metal claw loose, but it had smashed a big gap in the cliff's edge. It would be pretty damned hard for the ruum to use that part of the rock again!

He looked down. Sure enough, the ruum was back at the bottom. Jim Irwin grinned. Every time the thing clamped a hook over the bluff, he'd blow that hook loose. There was plenty of ammunition in his pocket and, until the moon rose, bringing a good light for shooting with it, he'd stick the gun's muzzle inches away if necessary. Besides, the thing—whatever it might be—was obviously too intelligent to keep up a hopeless struggle. Sooner or later it would accept the detour. And then, maybe the night would help to hide his trail.

Then—he choked and, for a brief moment, tears

came to his eyes. Down below, in the dimness, the squat, phlegmatic spheroid was extruding three hooked rods simultaneously in a fanlike spread. In a perfectly coordinated movement, the rods snagged the cliff's edge at intervals of about four feet.

Jim Irwin whipped the rifle to his shoulder. All right—this was going to be just like rapid-fire for record back at Benning. Only, at Benning, they didn't expect good shooting in the dark!

But the first shot was a bull's-eye, smacking the left-hand hook loose in a puff of rock dust. His second shot did almost as well, knocking the gritty stuff loose so the center barb slipped off. But even as he whirled to level at number three, Jim saw it was hopeless.

The first hook was back in place. No matter how well he shot, at least one rod would always be in position, pulling the ruum to the top.

Jim hung the useless rifle muzzle down from a stunted tree and ran into the deepening dark. The toughening of his body, a process of years, was paying off now. So what? Where was he going? What could he do now? Was there anything that could stop the damned thing behind him?

Then he remembered the dynamite.

Gradually changing his course, the weary man cut back towards his camp by the lake. Overhead the stars brightened, pointing the way. Jim lost all sense of time. He must have eaten as he wobbled along, for he wasn't hungry. Maybe he could eat at the lean-to . . . no, there wouldn't be time . . . take a benzedrine pill. No, the pills were all gone and the moon was up and he could hear the ruum close behind. Close.

Quite often phosphorescent eyes peered at him from the underbrush and once, just at dawn, a grizzly whoofed with displeasure at his passage.

Sometime during the night his wife, Cele, stood before him with outstretched arms. "Go away!" he rasped. "Go away! You can make it! It can't chase both of us!"

So she turned and ran lightly alongside of him. But when Irwin panted across a tiny glade, Cele faded away into the moonlight and he realized she hadn't been there at all.

Shortly after sunrise Jim Irwin reached the lake. The ruum was close enough for him to hear the dull sounds of its passage. Jim staggered, his eyes closed. He hit himself feebly on the nose, his eyes jerked open and he saw the explosive. The sight of the greasy sticks of dynamite snapped Irwin wide awake.

He forced himself to calmness and carefully considered what to do. Fuse? No. It would be impossible to leave fused dynamite in the trail and time the detonation with the absolute precision he needed. Sweat poured down his body, his clothes were sodden with it. It was hard to think. The explosion *must* be set off from a distance and at the exact moment the ruum was passing over it. But Irwin dared not use a long fuse. The rate of burning was not constant enough. Couldn't calibrate it perfectly with the ruum's advance. Jim Irwin's body sagged all over, his chin sank toward his heaving chest. He jerked his head up, stepped back—and saw the .22 pistol where he had left it in the lean-to.

His sunken eyes flashed.

Moving with frenetic haste, he took the half-filled case, piled all the remaining percussion caps among the loose sticks in a devil's mixture. Weaving out to the trail, he carefully placed box and contents directly on his earlier tracks some twenty yards from a rocky ledge. It was a risk—the stuff might go any time—but that didn't matter. He would far rather be blown to rags than end up living but paralyzed in the ruum's outdoor butcher's stall.

The exhausted Irwin had barely hunched down behind the thin ledge of rock before his inexorable pursuer appeared over a slight rise 500 yards away. Jim scrunched deeper into the hollow, then saw a vertical gap, a narrow crack between rocks. That was it, he thought vaguely. He could sight through the gap at the dynamite and still be shielded from the blast. If it was a shield . . . when that half-case blew only twenty yards away . . .

He stretched out on his belly, watching the ruum roll forward. A hammer of exhaustion pounded his ballooning skull. Jesus! When he had slept last? This was the first time he had lain down in hours. Hours? Ha! it was days. His muscles stiffened, locked into throbbing, burning knots. Then he felt the morning sun on his back, soothing, warming, easing . . . No! If he let go, if he slept now, it was the ruum's macrabre collection for Jim Irwin! Stiff fingers tightened around the pistol. He'd stay awake! If he lost—if the ruum survived the blast— there'd still be time to put a bullet through his brain.

He looked down at the sleek pistol, then out at the innocent-seeming booby trap. If he timed this right— and he would—the ruum wouldn't survive. No. He relaxed a little, yielding just a bit to the gently insistent sun. A bird whistled softly somewhere above him and a fish splashed in the lake.

Suddenly he was wrenched to full awareness. Damn! Of all times for a grizzly to come snooping about! With the whole of Irwin's camp ready for greedy looting, a fool bear had to come sniffing around the dynamite! The furred monster smelled carefully at the box, nosed around, rumbled deep displeasure at the alien scent of man. Irwin held his breath. Just a touch would blow a cap. A single cap meant . . .

The grizzly lifted his head from the box and growled hoarsely. The box was ignored, the offensive odor of man was forgotten. Its feral little eyes focussed on a plodding spheroid that was now only forty yards away. Jim Irwin snickered. Until he had met the ruum the grizzly bear of the North American continent was the only thing in the world he had ever feared. And now— why the hell was he so calm about it?—the two terrors of his existence were meeting head on and he was laughing. He shook his head and the great side muscles in his neck hurt abominably. He looked down at his pistol, then out at the dynamite. *These* were the only real things in his world.

About six feet from the bear, the ruum paused. Still in the grip of that almost idiotic detachment, Jim Irwin found himself wondering again what it was, where it had come from. The grizzly arose on its haunches, the embodiment of utter ferocity. Terrible teeth flashed white against red lips. The business-like ruum started to roll past. The bear closed in, roaring. It cuffed at the ruum. A mighty paw, armed with black claws sharper and stronger than scythes, made that cuff. It would have disemboweled a rhinoceros. Irwin cringed as that side-swipe knocked dust from the leathery sphere. The ruum was hurled back several inches. It paused, recovered, and with the same dreadful casualness it rippled on, making a wider circle, ignoring the bear.

But the lord of the woods wasn't settling for any draw. Moving with that incredible agility which has terrified Indians, Spanish, French and Anglo-Americans since the first encounter of any of them with his species, the grizzly whirled, side-stepped beautifully and hugged the ruum. The terrible, shaggy forearms tightened, the slavering jaws champed at the gray surface. Irwin half rose. "Go it!" he croaked. Even as he cheered the clumsy emperor of the wild, Jim thought it was an insane tableau: the village idiot wrestling with a beach ball.

Then silver metal gleamed bright against gray. There was a flash, swift and deadly. The roar of the king abruptly became a whimper, a gurgle and then there was nearly a ton of terror wallowing in death—its throat slashed open. Jim Irwin saw the bloody blade retract into the gray spheroid, leaving a bright red smear on the thing's dusty hide.

And the ruum rolled forward past the giant corpse, implacable, still intent on the man's spoor, his footprints, his pathway. Okay, baby, Jim giggled at the dead grizzly, this is for you, for Cele, for—for lots of poor dumb animals like us—come to, you damned fool, he cursed at himself. And aimed at the dynamite. And very calmly, very carefully, Jim Irwin squeezed the trigger of his pistol.

Briefly, sound first. Then giant hands lifted his body from where he lay, then let go. He came down hard, face in a patch of nettles, but he was sick, he didn't care. He remembered that the birds were quiet. Then there was a fluid thump as something massive struck the grass a few yards away. Then there was quiet.

Irwin lifted his head . . . all men do in such a case. His body still ached. He lifted sore shoulders and saw . . . an enormous, smoking crater in the earth. He also saw, a dozen paces away, gray-white because it was covered now with powdered rock, the ruum.

It was under a tall, handsome pine tree. Even as Jim watched, wondering if the ringing in his ears would ever stop, the ruum rolled toward him.

Irwin fumbled for his pistol. It was gone. It had dropped somewhere, out of reach. He wanted to pray, then, but couldn't get properly started. Instead, he kept thinking, idiotically, "My sister Ethel can't spell Nebuchadnezzar and never could. My sister Ethel—"

The ruum was a foot away now, and Jim closed his eyes. He felt cool, metallic fingers touch, grip, lift. His unresisting body was raised several inches, and juggled oddly. Shuddering, he waited for the terrible syringe with its green liquid, seeing the yellow, shrunken face of a lizard with one eyelid a-tremble.

Then, dispassionately, without either roughness or solicitude, the ruum put him back on the ground. When he opened his eyes, some seconds later, the sphere was rolling away. Watching it go, he sobbed dryly.

It seemed a matter of moments only, before he heard the seaplane's engine, and opened his eyes to see Walt Leonard bending over him.

*   *   *

Later, in the plane, 5000 feet above the valley, Walt grinned suddenly, slapped him on the back, and cried, "Jim, I can get a whirlybird, a four place job! Why, if we can snatch up just a few of those prehistoric lizards and things while the museum keeper's away, it's like you said—the scientists will pay us plenty."

Jim's hollow eyes lit up. "That the idea," he agreed. Then, bitterly: "I might just as well have stood in bed. Evidently the damned thing didn't want me at all. Maybe it wanted to know what I paid for these pants! Barely touched me, then let go. And how I ran!"

"Yeah," Walt said. "That was damned queer. And after that marathon. I admire your guts, boy." He glanced sideways at Jim Irwin's haggard face. "That night's run cost you plenty. I figure you lost over ten pounds."

Henry Kuttner started his professional writing career when he was a teenager. His early work was crude. To see how crude, compare his Elak of Atlantis stories with one of their obvious models, the classic Jirel of Joiry pieces by C. L. Moore (who later met and married him).

Early on, Kuttner put his hand to any form of writing that would earn him a buck. When Marvel Science Stories (not to be confused with other magazines of similar name) made a two-issue attempt to boost circulation with (what was for the 1930s) pornography, Kuttner wrote most of the stories under a variety of pseudonyms. According to Manly Wade Wellman, who was present, Kuttner told the informal writers' gathering in The Steuben Tavern that he was making a lot of money on his new assignment.

"You bet, Hank," said another of those present. "Kill a monster, grab a tit. Kill a monster, grab a tit."

But Kuttner continued learning his craft for as long as his short life let him practice it.

This isn't as common as you'd think. Science fiction has its share of one-shot authors, people who did one brilliant work and never equalled it no matter how long they kept trying. This is unfortunate (especially for the writers, I suppose); but you can attribute it to a flash of genius and decide you were lucky to get that one undeserved marvel.

Much more depressing to me are the writers who start out doing flawed work; not great, but good enough to get published because on balance the strengths outweigh the flaws. A solid foundation to build on.

Except that the next work, and the work they're doing ten years later, has precisely the same flaws as that original piece. They're never going to get any better. They don't even have a clue as to what they're doing wrong.

Writers like this don't come from any particular point in the literary spectrum. Sometimes they reach entry

*level because they were the darlings of this or that
writers' workshop, sure; but it's just as likely that their
first sale was a barbarian fantasy, because they happened to have written a novel of that sort in time to hit
one of the periodic booms which peak the sub-genre.*

*These writers depress me more than the "one-flash-of-
genius" type, because I've never claimed genius for my
own work. My first sale was a pastiche of August Derleth
pastiching early Lovecraft; it was just as bad as it
sounds, but it sold because Mr. Derleth was putting
together an original anthology and needed to fill ten
more pages. I know from personal experience that it's
possible to improve from a very slow start; but the
writers who never become better craftsmen show that I
might not have either.*

*Whereas Hank Kuttner proves just how good a crafts-
man can become if he continues to take risks. Consider,
for instance, the structure of "Happy Ending." . . .*

HAPPY ENDING

Henry Kuttner

This is the way the story ended: James Kelvin concentrated very hard on the thought of the chemist with the red mustache who had promised him a million dollars. It was simply a matter of tuning in on the man's brain, establishing a rapport. He had done it before. Now it was more important than ever that he do it this one last time. He pressed the button on the gadget the robot had given him, and thought hard.

Far off, across limitless distances, he found the rapport.

He clamped on the mental tight beam.

He rode it . . .

The red-mustached man looked up, gaped, and grinned delightedly.

"So there you are!" he said. "I didn't hear you come in. Good grief, I've been trying to find you for two weeks."

"Tell me one thing quick," Kelvin said. "What's your name?"

"George Bailey. Incidentally, what's yours?"

But Kelvin didn't answer. He had suddenly remembered the other thing the robot had told him about that gadget which established rapport when he pressed the button. He pressed it now—and nothing happened. The gadget had gone dead. Its task was finished, which obviously meant he had at last achieved health, fame and fortune. The robot had warned him, of course. The thing was set to do one specialized job. Once he got what he wanted, it would work no more.

So Kelvin got the million dollars.

And he lived happily ever after. . . .

This is the middle of the story:

As he passed aside the canvas curtain something—a carelessly hung rope—swung down at his face, knocking the horn-rimmed glasses askew. Simultaneously a vivid bluish light blazed into his unprotected eyes. He felt a curious, sharp sense of disorientation, a shifting motion that was almost instantly gone.

Things steadied before him. He let the curtain fall back into place, making legible again the painted inscription: HOROSCOPES—LEARN YOUR FUTURE—and he stood staring at the remarkable horomancer.

It was a—oh, impossible!

The robot said in a flat, precise voice, "You are James Kelvin. You are a reporter. You are thirty years old, unmarried, and you came to Los Angeles from Chicago today on the advice of your physician. Is that correct?"

In his astonishment Kelvin called on the Deity. Then he settled his glasses more firmly and tried to remember an exposé of charlatans he had once written. There was some obvious way they worked things like this, miraculous as it sounded.

The robot looked at him impassively out of its faceted eye.

"On reading your mind," it continued in the pedantic voice, "I find this is the year Nineteen Forty-nine. My plans will have to be revised. I had meant to arrive in the year Nineteen Seventy. I will ask you to assist me."

Kelvin put his hands in his pockets and grinned.

"With money, naturally," he said. "You had me going for a minute. How do you do it, anyhow? Mirrors? Or like Maezel's chess player?"

"I am not a machine operated by a dwarf, nor am I an optical illusion," the robot assured him. "I am an artifically created living organism, originating at a period far in your future."

"And I'm not the sucker you take me for," Kelvin remarked pleasantly. "I came in here to—"

"You lost your baggage checks," the robot said. "While wondering what to do about it, you had a few drinks and took the Wilshire bus at exactly—exactly eight-thirty-five post meridian."

"Lay off the mind-reading," Kelvin said. "And don't tell me you've been running this joint very long with a line like that. The cops would be after you. *If* you're a real robot, ha, ha."

"I have been running this joint," the robot said, "for approximately five minutes. My predecessor is unconscious behind that chest in the corner. Your arrival here was sheer coincidence." It paused very briefly, and Kelvin had the curious impression that it was watching to see if the story so far had gone over well.

The impression was curious because Kelvin had no feeling at all that there was a man in the large, jointed figure before him. If such a thing as a robot were possible, he would have believed implicitly that he confronted a genuine specimen. Such things being impossible, he waited to see what the gimmick would be.

"My arrival here was also accidental," the robot informed him. "This being the case, my equipment will have to be altered slightly. I will require certain substitute mechanisms. For that, I gather as I read your mind, I will have to engage in your peculiar barter system of economics. In a word, coinage or gold or silver certificates will be necessary. Thus I am—temporarily—a horomancer."

"Sure, sure," Kelvin said. "Why not a simple mugging? If you're a robot, you could do a super-mugging job with a quick twist of the gears."

"It would attract attention. Above all, I require secrecy. As a matter of fact, I am—" The robot paused, searched Kelvin's brain for the right phrase, and said, "—on the lam. In my era, time-traveling is strictly forbidden, even by accident, unless government-sponsored."

There was a fallacy there somewhere, Kelvin thought, but he couldn't quite spot it. He blinked at the robot intently. It looked pretty unconvincing.

"What proof do you need?" the creature asked. "I read your brain the minute you came in, didn't I? You must have felt the temporary amnesia as I drew out the knowledge and then replaced it."

"So that's what happened," Kelvin said. He took a cautious step backward. "Well, I think I'll be getting along."

"Wait," the robot commanded. "I see you have begun to distrust me. Apparently you now regret having suggested a mugging job. You fear I may act on the suggestion. Allow me to reassure you. It is true that I could take your money and assure secrecy by killing you, but I am not permitted to kill humans. The alternative is to engage in the barter system. I can offer you something valuable in return for a small amount of gold. Let me see." The faceted gaze swept around the tent, dwelt piercingly for a moment on Kelvin. "A horoscope," the robot said. "It is supposed to help you achieve health, fame and fortune. Astrology, however, is out of my line. I can merely offer a logical scientific method of attaining the same results."

"Uh-huh," Kelvin said skeptically. "How much? And why haven't *you* used that method?"

"I have other ambitions," the robot said in a cryptic

manner. "Take this." There was a brief clicking. A
panel opened in the metallic chest. The robot extracted
a small, flat case and handed it to Kelvin, who automatically closed his fingers on the cold metal.

"Be careful. Don't push that button until—"

But Kelvin had pushed it. . . .

He was driving a figurative car that had got out of
control. There was somebody else inside his head. There
was a schizophrenic, double-tracked locomotive that
was running wild and his hand on the throttle couldn't
slow it down an instant. His mental steering-wheel had
snapped.

Somebody else was thinking for him!

Not quite a human being. Not quite sane, probably,
from Kelvin's standards. But awfully sane from his own.
Sane enough to have mastered the most intricate principles of non-Euclidean geometry in the nursery.

The senses get synthesized in the brain into a sort of
common language, a master-tongue. Part of it was auditory, part pictorial, and there were smells and tastes
and tactile sensations that were sometimes familiar and
sometimes spiced with the absolutely alien. And it was
chaotic.

Something like this, perhaps. . . .

"—Big Lizards getting too numerous this season—tame
threvvars have the same eyes not on Callisto though—
vacation soon—preferably galactic—solar system claustrophobic—byanding tomorrow if square rootola and
upsliding three—"

But that was merely the word-symbolism. Subjec-
tively, it was far more detailed and very frightening.
Luckily, reflex had lifted Kelvin's finger from the button almost instantly, and he stood there motionless,
shivering slightly.

He was afraid now.

The robot said, "You should not have begun the
rapport until I instructed you. Now there will be dan-

ger. Wait." His eye changed color. "Yes . . . there is
. . . Tharn, yes. Beware of Tharn."

"I don't want any part of it," Kelvin said, quickly.
"Here, take this thing back."

"Then you will be unprotected against Tharn. Keep
the device. It will, as I promised, ensure your health,
fame and fortune, far more effectively than a—a horoscope."

"No, thanks. I don't know how you managed that
trick—sub-sonics, maybe, but I don't—"

"Wait," the robot said. "When you pressed that button, you were in the mind of someone who exists very
far in the future. It created a temporal rapport. You can
bring about that rapport any time you press the button."

"Heaven forfend," Kelvin said, still sweating a little.

"Consider the opportunities. Suppose a troglodyte of
the far past had access to your brain? He could achieve
anything he wanted."

It had become important, somehow, to find a logical
rebuttal to the robot's arguments. "Like St. Anthony—or
was it Luther?—arguing with the devil?" Kelvin thought
dizzily. His headache was worse, and he suspected he
had drunk more than was good for him. But he merely
said:

"How could a troglodyte understand what's in my
brain? He couldn't apply the knowledge without the
same conditioning I've had."

"Have you ever had sudden and apparently illogical
ideas? Compulsions? So that you seem forced to think of
certain things, count up to certain numbers, work out
particular problems? Well, the man in the future on
whom my device is focused doesn't know he's en rapport with you, Kelvin. But he's vulnerable to compulsions. All you have to do is concentrate on a problem
and then press the button. Your rapport will be
compelled—illogically, from his viewpoint—to solve
that problem. And you'll be reading his brain. You'll
find out how it works. There are limitations, you'll learn

those too. And the device will ensure health, wealth and fame for you."

"It would ensure anything, if it really worked that way. I could do anything. That's why I'm not buying!"

"I said there were limitations. As soon as you've successfully achieved health, fame, and fortune, the device will become useless. I've taken care of that. But meanwhile you can use it to solve all your problems by tapping the brain of the more intelligent specimen in the future. The important point is to concentrate on your problems *before* you press the button. Otherwise you may get more than Tharn on your track."

"Tharn? What—"

"I think an—an android," the robot said, looking at nothing. "An artificial human . . . However, let us consider my own problem. I need a small amount of gold."

"So that's the kicker," Kelvin said, feeling oddly relieved. He said, "I haven't got any."

"Your watch."

Kelvin jerked his arm so that his wristwatch showed. "Oh, no. That watch cost plenty."

"All I need is the gold-plating," the robot said, shooting out a reddish ray from its eye. "Thank you." The watch was now dull gray metal.

"Hey!" Kelvin cried.

"If you use the rapport device, your health, fame and fortune will be assured," the robot said rapidly. "You will be as happy as any man of this era can be. It will solve all your problems—including Tharn. Wait a minute." The creature took a backward step and disappeared behind a hanging Oriental rug that had never been east of Peoria.

There was silence.

Kelvin looked from his altered watch to the flat, enigmatic object in his palm. It was about two inches by two inches, and no thicker than a woman's vanity-case, and there was a sunken push-button on its side.

He dropped it into his pocket and took a few steps forward. He looked behind the pseudo-Oriental rug, to find nothing except emptiness and a flapping slit cut in the canvas wall of the booth. The robot, it seemed, had taken a powder. Kelvin peered out through the slit. There was the light and sound of Ocean Park amusement pier, that was all. And the silvered, moving blackness of the Pacific Ocean, stretching to where small lights showed Malibu far up the invisible curve of the coastal cliffs.

So he came back inside the booth and looked around. A fat man in a swami's costume was unconscious behind the carved chest the robot had indicated. His breath, plus a process of deduction, told Kelvin that the man had been drinking.

Not knowing what else to do, Kelvin called on the Deity again. He found suddenly that he was thinking about someone or something called Tharn, who was an android.

Horomancy . . . time . . . rapport . . . *no!* Protective disbelief slid like plate armor around his mind. A practical robot couldn't be made. He knew that. He'd have heard—he was a reporter, wasn't he?

Sure he was.

Desiring noise and company, he went along to the shooting gallery and knocked down a few ducks. The flat case burned in his pocket. The dully burnished metal of his wristwatch burned in his memory. The remembrance of that drainage from his brain, and the immediate replacement burned in his mind. Presently bar whiskey burned in his stomach.

He'd left Chicago because of sinusitis, recurrent and annoying. Ordinary sinusitis. Not schizophrenia or hallucinations or accusing voices coming from the walls. Not because he had been seeing bats or robots. That thing hadn't really been a robot. It all had a perfectly natural explanation. Oh, sure.

Health, fame and fortune. And if—

THARN!

The thought crashed with thunderbolt impact into his head.

And then another thought: I *am* going nuts!

A silent voice began to mutter insistently, over and over. "Tharn—Tharn—Tharn—Tharn—"

And another voice, the voice of sanity and safety, answered it and drowned it out. Half aloud, Kelvin muttered:

"I'm James Noel Kelvin. I'm a reporter—special features, leg work, rewrite. I'm thirty years old, unmarried, and I came to Los Angeles today and lost my baggage checks and—and I'm going to have another drink and find a hotel. Anyhow, the climate seems to be curing my sinusitis."

Tharn, the muffled drum-beat said almost below the threshold of realization. *Tharn, Tharn.*

Tharn.

He ordered another drink and reached in his pocket for a coin. His hand touched the metal case. And simultaneously he felt a light pressure on his shoulder.

Instinctively he glanced around. It was a seven-fingered, spidery hand tightening—hairless, without nails—and white as smooth ivory.

The one, overwhelming necessity that sprang into Kelvin's mind was a simple longing to place as much space as possible between himself and the owner of that disgusting hand. It was a vital requirement, but one difficult of fulfilment, a problem that excluded everything else from Kelvin's thoughts. He knew, vaguely, that he was gripping the flat case in his pocket as though that could save him, but all he was thinking was:

I've got to get away from here.

The monstrous, alien thoughts of someone in the future spun him insanely along their current. It could not have taken a moment while that skilled, competent, trained mind, wise in the lore of an unthinkable future, solved the random problem that had come so suddenly, with such curious compulsion.

Three methods of transportation were simultaneously clear to Kelvin. Two he discarded; motorplats were obviously inventions yet to come, and quirling—involving, as it did, a sensory coil-helmet—was beyond him. But the third method—

Already the memory was fading. And that hand was still tightening on his shoulder. He clutched at the vanishing ideas and desperately made his brain and his muscles move along the unlikely direction the future-man had visualized.

And he was out in the open, a cold night wind blowing on him, still in a sitting position, but with nothing but empty air between his spine and the sidewalk.

He sat down suddenly.

Passersby on the corner of Hollywood Boulevard and Cahuenga were not much surprised at the sight of a dark, lanky man sitting by the curb. Only one woman had noticed Kelvin's actual arrival, and she knew when she was well off. She went right on home.

Kelvin got up laughing with soft hysteria. "Teleportation," he said. "How did I work it? It's gone . . . Hard to remember afterward, eh? I'll have to start carrying a notebook again."

And then— "But what about Tharn?"

He looked around, frightened. Reassurance came only after half an hour had passed without additional miracles. Kelvin walked along the Boulevard, keeping a sharp lookout. No, Tharn, though.

Occasionally he slid a hand into his pocket and touched the cold metal of the case. Health, wealth and fortune. Why, he could—

But he did not press the button. Too vivid was the memory of that shocking, alien disorientation he had felt. The mind, the experiences, the habit-patterns of the far future were uncomfortably strong.

He would use the little case again—oh, yes. But there was no hurry. First, he'd have to work out a few angles.

His disbelief was completely gone. . . .

Tharn showed up the next night and scared the day-lights out of Kelvin again. Prior to that, the reporter had failed to find his baggage tickets, and was only consoled by the two hundred bucks in his wallet. He took a room—paying in advance—at a medium-good hotel, and began wondering how he might apply his pipe-line to the future. Very sensibly, he decided to continue a normal life until something developed. At any rate, he'd have to make a few connections. He tried the *Times*, the *Examiner*, the *News*, and some others. But these things develop slowly, except in the movies. That night Kelvin was in his hotel room when his unwelcome guest appeared.

It was, of course, Tharn.

He wore a very large white turban, approximately twice the size of his head. He had a dapper black mustache, waxed downward at the tips like the mus-tache of a mandarin, or a catfish. He stared urgently at Kelvin out of the bathroom mirror.

Kelvin had been wondering whether or not he needed a shave before going out to dinner. He was rubbing his chin thoughtfully at the moment Tharn put in an ap-pearance, and there was a perceptible mental lag be-tween occurrence and perception, so that to Kelvin it seemed that he himself had mysteriously sprouted a long moustache. He reached for his upper lip. It was smooth. But in the glass the black waxed hairs quivered as Tharn pushed his face up against the surface of the mirror.

It was so shockingly disorienting, somehow, that Kel-vin was quite unable to think at all. He took a quick step backward. The edge of the bathtub caught him behind the knees and distracted him momentarily, fortunately for his sanity. When he looked again there was only his own appalled face reflected above the wash-bowl. But

after a second or two the face seemed to develop a
cloud of white turban, and mandarin-like whiskers began to form sketchily.

Kelvin clapped a hand to his eyes and spun away. In
about fifteen seconds he spread his fingers enough to
peep through them at the glass. He kept his palm
pressed desperately to his upper lip, in some wild hope
of inhibiting the sudden sprouting of a moustache. What
peeped back at him from the mirror looked like himself.
At least, it had no turban, and it did not wear horn-
rimmed glasses. He risked snatching his hand away for
a quick look, and clapped it in place again just in time
to prevent Tharn from taking shape in the glass.

Still shielding his face, he went unsteadily into the
bedroom and took the flat case out of his coat pocket.
But he didn't press the button that would close a mental synapse between two incongruous eras. He didn't
want to do that again, he realized. More horrible, somehow, than what was happening now was the thought of
reentering that *alien* brain.

He was standing before the bureau, and in the mirror
one eye looked out at him between reflected fingers. It
was a wild eye behind the gleaming spectacle-lens, but
it seemed to be his own. Tentatively he took his hand
away. . . .

This mirror showed more of Tharn. Kelvin wished it
hadn't. Tharn was wearing white knee-boots of some
glittering plastic. Between them and the turban he
wore nothing whatever except a minimum of loincloth,
also glittering plastic. Tharn was very thin, but he
looked active. He looked quite active enough to spring
right into the hotel room. His skin was whiter than his
turban, and his hands had seven fingers each, all right.

Kelvin abruptly turned away, but Tharn was resource-
ful. The dark window made enough of a reflecting surface to show a lean, loin-clothed figure. The feet showed
bare, and they were less normal than Tharn's hands.

And the polished brass of a lampbase gave back the picture of a small, distorted face not Kelvin's own.

Kelvin found a corner without reflecting surfaces and pushed into it, his hands shielding his face. He was still holding the flat case.

Oh, fine, he thought bitterly. Everything's got a string on it. What good will this rapport gadget do me if Tharn's going to show up every day? Maybe I'm not crazy. I hope so.

Something would have to be done unless Kelvin was prepared to go through life with his face buried in his hands. The worst of it was that Tharn had a haunting look of familiarity. Kelvin discarded a dozen possibilities, from reincarnation to the *déjà vu* phenomenon, but—

He peeped through his hands, in time to see Tharn raising a cylindrical gadget of some sort and leveling it like a gun. That gesture formed Kelvin's decision. He'd *have* to do something, and fast. So, concentrating on the problem—*I want out!*—he pressed the button in the surface of the flat case.

And instantly the teleportation method he had forgotten was perfectly clear to him. Other matters, however, were obscure. The smells—someone was thinking—were adding up to a—there was no word for that, only a shocking visio-auditory ideation that was simply dizzying. Someone named Three Million and Ninety Pink had written a new flatch. And there was the physical sensation of licking a twenty-four-dollar stamp and sticking it on a postcard.

But, most important, the man in the future had had—or would have—a compulsion to think about the teleportation method, and as Kelvin snapped back into his own mind and time, he instantly used that method. . . .

He was falling.

Icy water smacked him hard. Miraculously he kept his grip on the flat case. He had a whirling vision of stars in a night sky, and the phosphorescent sheen of silvery light on a dark sea. Then brine stung his nostrils.

Kelvin had never learned how to swim.

As he went down for the last time, bubbling a scream, he literally clutched at the proverbial straw he was holding. His finger pushed the button down again. There was no need to concentrate on the problem; he couldn't think of anything else.

Mental chaos, fantastic images—and the answer.

It took concentration, and there wasn't much time left. Bubbles streamed up past his face. He felt them, but he couldn't see them. All around, pressing in avidly, was the horrible coldness of the salt water. . . .

But he did know the method now, and he knew how it worked. He thought along the lines the future mind had indicated. Something happened. Radiation—that was the nearest familiar term—poured out of his brain and did peculiar things to his lung-tissue. His blood cells adapted themselves. . . .

He was breathing water, and it was no longer strangling him.

But Kelvin had also learned that this emergency adaptation could not be maintained for very long. Teleportation was the answer to that. And surely he could remember the method now. He had actually used it to escape from Tharn only a few minutes ago.

Yet he could not remember. The memory was expunged cleanly from his mind. So there was nothing else to do but press the button again, and Kelvin did that, most reluctantly.

Dripping wet, he was standing on an unfamiliar street. It was no street he knew, but apparently it was in his own time and on his own planet. Luckily, teleportation seemed to have limitations. The wind was cold. Kelvin stood in a puddle that grew rapidly around his feet. He stared around.

He picked out a sign up the street that offered Turkish

Baths, and headed moistly in that direction. His thoughts were mostly profane. . . .

He was in New Orleans, of all places. Presently he was drunk in New Orleans. His thoughts kept going around in circles, and Scotch was a fine palliative, an excellent brake. He needed to get control again. He had an almost miraculous power, and he wanted to be alone to use it effectively before the unexpected happened again. Tharn. . . .

He sat in a hotel room and swigged Scotch. Gotta be logical!

He sneezed.

The trouble was, of course, that there were so few points of contact between his own mind and that of the future-man. Moreover, he'd got the rapport only in times of crisis. Like having access to the Alexandrian Library, five seconds a day. In five seconds you couldn't even start translating. . . .

Health, fame and fortune. He sneezed again. The robot had been a liar. His health seemed to be going fast. What about that robot? How had he got involved, anyway? He said he'd fallen into this era from the future, but robots are notorious liars. Gotta be logical. . . .

Apparently the future was peopled by creatures not unlike the cast of a Frankenstein picture. Androids, robots, so-called men whose minds were shockingly different . . . *Sneeze*. Another drink.

The robot had said that the case would lose its power after Kelvin had achieved health, fame and fortune. Which was a distressing thought. Suppose he attained those enviable goals, found the little push-button useless, and *then* Tharn showed up? Oh, no. That called for another shot.

Sobriety was the wrong condition in which to approach a matter that in itself was as wild as delirium tremens, even though, Kelvin knew, the science he had stumbled on was all theoretically quite possible. But not in this day and age. Sneeze.

The trick would be to pose the right problem and use the case at some time when you weren't drowning or being menaced by that bewhiskered android with his seven-fingered hands and his ominous rod-like weapon. Find the problem.

But that future-mind was hideous.

And suddenly, with drunken clarity, Kelvin realized that he was profoundly drawn to that dim, shadowy world of the future.

He could not see its complete pattern, but he sensed it somehow. He knew that it was *right*, a far better world and time than this. If he could *be* that unknown man who dwelt there, all would go well.

Man must needs love the highest, he thought wryly. Oh, well. He shook the bottle. How much had he absorbed? He felt fine.

Gotta be logical.

Outside the window street-lights blinked off and on. Neons traced goblin languages against the night. It seemed rather alien, too, but so did Kelvin's own body. He started to laugh, but a sneeze choked that off.

All I want, he thought, is health, fame and fortune. Then I'll settle down and live happily ever after, without a care or worry. I won't need this enchanted case after that. Happy ending.

On impulse he took out the box and examined it. He tried to pry it open and failed. His finger hovered over the button.

"How can I—" he thought, and his finger moved half an inch. . . .

It wasn't so alien now that he was drunk. The future man's name was Quarra Vee. Odd he had never realized that before, but how often does a man think of his own name? Quarra Vee was playing some sort of game vaguely reminiscent of chess, but his opponent was on a planet of Sirius, some distance away. The chessmen were all unfamiliar. Complicated, dizzying space-time gambits flashed through Quarra Vee's mind as Kelvin listened in. Then Kelvin's problem thrust through, the compulsion hit Quarra Vee, and—

It was all mixed up. There were two problems, really. How to cure a cold—coryza. And how to become healthy, rich and famous in a practically prehistoric era—for Quarra Vee.

A small problem, however, to Quarra Vee. He solved it and went back to his game with the Sirian.

Kelvin was back in the hotel room in New Orleans.

He was very drunk or he wouldn't have risked it. The method involved using his brain to tune in on another brain in this present twentieth century that had exactly the wave-length he required. All sorts of factors would build up to the sum total of that wave-length—experience, opportunity, position, knowledge, imagination, honesty— but he found it at last, after hesitating among three totals that were all nearly right. Still, one was righter, to three decimal points. Still drunk as a lord, Kelvin clamped on a mental tight beam, turned on the teleportation, and rode the beam across America to a well-equipped laboratory where a man sat reading.

The man was bald and had a bristling red moustache. He looked up sharply at some sound Kelvin made.

"Hey!" he said. "How did you get in here?"

"Ask Quarra Vee," Kelvin said.

"Who? *What?*" The man put down his book.

Kelvin called on his memory. It seemed to be slipping. He used the rapport case for an instant, and refreshed his mind. Not so unpleasant this time, either. He was beginning to understand Quarra Vee's world a little. He liked it. However, he supposed he'd forget that too.

"An improvement on Woodward's protein analogues," he told the red-moustached man. "Simple synthesis will do it."

"Who the devil are you?"

"Call me Jim," Kelvin said simply. "And shut up and

listen." He began to explain, as to a small, stupid child. (The man before him was one of America's foremost chemists.) "Proteins are made of amino acids. There are about thirty-three amino acids—"

"There aren't."

"There are. Shut up. Their molecules can be arranged in lots of ways. So we get an almost infinite variety of proteins. And all living things are forms of protein. The absolute synthesis involves a chain of amino acids long enough to recognize clearly as a protein molecule. That's been the trouble."

The man with the red moustache seemed quite interested. "Fischer assembled a chain of eighteen," he said, blinking. "Abderhalden got up to nineteen, and Woodward, of course, has made chains ten thousand units long. But as for testing—"

"The complete protein molecule consists of complete sets of sequences. But if you can test only one or two sections of an analogue you can't be sure of the others. Wait a minute." Kelvin used the rapport case again. "Now I know. Well, you can make almost anything out of syntheized protein. Silk, wool, hair—but the main thing, of course," he said, sneezing, "is a cure for coryza."

"Now look—" said the red-moustached man.

"Some of the viruses are chains of amino acids, aren't they? Well, modify their structure. Make 'em harmless. Bacteria too. And synthesize antibiotics."

"I wish I could. However, Mr.—"

"Just call me Jim."

"Yes. However, all this is old stuff."

"Grab your pencil," Kelvin said. "From now on it'll be solid, with riffs. The method of synthesizing and testing is as follows—"

He explained, very thoroughly and clearly. He had to use the rapport case only twice. And when he had finished, the man with the red moustache laid down his pencil and stared.

"This is incredible," he said. "If it works—"

"I want health, fame and fortune," Kelvin said stubbornly. "It'll work."

"Yes, but—my good man—"

However, Kelvin insisted. Luckily for himself, the mental testing of the red-moustached man had included briefing for honesty and opportunity, and it ended with the chemist agreeing to sign partnership papers with Kelvin. The commercial possibilities of the process were unbounded. Dupont or GM would be glad to buy it.

"I want lots of money. A fortune."

"You'll make a million dollars," the red-moustached man said patiently.

"Then I want a receipt. Have to have this in black and white. Unless you want to give me my million now."

Frowning, the chemist shook his head. "I can't do that. I'll have to run tests, open negotiations—but don't worry about that. Your discovery is certainly worth a million. You'll be famous, too."

"And healthy?"

"There won't be any more disease, after a while," the chemist said quietly. "That's the real miracle."

"Write it down," Kelvin clamored.

"All right. We can have partnership papers drawn up tomorrow. This will do temporarily. Understand, the actual credit belongs to you."

"It's got to be in ink. A pencil won't do."

"Just a minute, then," the red-moustached man said, and went away in search of ink. Kelvin looked around the laboratory, beaming happily.

Tharn materialized three feet away. Tharn was holding the rod-weapon. He lifted it.

Kelvin instantly used the rapport case. Then he thumbed his nose at Tharn and teleported himself far away.

He was immediately in a cornfield, somewhere, but

undistilled corn was not what Kelvin wanted. He tried
again. This time he reached Seattle.

That was the beginning of Kelvin's monumental two-
week combination binge and chase.

His thoughts weren't pleasant.

He had a frightful hangover, ten cents in his pocket,
and an overdue hotel bill. A fortnight of keeping one
jump ahead of Tharn, via teleportation, had frazzled his
nerves so unendurably that only liquor had kept him
going. Now even that stimulus was failing. The drink
died in him and left what felt like a corpse.

Kelvin groaned and blinked miserably. He took off
his glasses and cleaned them, but that didn't help.

What a fool.

He didn't even know the name of that chemist!

There was health, wealth and fame waiting for him
just around the corner, but what corner? Some day he'd
find out, probably when the news of the new protein
synthesis was publicized, but when would that be? In
the meantime, what about Tharn?

Moreover, the chemist couldn't locate him, either.
The man knew Kelvin only as Jim. Which had somehow
seemed a good idea at the time, but not now.

Kelvin took out the rapport case and stared at it with
red eyes. Quarra Vee, eh? He rather liked Quarra Vee
now. Trouble was, a half hour after his rapport, at most,
he would forget all the details.

This time he used the push-button almost as Tharn
snapped into bodily existence a few feet away.

The teleportation angle again. He was sitting in the
middle of a desert. Cactus and Joshua trees were all the
scenery. There was a purple range of mountains far
away.

No Tharn, though.

Kelvin began to be thirsty. Suppose the case stopped
working now? Oh, this couldn't go on. A decision hanging fire for a week finally crystallized into a conclusion
so obvious he felt like kicking himself. Perfectly obvious!

Why hadn't he thought of it at the very beginning?

He concentrated on the problem: How can I get rid of Tharn? He pushed the button. . . .

And, a moment later, he knew the answer. It would be simple, really.

The pressing urgency was gone suddenly. That seemed to release a fresh flow of thought. Everything became quite clear.

He waited for Tharn.

He did not have to wait long. There was a tremor in the shimmering air, and the turbaned, pallid figure sprang into tangible reality.

The rod-weapon was poised.

Taking no chances, Kelvin posed his problem again, pressed the button, and instantly reassured himself as to the method. He simply thought in a very special and peculiar way—the way Quarra Vee had indicated.

Tharn was flung back a few feet. The moustached mouth gaped open as he uttered a cry.

"Don't!" the android cried. "I've been trying to—"

Kelvin focused harder on his thought. Mental energy, he felt, was pouring out toward the android.

Tharn croaked, "Trying—you didn't—give me—chance—"

And then Tharn was lying motionless on the hot sand, staring blindly up. The seven-fingered hands twitched once and were still. The artificial life that had animated the android was gone. It would not return.

Kelvin turned his back and drew a long, shuddering breath. He was safe. He closed his mind to all thoughts but one, all problems but one.

How can I find the red-moustached man?

He pressed the button.

This is the way the story starts:

Quarra Vee sat in the temporal warp with his android Tharn, and made sure everything was under control.

"How do I look?" he asked.

"You'll pass," Tharn said. "Nobody will be suspicious in the era you're going to. It didn't take long to synthesize the equipment."

"Not long. Clothes—they look enough like real wool and linen, I suppose. Wristwatch, money—everything in order. Wristwatch—that's odd, isn't it? Imagine people who need machinery to tell time!"

"Don't forget the spectacles," Tharn said.

Qurra Vee put them on. "Ugh. But I suppose—"

"It'll be safe. The optical properties in the lenses are a guard you may need against dangerous mental radiations. Don't take them off, or the robot may try some tricks."

"He'd better not," Quarra Vee said. "That so-and-so runaway robot! What's he up to, anyway, I wonder? He always was a malcontent, but at least he knew his place. I'm sorry I ever had him made. No telling what he'll do, loose in a semi-prehistoric world, if we don't catch him and bring him home."

"He's in that horomancy booth," Tharn said, leaning out of the time-warp. "Just arrived. You'll have to catch him by surprise. And you'll need your wits about you, too. Try not to go off into any more of those deep-thought compulsions you've been having. They could be dangerous. That robot will use some of his tricks if he gets the chance. I don't know what powers he's developed by himself, but I do know he's an expert at hypnosis and memory erasure already. If you aren't careful he'll snap your memory-track and substitute a false brain-pattern. Keep those glasses on. If anything should go wrong, I'll use the rehabilitation ray on you, eh?" And he held up a small rod-like projector.

Quarra Vee nodded.

"Don't worry. I'll be back before you know it. I have an appointment with that Sirian to finish our game this evening."

It was an appointment he never kept.

Quarra Vee stepped out of the temporal warp and

strolled along the boardwalk toward the booth. The clothing he wore felt tight, uncomfortable, rough. He wriggled a little in it. The booth stood before him now, with its painted sign.

He pushed aside the canvas curtain and something—a carelessly hung rope—swung down at his face, knocking the horn-rimmed glasses askew. Simultaneously a vivid bluish light blazed into his unprotected eyes. He felt a curious, sharp sensation of disorientation, a shifting motion that almost instantly was gone.

The robot said, "You are James Kelvin."

"Ancient, My Enemy" involves hunting as a form of ritual; but hunting has always been one of the most highly ritualized of human activities, in advanced societies whose members hunt for sport as well as among primitive peoples to whom hunted protein provides the margin of survival.

If you take hunting to be the searching out and slaughter of wild animals, then everything that complicates the process is undesirable and even silly. In certain cases, that attitude is undoubtedly the correct one.

Alexander Lake, who hunted extensively in Africa during the middle of this century, described with amusement the laborious efforts of Colonel J. H. Patterson to kill the man-eating lions of Tsavo. Patterson was successful, but not until the lions had killed and eaten nearly a hundred natives and Indian construction workers.

By contrast, a native servant of Lake's dispatched a lion within a day of when the beast killed an old woman in her hut. The lion had been frightened off its kill. Lake's servant waited near the site that night. When the fellow heard growls in the hut, indicating that the lion had returned to finish its dinner, he tossed a grenade through the doorway.

Sporting? Hell, no. But that *cat* didn't kill any more old ladies.

In general, however, killing isn't the only purpose of the hunt. Sometimes it isn't even part of the purpose. The ritual itself is clearly the desired end when foxhunters in immaculate turn-outs ride to their hounds.

Bag limits decrease an individual's annual take of game—in order to increase the game available over a long period. Earlier societies achieved a similar end by letting the nobility atop the social pyramid slaughter game as it chose—and hanging inferior personages who dared to hunt the nobles' game.

Sometimes the limitations with which hunting is entwined have nothing whatever to do with the process of

77

killing animals. This is not to say they're without purpose. Throughout many of the United States, deer hunters are required to wear blaze orange. Their clothing doesn't make them more effective hunters, but it aids in implementing the desired public purpose of keeping hunters from shooting one another.

Primitive hunting rites generally seem meaningless to civilized men who don't share the primitives' worldview. Occasionally the practical reality behind the "superstitious taboos" becomes all too evident.

While the Manchus ruled China, marmot-hunting in Manchuria was limited to local nomads who had a wide variety of restrictions on how the animals (whose pelts were valuable) could be hunted. The nomads always shot marmots instead of catching the beasts in traps. Marmots which acted abnormally were taboo; and if a number of marmots in a colony acted strangely, the nomads broke camp and moved out of the area.

The Manchu dynasty collapsed early in this century. Chinese hunters moved into Manchuria to get their share of the lucrative fur trade, ignoring local superstitions.

Shortly afterwards came a terrible death toll among humans living along the railways and in Harbin, Manchuria's main port. Trapped marmots gave no indication of their state of health, so the civilized Chinese were shipping back the skins of beasts infected with bubonic plague. . . .

ANCIENT,
MY ENEMY

Gordon R. Dickson

They stopped at the edge of the mountains eight hours after they had left the hotel. The day was only a dim paling of the sky above the ragged skyline of rock to the east when they set up their shelter in a little level spot—a sort of nest among the granitic cliffs, ranging from fifty to three hundred meters high, surrounding them.

With the approach of dawn the Udbahr natives trailing them had already begun to seek their own shelters, those cracks in the rock into which they would retreat until the relentless day had come and gone again and the light of the nearer moon called them out. Already holed up high among the rocks, some of the males had begun to sing.

"What's he saying? What do the words mean?" demanded the girl graduate student, fascinated. Her name was Willy Fairchild and in the fading light of the nearer moon she showed tall and slim, with short whitish-blonde hair around a thin-boned face.

Kiev Archad shrugged. He listened a moment.

79

He translated:

> *You desert me now, female,*
> *Because I am crippled,*
> *And yet all my fault was*
> *That I did not lack courage.*
> *Therefore I will go now to the*
> *high rocks to die,*
> *And another will take you.*
> *For what good is a warrior*
> *Whose female forsakes him?*

Kiev stopped translating.

"Go on," said Willy. The song was still mournfully falling upon them from the rocks above.

"There isn't any more," said Kiev. "He just keeps singing it over and over again. He'll go on singing until it's time to seal his hole and keep the heat from drying him up."

"Oh," said Willy. "Is he really crippled, do you think?"

Kiev shrugged again.

"I doubt it," he said. "If he were really hurt he'd be keeping quiet, so none of the other males could find him. As it is, he's probably just hoping to lure another one of them close—so that he can kill himself a full meal before the sun rises."

She gasped.

He looked at her. "Sorry," he said. "If you weren't printed with the language, maybe you weren't printed with the general info—"

"Like the fact that they're cannibals? Of course I was," she said. "It doesn't disturb me at all. Cannibalism is perfectly reasonable in an environment like this where the only other protein available is rock rats—and everything else, except humans, is carbohydrates."

She glanced at one of the several moonplants growing like outsize mushrooms from the rocky rubble of the surface beside the shelter's silver walls. They had already pulled their petals into the protection of horny overhoods. But they had not yet retreated into the ground.

"After all," she said into his silence, "my field's anthropopathic history. People who disturb easily just don't take that up for a study. There were a number of protein-poor areas back on Earth and so-called primitive local people became practical cannibals out of necessity."

"Oh," said Kiev. He wriggled his wide shoulders briefly against the short pre-dawn chill. "We'd better be getting inside and settled. You'll need as much rest as you can get. We'll have to strike the shelter so as to start our drive at sunset."

"Sunset?" She frowned. "It'll still be terribly hot, won't it? What drive?"

He turned sharply to look at her.

"I thought—if you knew about their eating habits—"

"No," she said, interested. "No one said anything to me about drives."

"We've been picking up a gang of them ever since we left the hotel," he said. "And we're protein, too, just as you say. Or at least, enough like their native protein for them to hope to eat us. Sooner or later, if there get to be enough of them, they'll attack—if we don't drive them first."

"Oh, I see. You scare them off before they can start something."

"Something like that—yes." He turned, ran his finger down the closure of the shelter and drew back the flap. "That's why Wadjik and Shant came this far with us—so we could have four men for the drive. Come on, we've got to get inside."

She went past him into the shelter.

Inside, Johnson and the other prospecting team of Wadjik and Shant—who would split with them next evening—were already cosy. Johnson was hunched in his thermal sleeping bag, reading. Wadjik and Shant were at a card table playing bluet. Johnson turned his dark face to Kiev and Willy as they came in.

He said, "I laid your bags out for you—beyond the stores."

"Regular nursemaid," said Wadjik without looking up from his cards.

"Wad," said Johnson, quietly. "You and Shanny can shelter up separately if you want." His bare arms and chest swelled with muscle above the partly open slit of his thermal bag. He was not as big as Wadjik or Kiev but he was the oldest and knew the mountains better than any of them.

"Two more cards," said Wadjik looking to Shant.

The grey-headed man dealt.

Kiev led the way around the card table. Two unrolled thermal bags occupied the floor space next to the entrance to the lavatory partition that gave privacy to the shelter's built-in chemical toilet. Kiev gave the one nearest to the partition to Willy and unrolled the other next to the pile of stores.

The pile was really not much as a shelter divider. By merely lifting himself on one elbow, once he was in his bag, Kiev was able to see the other three bags and Johnson, reading. The card players, sitting up at their table, could look down on both Kiev and Willy—but, of course, once it really started to heat up, they would be in their sacks too.

Kiev undressed within his thermal bag, handing his clothes out as he took them off and keeping his back turned to the girl. When at last he turned to her he saw that, while she was also in her bag, she still wore a sort of light blouse or skivvy shirt—he had no idea what the proper name for it was.

"That's all right for now," he said, nodding at the blouse. "But later on you'll be wanting to get completely down into the bag for coolness, anyhow, so it won't matter for looks. And any kind of cloth between you and the bag's inner surface cuts its efficiency almost in half."

"I don't see why," she answered stiffly.

"They didn't tell you that either?" he asked. "Part of the main idea behind using the thermal bag is that we don't have to carry too heavy an air-conditioning unit. If you take heat from anything, even a human body, you've got to pump it somewhere else. That's what an air-conditioning unit does. But these bags are stuffed between the walls with a chemical heat-absorbent—"

He went on, trying to explain to her that the bag could soak up the heat from her naked body over a fourteen-hour period without getting so full of heat it lost its cooling powers. But the lining of the bag was built to operate in direct contact with the human skin. Anything like cloth in between caused a build-up of stored heat that would overload the bag before the fourteen hours until cool-off was over. It was not just a matter of comfort—she would be risking heat prostration and even death.

She listened stiffly. He did not know if he had convinced her or not. But he got the feeling that when the time finally came she would get rid of the garment. He lay back on his own bag, closed his eyes and tried to get some sleep. In another four hours sleep would be almost impossible even in the bags.

Wadjik and Shant were fools with their cards. A man could tough out a drive with only a couple of hours of sleep; but what if some accident during the next shelter stop kept him from getting any sleep at all? He could be half-dead with heat and exhaustion by the following cool-off, his judgment gone and his reflexes shot. One little bit of bad luck could finish him off. Characters like Johnson had survived in the mountains all these years by always keeping in shape. After four trips into the grounds Kiev had made up his mind to do the same thing.

*   *   *

He slept. The heat woke him.

He found he had instinctively slid down into his bag and sealed it up to the neck without coming fully awake. Opening his eyes now, feeling the blasting dryness and quivering heat of the air against his already parched face, he first pulled his head down completely into the bag and took a deep breath. The hot air from above, pulled momentarily into the bag, cooled on his dust-dry throat and mouth. He worked some saliva into existence, swallowed several times and then, sitting up, pushed his head and one arm out of the bag. He found his salve and began to grease his face and neck.

He glanced over at Willy as he worked. She was lying muffled in her thermal bag, watching him, her features shining with salve.

"You take that shirt off?" he asked.

She nodded briefly. He looked over past the deserted card table at the three other thermal bags. Johnson, encased to his nose, slept with the ease of an old prospector, his upper face placidly shining with salve. Shant was out of sight in his bag—all but his close-cut cap of grey hair. Wadjik was propped up against a case from the stores, his heavy-boned face under its uncombed black hair absent-eyed, staring at and through Kiev.

"Wad," said Kiev, "better get Shanny up out of that. He'll overload his sack in five hours if he goes to sleep breathing down there like that."

Wadjik's eyes focused. He grinned unpleasantly and rolled over on his side. He bent in the middle and kicked the foot of his thermal bag hard against the side of Shant's. Shant's head popped into sight.

"You go to sleep down there," Wad snarled, "and you won't live until sunset."

"Oh—sure, Wad. Sorry," Shant said, quickly.

A short silence fell. Wadjik had gone back to staring through unfocused eyes. Johnson woke but the only sign he gave was the raising of his eyelids. He did not move in his bag. Around them all, now, the heat was becoming a living thing—an invisible but sentient presence, a demon inside the shelter who could be felt growing stronger almost by the second. The shelter's little air conditioner hummed, keeping the air about them moving and just below unbreathable temperature.

"Kiev," said Wadjik, suddenly. "Was that old Hehog you and Willy were listening to out there, just before dawn?"

"Yes," said Kiev.

"This time we'll get him."

"Maybe," said Kiev.

"No maybe. I mean it, man."

"We'll see," said Kiev.

A movement came beside Kiev. Willy sat up in her bag.

"Mr. Wadjik—"

"Joe. I told you—Joe."

Wadjik grinned at her.

"All right. Joe. Do you mean you don't know which Udbahr male that was—the one who was singing? Don't you know why I'm going to these prospecting grounds of yours? Don't you know about the remains of a city there built by these same Udbahrs?"

"Sure, I've seen it. What of it?"

"I'm telling you what of it! They had a high level of civilization once—or at least a higher level than now. But that doesn't mean anything to you—"

"They degenerated. That's what it means to me. They're cannibal degenerates. And you want me to treat them like human beings—"

"I want you to treat them like intelligent beings— which they are. Even an uneducated, brutal, stupid man like you ought to understand—"

"Listen to who's talking. The kid historian speaks. I thought you were still in school, writing a thesis. You didn't tell me you'd been at this for years—"

"I may be only a graduate student but I've learned a few things you never did—"

Looking past Wadjik's heat-reddened face, flaming under its salve, Kiev saw the upper part of Johnson's countenance beyond. Johnson seemed to be calmly listening. There was nothing to do, Kiev knew, but listen. It was the heat—the sickening intoxication of the deadly heat in the shelter—that was making the argument. When the heat reached its most relentless intensity only the instinct keeping men in their thermal bags stopped them from killing each other.

Wadjik finally broke off the argument by drawing down into his bag and rolling across the floor of the shelter to the lavatory door. He pressed the bottom latch through his bag, opened the door, rolled inside and shut himself off from the rest of the room. Willy fell silent.

Kiev looked sideways at her.

"It's no use," he whispered to her. "Save your energy."

She turned and glared at him.

"And I thought you were different!" She spat and slid down, head and all, into her bag.

Kiev backed into his own cocoon. Fuelled by the feverishness induced by the heat, his mind ran on. They were all a little crazy, he thought, all who had taken up prospecting. Crazy or they had something to hide in their pasts that would keep them from ever leaving this planet.

But a man who was clean elsewhere, could become rich in five years if he kept his head—and kept his health—both on the trips and back in civilization. On Kiev's first trip into the mountains, two years ago, he had not known what he was after. Just a lot of money, he had thought, to blow back at the hotels. But now he knew better. He was going to take it cool and calm, like Johnson—who could never leave the planet.

Kiev meant to keep his own backtrail clear. And he would leave when the time came with enough to buy him citizenship and a good business franchise back on one of the Old Worlds. He had his picture of the future clear in his mind. A modern home on a settled world, a steady, good income. Status. A family.

He had seen enough of the wild edges of civilization. Leave the rest of it to the new kids coming out. He was still young but he could look ahead and see thirty up there waiting for him.

His thoughts rambled on through the deadly hours as his body temperature was driven slowly upward by the heat. In the end his mind rambled and staggered. He awoke suddenly.

He had passed from near-delirium into sleep without realizing it. The deadly heat of mid-afternoon had broken towards cool-off and with the first few degrees of relief within the shelter he, like all the rest, had dropped immediately into exhausted slumber. By now—he glanced at the wristwatch on the left sleeve of his outergear—the hour was nearly sunset.

He looked about the shelter. Willy, Shant, Wadjik, Johnson were still sleeping.

"Hey," he croaked at them, speaking above a whisper for the first time in hours. "Time for the drive. Up and at 'em."

In forty-five minutes they were all dressed, fed and outside, with the shelter folded and packed, along with the other equipment, on grav-sleds ready to travel. Wadjik and Shant took off to the north, towing their own grav-sled. Kiev and Johnson were left with their sled and the girl. They looked at her thoughtfully. The sun was already down below the peaks to the west. But three-quarters of the sky above them was still white with a glare too bright to look at directly and the heat, even with outersuit and helmet sealed, made every movement a new cause for perspiration. The climate units of the suits whined with their effort to keep the occupants dry and cool.

"I'm not going to join you," Willy snapped. "I won't be a party to any killing of the natives."

"We can't leave you behind," Kiev answered. "Unless you can handle a gun—and will use it. If any of the males break away from the drive they'll double back and you'd make an easy meal."

Inside the transparent helmet her fact was pale even in the heat.

"You can stick with the grav-sled," said Kiev. "You don't have to join the drive. Just keep up."

She did not look at him or speak. She was not going to give him the satisfaction of an answer, he thought.

"Move out, then," said Johnson.

They began to climb the cliffs towards the brightness in the sky, the grav-sled trailing behind them on slave circuit, its load piled high. Willy, looking small in her suit, trudged behind it. Under the crown of the cliffs they turned about, deployed to cover both sides of the clearing below and began their drive.

They worked forward, each man firing into every rock niche or cranny that might have an Udbahr sealed up within it. Deep, booming sounds—made by the air and moisture within each cranny exploding outward—began to echo between the cliffs. Soon a shout came over Kiev's suit intercom in Johnson's deep voice.

"One running! One running! Eleven o'clock, sixty meters, down in the cleft there."

Kiev jerked his gaze ahead and caught a glimpse of an adult-sized, humanlike, brown figure with a greenishly naked, round skull and large tarsier-like eyes, vanishing up a narrow cut.

"No clothing," called Kiev over the intercom. "Must be a female, or a young male."

"Or maybe old Hehog playing it incognito—" Johnson began but was interrupted.

"One running! One running!" bellowed Wadjik's voice distantly over the intercom. "Two o'clock, near clifftop."

"One running! Deep in the pass there at three o'clock!" chimed in Johnson, again. "Keep them moving!"

The sounds of the blasting attack were now routing

out Udbahrs who had denned up for the day. Most were females or young, innocent of either clothing or weapons. But here and there was a heavier, male figure, running with spear or throwing-stick in hand and wearing anything from a rope of twisted rock vines or rat furs around his waist to some tattered article of clothing, stolen, scavenged—or just possibly taken as a war prize—from the dead body of a human prospector.

The males were slowed by their insistence on herding the females and the young ahead of them. They always did this, even though nearly all prospectors made it a point to kill only the grown males—the warriors who were liable to attack if left alive. The pattern was old, familiar—one of the things that made most prospectors swear the Udbahrs had to be animal rather than intelligent. The females and young were gathering into a herd as they ran, joining up beyond the screen of the males following them. When the herd was complete— when all who should be in it had been accounted for— the males would choose their ground, stop and turn to fight and hold up the pursuers while the females and young escaped.

They always reacted the same way, no matter whether the tactic were favorable or not in the terrain where they were being driven. Kiev thought suddenly. Everything the Udbahrs did was by rote. And strange to creatures who reasoned like men. No matter what Willy said, it was hard to think of them as any kind of people— let alone people with whom you could become involved. For example, if he, Johnson, Shant and Wadjik quit driving the natives now and pulled back, the Udbahr males would immediately turn around and start trying to kill each other. It was only when they were being driven or were joining for an attack on prospectors that the males had ever been known to cooperate.

So, as it always went, it went this sunset hour on the Udbahr Planet. By the time the last light of the day star was beginning to evaporate from the western sky and the great ghostly circle of the nearer moon was beginning to be visible against a more reasonably lighted sky, some half dozen of the Udbahr males disappeared suddenly among the boulders and rocks at the mouth of a pass down which the herd of females and young were vanishing.

"Hold up," Johnson gasped over the intercom. "Hold it up. They've forted. Stop and breathe."

Kiev checked his weary legs and collapsed into sitting position on a boulder, panting. His body was damp all over in spite of the efforts of his suit to keep him dry. His head rang with a headache induced by exhaustion and the heat.

The Udbahr males hidden among the rocks near the mouth of the pass began to sing their individual songs of defiance.

Kiev's breathing eased. His headache receded to a dull ache and finally disappeared. The last of the daylight was all but gone from the sky behind them. The nearer moon, twice as large as the single moon of Earth by which all moons were measured, was sharply outlined, bright in the sky, illuminating the scene with a sort of continuing twilight.

"What're you waiting for?" Willy's voice said dully in his earphones. "Why don't you go and kill them?"

He turned to look for her and was astonished to find her, with the grav-sled, almost beside him. She had sat down on the ground, her back bowed as if in deep discouragement, her face turned away and hidden from him within the transparent helmet.

"They'll come to us," he muttered, without thinking.

Suddenly she curled up completely into a huddled ball of silver outerwear suit and crystalline helmet. The sheer, unutterable anguish of her pose squeezed at his throat.

He dropped down to his knees beside her and put his arms around her. She did not respond.

"You don't understand—" he said. And then he had the sense to tongue off the interphone and speak to her directly and privately through the closeness of their helmets, alone. "You don't understand."

"I do understand. You like to do this. You like it."

Her voice was muffled, dead.

His heart turned over at the sound of it and suddenly, unexpectedly, he realized that he had somehow managed to fall in love with her. He felt sick inside. It was all wrong—all messed up. He had meant to go looking for a woman—but eventually, after he'd made his stake and gone back to some civilized world. He had not planned anything like this involvement with a girl he had known only five days and who had all sorts of wild notions about how things should be. He did not know what to do except kneel there, holding her.

"If you don't like it why do you do it?" her voice said. "If you really don't like it—then don't do it. Now. Let these go."

"I can't," he said.

The singing broke off suddenly in a concerted howl from the Udbahr males, mingled with a triumphant cry over the intercom from Wadjik.

"Got one." And then: "Look out. Stones."

Kiev jerked into the shelter of a boulder, dragging Willy with him. Two rocks, each about half the size of his fist, dug up the ground where they had crouched together.

"You see?"

He pushed her roughly from him and drew his sidearm. Leaning around the boulder, he searched the rocks of the slope below the pass, watching the vernier needle of the heat-indicator slide back and forth on the weapon's barrel. It jumped suddenly and he stopped moving.

He peered into the gun's rear sights, thumbing the near lens to telescopic. He held his aim on the warm location, studying the small area framed in the sight screen. Suddenly he made it out—a tiny patch of brown between a larger boulder and a bit of upright, broken rock.

He aimed carefully.

"Don't do it."

He jerked involuntarily, sending his beam wide of the mark at the sound of her voice. A patch of bare gravel boomed and flew. The bit of brown color disappeared from between the rocks. He leaned the front of his helmet wearily against the near side of the boulder before him.

"Damn you," he said helplessly. "What are you doing to me?"

"I'm trying to save you," she said fiercely, "from being a murderer."

Another stone hit the top of the boulder behind which they hid and caromed off their heads.

"How about saving me from that?" he said emptily. "Don't you understand? If we don't kill them they'll try to kill us—"

"I don't believe it." She, too, had shut off her intercom. Her voice came to him distantly through two thicknesses of transparent material. "Have you ever tried? Has anyone ever tried?"

Another sudden valley of stones was followed by more dull explosions as the heat of the human weapons found and destroyed live targets. Shant and Wadjik were howling in triumph and shooting steadily.

"We got five—they're on the run," Shant whooped. "Kiev! Johnson! They're on the run!"

The explosions ceased. Kiev peered cautiously around his boulder, stood up slowly. Wadjik, Shant, and Johnson had risen from positions in a semicircle facing the distant pass.

"Any get away?" Johnson was asking.

"One, maybe two—" Shant cut himself short. "Look out—duck. Twelve o'clock, fifty meters."

At once Kiev was again down behind his boulder. He dragged down Willy, tongued on his intercom.

"What is it?"

"That chunk of feldspar about a meter high—"

Kiev looked down the slope until his eyes found the rock. A glint that came and went behind and above it, winking in the waxing light of the nearer moon that now seemed as bright as a dull, cloudy day back on Earth. The flash came and went, came and went.

Kiev recognized it presently as a reflection from the top curve of a transparent helmet bobbing back and forth like the head of someone dancing just behind the boulder. A male Udbahr's voice began to sing behind the rock.

> Man with a head-and-a-half
> come and get your half-head.
> Man with a head-and-a-half
> Come so I can kill you.
> Ancient, my enemy.
> Ancient, my enemy—

"Hehog," snapped Johnson's voice over the intercom.

Silence held for a minute. Then Wadjik's voice came thinly through the phones.

"What are you waiting for, Kiev?"

Kiev said nothing. The transparent curve of the helmet top rose again, bobbed and danced behind the boulder. It danced higher. Within it now was a bald, round, greenish skull with reddish, staring tarsier eyes and—finally revealed—the lipless gash of a fixedly grinning mouth.

"What is it? What's Wadjik mean?" Willy asked.

Her voice rang loud in Kiev's helmet phones. She had reactivated her intercom.

"It's Hehog down there," Kiev said between stiff jaws. "That's my helmet he's wearing. He's had it ever since he first took it off me my first trip into the mountains."

"Took it off you?"

"I was new. I'd never been on a drive before," muttered Kiev. "I got hit in the chest by a stone, had the wind knocked out of me. Next thing I knew Hehog was lifting off my helmet. My partners came up shooting and drove him off."

"What about it, Kiev?" The voice was Johnson's. "Do you want us to spread out and get behind him? Or you want to go down and get the helmet by yourself?"

Kiev grunted under his breath, took his sidearm into his left hand and flexed the cramped fingers of his right. They had been squeezing the gunbutt as if to mash it out of all recognizable shape.

"I'm going alone," he said over the intercom. "Stay back."

He got his heels under him and was ready to rise when he was unexpectedly yanked backward to the gravel. Willy had pulled him down.

"You're not going."

He tongued off his intercom, turned and jerked her hand loose from his suit.

"You don't understand," he shouted at her through his helmet. "That's the trouble with you. You don't understand a damn thing."

He pushed her from him, rose and dived for the protection of a boulder four meters down the slope in front of him and a couple of meters to his right.

A flicker of movement came from below as he moved— the upward leap of a throwing-stick behind the rock where Hehog hid. Kiev glimpsed something dark racing through the air towards him. A rock fragment struck and burst on the boulder-face, spraying him with stone chips and splinters.

Reckless now, he threw himself towards the next bit of rock cover farther down the slope. His foot caught on a stony outcropping in the shale. He tripped and rolled, tumbling helplessly to a stop beside the very boulder behind which Hehog crouched, throwing-stick in one hand, stone-tipped spear in the other.

Kiev sprawled on his back. He stared helplessly up into the great eyes and humorlessly grinning mouth looming over him inside the other helmet less than an arm's length away. The spear twitched in the brown hand—but that was all.

Hehog stared into Kiev's eyes. Kiev was aware of Willy and the others shouting through his helmet phones. A couple of shots blasted grooves into the boulder-top above his head. And with a sudden, wordless cry Hehog bounded to his feet and dodged away among the boulder towards the pass.

The bright beams of shots from the human guns followed him but lost him. He vanished into the pass.

Kiev climbed to his feet, shaking inside. He awoke to the fact that he was still holding his sidearm. A bitter understanding broke upon him with the hard, unsparing clarity of an Udbahr Planet dawn.

He could have shot Hehog at point-blank range during the moment he had spent staring frozenly at the spear in Hehog's hand and at the great-eyed, grinning head within the helmet. Hehog had to have seen the gun. And that would have been why he had not tried to throw the spear.

Kiev cursed blackly. He was still cursing when the others slid down the loose rock of the slope to surround him.

"What happened?" demanded Shant.

"He—" Kiev discovered that his intercom was still off. He tongued it on. "He got away."

"We know he got away," said Wadjik. "What we want to know is how come?"

"You saw," Kiev snapped. "I fell. He had me. You scared him off."

"He had you? I thought you had *him,* damn it!"

"All right, he's gone," Johnson said. "That's the main thing. Leave the other bodies for whoever wants to eat them. We've had a good drive. We'll split up, now." He looked at Wadjik and Shant. "See you back in civilization."

Wadjik cursed cheerfully.

"Team with the heaviest load buys the drinks," he said. "Come on, Shanny."

The two of them turned away, dragging their loaded grav-sled through the air behind them.

Kiev, Willy and Johnson reached Dead City a good two hours before dawn. They had time to pick out one of the empty, windowless houses, half-cave, half-building, to use as permanent headquarters. Tomorrow night they would cut stone to fill the open doorway but for today the shelter, fitted double-thick into the opening, would do well enough.

No singing came from the surrounding cliffs. Johnson crawled in. Kiev lingered to speak to Willy.

"You don't have to worry." The words were not what he had planned to say. "The Udbahr are scared of this place."

"I know." She did not look at him. "Of course. I know more about this city and the Udbahrs than even Mr. Johnson does. There's a taboo on this place for them."

"Yes." Kiev looked down at his gloved right hand and spread the fingers, still feeling the hard butt of his sidearm clamped inside them. "About earlier tonight, with Hehog—"

"It's all right," she said softly, looking unexpectedly up at him. Her intercom was off and her voice came to him through her helmet. In the combination of the low-angled moonlight and the first horizon glow of the dawn, her face seemed luminescent. "I know you did it for me—after all."

He stared at her.

"Did what?"

She still spoke softly: "I know why you let that

Udbahr male live. It was because of what I'd said, wasn't it? But you need to be ashamed of nothing. You simply haven't gone bad inside, like the others. Don't worry—I won't tell anyone."

She took his arm gently with both hands, and lifted her head as if—had they been unhelmeted—she might have kissed his cheek. Then she turned and disappeared into the cave.

He followed her after some moments. A small filter panel in the shelter had let a little of the terrible daylight through the illumination. Here artificial lighting had to be on. Kiev saw by it that she had piled stores and opened some of her own gear to set up a four-foot wall that gave her individual privacy.

He laid out his own thermal bag. The heat was quite bearable behind the insulation of the thick-walled building as the day began. Kiev fell into a deep, exhausted sleep that seemed completely dreamless.

He awoke without warning. Instantly alert, he rose to an elbow.

The light was turned down. He heard no sound from Willy. Johnson snored.

Kiev remained stiffly propped on one elbow. A feeling of danger prickled his skin. He found his ears were straining for some noise that did not belong here.

He listened.

For a long moment he heard only the snoring and beyond it silence. Then he heard what had awakened him. It came again, like the voice of some imprisoned spirit—not from beyond the wall but from under the stone floor on which he lay.

> *Man with a head-and-a-half,*
> *come and get your half-head.*
> *Man with a head-and-a-half,*
> *Come, so I can kill you.*
> *Ancient, my enemy.*
> *Ancient, my enemy.*

The singing broke off suddenly. Kiev jerked bolt upright and the thermal bag fell down around his waist. Suddenly more loudly through the rock, and nearer, the voice echoed in the dim interior of the stone building:

> *Only for ourselves is the killing*
> *of each other!*
> *Man with a head-and-a-half,*
> *come and get your half-head.*
> *Man with a head-and-a-half . . .*

The singing continued. Fury uprushed like vomit in Kiev. He swore, tearing off his thermal bag and pawing through his piled outerwear. His fingers closed on the butt of the weapon. He jerked it clear, aimed it at the section of the floor from which the singing was coming and pressed the trigger.

Light, heat and thunder shredded the sleeping quiet of the dimly lit room. Kiev held the beam steady, a hotter rage inside him than he could express with the rock-rending gun. He felt his arm seized. The sidearm was torn from his grip. He whirled to find Johnson holding the weapon out of reach.

"Give me that," Kiev said thickly.

"Wake up," Johnson said, low-voiced. "What's got into you?"

"Didn't you hear?" Kiev shouted at him. "That was Hehog—Hehog! Down there!"

He pointed at the hole with its melted sides, half a meter deep into the floor of the building.

"I heard," said Johnson. "It was Hehog, all right. There must be tunnels under some of these buildings."

Willy chimed in.

"But Udbahrs don't—"

Kiev and Johnson turned to see her staring at them over the top of her barricade. Kiev became suddenly conscious that, like Johnson, he was completely without clothes.

Willy's face disappeared abruptly. Kiev turned back to look at the hole his gun had burned in the stone. It showed no breakthrough into further darkness at the bottom.

"All right," he said shakily. "I'm sorry. I woke up hearing him and just jumped—that's all. We can shift to another building tomorrow. And sound for tunnels before we move in."

Johnson turned and returned to his thermal bag. Kiev resumed his cocoon. He lay on his back, hands behind his head, staring up at the shadowy ceiling.

. . . Ancient, my enemy . . . ancient, my enemy . . .

The memory of Hehog's chant continued to run through his head.

You and me, Hehog. I'll show you, Udbahr . . .

And some time he fell asleep.

They moved camp the next night, as soon as the sun was down. Kiev and Johnson quarried large chunks of rock from the wall on an adjoining building, melted them into place to fill up the new door opening, except for the entrance unit, which was set up double as a heat lock and fitted into place.

Now the shelter air conditioner could keep the whole interior of the new building comfortable all day long. The night was half over by the time they finished.

Kiev and Johnson had some four hours left to trek to their prospecting area. The gold ore deposits in the neighborhood of Dead City were almost always in pipes and easily worked out in a few days by men with the proper equipment.

Kiev hesitated.

"I'll stay," he said. "With Hehog around, someone's got to stay with Miss Fairchild."

Johnson regarded him thoughtfully.

"You're right. If we leave her here alone Hehog's sure to get her. And who would sell us gear for our next

trip if word got out about how we left her to be killed?"
He hesitated. "Tell you what—we'll draw straws."

Kiev said, "I'll stay. Drop back in a week. I'll tell you
then if I need you to take over."

Johnson nodded. He turned away and began his
packing—food, weapons, equipment, a water drill for
tapping the moonflower root systems. Also, a breathing
membrane for sealing the caves they would be denning
up in by day. Kiev, squatting, making a final check of
the seal around the entrance, saw a shadow fall across a
seam he was examining.

He stood up, turned and saw Willy down the street,
taking solidographs of one of the buildings. Johnson
stood just behind him, equipment already on his
backpack.

"We haven't had a chance to talk," Johnson said.

"No."

"Let me say now what I've wanted to say. Why don't
you pack up and go back—and take the girl with you?"

"I've got my stake to make out here—like everybody
else."

"You know there's more to the situation. Hehog's
changed everything. Also, there's the girl—we both
know what I mean. And there's something else—something I don't think you're aware of."

"What?"

"You've heard how sometimes the males—if they've
just fed so they aren't hungry and there's only one of
them around—will come into your camp and sit down
to talk?"

Kiev frowned at him.

"I've heard of it," he said. "It's never happened to
me."

"It's happened to me," said Johnson. "They ask you
things that'd surprise you. Surprise you what they tell
you, too. You know why Hehog's broken taboo and
come right into Dead City?"

"Do you?"

Johnson nodded.

"There's a thing the Udbahrs believe in," Johnson said. "They figure that when they eat someone they eat his soul, too?"

"Sure," said Kiev. "And that soul stays inside them until they're killed. Then, when they die, if no one else eats them right away, all the souls of all the bodies they've eaten in their lives fly loose and take over the bodies of pups too young to have strong souls of their own."

Johnson nodded. He tilted his head at the distant figure of Willy.

"You've been learning from her," he said.

"Her? As a matter of fact, I have," said Kiev. "But you were the one who told me about Udbahr cannibalism—a year or more ago."

"Did I?" Johnson looked at him. "Did I tell you about Ancient Enemies?"

Kiev shook his head.

"Once in a while a couple of males get a real feud going. It's not an ordinary hate. It's almost a noble thing—if you follow me. And from then on the feud never stops, no matter how many times they both die. Every time one is killed and born again—when he grows up it's turn to kill the other one. The next time the roles are reversed. You follow me?"

Kiev frowned.

"No."

"Figure both souls live forever through any number of bodies. They take turns killing each other physically." Johnson looked strangely at Kiev. "The only thing is that no soul ever remembers from one body to the next—they never know whose turn it is to be killed and which one's to be the killer. So they just keep running into each other until the soul of one of them tells him, 'Go!' Then he kills the other and goes off to wait to die."

Johnson stopped speaking. Kiev stared.

"You mean Hehog thinks he and I—he thinks we're these Ancient Enemies?"

"Night before last," said Johnson, "you and he were face to face, both armed—and neither one of you killed the other. Yesterday—while we were denned up—he showed up here in the Dead City where it's taboo for him to be. Being Ancient Enemies is the only thing that'd set him free of a taboo like that. What do you think?"

Kiev turned for a second look down the street at Willy.

"Hehog's not going to leave you alone if I'm right," said Johnson. "And he's smart. He might even get away with killing one or two of us so he could stay close to you. And the easiest one for him to kill would be that girl. And it's true what I said. We lose a human woman out here and no supplier's going to touch us with a ten-foot pole."

"Yeah," said Kiev.

"I'm not afraid of Hehog, myself. But I've got no place else to go. I plan to die out here some day—but not yet for a few trips. Take the girl and head back. Give up the mountains while you still can. Kiev—I mean it."

"You can't make us leave," Kiev said slowly.

"No," said Johnson. His face looked old and dark as weather-stained oak. "But you keep that girl here and Hehog'll get her. She doesn't know anything but books and she doesn't understand someone like Hehog. She doesn't even understand us." He took a step back. "So long, partner," he said. "See you in three nights—maybe."

He turned and walked away slowly, leaning forward against the weight of the pack, until he was lost among the rocks of the western cliffs.

Kiev turned and saw the small shape of Willy even farther down the street, still taking pictures.

He continued to think for the next two days and nights, which were quiet. He spent most of his time

studying the aerial maps near Dead City he had planned
to work during this trip. Actually he was getting his
ideas in order for explanation to Willy, who seemed to
be having the time of her life. She was measuring and
photographing Dead City inch by inch, as excited over
it as if it were one large Christmas present. She had
changed towards him, too, teasing him and doing for
him, by turns.

Hehog did not sing from underground in the new
building.

On the third night Kiev invited himself along on her
work with the City.

He realized now that what Johnson had told him was
true. Johnson's words had been the final shove he had
needed to make up his mind. The fact that he and Willy
had met less than a week ago meant nothing. Out here
things were different.

He had worried about how he would bring up the
subject of his future—and hers. But it turned out that
he had no need to bring it up. It was already there.
Almost before he knew it they were talking as if certain
things were understood and taken for granted.

He said, "I've got at least five more trips to make to
get the stake I need for a move back to the Old Worlds.
You'd have to wait."

"But you don't need to keep coming back here," she
said. "I know how you can make the rest of the money
you need without even one more trip. I know because a
publishing company talked to me about doing something like it. There's a steady market for information
about humanoids like the Udbahrs. Books, lectures.
Acting as industrial and economic consultant—"

He stared at her.

"I couldn't do anything like that," he said. "I'm no
good with words and theories—"

"You don't have to be. All you have to do is tell what
you've seen and done on these trips of yours. You'll
collect enough on advance bookings alone for us to go

back to any Old World you want—after I get my doctor-ate, of course—and settle down there. Don't forget I've got my work, too. I'll be teaching." She stared at him eagerly. "And think of what you'll be achieving. Intelligent natives are being killed off or exploited on new worlds like this one simply because there's no local concern over them and because our civilization hasn't understood them enough to make the necessary concessions for them to accept it. You could be the one to get the ball rolling that could save the Udbahrs from being hunted down and killed off—"

"By people like me, you mean," he said, a little sourly.

"Not you. You haven't yet been infected with the sort of killing lust Wadjik and Shant—and even Johnson —have."

"It isn't a lust. Out here you have to kill the Udbahrs to keep them from killing you."

She looked at him sharply.

"Yes—if you're a savage," she said. "As the Udbahrs are savages. I couldn't love an Udbahr. I could only love a man who was civilized—able to keep the savage part inside him chained up. That Ancient Enemy business Hehog sang to you—that's the way a savage thinks. I don't expect you not to have the psychological capacity to lust for killing—but if you're a healthy-minded man you can keep that sort of Ancient Enemy locked up inside you. You don't have to let him take you over."

He opened his mouth to make one more stubborn effort to explain himself to her, then closed it again rather helplessly. He found a certain uncomfortable rightness in part of what she was saying. Although from that rightness she went off into left field somewhere to an area where he was sure she was wrong. While he groped for words to express himself the still air around him was suddenly torn by the sound of a gun-bolt explosion.

He found himself running towards the building they had set up as their headquarters, sidearm in his hand, the sound of Willy's voice and footsteps following him. The distance was not great and he did not slow down for her. Better if he made it first—or if she did not come at all until he knew what had happened.

He rounded the corner of the building and saw the shelter entrance hanging in blackened tatters. He dove past it. By some miracle the light was still burning against the ceiling but the interior it illuminated was a scene of wreckage. Concussion and heat from the bolt had torn apart or scorched everything in the place.

With a wild coldness inside him, he pawed swiftly through the rubble for whatever was usable. Two thermal sleeping bags were still in working condition, though their outer covering was charred in spots and stinking of burned plastic. Food containers were ripped open and their contents destroyed. The water drill was workable and most of one air membrane was untouched.

"What happened? Who did it? Kiev—"

He awoke to the fact that Willy was with him again, literally pulling at him to get his attention. He came erect wearily.

"I don't know," he said, dully. "Maybe some prospector has gone out of his head entirely. Or—"

He hesitated.

"Or what?"

He looked at her.

"Or an Udbahr male has gotten hold of the gun of a dead prospector."

Her face thinned and whitened under the light of the overhead lamp.

"A dead—"

She did not finish.

"That's right," he said. "One of our people, it could be—Wadjik, Shant, or Johnson."

"How could a savage who knows only sticks and stones kill an experienced, armed man?"

Willy sounded outraged.

"All sorts of animals kill people." He felt sick inside, hating himself for not having set up at least a trigger wire to guard the building area. "We've got to get out of here. We can't spend another night in a building, anyway, without a shelter entrance."

"Where'll we go?"

"We'll head towards Johnson," Kiev said. "He isn't digging so far away that we shouldn't be able to make it before dawn—if he isn't dead."

They started out on the bearing Johnson had taken and soon left the city behind them. Fully risen moon-flowers—some of them giants over three meters high—surrounded them. They were lost in a forest of strange, pale beauty, where by day there would only be the bare, heat-blasted mountainside.

"Aren't we likely to pass him and not even see him?" asked Willy.

"No," Kiev said absently. "He'll be following contours at a constant elevation. So are we. When he gets close enough, we'll hear static in our earphones."

He did not again mention the possibility of Johnson's being dead—partly because he wanted to be easy on himself.

They tramped on in silence. Kiev's mind was busy among the number of problems opened up by their present situation. After about an hour he heard the hiss of interference in his helmet phones that signalled the approach of another transmitting unit.

He stopped so suddenly that Willy bumped into him. He rotated his helmet slowly, listening for the maximum noise. When he found it, he spoke.

"Johnson? Johnson, can you hear me?"

"Thought it was you, Kiev." Johnson's voice came distorted and weakened by rock distance. "The girl with you? What's up?"

"Somebody fired a gun into our building," said Kiev. "I scraped together a sort of maintenance kit out of what was left—but I'm carrying all the salvage."

"I see." Johnson did not waste breath on speculation. "Stop where you are and wait for me. We better head back towards Wad's and Shanny's diggings as soon as we're together. No point your burning energy trying to meet me halfway."

"Right."

Kiev loosened his pack and sat down with his back to the trunk of a moonflower. Willy sat beside him. She said nothing and, busy with his own thoughts still, he hardly noticed her silence.

By the time Johnson found them Kiev had already worked out the new compass heading from their present location to the diggings where Wadjik and Shant had planned to work. A little over three hours of the night remained.

"Do you think we can make it before dawn?" Kiev asked as the three of them started out on the new heading. "You've been through that area before, haven't you?"

Johnson nodded.

"I don't know," he said. "It'll be faster going once the moonflowers are down." He looked at Willy. "We'll be pushing on as fast as we can. Think you can keep up?"

"Yes," she said without looking at him. Her voice was dull.

"Good. If you start really to give out, though, speak up. Don't overdo it to the point where we have to carry you. All right?"

"Yes."

They continued their march. Soon the moonflowers had drawn in their petals until they were hardly visible under the hoods and begun their retreat into the ground. The men were now able to see, across the tops of the hoods, the general shape of the terrain and pick the most direct route from contour point to contour point. Willy walked between them. The moonflower hoods still stood above her head—tall as she was for a woman—but did not seem to bother her. She looked at nothing.

Johnson glanced at Kiev across the top of her helmet, and tongued off his helmet phones. He let her walk slightly ahead, then leaned towards Kiev until their helmets touched.

"I told you," Johnson said softly through the helmet contact. "She didn't understand or believe. We were something out of books to her—so were the Udbahrs. Now she's trying hard to keep on not believing. You see why I told you yesterday to get out of here?"

Kiev said nothing.

Johnson pulled back his helmet, tongued his intercom back on, kept walking.

After a while the sky began to whiten ominously. The nearer moon was low and paling on the horizon behind. Johnson halted. Kiev and Willy also stopped.

"It's no good," said Johnson, over the intercom to Kiev. "We're going to have to take time to find a hole to crawl into before day. We're going to have to quit and wait for night."

Kiev nodded.

"A hole?" echoed Willy.

Kiev looked at Johnson. Johnson shrugged. The message of the shrug was clear—there were no caves in this area. But they hunted until Johnson called a halt.

"This will have to do."

He pointed to a crack in a rock face. He and Kiev attacked the crack with mining tools and their guns.

Twenty minutes' work hollowed out a burrow three meters in circular diameter, with an entrance two feet square. Above the entrance the crack had been sealed with melted rock. The trio crawled inside and fitted the breathing membrane in place against the opening.

Kiev waited until all were undressed and in their thermal bags before setting the light he had saved from the building in place against the rocky ceiling. The cramped closeness of their enclosure came to solid life around them. The den was beginning to heat up.

The place had no air-conditioning unit—the shelter had been a palace by comparison. Even Kiev had to struggle against the intoxicating effect of the heat and the claustrophobic panic of the enclosed space. Willy went out of her head before noon. Kiev and Johnson had to hold her in her thermal bag. Shortly after that she went into syncope and stayed unconscious until cool-off.

Haggard with exhaustion, Kiev leaned on one elbow above her, staring down into her face, now smoothed out into natural sleep. Teetering on the verge of irresistible unconsciousness himself, he felt in him the strange clear-headedness of utter weariness. She had been right, he thought, about that primitive part in him and all men—the Ancient Enemy. The prospectors did not so much fight the Udbahr males out here as something in themselves that corresponded to its equivalent in the Udbahrs. The lust for killing. A lust that could get you to the point where you no longer cared if you were killed yourself.

Kiev never finished the thought. When he opened his eyes the membrane was down from the entrance and outside was the cool and blessed moonlight.

He crawled out to find Willy and Johnson already packing gear.

"Got to move, Kiev," said Johnson, seeing him. "If Wad and Shanny are alive and headed home we want to take out after them as soon as possible. One long night's walk can put us back at the hotel."

"The hell you say." Kiev was astonished. "They didn't come all the way out with us and then cut that far back to find a a digging area."

"No," Johnson said, "But from here we can hit a different pass through the border range. Going back that way makes the hypotenuse of a right triangle. Coming out we would have dog-legged it to reach this point like doing the triangle's other two sides. You understand?"

Within half an hour they were on their way. And within an hour, as they were coming around a high spire of rock, Johnson put out his arm and stopped.

"Wait here, Willy," Johnson said. "Come on, Kiev."

The two men rounded the rock and stopped, staring down into a small open area. They saw the scattered remains of the working equipment and of Wadjik and Shant. At least one day under the open sun had mummified their bodies. Wadjik lay on his back with the broken shaft of a spear through his chest. But Shant had been pegged out and left to die.

Their outerwear and guns were gone.

"I thought I saw sign of at least half a dozen males back there," Johnson said. "Hehog, all right—with help. He must be swinging some real clout with the other males to have kept them from eating these two right away." He glanced hard at Kiev. "And all for you."

Kiev stared.

"Me? You mean Hehog tied Shanny up and left him like that on purpose—just so I could come along and see it?"

"You begin to see what Ancient Enemy means?" he responded. "We're in trouble, Kiev. Two guns missing and one of the local males grown into a real hoodoo. We'll get moving for civilization right now."

"You're going to bury them first," Willy said.

The men swung around. She was standing just behind them, looking at them. Her gaze dropped, fixed on the bodies below. For a second Kiev thought that the sight had sent her completely out of her mind. Then he saw that her eyes were clear and sane.

Johnson said, "We haven't time—and, anyway, the Udbahrs would come back to dig them up again when they were hungry enough."

"He's right, Willy," said Kiev. "We've got to go—
fast." He thought of something else and swung back to
Johnson. "That pass you talked about—they'll be laying
for us there, Hehog and the other males he's got together. It's the straightest route home, you say, and
they know prospectors always head straight out of the
mountains when they get into trouble."

Johnson shook his head.

"Don't think so," he said. "You're his Ancient Enemy, looking for that one spot where you and he come
face to face and one of you gets the word to kill the
other. He'll be right around this area, waiting for us to
start hunting for him. If we move fast we've got as good
a chance as anyone ever had to get out of these mountains alive."

*

Johnson set a hard pace. Several times—before the
nearer moon was high in the sky and the moonflowers
were stretching to full bloom—Willy tripped and would
have gone down if Kiev had not caught her. But she
did not complain. In fact, she said nothing at all. Shortly
after midnight, they broke out from under the umbrel-
las of a clump of moonflower petals and found themselves in the pass Johnson had talked about.

"We made it," said Johnson, stopping. Kiev also
stopped. Willy, stumbling with weariness, blundered
into him. She clung to him like a child—and at that
moment a thin, bright beam came from among the
trunks of the moonflowers behind them.

The side of Johnson's outerwear burst in dazzle and
smoke.

Johnson lunged forward, Kiev and Willy ran behind
him. Three more bright beams flickered around them
as they lurched over the lip of the pass, took half a
dozen long, staggering, tripping strides down the far
side and dived to shelter behind some waist-high chunks
of granite.

Male Udbahr voices began to sing on the far side of the pass.

Johnson coughed. Kiev looked at him and Johnson quickly turned his helmet away, so that the face plate was hidden.

"Move out," Johnson said, in a thick voice, like that of a man with a frog in his throat.

"Are you crazy?"

Kiev had his sidearm out. He sighted around the granite boulder before him and sent a beam high into the rock wall beyond the lip of the pass, on the other side. The rock boomed loudly and flew in fragments. The singing stopped. After a moment it started again.

"I can't help you now," Johnson said, still keeping his face turned away. "Move out, I tell you."

"You think I'm going to leave you?"

Kiev sent off another bolt into the rock face beyond the lips of the pass. This time the singing hardly paused.

"Don't waste your charges," Johnson said hoarsely. "Get out. An hour puts you—hotel."

He had to stop in mid-sentence to cough.

"Forget it, partner," said Kiev. "With my gun and yours I can hold that pass until morning. They can't come through."

Johnson gave an ugly laugh.

"What partner—" he asked. "This partnership's dissolved. And what'll you do when dawn comes? Cook? You're still a good hour's trek from the hotel."

Kiev became aware that Willy was tugging at his arm. She motioned with her head for him to follow her. He did. She slid back down among the rocks until they were a good four meters from where Johnson lay, head towards the pass.

Willy tongued off her intercom and touched her helmets to his.

"He's dying," she said to him through the helmets.

"All right."

Kiev stared at her as if she were Hehog himself.

"You couldn't get him to the hotel in time to save his life even if there weren't any Udbahrs behind us. And we'll never make the hotel unless he stays there and keeps them from following us."

"So?"

She took hold of his shoulders and tried to shake him but he was too heavy and too unmoving with purpose.

"Be sensible." She was almost crying. "Don't you see it's something he wants to do? He wants to save us—"

Kiev stared at her stonily.

"Shanny's dead," Kiev said. "Wad's dead. You want me to leave Johnson?"

She did begin to cry at that, the tears running down her pale face inside her helmet.

"All right, hate me," she said. "Why shouldn't I want to live? This is all your fault—not mine. I didn't kill your partner. I didn't make Hehog your special enemy. All I did was love you. If you were back there I wouldn't leave you, either. But that wouldn't make my staying sensible."

"Go on if you want," he said coldly.

"You know I can't find the hotel by myself!" she said. "You know I'm not going to leave you. Maybe you've got a right to kill yourself—maybe you've even got a right to kill me. But have you got the right to kill me for something that's got nothing to do with me?"

He closed his eyes against the sight of her face. After seconds he opened his eyes, looked away from her, and began to crawl back up the slope until he once more lay beside Johnson.

"It's Willy," he said, not looking at the other man.

"Sure. That's right," said Johnson hoarsely.

A flicker of dark movement came from one side of the pass and his gun spat. The pass was clear of pursuers again.

"Damn you both," Kiev said, emptily.

"Sure, boy," said Johnson. "Don't waste time, huh?"

Kiev lay where he was. The nearer moon was descending in the sky a little above and to the right of the pass.

"I'll leave my gun," Kiev said at last.

"Don't need it," Johnson said.

Kiev reached out and took Johnson's gloved hand in his own. Through the fabric the return pressure of the other man's grip was light and feeble.

"Get out," said Johnson. "I told you I figured on ending out here."

"You told me not for some trips yet."

"Changed my mind." Johnson let go of Kiev's hand and closed his eyes. His voice was not much more than a whisper. "I think instead I'll make it this trip."

He did not say any more. After a long minute Kiev spoke to him again.

"Johnson—"

Johnson did not answer. Only the gun in his hand spat light briefly into the wall of the pass. Kiev stared a second longer, then turned and went sliding down the hill to where Willy crouched.

"We go fast," said Kiev.

They went away without looking back. Twice they heard the sound of a gun behind them. Then intervening rocks cut off whatever else they might have heard. They walked without pausing. After about an hour Willy began to stumble with exhaustion and clung to him. Kiev put his arm around her; they hobbled along together, leaning into the pitch of the upslopes, sliding in the loose rock of downslopes.

The moon was low on the stony horizon behind them. Ahead came the first whitening in the sky that said dawn was less than two hours away. Willy staggered and leaned more heavily upon Kiev. Looking down at her face through the double transparencies of both helmets, Kiev saw that she was stumbling along with her eyes tightly closed, her face hardened into a colorless mask of effort. A strand of hair had fallen forward over one closed eye and his heart lurched at the sight of it.

Not from the first had he ever thought of her as beautiful. Now, gaunt with effort, hair disarrayed, she was less so than ever—and yet he had never loved and wanted her more. It was because of the mountains, he thought. And Hehog, Wad, Shanny—and Johnson. Each time he had paid out one of them for her, the worth of her had gone up that much. Now she was equal to the total of all of them together.

She stumbled again, almost lost her footing. A wordless little sound was jolted out from between her clenched teeth, though her eyes stayed closed.

"Walk," he said savagely, jerking her upright and onward. "Keep walking." They were on the Track, now, the curving trail that all the prospectors took out of the valley of the Border Hotel. "Keep walking," he muttered to her. "Just around the curve there—"

A bolt from a gun behind them boomed suddenly against the cliff-base to their right. Rock chips rained down Willy's knees. She lurched towards the shelter of the nearest boulder.

He jerked her upright.

"Run for it, run—"

Jolting, stumbling, they ran while bolts from the gun boomed.

"They can't shoot worth—" Kiev muttered through his teeth.

He stopped talking. Because at that moment they rounded a curve and saw the sprawling concrete shape of the Border Hotel and its grounds—and saw Hehog, holding a sidearm, stepping out from behind a rock twenty feet ahead.

In that instant time itself seemed to hesitate. Kiev's weary legs had checked at his sight of Hehog. He started forward again at a walk, half-carrying Willy. Her eyes were still closed.

He thought, *She doesn't see Hehog.*

He marched on. Hehog brought up the gun, aimed it—but he, too, seemed caught in the suspension of time. He wore the helmet he had taken from Kiev two years before and now he also wore the white jacket of Shant's outerwear suit—which almost fitted him. He stood waiting, one sidearm in a jacket pocket, one in his hand, aimed.

Kiev stumped towards him, bringing Willy. Kiev's eyes were on the bulging eyes of Hehog. Their gazes locked. The only sound was the noise of Kiev's boots scuffing the rock underfoot. From the hotel in the valley below, no sound. From the other Udbahr males that had been firing at them from behind, no sound.

Kiev marched on, Hehog growing before him. The great eyes danced in Kiev's vision. There was a wild emptiness in Kiev now, an insane certainty. He did not move aside to avoid Hehog. They were ten feet apart— they were five—they would collide—

Hehog stepped back. Without shifting the line of his advance an inch, without moving his eyes to follow Hehog, Kiev marched past him. The trail to the hotel sloped suddenly more sharply under Kiev's feet and now he looked only at what was manmade. All the Udbahrs were behind him. And behind him he heard Hehog beginning to sing softly.

> *Man with a head-and-a-half,*
> *come and get your half-head,*
> *Man with a head-and-a-half,*
> *Come, so I can kill you . . .*

The song faded behind him until his shambling feet carried him in through the great airdoor of the hotel and all things ended at once.

He was nearly four days recovering and three days after that sitting around the Border Hotel, making plans for the future with Willy. They had adjoining rooms, each with a balcony looking out to the dawnrise side of the hotel. Heavy filterglass doors shut out the sunlight and protected the rooms' air-conditioned interiors during the daytime. Kiev had agreed to go back to the Old Worlds with Willy, to get married and write and tell what he knew. There was nothing wrong with making a living any way you could back on the Old Worlds, even if it meant writing and lecturing. Only once did Willy bring up the subject of the mountains.

"Why did Hehog let us pass?" she asked.

He stared at her.

"I thought that your eyes were closed."

"I opened them when you halted. I closed them when I saw him. I thought it was all over then—and that he was going to kill us both. But you started walking and he let us pass. Why?"

Kiev looked down at the thick brown carpet.

"Hehog's never going to get the message," he said to the carpet.

"What?"

"Ancient Enemies—Johnson told me. Hehog thinks he and I are something special to each other with this Ancient Enemies business. We're doomed to have one of us kill the other. We're supposed to keep coming together until one of us gets the message to kill. Then the other just lets it happen. Because he's doomed—there's nothing he can do about it."

He stopped talking. For a minute she said nothing, either, as if she was waiting for him to go on explaining.

"Hehog didn't get the message when we walked past him?" she said, at last. "Is that it?"

"He'll never get the message," said Kiev dully. "He had two clear chances at me and he didn't do anything. It means he thinks he's the one who's doomed. He's waiting to die—for me to kill him."

"To kill him? Why would he want you to kill him?"

Kiev shrugged.

"Answer me."

"How do I know?" Kiev said exhaustedly. "Maybe he's getting old. Maybe he thinks it's just time for him to die—maybe his mate's dead."

There was momentary, somehow ugly silence. Then Willy spoke again.

"Kiev."

"What?"

"Look up here," she said, sharply. "I want you to look at me."

He raised his gaze slowly from the thick carpet and saw her face as stiffly fixed as it had been in the helmet on the last long kilometer to the hotel.

"Listen to me, Kiev," she said. "I love you and I want to live with you more than anything else for the rest of my life—and I'll do anything for you I can do. But there's one thing I can't do. I just can't."

He frowned at her, uneasy and restless.

"I can't help it," she said. "I thought we were getting away from it here and that it didn't matter. But it does. If I can feel it there in you I go dead inside—I just can't love you any more. That's all there is to it."

"What?" he asked.

Her hands made themselves into ineffective small fists in her lap, then uncurled and lay limp.

"There are so many things I love about you," she said emptily, "I thought I could ignore this one thing. But I can't think so any more. Not since we saw those two dead men—and not since the walk back here. Our love is just never going to work if you still want—want to kill. Do you understand? If you're still wanting to kill it just won't work out for us. Do you understand, Kiev?"

The bottom seemed to fall out of his stomach. He was abruptly sick.

"I told you that's all over!" he shouted furiously at her. "I don't want to kill anything!"

"You don't have to promise." She rose to her feet, her face still tight. "It doesn't matter if you promise. It only matters if you're telling the truth."

She turned and walked to the door of his hotel room.

"It's almost dawn," she said. "I'm going down to see if the authorization of our spaceship tickets has come through for today's flight—before the sun shuts off communications. I'll be back in half an hour."

She went out. The door made no noise closing behind her.

He turned and flopped on the bed, stared up at the ceiling. Everything was wonderful—or was it? He tried to think about the future in safety of the Old Worlds but his mind would not focus. After a bit he rose and walked out to the balcony.

Before him stood the ramparts of the cliffs. On the balcony was an observation scope. He bent over it and fiddled with its controls until the boulders a kilometer away seemed to hang a dozen meters in front of him.

He turned the sound pick-up on.

It was nearly time for the Udbahrs to be hunting their dens for the day but he heard no singing. He panned the scope, searching the rocks. There it came—a faint wisp of melody.

He searched the rock. The stone blurred before him. He lost then found the song again and closed in on it until the image in the screen of the scope locked on the figure of a male Udbahr standing deep between two tall boulders—an Udbahr wearing a transparent helmet and white jacket, with a sidearm in his hand.

The song came suddenly loud and clear.

> *Ancient, my enemy. Ancient,*
> *my enemy.*
> *No one but ourselves has the*
> *killing of each other . . .*
> *Man with a head-and-a-half,*
> *come and get your half-head.*
> *Man with a head-and-a-half*

Kiev stepped back from the scope. His head pounded suddenly. His stomach knotted. His throat ached. A fever blazed through him and his skin felt dusty. He turned and strode across the room to his bag. He ploughed through it, throwing new shoes, pants and shirts aside.

His hand closed on the last hard item at the bottom. His gun. He jerked out the weapon, snatched up the long barrel for distance shooting and was snapping it into position on the gun even as he was striding towards the balcony.

He applied the magnetic clamp of the gunbutt to the scope and thumbed up the near lens of the telescope sight. The red cross-hairs wavered, searched, found Hehog. It was a long shot. The lenses of the sight level on the Udbahr in a straight line; but below them, on their gimbals, the barrel of the automatically sighting weapon was angled so that it seemed to point clear over the cliffs at the day that was coming. Kiev's dry and shaking fingers curled around the butt. His forefinger reached towards the firing button and instantly all the shaking was over.

His grip was steady. His blood was ice but the fever still burned in his brain. As clearly as a vision before him, he saw the mummified figures of Wadjik and Shant—and Johnson as he had last seen the old man.

Kiev pressed the firing button.

From the cliffside came the sound of a distant explosion. A puff of rockdust plumed towards the whitening sky. A rising murmur, a mountain buzz of voices began beyond the walls of his room. People began to appear on the surroundings balconies.

Kiev faded back two steps, silent as a thief. Hidden in the shadows of the balcony he could still see what the others could not.

Hehog lay beside one of the two boulders between which he had been standing. A blackish stain was spread-

ing on the right side of his white jacket and the sidearm had fallen from his grip.

He was plainly dying. But he was not yet dead. He
began to sing again.

> *Man with a head-and-a-half*
> *. . . come and get your. . . half-head.*
> *Man with a head-and-a . . .*

Through the pick-up of the scope Kiev, frozen in the
shadows, could hear the Udbahr's voice weakening.
Then the door to the room slammed open behind him.

"Kiev, did you hear it? Someone shot from the
Hotel—"

Willy's voice broke off.

He turned and saw her just inside the door. She was
gazing past him at the scope with its picture of Hehog
and the sound of Hehog's weakening song coming from
it. She stared at it. Then, slowly, as if she was being
forced against her will, her eyes shifted until they met
his.

All the feeling in him that the sight of Hehog had
triggered into life went out of him with a rush, leaving
him empty as a disembowelled man.

"Willy—"

He took a step towards her. Her face twitched as if
with a sudden, sharp, unbearable pain and her hand
come up reflexively as if to push him away, though they
were still more than half a room apart.

Her throat worked but she made no sound. She
struggled for an instant, then shook her head briefly.
Still holding up her hand as if to fend him off, she
backed away from him. The door opened behind her
and let her out.

The door closed, leaving him alone. He swung slowly
back to face the scope. Hehog still lay framed in the
lens and above that image the ominous light of day was
fast whitening the sky.

Hehog was still feebly singing; but the song had changed. Now it was the song Willy had asked Kiev to translate when she had first heard an Udbahr male. Kiev turned and flung himself facedown on the bed, his arms over his head to shut out the sound. But the song came through to him.

> *You desert me now, female,*
> *Because I am crippled.*
> *And yet, all my fault was*
> *That I did not lack courage.*
> *Therefore I will go now to the*
> *high rocks to die.*
> *And another will take you . . .*

The slow rumble of the heavy, opaque, thermal glass, sliding automatically across the entrance to the balcony, silenced the song in Kiev's ears. Beyond the dark glass the sun of day broke at last over the rim of the cliffs and sent its fierce light slanting down. There was no mercy in that relentless light and all living things who did not hide before it died.

In the front of this volume, I thank people who helped me put it together. Using "Rough Beast" as an (extreme) example, I'd like to demonstrate how crucial their help was to the project. (It will also suggest why my WATS line service calls me every month to make sure that I'm pleased with their performance.)

Jim Baen (editor and publisher; but also my friend, which is why we were shooting the bull about this project) mentioned a story that really needed to be in the collection. You see, this spaceship crashes on Earth releasing an utterly-ferocious monster. The aliens warn the nearest humans, but they can't interfere in time to stop the ravening beast before it—

Yeah, sure I remembered the story! Thought it was in Analog in the early '60s. Hadn't a clue as to the author, but I was almost certain of the title: "What Rough Beast?"

So I checked an index at Karl Wagner's house and found to my amazement that the story was by Damon Knight—hadn't seemed like his sort of story, the way I recalled it. It was in F&SF, not Analog, but that was no problem. I went home and found the issue in my set of F&SFs.

Wrong story. (I remembered that Knight story also; an excellent piece. It just wasn't the right one.) Either I had the title wrong, or there was a glitch in the index.

I was more sure than ever that Analog was the source, so I (with the considerable help of my wife; I have my abilities, but most of the time I couldn't find my fanny with both hands) searched my Analogs for the period. I had a subscription throughout the '60s, but I don't at present have either a complete or an organized set . . . and I didn't find anything remotely like the story Jim and I remembered.

Next was picking the brains of my friends. Nobody came up with the story off the top of their head; but the Miesel clan was going to visit the Coulsons in a few days. Buck Coulson has an exceptional magazine collection, and they would search it together.

No luck. To get ahead of myself, they'd understood that I'd already checked Analog, so they searched everything else . . .

I was at a dead end until Charles Waugh called me on another project and I—diffidently, because Charles and Marty Greenberg are professional anthologizers as well as being tenured academics—asked if the story rang any bells with him.

I was embarrassed to ask, but Charles' help was as expert and unhesitating as I should have expected: the story was "Rough Beast" (thus my problem when I checked the index under "What") by Roger Dee—Analog for March, 1962.

But "Rough Beast" had been the last Roger Dee story published, and Charles didn't known how I could get in touch with the author to arrange permission to reprint.

I had a line on that. At a convention about ten years ago, Jerry Page—a friend and fellow SF-writer—had mentioned (I thought) meeting Roger Dee, an under-appreciated Southern SF writer.

So I phoned Jerry, who hadn't met the writer himself but knew someone who had. Jerry told me the correct name, Roger D. Aycock, and thought he was a postal employee in a particular Georgia city. A few hours later, Jerry called back to correct himself: it was a different city.

So what the hell: I phoned information to see if there was a listing for Roger D. Aycock in that city. There was; I tried it; and Mr. Aycock couldn't have been more gracious and pleased to do business with me.

Oh—and Buck Coulson quickly photocopied the story for me when I gave him the cite.

There are probably more efficient ways to have achieved the desired end. But friends like mine make it possible to succeed despite a lot of fumbling.

ROUGH BEAST

Roger Dee

The field of the experimental Telethink station in the Florida Keys caught the fleeing Morid's attention just as its stolen Federation lifeboat plunged into the outer reaches of nightside atmosphere.

The Morid reacted with the instant decision of a harried wolf stumbling upon a dark cave that offers not only sanctuary but a lost lamb for supper as well. With the pursuing Federation ship hot on its taloned heels, the Morid zeroed on the Telethink signals—fuzzy and incomprehensibly alien to its viciously direct mentality, but indicating life and therefore food—and aimed straight for their source.

The lifeboat crashed headlong in the mangroves fringing Dutchman's Key, perhaps ten miles west of the Oversea Highway and less than two from the Telethink station. The Morid emerged in snarling haste, anticipating the powerplant's explosion by a matter of seconds, and vanished like a magenta-furred juggernaut into the moonlit riot of vegetation that crowded back from the mangroved strip of beach. The Morid considered it a success.

The lifeboat went up in a cataclysmic roar and flare of bluish light that brought Vann, the Telethink operator on duty, out of his goldberg helmet with a prickly conviction of runaway range missiles. It all but blinded and deafened Ellis, his partner, who was cruising with a portable Telethink in the station launch through a low-lying maze of islands a quarter of a mile from Dutchman's Key.

Their joint consternation was lost on the Morid because both at the moment were outside its avid reach. The teeming welter of life on Dutchman's Key was not. The Morid headed inland, sensing abundant quarry to satisfy the ravening hunger that drove it and, that craving satisfied, to offer ample scope to its joy of killing.

The Morid's escape left Xaxtol, Federation ship's commander, in a dilemma bordering upon the insoluble.

It would have been bad enough to lose so rare a specimen even on a barren world, but to have one so voracious at large upon one so teeming—as the primitive Telethink signals demonstrated—with previously unsuspected intelligence was unthinkable.

This, at the outset, was Xaxtol's problem:

Forbidden by strictest Galactic injunction, he could not make planetfall and interfere with a previously unscouted primitive culture. Contrariwise, neither could civilized ethic condone his abandoning such an unsuspecting culture to the bloody mercies of a Morid without every effort to correct his blunder.

Hanging in stationary orbit in order to keep a fixed relation to the Morid's landing site, the Federation commander debated earnestly with his staff until a sudden quickening of the barbarous Telethink net made action imperative.

Two of an autochthons were isolated on a small island with the Morid. Unwarned, they were doomed.

So he grouped his staff about him—sitting, crouching, coiling or hovering, as individual necessity demanded—and as one entity put the whole into rapport with the all-but-meaningless signals that funneled up from the Telethink station in the Florida Keys.

And, in doing so, roused a consternation as great as his own and infinitely more immediate.

The flash brought Vann away from the Telethink console and out of the quonset station to stare shakenly across the tangle of mangroved islands to the west. Weyman came out a moment later, on the run, when the teeth-jarring blast of the explosion woke him. They stood together on the moon-bright sand and Vann relayed in four words the total of his information.

"It fell over there," Vann said.

A pale pinkish cloud of smoke and steam rose and drifted phosphorescently toward a noncommittal moon.

"Second key out," Weyman said. "That would be Dutchman's, where the hermit lives."

Vann nodded, drawing minimal reassurance from the fact that there had been no mushroom. "It shouldn't be atomic."

The Gulf breeze was steady out of the west, freighted with its perpetual salt-and-mangrove smell.

"The Geigers will tell us soon enough," Weyman said. "Not that it'll help us, with Ellis out in the launch."

They looked at each other in sudden shock of joint realization.

"The launch," Vann said. "Ellis is out there with the portable Telethink rig. We were working out field-strength ratios for personal equipment—"

They dived for the quonset together. Vann, smaller and more agile than the deliberate Weyman, reached the Telethink first.

"Nothing but the regular standby carried from Washington," Vann said. "Ellis may have been directly under the thing when it struck. He was working toward Dutchman's Key, hoping for a glimpse of the hermit."

"Maybe he wasn't wearing the Telethink when the blast came," Weyman said. Then, with characteristic practicality: "Better image Washington about this while we're waiting for Ellis to report in. Can't use the net radio—we'd start a panic."

Vann settled himself at the console.

"I'll try. That is, if I can get across anything beyond the sort of subliminal rot we've been trading lately."

He signaled for contact and felt the Washington operator's answering surge of subconscious resentment at being disturbed. With the closing of the net the now-familiar giddiness of partial rapport came on him, together with the oppressive sense of bodily sharing.

There was a sudden trickle of saliva in his mouth and he resisted the desire to spit.

"Washington is having a midnight snack," Vann said. "Rotted sardines and Limburger, I think."

He made correction when the Washington operator radiated indignation. "Goose liver and dill pickles, then but you wouldn't guess it. Salt tastes like brass filings."

Wyman said shortly, "Get on with it. You can clown later."

Vann visualized the flare of explosion and winced at the panicky hammer-and-sickled surmise that came back to him.

"How would I know?" he said aloud. "We have a man out—"

He recalled the inherent limitation of phonetics then and fell back upon imagery, picturing Ellis' launch heading toward an island luridly lighted by the blast. For effect he added, on the key's minuscule beach, a totally imaginary shack of driftwood, complete with bearded hermit.

He knew immediately when authority arrived at the other end of the net. There was mental backwash of conversation that told him his orders even before the Washington operator set himself for their relay.

"They want an eyewitness account from Ellis," he told Weyman. "As if—"

Ellis broke into the net at that moment, radiating a hazy image—he was still partially blinded from the glare of the blast—of a lowering key overhung by a dwindling pall of pinkish smoke. In the foreground of lagoon and mangroves stood a stilted shack not unlike the one Vann had pictured, but without the hermit.

Instead, the rickety elevation of thatched porch was a blot of sable darkness relieved only by a pair of slanted yellow eyes gleaming close to the floor.

Climactically, Xaxtol entered the net then with an impact of total information that was more than the human psyche, conditioned to serialized thinking by years of phonetic communication, could bear.

The Washington operator screamed and tore off his helmet, requiring restraint until he could compose himself enough to relay his message.

Ellis, in his launch, fainted dead away and ran the boat headlong, aground on the beach of Dutchman's Key.

Vann reeled in his chair, teetering between shock and lunacy, until Weyman caught him and slid the Telethink from his head. It was minutes before Vann could speak; when he did, it was with a macabre flippancy that Weyman found more convincing than any dramatics.

"It's come," Vann said. "There's an interstellar ship out there with a thousand-odd crew that would give Dali himself nightmares."

Weyman had to shake him forcibly before he could continue.

"They're sorry they can't put down and help us," Vann said. "Galactic regulations, it seems. But they feel they should warn us that they've let some sort of bloodthirsty jungle monster—a specimen they were freighting to an interplanetary zoo—escape in a lifeboat. It's loose down here."

"Dutchman's Key," Weyman breathed. "What kind of brute could live through a blast like *that?*"

"It left the lifeboat before the power plant blew," Vann said. "They're tracking its aura now. It's intelligent to a degree—about on par with ourselves, I gather—and it's big. It's the largest and most vicious life form they've met in kilo-years of startrading."

He frowned over a concept unsuited to words, "Longer than thousands. Their culture goes back so far that the term doesn't register."

"Ellis," Weyman said. "Tell him to sheer off. Tell him to keep away from that island."

Vann clapped on the Telethink helmet and felt real panic when he found the net vacant except for a near-hysterical Washington operator.

"Aliens are off the air," he said. "But I can't feel Ellis."

"Maybe he isn't wearing his Telethink. I'll try his launch radio."

He had the microphone in his hand when Vann said, "They got the message in Washington, and they're petrified. I asked for a copter to pick up Ellis—and the hermit, if they can reach them before this *thing* does—but they're thinking along different lines. They're sending a squadron of jet bombers with nonatomic HE to make sure the beast doesn't escape to the mainland and devastate the countryside."

Weyman said incredulously, "They'll blow the key to bits. What about Ellis and the hermit?"

"Ellis is to evacuate him if possible. They're giving us twenty minutes before the jets come. After that—"

He didn't have to finish.

At midnight old Charlie Trask was wading knee-deep in the eastside grass flats of his private lagoon, methodically netting shrimp that darted to the ooze-clouded area stirred up by his ragged wading shoes. An empty gunny sack hung across one shoulder, ready for the coon oysters he would pick from mangrove roots on his way back to his shack.

In his dour and antisocial way, Charlie was content. He had nearly enough shrimp for boiling and for bait, with the prospect of coon-oyster stew in the offing. He had tobacco for his pipe and cartridges for his single-shot .22 rifle and a batch of potent homebrew ready for the bottling.

What more could a man want?

The blast and glare of the Morid's landing on the western fringe of his key jarred Charlie from his mellow mood like a clear-sky thunderbolt. The concussion rattled what teeth remained to him and brought a distant squall from his cat, a scarred and cynical old tom named Max, at the shack.

Damn rockets; was Charlie's instant thought. *Fool around till they blow us all to hell.*

The rosy phosphorescence drifting up from the mangroves a quarter of a mile away colored his resentment with alarm. A blast like that could start a fire, burn across the key and gut his shack.

Grumbling at the interruption of his midnight foray, Charlie crimped the lid tight on his shrimp bucket and stalked back along the lagoon toward his shack. The coon oysters would have to wait.

Five minutes later he reached his personal castle, perched on precarious piling in a gap hewn from the mangroves. The moon made it, to Charlie, a thing of black-and-silver beauty, with Max's yellow eyes gleaming from the porch floor like wicked, welcoming beacons.

Still muttering, Charlie waded out of the shallow-water ooze and stumped in squishing shoes up the ladder to his shack. The shrimp bucket he hung on a wall peg out of Max's calculating reach. He found his pipe in the kitchen and loaded and lighted it, deliberately because the capacity for haste was not in him. His homebrew crock bubbled seductively and he took time out to raise the grimy toweling that covered it and sniff appreciatively.

"Ready to cap by the time I come back and get the shrimp graded," he told Max.

He changed his dripping brogans for a pair of snake-proof boots and took down his .22 rifle from its pegs, not because he really imagined that anyone might have lived through such a blast but because strangers—them radio fellows two keys east, for instance—might take it into their heads to come prying around.

He was halfway across the key when the drone of Ellis' launch entering his lagoon justified his suspicions.

Charlie's investigation was soon over.

A dying plume of steam rising from a circle of battered mangroves told him that no danger of fire impended, and he turned back in relief. It did not occur to him that the pilot of this hypothetical rocket might be lying desperately injured in the shallow water, at the mercy of sharks and crocodiles. If it had, he would not have moved to help. Any fool who got himself into such a spot, in Charlie's rude philosophy, could get himself out.

The drone of the launch's engine was loud when he reached his shack. The boat, handled by a pilot grotesque in what Charlie took at first for a diver's helmet, was heading directly for his landing at an unsafe speed.

"Serve him right if he shoals on a oyster bed and rips his bottom," Charlie said.

As if on cue, the boat swerved sharply. Its pilot came half erect, arms flung wide in a convulsive gesture. The engine roared wildly; the boat heeled, slamming its occupant against the right gunwale, and blasted straight for Charlie's shack.

Miraculously, it missed the shack's piling and lunged half its length upon the sand. The engine-roar died instantly. The pilot was thrown headlong overside, goldberg helmet flying off in mid-arc, to lie stunned at the foot of Charlie's ladder.

Callously, Charlie stepped over Ellis' twitching form and stumped up the ladder to his shack. Max, who had taken to the porch rafters at the crash of the launch, came meowing gingerly down to meet him.

"It's all right," Charlie told him. "Just some fool that don't know how to handle a boat."

He leaned his rifle against the wall and brought a split-bamboo chair from the kitchen. He was not too late; the bucket, when he took it from its peg, still slithered satisfactorily with live shrimp.

The squawking of the launch radio roused Ellis. He groaned and sat up, dazed and disoriented by the combined shock of Xaxtol's telepathic bombshell and his own rude landing, just as Weyman gave up his attempt at radio contact. In the silence that fell, Ellis would have fainted again except for the chilling knowledge that he was unarmed and afoot on the same key with a man-eating alien monster that might make its appearance at any moment.

He collected wits and breath to stave off the black pall of shock that still threatened.

"Come down from there and help me push the launch off," he called up to Charlie Trask. "We've got to get off this key. Fast!"

Charlie separated a menu-sized shrimp from his bucket.

"You grounded her," he said sourly. "Push her off yourself."

"Listen," Ellis said desperately. "That blast was a ship from space, from another star. A wild animal escaped from it, something worse than you ever dreamed of. We've got to get out of here before it finds us."

Charlie grunted and chose another shrimp.

The Morid, as Xaxtol had pictured it, rose vividly in Ellis' memory, fanged and shaggy and insatiably voracious, a magenta-furred ursine embodiment of bloodlust made the worst by its near-human intelligence.

He described it in dogged haste, his eyes frozen to the tangle of inland underbrush behind the shack.

"No such varmint in these kays," old Charlie said.

The launch radio blared again in Weyman's voice, speaking urgently of jet bombers and deadlines. A glance at his watch brought Ellis up from the sand in galvanic resolution.

"In twelve minutes," he said grimly, "a squadron of planes will pinpoint this key and blast it out of the water. I'm not going to be eaten alive or blown to bits arguing with you. If I can't push the launch off alone, I'll swim."

He scooped up his fallen Telethink helmet and ran for the launch. At the fourth step his foot caught in the iron-hard stump of mangrove root that had been chopped off inches above the sand and he fell heavily. Pain blinded him; his right ankle lanced with fire and went numb.

He fought to rise and fell again when the ankle collapsed under him.

"*Hell*," he said, just before blackness claimed him for the second time, "I've broken my leg!"

His twelve minutes had dwindled to seven when Ellis roused. He tried to stand, his twisted ankle momentarily forgotten, and gave it up when the mangroves spun dizzily before his eyes. He couldn't afford to pass out again.

He made one last-ditch bid for help.

"My leg's broken," he yelled up at old Charlie Trask. "Get down here and lend a hand!"

Charlie glowered and said nothing.

Max bounded down the ladder, tail stiffly erect and scarred ears cocked at the underbrush in baleful curiosity.

"The thing is coming this way," Ellis called. "Your cat scents it. Will you let us all be killed?"

Charlie Trask graded another shrimp.

Swearing bitterly, Ellis caught up his Telethink helmet and slid it over his head. He found the net in a welter of confusion. Washington demanded further information; Vann, at the station, was calling him frantically. His own scramble for help-images only added to the mental babel.

On the Federation ship, confusion was nearly as rampant.

Xaxtol's dilemma still held: he could not make planetfall—time was too short for aid now, in any case—but neither could he, with clear Galactic conscience, desert the harried primitives below while hope remained.

Ellis' predicament forced Xaxtol to decision; he could only follow the Morid's aura and relay its progress.

It could not be helped that the relayed image was blurred of definition and weirdly askew; the Morid's visual and auditory range differed so sharply from either human or Galactic that even over the ship's wonderfully selective telecommunicator little of the Morid's immediate surroundings came through clearly. Its aura arrived with a burning intensity that turned Xaxtol and his group faint with empathetic horror, but the fact that the Morid had just made its first kill obliterated all detail for the moment beyond a shocking welter of blood and torn flesh.

Ellis fared a little better under the second telepathic blast than under the first—he managed to snatch off his Telethink helmet just in time.

"The thing just killed something out there," he yelled at Charlie Trask. "It's coming this way. Are you going to sit there and—"

Charlie graded his last edible shrimp, took up his bucket and went inside. The leisurely clinking of homebrew bottles drifted after him, clear and musical on the still, hot air.

Ellis looked at his watch and considered prayer. He had three minutes left.

* * *

When the Morid came, Ellis was sitting dumbly on the sand, nursing his broken ankle and considering with a shock-detached part of his mind a fragmentary line of some long-forgotten schooldays poem.

What rough beast is this . . . the rest eluded him.

The underbrush beyond the shack rustled and the Morid's ravening image sprang to Ellis' mind with a clarity that shook his three net-participants to the core—one of them past endurance.

Vann, in the station, said *"Dear God,"* and braced himself for the end. In Washington, the operator fainted and had to be dragged from his console.

Aboard the Federation ship, Xaxtol radiated a shaken "Enough!" and tentacled a stud that sent his craft flashing on its way through subspace.

At Charlie Trask's shack, Max bounded across the clearing and into the brush. There followed a riot of squalling and screaming that brought Charlie out of his shack on the run. Ellis sat numbly, beyond shock, waiting for the worst.

Unaccountably, the worst was delayed.

Charlie came back, clutching a protesting Max by the scruff of the neck, and threw down something at Ellis' feet. Something small and limp and magenta-furred, smeared with greenish blood and very, very dead.

"There's your varmint," said Charlie.

With one minute remaining before the promised bombers roared over, Ellis, with a frozen clarity he had not dreamed he possessed, radiated a final message before he fainted again.

"Call off the jets," he said, in effect. "It's over. The beast is dead. The hermit's cat killed it.

An hour later at the station, his ankle bandaged and his third cup of coffee in hand, Ellis could review it all with some coherence.

"We didn't consider the business of relative size," he

said. "Neither did our Galactic friends. Apparently they're small, and so are all the species they've met with before. Maybe we're something unique in the universe, after all. And maybe it's a good thing they didn't land and learn how unique."

"It figures," Weyman said. "Washington let it out on the air that DF stations made a fix on the spaceship before it jumped off. It measured only twenty-two feet."

Vann said wonderingly, "And there were hundreds of them aboard. Gentlemen, we are Brobdingnagians in a universe of Lilliputians."

"I've been trying," Ellis said irrelevantly, "to recall a poem I read once in school. I've forgotten the author and all the verse but one line. It goes—"

"*What rough beast is this,*" Vann quoted. "You were thinking about it hard enough when the debacle in the brush took place. The image you radiated was rough enough—it shocked the pants off us."

"And off the Galactics," Weyman said. "The shoe is on the other foot now, I think."

He went to the quonset door and looked out and up, listening. "Jets. The Washington brass on its way to cross-examine us."

"The other foot?" Vann said. "Don't be cryptic, man. Whose foot?"

"Theirs," Ellis said. "Don't you see? One of these days we'll be going out there to make our own place in the galaxy. With our size and disposition, how do you think we'll seem to those gentle little people?"

Vann whistled in belated understanding.

"Rough," he said.

Often the dates picked for the end or beginning of a process are wholly arbitrary. The government in Ravenna in 476 AD had a lot of problems on its hands—but what else was new? It's unlikely that anybody in the imperial administration felt that he's just experienced the Fall of the Roman Empire.

Similarly, the end of the Golden Age of Science Fiction is an arbitrary date. With the May, 1943, issue, Street and Smith reduced the page-size of Astounding *from "bedsheet" to "pulp" dimensions. The change was necessitated by wartime paper shortages; it had no effect on the magazine's contents or editorial policies.*

But the war did have *an effect on the contents and policies of all fiction magazines, not just John Campbell's* Astounding—*the acknowledged premier of the SF field. One factor was the way top writers gravitated into war service or the military. That didn't mean those who remained were bad, but it made a drastic change in what SF's leading market would be able to print "for the duration."*

More damaging—because it was universal—was the shift in emphasis from "story" to "war." Ed Price was told by an editor (not Campbell) rejecting a story of his, "Sure it's good. But what does it do for the war effort?"

Generally that wasn't a question editors had to ask. Writers were just as patriotic as other Americans. Those who weren't fit for military service because of health or age—Ed had served in France during World War I—often felt an especial need to show they were doing their part.

This was natural enough. It wasn't until the death camps were liberated toward the end of the war that Americans fully realized what German civilization was attempting to do to Europe; but the incredible brutality of the modern Japanese had been a matter of record ever since their invasion of Manchuria in 1930.

While the focus of writers and editors on something

other than stories was understandable, it didn't have a good effect on fiction—as anyone who browses the SF magazines of the period will agree. The down-sizing of Astounding accompanied rather than caused the change; but it provides a useful terminus. (Incidentally, it doesn't require a war against world-threatening evil to achieve the same unfortunate result. Witness the current magazines in the fields, rushing toward a cliff behind the banner of Literary Quality.)

The end of the Golden Age of Science Fiction is an arbitrary date. The beginning—July, 1939—is not. The August, 1939, issue of Astounding ran the first story by Robert Heinlein. The previous issue ran the first story by another great author, A. E. van Vogt.

This story.

BLACK DESTROYER

A. E. Van Vogt

On and on Coeurl prowled! The black, moonless, almost starless night yielded reluctantly before a grim reddish dawn that crept up from his left. A vague, dull light it was, that gave no sense of approaching warmth, no comfort, nothing but a cold, diffuse lightness, slowly revealing a nightmare landscape.

Black, jagged rock and black, unliving plain took form around him, as a pale-red sun peered at last above the grotesque horizon. It was then Coeurl recognized suddenly that he was on familiar ground.

He stopped short. Tenseness flamed along his nerves. His muscles pressed with sudden, unrelenting strength against his bones. His great forelegs—twice as long as his hindlegs—twitched with a shuddering movement that arched every razor-sharp claw. The thick tentacles that sprouted from his shoulders ceased their weaving undulation, and grew taut with anxious alertness.

141

Utterly appalled, he twisted his great cat head from side to side, while the little hairlike tendrils that formed each ear vibrated frantically, testing every vagrant breeze, every throb in the ether.

But there was no response, no swift tingling along his intricate nervous system, not the faintest suggestions anywhere of the presence of the all-necessary id. Hopelessly, Coeurl crouched, an enormous catlike figure silhouetted against the dim reddish skyline, like a distorted etching of a black tiger resting on a black rock in a shadow world.

He had known this day would come. Through all the centuries of restless search, this day had loomed ever nearer, blacker, more frightening—this inevitable hour when he must return to the point where he began his systematic hunt in a world almost depleted of id-creatures.

The truth struck in waves like an endless, rhythmic ache at the seat of his ego. When he had started, there had been a few id-creatures in every hundred square miles, to be mercilessly rooted out. Only too well Coeurl knew in this ultimate hour that he had missed none. There was no id-creatures left to eat. In all the hundreds of thousands of square miles that he had made his own by right of ruthless conquest—until no neighboring coeurl dared to question his sovereignty—there was no id to feed the otherwise immortal engine that was his body.

Square foot by square foot he had gone over it. And now—he recognized the knoll of rock just ahead, and the black rock bridge that formed a queer, curling tunnel to his right. It was in that tunnel he had lain for days, waiting for the simple-minded, snakelike id-creature to come forth from its hole in the rock to bask in the sun—his first kill after he had realized the absolute necessity of organized extermination.

He licked his lips in brief gloating memory of the moment his slavering jaws tore the victim into precious toothsome bits. But the dark fear of an idless universe swept the sweet remembrance from his consciousness, leaving only certainty of death.

He snarled audibly, a defiant, devilish sound that quavered on the air, echoed and re-echoed among the rocks, and shuddered back along his nerves—instinctive and hellish expression of his will to live.

And then—abruptly—it came.

He saw it emerge out of the distance on a long downward slant, a tiny glowing spot that grew enormously into a metal ball. The great shining globe hissed by above Coeurl, slowing visibly in quick deceleration. It sped over a black line of hills to the right, hovered almost motionless for a second, then sank down out of sight.

Coeurl exploded from his startled immobility. With tiger speed, he flowed down among the rocks. His round, black eyes burned with the horrible desire that was an agony within him. His ear tendrils vibrated a message of id in such tremendous quantities that his body felt sick with the pangs of his abnormal hunger.

The little red sun was a crimson ball in the purple-black heavens when he crept up from behind a mass of rock and gazed from its shadows at the crumbling, gigantic ruins of the city that sprawled below him. The silvery globe, in spite of its great size, looked strangely inconspicuous against that vast, fairylike reach of ruins. Yet about it was a leashed aliveness, a dynamic quiescence that, after a moment, made it stand out, dominating the foreground. A massive, rock-crushing thing of metal, it rested on a cradle made by its own weight in the harsh, resisting plain which began abruptly at the outskirts of the dead metropolis.

Coeurl gazed at the strange, two-legged creatures who stood in little groups near the brilliantly lighted opening that yawned at the base of the ship. His throat thickened with the immediacy of his need; and his brain grew dark with the first wild impulse to burst forth in furious charge and smash these flimsy, helpless-looking creatures whose bodies emitted the id-vibrations.

Mists of memory stopped that mad rush when it was still only electricity surging through his muscles. Memory that brought fear in an acid stream of weakness, pouring along his nerves, poisoning the reservoirs of his strength. He had time to see that the creatures wore things over their real bodies, shimmering transparent material that glittered in strange, burning flashes in the rays of the sun.

Other memories came suddenly. Of dim days when the city that spread below was the living, breathing heart of an age of glory that dissolved in a single century before flaming guns whose wielders knew only that for the survivors there would be an ever-narrowing supply of id.

It was the remembrance of those guns that held him there, cringing in a wave of terror that blurred his reason. He saw himself smashed by balls of metal and burned by searing flame.

Came cunning—understanding of the presence of these creatures. This, Coeurl reasoned for the first time, was a scientific expedition from another star. In the olden days, the coeurls had thought of space travel, but disaster came too swiftly for it ever to be more than a thought.

Scientists meant investigation, not destruction. Scientists in their way were fools. Bold with his knowledge, he emerged into the open. He saw the creatures become aware of him. They turned and stared. One, the smallest of the group, detached a shining metal rod from the sheath, and held it casually in one hand. Coeurl loped on, shaken to his core by the action; but it was too late to turn back.

Commander Hal Morton heard Gregory Kent, the chemist, laugh with the embarrassed half gurgle with which he invariably announced inner uncertainty. He saw Kent fingering the spindly metalite weapon.

Kent said: "I'll take no chances with anything as big as that."

Commander Morton allowed his own deep chuckle to echo along the communicators. "That," he grunted finally, "is one of the reasons why you're on this expedition, Kent—because you never leave anything to chance."

His chuckle trailed off into silence. Instinctively, as he watched the monster approach them across that black rock plain, he moved forward until he stood a little in advance of the others, his huge form bulking the transparent metalite suit. The comments of the men pattered through the radio communicator into his ears:

"I'd hate to meet that baby on a dark night in an alley."

"Don't be silly. This is obviously an intelligent creature. Probably a member of the ruling race."

"It looks like nothing else than a big cat, if you forget those tentacles sticking out from its shoulders, and make allowances for those monster forelegs."

"Its physical development," said a voice, which Morton recognized as that of Siedel, the psychologist, "presupposes an animal-like adaptation to surroundings, not an intellectual one. On the other hand, its coming to us like this is not the act of an animal but of a creature possessing mental awareness of our possible identity. You will notice that its movements are stiff, denoting caution, which suggests fear and consciousness of our weapons. I'd like to get a good look at the end of its tentacles. If they taper into handlike appendages that can really grip objects, then the conclusion would be inescapable that it is a descendant of the inhabitants of this city. It would be a great help if we could establish communication with it, even though appearance indicates that it had degenerated into a historyless primitive."

Coeurl stopped when he was still ten feet from the foremost creature. The sense of id was so overwhelming that his brain drifted to the ultimate verge of chaos. He felt as if his limbs were bathed in molten liquid; his very vision was not quite clear, as the sheer sensuality of his desire thundered through his being.

The men—all except the little one with the shining metal rod in his fingers—came closer. Coeurl saw that they were frankly and curiously examining him. Their lips were moving and their voices beat in a monotonous, meaningless rhythm on his ear tendrils. At the same time he had the sense of waves of a much higher frequency—his own communication level—only it was a machinelike clicking that jarred his brain. With a distant effort to appear friendly, he broadcast his name from his ear tendrils, at the same time pointing at himself with one curving tentacle.

Gourlay, chief of communications, drawled: "I got a sort of static in my radio when he wiggled those hairs, Morton. Do you think—"

"Looks very much like it," the leader answered the unfinished question. "That means a job for you, Gourlay. If it speaks by means of radio waves, it might not be altogether impossible that you can create some sort of television picture of its vibrations, or teach him the Morse code."

"Ah," said Siedel. "I was right. The tentacles each develop into seven strong fingers. Provided the nervous system is complicated enough, those fingers could, with training, operate any machine."

Morton said: "I think we'd better go in and have some lunch. Afterward, we've got to get busy. The material men can set up their machines and start gathering data on the planet's metal possibilities, and so on. The others can do a little careful exploring. I'd like some notes on architecture and on the scientific development of this race, and particularly what happened to wreck the civilization. On earth civlzation after civilization crumbled, but always a new one sprang up in its dust. Why didn't that happen here? Any questions?"

"Yes. What about pussy? Look, he wants to come in with us."

Commander Morton frowned, an action that emphasized the deep-space pallor of his face. "I wish there was some way we could take it in with us, without forcibly capturing it. Kent, what do you think?"

"I think we should first decide whether it's an it or a him, and call it one or the other. I'm in favor of him. As for taking him in with us—" The little chemist shook his head decisively. "Impossible. This atmosphere is twenty-eight per cent chlorine. Our oxygen would be pure dynamite to his lungs."

The commander chuckled. "He doesn't believe that, apparently." He watched the catlike monster follow the first two men through the great door. The men kept an anxious distance from him, then glanced at Morton questioningly. Morton waved his hand. "O.K. Open the second lock and let him get a whiff of the oxygen. That'll cure him."

A moment later, he cursed his amazement. "By Heaven, he doesn't even notice the difference! That means he hasn't any lungs or else the chlorine is not what his lungs use. Let him in! You bet he can go in! Smith, here's a treasure house for a biologist—harmless enough if we're careful. We can always handle him. But what a metabolism!"

Smith, a tall, thin, bony chap with a long, mournful face, said in an oddly forceful voice: "In all our travels, we've found only two higher forms of life. Those dependent on chlorine, and those who need oxygen—the two elements that support combustion. I'm prepared to stake my reputation that no complicated organism could ever adapt itself to both gases in a natural way. At first thought I should say there is an extremely advanced form of life. This race long ago discovered truths of biology that we are just beginning to suspect. Morton, we mustn't let this creature get away if we can help it."

"If his anxiety to get inside is any criterion," Com-

mander Morton laughed, "then our difficulty will be to
get rid of him."

He moved into the lock with Coeurl and the two
men. The automatic machinery hummed; and in a few
minutes they were standing at the bottom of a series of
elevators that led up to the living quarters.

"Does that go up?" One of the men flicked a thumb
in the direction of the monster.

"Better send him up alone, if he'll go in."

Coeurl offered no objection, until he heard the door
slam behind him; and the closed cage shot upward. He
whirled with a savage snarl, this reason swirling into
chaos. With one leap, he pounced at the door. The
metal bent under his plunge, and the desperate pain
maddened him. Now, he was all trapped animal. He
smashed at the metal with his paws, bending it like so
much tin. He tore great bars loose with his thick tentacles. The machinery screeched; there were horrible
jerks as the limitless power pulled the cage along in
spite of projecting pieces of metal that scraped the
outside walls. And then the cage stopped, and he
snatched off the rest of the door and hurtled into the
corridor.

He waited there until Morton and the men came up
with drawn weapons. "We're fools," Morton said. "We
should have shown him how it works. He thought we'd
double-crossed him."

He motioned to the monster, and saw the savage
glow fade from the coal-black eyes as he opened and
closed the door with elaborate gestures to show the
operation.

Coeurl ended the lesson by trotting into the large
room to his right. He lay down on the rugged floor, and
fought down the electric tautness of his nerves and
muscles. A very fury of rage against himself for his
fright consumed him. It seemed to his burning brain
that he had lost the advantage of appearing a mild and

harmless creature. His strength must have startled and
dismayed them.

It meant greater danger in the task which he now
knew he must accomplish: To kill everything in the
ship, and take the machine back to their world in
search of unlimited id.

With unwinking eyes, Coeurl lay and watched the
two men clearing away the loose rubble from the metal
doorway of the huge old building. His whole body
ached with the hunger of his cells for id. The craving
tore through his palpitant muscles, and throbbed like a
living thing in his brain. His every nerve quivered to
be off after the men who had wandered into the city.
One of them, he knew, had gone—alone.

The dragging minutes fled; and still he restrained
himself, still he lay there watching, aware that the men
knew he watched. They floated a metal machine from
the ship to the rock mass that blocked the great half-
open door, under the direction of the third man. No
flicker of their fingers escaped his fierce stare, and
slowly, as the simplicity of the machinery became apparent to him, contempt grew upon him.

He knew what to expect finally, when the flame
flared in incandescent violence and ate ravenously at
the hard rock beneath. But in spite of his preknowledge,
he deliberately jumped and snarled as if in fear, as that
white heat burst forth. His ear tendrils caught the
laughter of the men, their curious pleasure at his simu-
lated dismay.

The door was released, and Morton came over and
went inside with the third man. The latter shook his
head.

"It's a shambles. You can catch the drift of the stuff.
Obviously, they used atomic energy, but . . . but it's in
wheel form. That's a peculiar development. In our science, atomic energy brought in the nonwheel machine.
It's possible that here they've progressed further to a

new type of wheel mechanics. I hope their libraries are better preserved than this, or we'll never know. What could have happened to a civilization to make it vanish like this?"

A third voice broke through the communicators: "This is Siedel. I heard your question, Pennons. Psychologically and sociologically speaking, the only reason why a territory becomes uninhabited is lack of food."

"But they're so advanced scientifically, why didn't they develop space flying and go elsewhere for their food?"

"Ask Gunlie Lester," interjected Morton. "I heard him expounding some theory even before we landed."

The astronomer answered the first call. "I've still got to verify all my facts, but this desolate world is the only planet revolving around that miserable red sun. There's nothing else. No moon, not even a planetoid. And the nearest star system is *nine hundred light-years* away.

"So tremendous would have been the problem of the ruling race of this world, that in one jump they would not only have had to solve interplanetary but interstellar space traveling. When you consider how slow our own development was—first the moon, then Venus— each success leading to the next, and after centuries to the nearest stars; and last of all to the anti-accelerators that permitted galactic travel—considering all this, I maintain it would be impossible for any race to create such machines without practical experience. And, with the nearest star so far away, they had no incentive for the space adventuring that makes for experience."

Coeurl was trotting briskly over to another group. But now, in the driving appetite that consumed him, and in the frenzy of his high scorn, he paid no attention to what they were doing. Memories of past knowledge, jarred into activity by what he had seen, flowed into his consciousness in an ever developing and more vivid stream.

From group to group he sped, a nervous dynamo— jumpy, sick with his awful hunger. A little car rolled up, stopping in front of him, and a formidable camera whirred as it took a picture of him. Over on a mound of rock, a gigantic telescope was rearing up toward the sky. Nearby, a disintegrating machine drilled its searing fire into an ever-deepening hole, down and down, straight down.

Coeurl's mind became a blur of things he watched with half attention. And ever more imminent grew the moment when he knew he could no longer carry on the torture of acting. His brain strained with an irresistible impatience; his body burned with the fury of his eagerness to be off after that man who had gone alone into the city.

He could stand it no longer. A green foam misted his mouth, maddening him. He saw that, for the bare moment, nobody was looking.

Like a shot from a gun, he was off. He floated along in great, gliding leaps, a shadow among the shadows of the rocks. In a minute, the harsh terrain hid the space-ship and the two-legged beings.

Coeurl forgot the ship, forgot everything but his purpose, as if his brain had been wiped clear by a magic, memory-erasing brush. He circled widely, then raced into the city, along deserted streets, taking short cuts with the ease of familiarity, through gaping holes in time-weakened walls, through long corridors of moldering buildings. He slowed to a crouching lope as his ear tendrils caught the id vibrations.

Suddenly, he stopped and peered from a scatter of fallen rock. The man was standing at what must once have been a window, sending the glaring rays of his flashlight into the gloomy interior. The flashlight clicked off. The man, a heavy-set, powerful fellow, walked off with quick, alert steps. Coeurl didn't like that alertness. It presaged trouble; it meant lightning reaction to danger.

Coeurl waited till the human being had vanished around a corner, then he padded into the open. He was running now, tremendously faster than a man could walk, because his plan was clear in his brain. Like a wraith, he slipped down the next street, past a long block of buildings. He turned the first corner at top speed; and then, with dragging belly, crept into the half-darkness between the building and a huge chunk of débris. The street ahead was barred by a solid line of loose rubble that made it like a valley, ending in a narrow, bottlelike neck. The neck had its outlet just below Coeurl.

His ear tendrils caught the low-frequency waves of whistling. The sound throbbed through his being; and suddenly terror caught with icy fingers at his brain. The man would have a gun. Suppose he leveled one burst of atomic energy—*one burst*—before his own muscles could whip out in murder fury.

A little shower of rocks streamed past. And then the man was beneath him. Coeurl reached out and struck a single crushing blow at the shimmering transparent headpiece of the spacesuit. There was a tearing sound of metal and a gushing of blood. The man doubled up as if part of him had been telescoped. For a moment, his bones and legs and muscles combined miraculously to keep him standing. Then he crumpled with a metallic clank of his space armor.

Fear completely evaporated, Coeurl leaped out of hiding. With ravenous speed, he smashed the metal and the body within it to bits. Great chunks of metal, torn piecemeal from the suit, sprayed the ground. Bones cracked. Flesh crunched.

It was simple to tune in on the vibrations of the id, and to create the violent chemical disorganization that freed it from the crushed bone. The id was, Coeurl discovered, mostly in the bone.

He felt revived, almost reborn. Here was more food than he had had in the whole past year.

Three minutes, and it was over, and Coeurl was off like a thing fleeing dire danger. Cautiously, he approached the glistening globe from the opposite side to that by which he had left. The men were all busy at their tasks. Gliding noiselessly, Coeurl slipped unnoticed up to a group of men.

Morton stared down at the horror of tattered flesh, metal and blood on the rock at his feet, and felt a tightening in his throat that prevented speech. He heard Kent say:

"He would go alone, damn him!" The little chemist's voice held a sob imprisoned; and Morton remembered that Kent and Jarvey had chummed together for years in the way only two men can.

"The worst part of it is," shuddered one of the men, "it looks like a senseless murder. His body is spread out like little lumps of flattened jelly, but it seems to be all there. I'd almost wager that if we weighed everything here, there'd still be one hundred and seventy-five pounds by earth gravity. That'd be about one hundred and seventy pounds here."

Smith broke in, his mournful face lined with gloom: "The killer attacked Jarvey, and then discovered his flesh was alien—uneatable. Just like our big cat. Wouldn't eat anything we set before him—" His words died out in sudden, queer silence. Then he said slowly: "Say, what about that creature? He's big enough and strong enough to have done this with his own little paws."

Morton frowned. "It's a thought. After all, he's the only living thing we've seen. We can't just execute him on suspicion, of course—"

"Besides," said one of the men, "he was never out of my sight."

Before Morton could speak, Siedel, the psychologist, snapped, "Positive about that?"

The man hesitated. "Maybe he was for a few minutes. He was wandering around so much, looking at everything."

"Exactly," said Siedel with satisfaction. He turned to Morton. "You see, commander, I, too, had the impression that he was always around; and yet, thinking back over it, I find gaps. There were moments—probably long minutes—when he was completely out of sight."

Morton's face was dark with thought, as Kent broke in fiercely: "I say, take no chances. Kill the brute on suspicion before he does any more damage."

Morton said slowly: "Korita, you've been wandering around with Cranessy and Van Horne. Do you think pussy is a descendant of the ruling class of this planet?"

The tall Japanese archeologist stared at the sky as if collecting his mind. "Commander Morton," he said finally, respectfully, "there is a mystery here. Take a look, all of you, at that majestic skyline. Notice the almost Gothic outline of the architecture. In spite of the megalopolis which they created, these people were close to the soil. The buildings are not simply ornamented. They are ornamental in themselves. Here is the equivalent of the Doric column, the Egyptian pyramid, the Gothic cathedral, growing out of the ground, earnest, big with destiny. If this lonely, desolate world can be regarded as a mother earth, then the land had a warm, a spiritual place in the hearts of the race.

"The effect is emphasized by the winding streets. Their machines prove they were mathematicians, but they were artists, first; and so they did not create the geometrically designed cities of the ultra-sophisticated world metropolis. There is a genuine artistic abandon, a deep joyous emotion written in the curving and unmathematical arrangements of houses, buildings and avenues; a sense of intensity, of divine belief in an inner certainty. This is not a decadent, hoary-with-age civilization, but a young and vigorous culture, confident, strong with purpose.

"There it ended. Abruptly, as if at this point culture

had its Battle of Tours, and began to collapse like the ancient Mohammedan civilization. Or as if in one leap it spanned the centuries and entered the period of contending states. In the Chinese civilization that period occupied 480-230 B. C., at the end of which the State of Tsin saw the beginning of the Chinese Empire. This phase Egypt experienced between 1780-1580 B. C., of which the last century was the 'Hyksos'—unmentionable—time. The classical experienced it from Chæronea—338—and, at the pitch of horror, from the Gracchi—133—to Actium—31 B. C. The West European Americans were devasted by it in the nineteenth and twentieth centuries, and modern historians agree that, nominally, we entered the same phase fifty years ago; though, of course, we have solved the problem.

"You may ask, commander, what has all this to do with your question? My answer is: there is no record of a culture entering abruptly into the period of contending states. It is always a slow development; and the first step is a merciless questioning of all that was once held sacred. Inner certainties cease to exist, are dissolved before the ruthless probings of scientific and analytic minds. The skeptic becomes the highest type of being.

"I say that this culture ended abruptly in its most flourishing age. The sociological effects of such a catastrophe would be a sudden vanishing of morals, a reversion to almost bestial criminality, unleavened by any sense of ideal, a callous indifference to death. If this . . . this pussy is a descendant of such a race, then he will be a cunning creature, a thief in the night, a coldblooded murderer, who would cut his own brother's throat for gain."

"That's enough!" It was Kent's clipped voice. "Commander, I'm willing to act the role of executioner."

Smith interrupted sharply: "Listen, Morton, you're not going to kill that cat yet, even if he is guilty. He's a biological treasure house."

Kent and Smith were glaring angrily at each other. Morton frowned at them thoughtfully, then said: "Korita, I'm inclined to accept your theory as a working basis. But one question: Pussy comes from a period earlier than our own? That is, we are entering the highly civilized era of our culture, while he became suddenly historyless in the most vigorous period of his. *But* it is possible that his culture is a later one on this planet than ours is in the galactic-wide system we have civilized?"

"Exactly. His may be the middle of the tenth civilization of his world; while ours is the end of the eighth sprung from earth, each of the ten, of course, having been builded on the ruins of the one before it."

"In that case, pussy would not know anything about the skepticism that made it possible for us to find him out so positively as a criminal and murderer?"

"No; it would be literally magic to him."

Morton was smiling grimly. "Then I think you'll get your wish, Smith. We'll let pussy live; and if there are any fatalities, now that we know him, it will be due to rank carelessness. There's just the chance, of course, that we're wrong. Like Siedel, I also have the impression that he was always around. But now—we can't leave poor Jarvey here like this. We'll put him in a coffin and bury him."

"No, we won't!" Kent barked. He flushed. "I beg your pardon, commander. I didn't mean it that way. I maintain pussy wanted something from that body. It looks to be all there, but something must be missing. I'm going to find out what, and pin this murder on him so that you'll have to believe it beyond the shadow of a doubt."

It was late night when Morton looked up from a book and saw Kent emerge through the door that led from the laboratories below.

Kent carried a large, flat bowl in his hands; his tired

eyes flashed across at Morton, and he said in a weary, yet harsh, voice: "Now watch!"

He started toward Coeurl, who lay sprawled on the great rug, pretending to be asleep.

Morton stopped him. "Wait a minute, Kent. Any other time, I wouldn't question your actions, but you look ill; you're overwrought. What have you got there?"

Kent turned, and Morton saw that his first impression had been but a flashing glimpse of the truth. There were dark pouches under the little chemist's gray eyes— eyes that gazed feverishly from sunken cheeks in an ascetic face.

"I've found the missing element," Kent said. "It's phosphorus. There wasn't so much as a square millimeter of phosphorus left in Jarvey's bones. Every bit of it had been drained out—by what super-chemistry I don't know. There are ways of getting phosphorus out of the human body. For instance, a quick way was what happened to the workman who helped build this ship. Remember, he fell into fifteen tons of molten metalite—at least, so his relatives claimed—but the company wouldn't pay compensation until the metalite, on analysis, was found to contain a high percentage of phosphorus—"

"What about the bowl of food?" somebody interrupted. Men were putting away magazines and books, looking up with interest.

"It's got organic phosphorus in it. He'll get the scent, or whatever it is that he uses instead of scent—"

"I think he gets the vibrations of things," Gourlay interjected lazily. "Sometimes, when he wiggles those tendrils, I get a distinct static on the radio. And then, again, there's no reaction, just as if he's moved higher or lower on the wave scale. He seems to control the vibrations at will."

Kent waited with obvious impatience until Gourlay's last word, then abruptly went on: "All right, then, when he gets the vibration of the phosphorus and reacts to it like an animal, then—well, we can decide what we've proved by his reaction. May I go ahead, Morton?"

"There are three things wrong with your plan," Morton said, "In the first place, you seem to assume that he is only animal; you seem to have forgotten he may not be hungry after Jarvey; you seem to think that he will not be suspicious. But set the bowl down. His reaction may tell us something."

Coeurl stared with unblinking black eyes as the man set the bowl before him. His ear tendrils instantly caught the id-vibrations from the contents of the bowl— and he gave it not even a second glance.

He recognized this two-legged being as the one who had held the weapon that morning. Danger! With a snarl, he floated to his feet. He caught the bowl with the fingerlike appendages at the end of one looping tentacle, and emptied its contents into the face of Kent, who shrank back with a yell.

Explosively, Coeurl flung the bowl aside and snapped a hawser-thick tentacle around the cursing man's waist. He didn't bother with the gun that hung from Kent's belt. It was only a vibration gun, he sensed—atomic powered, but not an atomic disintegrator. He tossed the kicking Kent onto the nearest couch—and realized with a hiss of dismay that he should have disarmed the man.

Not that the gun was dangerous—but, as the man furiously wiped the gruel from his face with one hand, he reached with the other for his weapon. Coeurl crouched back as the gun was raised slowly and a white beam of flame was discharged at his massive head.

His ear tendrils hummed as they canceled the efforts of the vibration gun. His round, black eyes narrowed as he caught the movement of men reaching for their metalite guns. Morton's voice lashed across the silence.

"Stop!"

*   *   *

Kent clicked off his weapon; and Coeurl crouched down, quivering with fury at this man who had forced him to reveal something of his power.

"Kent," said Morton coldly, "you're not the type to lose your head. You deliberately tried to kill pussy, knowing that the majority of us are in favor of keeping him alive. You know what our rule is: If anyone objects to my decisions, he must say so *at the time*. If the majority object, my decisions are overruled. In this case, no one but you objected, and, therefore, your action in taking the law into your own hands is most reprehensible, and automatically debars you from voting for a year."

Kent stared grimly at the circle of faces. "Korita was right when he said ours was a highly civilized age. It's decadent." Passion flamed harshly in his voice. "My God, isn't there a man here who can see the horror of the situation? Jarvey dead only a few hours, and this creature, whom we all know to be guilty, lying there unchained, planning his next murder; and the victim is right here in this room. What kind of men are we— fools, cynics, ghouls—or is it that our civilization is so steeped in reason that we can contemplate a murderer sympathetically?"

He fixed brooding eyes on Coeurl. "You were right, Morton, that's no animal. That's a devil from the deepest hell of this forgotten planet, whirling its solitary way around a dying sun."

"Don't go melodramatic on us," Morton said. "Your analysis is all wrong, so far as I am concerned. We're not ghouls or cynics; we're simply scientists, and pussy here is going to be studied. Now that we suspect him, we doubt his ability to trap any of us. One against a hundred hasn't a chance." He glanced around. "Do I speak for all of us?"

"Not for me, commander!" It was Smith who spoke, and, as Morton stared in amazement, he continued: "In the excitement and momentary confusion, no one seems to have noticed that when Kent fired his vibration gun, the beam hit this creature squarely on is cat head—and didn't hurt him."

Morton's amazed glance went from Smith to Coeurl, and back to Smith again. "Are you certain it hit him? As you say, it all happened so swiftly—when pussy wasn't hurt I simply assumed that Kent had missed him."

"He hit him in the face," Smith said positively. "A vibration gun, of course, can't even kill a man right away—but it can injure him. There's no sign of injury on pussy, though, not even a singed hair."

"Perhaps his skin is a good insulation against heat of any kind."

"Perhaps. But in view of our uncertainty, I think we should lock him up in the cage."

While Morton frowned darkly in thought, Kent spoke up. "Now you're talking sense, Smith."

Morton asked: "Then you would be satisfied, Kent, if we put him in the cage?"

Kent considered, finally: "Yes. If four inches of micro-steel can't hold him, we'd better give him the ship."

Coeurl followed the men as they went out into the corridor. He trotted docilely along as Morton unmistakably motioned him through a door he had not hitherto seen. He found himself in a square, solid metal room. The door clanged metallically behind him; he felt the flow of power as the electric lock clicked home.

His lips parted in a grimace of hate, as he realized the trap, but he gave no other outward reaction. It occurred to him that he had progressed a long way from the sunk-into-primitiveness creature who, a few hours before, had gone incoherent with fear in an elevator cage. Now, a thousand memories of his powers were reawakened in his brain; ten thousand cunnings were, after ages of disuse, once again part of his very being.

He sat quite still for a moment on the short, heavy haunches into which his body tapered, his ear tendrils examining his surroundings. Finally, he lay down, his eyes glowing with contemptuous fire. The fools! The poor fools!

It was about an hour later when he heard the man— Smith—fumbling overhead. Vibrations poured upon him, and for just an instant he was startled. He leaped to his feet in pure terror—and then realized that the vibrations were vibrations, not atomic explosions. Somebody was taking pictures of the inside of his body.

He crouched down again, but his ear tendrils vibrated, and he thought contemptuously: the silly fool would be surprised when he tried to develop those pictures.

After a while the man went away, and for a long time there were noises of men doing things far away. That, too, died away slowly.

Coeurl lay waiting, as he felt the silence creep over the ship. In the long ago, before the dawn of immortality, the coeurls, too, had slept at night; and the memory of it had been revived the day before when he saw some of the men dozing. At last, the vibration of two pairs of feet, pacing, pacing endlessly, was the only human-made frequency that throbbed on his ear tendrils.

Tensely, he listened to the two watchmen. The first one walked slowly past the cage door. Then about thirty feet behind him came the second. Coeurl sensed the alertness of these men; knew that he could never surprise either while they walked separately. It meant—he must be doubly careful!

Fifteen minutes, and they came again. The moment they were past, he switched his senses from their vibrations to a vastly higher range. The pulsating violence of the atomic engines stammered its soft story to his brain. The electric dynamos hummed their muffled song of pure power. He felt the whisper of that flow through the wires in the walls of his cage, and through the electric lock of his door. He forced his quivering body into straining immobility, his senses seeking, searching, to tune in on that sibilant tempest of energy. Suddenly, his ear tendrils vibrated in harmony—he caught the surging change into shrillness of that rippling force wave.

There was a sharp click of metal on metal. With a gentle touch of one tentacles, Coeurl pushed open the door, and glided out into the dully gleaming corridor. For just a moment he felt contempt, a glow of superiority, as he thought of the stupid creatures who dared to match their wit against a coeurl. And in that moment, he suddenly thought of other coeurls. A queer, exultant sense of race pounded through his being; the driving hate of centuries of ruthless competition yielded reluctantly before pride of kinship with the future rulers of all space.

Suddenly, he felt weighed down by his limitations, his need for other coeurls, his aloneness—one against a hundred, with the stake all eternity; the starry universe itself beckoned his rapacious, vaulting ambition. If he failed, there would never be a second chance—no time to revive long-rotted machinery, and attempt to solve the secret of space travel.

He padded along on tensed paws—through the salon—into the next corridor—and came to the first bedroom door. It stood half open. One swift flow of synchronized muscles, one swiftly lashing tentacle that caught the unresisting throat of the sleeping man, crushing it, and the lifeless head rolled crazily, the body twitched once.

Seven bedrooms; seven dead men. It was the seventh taste of murder that brought a sudden return of lust, a pure, unbounded desire to kill, return of a millennium-old habit of destroying everything containing the precious id.

As the twelfth man slipped convulsively into death, Coeurl emerged abruptly from the sensuous joy of the kill to the sound of footsteps.

They were not near—that was what brought wave

after wave of fright swirling into the chaos that suddenly became his brain.

The watchmen were coming slowly along the corridor toward the door of the cage where he had been imprisoned. In a moment, the first man would see the open door—and sound the alarm.

Coeurl caught at the vanishing remnants of his reason. With frantic speed, careless now of accidental sounds, he raced—along the corridor with its bedroom doors—through the salon. He emerged into the next corridor, cringing in awful anticipation of the atomic flame he expected would stab into his face.

The two men were together, standing side by side. For one single instant, Coeurl could scarcely believe his tremendous good luck. Like a fool the second had come running when he saw the other stop before the open door. They looked up, paralyzed, before the nightmare of claws and tentacles, the ferocious cat head and hate-filled eyes.

The first man went for his gun, but the second, physically frozen before the doom he saw, uttered a shriek, a shrill cry of horror that floated along the corridors—and ended in a curious gurgle, as Coeurl flung the two corposes with one irresistible motion the full length of the corridor. He didn't want the dead bodies found near the cage. That was his one hope.

Shaking in every nerve and muscle, conscious of the terrible error he had made, unable to think coherently, he plunged into the cage. The door clicked softly shut behind him. Power flowed once more through the electric lock.

He crouched tensely, simulating sleep, as he heard the rush of many feet, caught the vibration of excited voices. He knew when somebody actuated the cage audioscope and looked in. A few moments now, and the other bodies would be discovered.

*   *   *

"Siedel gone!" Morton said numbly. "What are we going to do without Siedel? And Breckenridge! And Coulter and— Horrible!"

He covered his face with his hands, but only for an instant. He looked up grimly, his heavy chin outthrust as he stared into the stern faces that surrounded him. "If anybody's got so much as a germ of an idea, bring it out."

"Space madness!"

"I've thought of that. But there hasn't been a case of a man going mad for fifty years. Dr. Eggert will test everybody, of course, and right now he's looking at the bodies with that possibility in mind."

As he finished, he saw the doctor coming through the door. Men crowded aside to make way for him.

"I heard you, commander," Dr. Eggert said, "and I think I can say right now that the space-madness theory is out. The throats of these men have been squeezed to a jelly. No human being could have exerted such enormous strength without using a machine."

Morton saw that the doctor's eyes kept looking down the corridor, and he shook his head and groaned:

"It's no use suspecting pussy, doctor. He's in his cage, pacing up and down. Obviously heard the racket and— Man alive! You can't suspect him. That cage was built to hold literally *anything*—four inches of microsteel—and there's not a scratch on the door. Kent, even you won't say, 'Kill him on suspicion,' because there can't be any suspicion, unless there's a new science here, beyond anything we can imagine—"

"On the contrary," said Smith flatly, "we have all the evidence we need. I used the telefluor on him—you know the arrangement we have on the top of the cage—and tried to take some pictures. They just blurred. Pussy jumped when the telefluor was turned on, as if he felt the vibrations.

"You all know what Gourlay said before? This beast can apparently receive and send vibrations of any lengths.

The way he dominated the power of Kent's gun is final proof of his special ability to interfere with energy."

"What in the name of all the hells have we got here?" One of the men groaned. "Why, if he can control that power, and sent it out in any vibrations, there's nothing to stop him killing all of us."

"Which proves," snapped Morton, "that he isn't invincible, or he would have done it long ago."

Very deliberately, he walked over to the mechanism that controlled the prison cage.

"You're not going to open the door!" Kent gasped, reaching for his gun.

"No, but if I pull this switch, electricity will flow through the floor, and electrocute whatever's inside. We've never had to use this before, so you had probably forgotten about it."

He jerked the switch hard over. Blue fire flashed from the metal, and a bank of fuses above his head exploded with a single bang.

Morton frowned. "That's funny. Those fuses shouldn't have blown! Well, we can't even look in, now. That wrecked the audios, too."

Smith said: "If he could interfere with the electric lock, enough to open the door, then he probably probed every possible danger and was ready to interfere when you threw that switch."

"At least, it proves he's vulnerable to our energies!" Morton smiled grimly. "Because he rendered them harmless. The important thing is, we've got him behind four inches of the toughest of metal. At the worst we can open the door and ray him to death. But first, I think we'll try to use the telefluor power cable—"

A commotion from inside the cage interrupted his words. A heavy body crashed against a wall, followed by a dull thump.

"He knows what we were trying to do!" Smith grunted to Morton. "And I'll bet it's a very sick pussy in there.

What a fool he was to go back into the cage and does he realize it!"

The tension was relaxing; men were smiling nervously, and there was even a ripple of humorless laughter at the picture Smith drew of the monster's discomfiture.

"What I'd like to know," said Pennons, the engineer, "is, why did the telefluor metal dial jump and waver at full power when pussy made that noise? It's right under my nose here, and the dial jumped like a house afire!"

There was silence both without and within the cage, then Morton said: "It may mean he's coming out. Back, everybody, and keep your guns ready. Pussy was a fool to think he could conquer a hundred men, but he's by far the most formidable creature in the galactic system. He may come out of that door, rather than die like a rat in a trap. And he's just tough enough to take some of us with him—if we're not careful."

The men backed slowly in a solid body; and somebody said: "That's funny. I thought I heard the elevator."

"Elevator!" Morton echoed. "Are you sure, man?"

"Just for a moment I was!" The man, a member of the crew, hesitated. "We were all shuffling our feet—"

"Take somebody with you, and go look. Bring whoever dared to run off back here—"

There was a jar, a horrible jerk, as the whole gigantic body of the ship careened under them. Morton was flung to the floor with a violence that stunned him. He fought back to consciousness, aware of the other men lying all around him. He shouted: "Who the devil started those engines!"

The agonizing acceleration continued; his feet dragged with awful exertion, as he fumbled with the nearest audioscope, and punched the engine-room number. The picture that flooded onto the screen brought a deep bellow to his lips:

"It's pussy! He's in the engine room—and we're heading straight out into space."

The screen went black even as he spoke, and he could see no more.

It was Morton who first staggered across the salon floor to the supply room where the spacesuits were kept. After fumbling almost blindly into his own suit, he cut the effects of the body-torturing acceleration, and brought suits to the semiconscious men on the floor. In a few moments, other men were assisting him; and then it was only a matter of minutes before everybody was clad in metalite, with anti-acceleration motors running at half power.

It was Morton then who, after first looking into the cage, opened the door and stood, silent as the others crowded about him, to stare at the gaping hole in the rear wall. The hole was a frightful thing of jagged edges and horribly bent metal, and it opened upon another corridor.

"I'll swear," whispered Pennons, "that it's impossible. The ten-ton hammer in the machine shops couldn't more than dent four inches of micro with one blow—and we only heard one. It would take at least a minute for an atomic disintegrator to do the job. Morton, this is a super-being."

Morton saw that Smith was examining the break in the wall. The biologist looked up. "If only Breckenridge weren't dead! We need a metallurgist to explain this. Look!"

He touched the broken edge of the metal. A piece crumbled in his finger and slithered away in a fine shower of dust to the floor. Morton noticed for the first time that there was a little pit of metallic debris and dust.

"You've hit it." Morton nodded. "No miracle of strength here. The monster merely used his special powers to interfere with the electronic tensions holding the metal together. That would account, too, for the drain on the telefluor power cable that Pennons noticed. The thing used the power with his body as a transforming medium, smashed through the wall, ran down the corridor to the elevator shaft, and so down to the engine room."

"In the meantime, commander," Kent said quietly, "we are faced with a super-being in control of the ship, completely dominating the engine room and its almost unlimited power, and in possession of the best part of the machine shops."

Morton felt the silence, while the men pondered the chemist's words. Their anxiety was a tangible thing that lay heavily upon their faces; in every expression was the growing realization that here was the ultimate situation in their lives; their very existence was at stake and perhaps much more. Morton voiced the thought in everybody's mind:

"Suppose he wins. He's utterly ruthless, and he probably sees galactic power within his grasp."

"Kent is wrong," barked the chief navigator. "The thing doesn't dominate the engine room. We've still got the control room, and that gives us *first* control of all the machines. You fellows may not know the mechanical set-up we have; but, though he can eventually disconnect us, we can cut off all the switches in the engine room now. Commander, why didn't you just shut off the power instead of putting us into spacesuits? At the very least you could have adjusted the ship to the acceleration."

"For two reasons," Morton answered. "Individually, we're safer within the force fields of our spacesuits. And we can't afford to give up our advantages in panicky moves."

"Advantages! What other advantages have we got?"

"We know things about him," Morton replied. "And right now, we're going to make a test. Pennons, detail five men to each of the four approaches to the engine room. Take atomic disintegrators to blast through the big doors. They're all shut, I noticed. He's locked himself in.

"Selenski, you go up to the control room and shut off everything except the drive engines. Gear them to the master switch, and shut them off all at once. One thing, though—leave the acceleration on full blast. No antiacceleration must be applied to the ship. Understand?"

"Aye, sir!" The pilot saluted.

"And report to me through the communicators if any of the machines start to run again." He faced the men. "I'm going to lead the main approach. Kent, you take No. 2; Smith, No. 3, and Pennons, No. 4. We're going to find out right now if we're dealing with unlimited science, or a creature limited like the rest of us. I'll bet on the second possibility."

Morton had an empty sense of walking endlessly, as he moved, a giant of a man in his transparent space armor, along the glistening metal tube that was the main corridor of the engine-room floor. Reason told him the creature had already shown feet of clay, yet the feeling that here was an invincible being persisted.

He spoke into the communicator: "It's no use trying to sneak up on him. He can probably hear a pin drop. So just wheel up your units. He hasn't been in that engine room long enough to do anything.

"As I've said, this is largely a test attack. In the first place, we could never forgive ourselves if we didn't try to conquer him now, before he's had time to prepare against us. But, aside from the possibility that we can destroy him immediately, I have a theory.

"The idea goes something like this: Those doors are built to withstand accidental atomic explosions, and it will take fifteen minutes for the atomic disintegrators to smash them. During that period the monster will have no power. True, the drive will be on, but that's straight atomic explosion. My theory is, he can't touch stuff like that; and in a few minutes you'll see what I mean—I hope."

His voice was suddenly crisp: "Ready, Selenski?"

"Aye, ready."

"Then cut the master switch."

The corridor—the whole ship, Morton knew—was abruptly plunged into darkness. Morton clicked on the dazzling light of his spacesuit; the other men did the same, their faces pale and drawn.

"Blast!" Morton barked into his communicator.

The mobile units throbbed; and then pure atomic flame ravened out and poured upon the hard metal of the door. The first molten droplet rolled reluctantly, not down, but up the door. The second was more normal. It followed a shaky downward course. The third rolled sideways—for this was pure force, not subject to gravitation. Other drops followed until a dozen streams trickled sedately yet unevenly in every direction—streams of hellish, sparkling fire, bright as fairy gems, alive with the coruscating fury of atoms suddenly tortured, and running blindly, crazy with pain.

The minutes ate at time like a slow acid. At last Morton asked huskily:

"Selenski?"

"Nothing yet, commander."

Morton half whispered: "But he must be doing something. He can't be just waiting in there like a cornered rat, Selenski?"

"Nothing, commander."

Seven minutes, eight minutes, then twelve.

"Commander!" It was Selenski's voice, taut. "He's got the electric dynamo running."

Morton drew a deep breath, and heard one of his men say:

"That's funny. We can't get any deeper. Boss, take a look at this."

Morton looked. The little scintillating streams had frozen rigid. The ferocity of the disintegrators vented in vain against metal grown suddenly invulnerable.

Morton sighed. "Our test is over. Leave two men

guarding every corridor. The others come up to the control room."

He seated himself a few minutes later before the massive control keyboard. "So far as I'm concerned the test was a success. We know that of all the machines in the engine room, the most important to the monster was the electric dynamo. He must have worked in a frenzy of terror while we were at the doors."

"Of course, it's easy to see what he did," Pennons said. "Once he had the power he increased the electronic tensions of the door to their ultimate."

"The main thing is this," Smith chimed in. "He works with vibrations only so far as his special powers are concerned, and the energy must come from outside himself. Atomic energy in its pure form, not being vibration, he can't handle any differently than we can."

Kent said glumly: "The main point in my opinion is that he stopped us cold. What's the good of knowing that his control over vibrations did it? If we can't break through those doors with our atomic disintegrators, we're finished."

Morton shook his head. "Not finished—but we'll have to do some planning. First, though, I'll start these engines. It'll be harder for him to get control of them when they're running."

He pulled the master switch back into place with a jerk. There was a hum, as scores of machines leaped into violent life in the engine room a hundred feet below. The noises sank to a steady vibration of throbbing power.

Three hours later, Morton paced up and down before the men gathered in the salon. His dark hair was uncombed; the space pallor of his strong face emphasized rather than detracted from the outthrust aggressiveness of his jaw. When he spoke, his deep voice was crisp to the point of sharpness:

"To make sure that our plans are fully co-ordinated,

I'm going to ask each expert in turn to outline his part in the overpowering of this creature. Pennons first!"

Pennons stood up briskly. He was not a big man, Morton thought, yet he looked big, perhaps because of his air of authority. This man knew engines, and the history of engines. Morton had heard him trace a machine through its evolution from a simple toy to the highly complicated modern instrument. He had studied machine development on a hundred planets; and there was literally nothing fundamental that he didn't know about mechanics. It was almost weird to hear Pennons, who could have spoken for a thousand hours and still only have touched upon his subject, say with absurd brevity:

"We've set up a relay in the control room to start and stop every engine rhythmically. The trip lever will work a hundred times a second, and the effect will be to create vibrations of every description. There is just a possibility that one or more of the machines will burst, on the principle of soldiers crossing a bridge in step—you've heard that old story, no doubt—but in my opinion there is no real danger of a break of that tough metal. The main purpose is simply to interfere with the interference of the creature, and smash through the doors."

"Gourlay next!" barked Morton.

Gourlay climbed lazily to his feet. He looked sleepy, as if he was somewhat bored by the whole proceedings, yet Morton knew he loved people to think him lazy, a good-for-nothing slouch, who spent his days in slumber and his nights catching forty winks. His title was chief communication engineer, but his knowledge extended to every vibration field; and he was probably, with the possible exception of Kent, the fastest thinker on the ship. His voice drawled out, and—Morton noted—the very deliberate assurance of it had a soothing effect on the men—anxious faces relaxed, bodies leaned back more restfully:

"Once inside," Gourlay said, "we've rigged up vibration screens on pure force that should stop nearly everything he's got on the ball. They work on the principle of reflection, so that everything he sends will be reflected back to him. In addition, we've got plenty of spare electric energy, that we'll just feed him from mobile copper cups. There must be a limit to his capacity for handling power with those insulated nerves of his."

"Selenski!" called Morton.

The chief pilot was already standing, as if he had anticipated Morton's call. And that, Morton reflected, was the man. His nerves had that rocklike steadiness which is the first requirement of the master controller of a great ship's movements; yet that very steadiness seemed to rest on dynamite ready to explode at its owner's volition. He was not a man of great learning, but he "reacted" to stimuli so fast that he always seemed to be anticipating.

"The impression I've received of the plan is that it must be cumulative. Just when the creature thinks that he can't stand any more, another thing happens to add to his trouble and confusion. When the uproar's at its height, I'm supposed to cut in the anti-accelerators. The commander thinks with Gunlie Lester that these creatures will know nothing about anti-acceleration. It's a development, pure and simple, of the science of interstellar flight, and couldn't have been developed in any other way. We think when the creature feels the first effects of the anti-acceleration—you all remember the caved-in feeling you had the first month—it won't know what to think or do."

"Korita next."

"I can only offer you encouragement," said the archeologist, "on the basis of my theory that the monster has all the characteristics of a criminal of the early ages of any civilization, complicated by an apparent reversion to primitiveness. The suggestion has been made by Smith that his knowledge of science is puzzling, and could only mean that we are dealing with an actual inhabitant, not a descendant of the inhabitants of the dead city we visited. This would ascribe a virtual immortality to our enemy, a possibility which is borne out by his ability to breathe both oxygen and chlorine—or neither—but even that makes no difference. He comes from a certain age in his civilization; and he has sunk so low that his ideas are mostly memories of that age.

"In spite of all the powers of his body, he lost his head in the elevator the first morning, until he remembered. He placed himself in such a position that he was forced to reveal his special powers against vibrations. He bungled the mass murders a few hours ago. In fact, his whole record is one of the low cunning of the primitive, egotistical mind which has little or no conception of the vast organization with which it is confronted.

"He is like the ancient German soldier who felt superior to the elderly Roman scholar, yet the latter was part of a mighty civilization of which the Germans of that day stood in awe.

"You may suggest that the sack of Rome by the Germans in later years defeats my argument; however, modern historians agree that the 'sack' was an historical accident, and not history in the true sense of the word. The movement of the 'Sea-peoples' which set in against the Egyptian civilization from 1400 B. C. succeeded only as regards the Cretan island-realm—their mighty expedition is against the Libyan and Phoenician coasts, with the accompaniment of Viking fleets, failed as those of the Huns failed against the Chinese Empire. Rome would have been abandoned in any event. Ancient, glorious Samarra was desolate by the tenth century; Pataliputra, Asoka's great capital, was an immense and completely uninhabited waste of houses when the Chinese traveler Hsinan-tang visited it about A. D. 635.

"We have, then, a primitive, and that primitive is

now far out in space, completely outside of his natural habitat. I say, let's go in and win."

One of the men grumbled, as Korita finished: "You can talk about the sack of Rome being an accident, and about this fellow being a primitive, but the facts are facts. It looks to me as if Rome is about to fall again; and it won't be no primitive that did it, either. This guy's got plenty of what it takes."

Morton smiled grimly at the man, a member of the crew. "We'll see about that—right now!"

In the blazing brilliance of the gigantic machine shop, Coeurl slaved. The forty-foot, cigar-shaped spaceship was nearly finished. With a grunt of effort, he completed the laborious installation of the drive engines, and paused to survey his craft.

Its interior, visible through the one aperture in the outer wall, was pitifully small. There was literally room for nothing but the engines—and a narrow space for himself.

He plunged frantically back to work as he heard the approach of the men, and the sudden change in the tempest-like thunder of the engines—a rhythmical off-and-on hum, shriller in tone, sharper, more nerve-racking than the deep-throated, steady throb that had preceded it. Suddenly, there were the atomic disintegrators again at the massive outer doors.

He fought them off, but never wavered from his task. Every mighty muscle of his powerful body strained as he carried great loads of tools, machines and instruments, and dumped them into the bottom of his makeshift ship. There was no time to fit anything into place, no time for anything—no time—no time.

The thought pounded at his reason. He felt strangely weary for the first time in his long and vigorous existence. With a last, tortured heave, he jerked the gigantic sheet of metal into the gaping aperture of the ship—and stood there for a terrible minute, balancing it precariously.

He knew the doors were going down. Half a dozen disintegrators concentrating on one point were irresistibly, though slowly, eating away the remaining inches. With a gasp, he released his mind from the doors and concentrated every ounce of his mind on the yard-thick outer wall, toward which the blunt nose of his ship was pointing.

His body cringed from the surging power that flowed from the electric dynamo through his ear tendrils into that resisting wall. The whole inside of him felt on fire, and he knew that he was dangerously close to carrying his ultimate load.

And still he stood there, shuddering with the awful pain, holding the unfastened metal plate with hard-clenched tentacles. His massive head pointed as in dread fascination at that bitterly hard wall.

He heard one of the engine-room doors crash inward. Men shouted; disintegrators rolled forward, their raging power unchecked. Coeurl heard the floor of the engine room hiss in protest, as those beams of atomic energy tore everything in their path to bits. The machines rolled closer; cautious footsteps sounded behind them. In a minute, they would be at the flimsy doors separating the engine room from the machine shop.

Suddenly Coeurl was satisfied. With a snarl of hate, a vindictive glow of feral eyes, he ducked into his little craft, and pulled the metal plate down into place as if it was a hatchway.

His ear tendrils hummed, as he softened the edges of the surrounding metal. In an instant, the plate was more than welded—it was part of his ship, a seamless, rivetless part of a whole that was solid opaque metal except for two transparent areas, one in the front, one in the rear.

His tentacle embraced the power drive with almost sensuous tenderness. There was a forward surge of his fragile machine, straight at the great outer wall of the machine shops. The nose of the forty-foot craft touched—and the wall dissolved in a glittering shower of dust.

Coeurl felt the barest retarding movement; and then he kicked the nose of the machine out into the cold of space, twisted it about, and headed back in the direction from which the big ship had been coming all these hours.

Men in space armor stood in the jagged hole that yawned in the lower reaches of the gigantic globe. The men and the great ship grew smaller. Then the men were gone; and there was only the ship with its blaze of a thousand blurring portholes. The ball shrank incredibly, too small now for individual portholes to be visible.

Almost straight ahead, Coeurl saw a tiny, dim, reddish ball—his own sun, he realized. He headed toward it at full speed. There were caves where he could hide and with other coeurls build secretly a spaceship in which they could reach other planets safely—now that he knew how.

His body ached from the agony of acceleration, yet he dared not let up for a single instant. He glanced back, half in terror. The globe was still there, a tiny dot of light in the immense blackness of space. Suddenly it twinkled and was gone.

For a brief moment, he had the empty, frightened impression that just before it disappeared, it moved. But he could see nothing. He could not escape the belief that they had shut off all their lights, and were sneaking up on him in the darkness. Worried and uncertain, he looked through the forward transparent plate.

A tremor of dismay shot through him. The dim red sun toward which he was heading was not growing larger. It was *becoming smaller* by the instant, and it grew visibly tinier during the next five minutes, became a pale-red dot in the sky—and vanished like the ship.

Fear came then, a blinding surge of it, that swept through his being and left him chilled with the sense of the unknown. For minutes, he stared frantically into the space ahead, searching for some landmark. But only the remote stars glimmered there, unwinking points against a velvet background of unfathomable distance.

Wait! One of the points was growing larger. With every muscle and nerve tensed, Coeurl watched the point become a dot, a round ball of light—red light. Bigger, bigger it grew. Suddenly, the red light shimmered and turned white—and there, before him, was the great globe of the spaceship, lights glaring from every porthole, the very ship which a few minutes before he had watched vanish behind him.

Something happened to Coeurl in that moment. His brain was spinning like a flywheel, faster, faster, more incoherently. Suddenly, the wheel flew apart into a million aching fragments. His eyes almost started from their sockets as, like a maddened animal, he raged in his small quarters.

His tentacles clutched at precious instruments and flung them insensately; his paws smashed in fury at the very walls of his ship. Finally, in a brief flash of sanity, he knew that he couldn't face the inevitable fire of atomic disintegrators.

It was a simple thing to create the violent disorganization that freed every drop of id from his vital organs.

They found him lying dead in a little pool of phosphorus.

"Poor pussy," said Morton. "I wonder what he thought when he saw us appear ahead of him, after his own sun disappeared. Knowing nothing of anti-accelerators, he couldn't know that we could stop short in space, whereas it would take him more than three hours to decelerate; and in the meantime he'd be drawing farther and farther away from where he wanted to go. He couldn't know that by stopping, we flashed past him at millions of miles a second. Of course, he didn't have a chance once

he left our ship. The whole world must have seemed
topsy-turvy."

"Never mind the sympathy," he heard Kent say behind him. "We've got a job—to kill every cat in that
miserable world."

Korita murmured softly: "That should be simple. They
are but primitives; and we have merely to sit down, and
they will come to us, cunningly expecting to delude
us."

Smith snapped: "You fellows make me sick! Pussy
was the toughest nut we ever had to crack. He had
everything he needed to defeat us—"

Morton smiled as Korita interrupted blandly: "Exactly, my dear Smith, except that he reacted according
to the biological impulses of his type. His defeat was
already foreshadowed when we unerringly analyzed him
as a criminal from a certain era of his civilization.

"It was history, honorable Mr. Smith, our knowledge
of history that defeated him," said the Japanese archeologist, reverting to the ancient politeness of his race.

According to the indices, "Collecting Team" was the title of this story when it was reprinted in the June, 1957, issue of Authentic Science Fiction. *The original publication was in* Super-Science Stories, *for December, 1956, where the piece was entitled "Catch 'Em All Alive!"*

I asked Bob which text he preferred. He didn't have any recollection of the variant title; didn't recall the early reprint at all (take a look at a Silverberg bibliography and you'll understand why that might be); and said whatever text I pleased was fine with him.

So what the hell: I used a 1971 Ballantine collection to avoid photocopying a thirty-year-old magazine.

The SF genre and the greater field of literature are fortunate that Robert Silverberg continues to write prolifically. Because of my tastes and present purposes, I am fortunate that he wrote so much and so well thirty years ago.

COLLECTING
TEAM

Robert Silverberg

From fifty thousand miles up, the situation looked promising. It was a middle-sized, brown-and-green, inviting-looking planet, with no sign of cities or any other such complications. Just a pleasant sort of place, the very sort we were looking for to redeem what had been a pretty futile expedition.

I turned to Clyde Holdreth, who was staring reflectively at the thermocouple.

"Well? What do you think?"

"Looks fine to me. Temperature's about seventy down there—nice and warm, and plenty of air. I think it's worth a try."

Lee Davison came strolling out from the storage hold, smelling of animals, as usual. He was holding one of the blue monkeys we pickled up on Alpheraz, and the little beast was crawling up his arm. "Have we found something, gentlemen?"

"We've found a planet," I said. "How's the storage space in the hold?"

"Don't worry about that. We've got room for a whole

183

zoofull more, before we get filled up. It hasn't been a very fruitful trip."

"No," I agreed. "It hasn't. Well? shall we go down and see what's to be seen?"

"Might as well," Holdreth said. "We can't go back to Earth with just a couple of blue monkeys and some anteaters, you know."

"I'm in favor of a landing too," said Davison. "You?"

I nodded. "I'll set up the charts, and you get your animals comfortable for deceleration."

Davison disappeared back into the storage hold, while Holdreth scribbled furiously in the logbook, writing down the coordinates of the planet below, its general description, and so forth. Aside from being a collecting team for the zoological department of the Bureau of Interstellar Affairs, we also double as a survey ship, and the planet down below was listed as *unexplored* on our charts.

I glanced out at the mottled brown-and-green ball spinning slowly in the viewport, and felt the warning twinge of gloom that came to me every time we made a landing on a new and strange world. Repressing it, I started to figure out a landing orbit. From behind me came the furious chatter of the blue monkeys as Davison strapped them into their acceleration cradles, and under that the deep, unmusical honking of the Rigelian anteaters, noisily bleating their displeasure.

The planet was inhabited, all right. We hadn't had the ship on the ground more than a minute before the local fauna began to congregate. We stood at the viewport and looked out in wonder.

"This is one of those things you dream about," Davison said, stroking his little beard nervously. "Look at them! There must be a thousand different species out there."

"I've never seen anything like it," said Holdreth.

I computed how much storage space we had left and how many of the thronging creatures outside we would be able to bring back with us. "How are we going to decide what to take and what to leave behind?"

"Does it matter?" Holdreth said gaily. "This is what you call an embarrassment of riches, I guess. We just grab the dozen most bizarre creatures and blast off—and save the rest for another trip. It's too bad we wasted all that time wandering around near Rigel."

"We *did* get the anteaters," Davison pointed out. They were his finds, and he was proud of them.

I smiled sourly. "Yeah. We got the anteaters there." The anteaters honked at that moment, loud and clear. "You know, that's one set of beasts I think I could do without."

"Bad attitude," Holdreth said. "Unprofessional."

"Whoever said I was a zoologist, anyway? I'm just a spaceship pilot, remember. And if I don't like the way those anteaters talk—and—smell—I see no reason why I—"

"Say, look at that one," Davison said suddenly.

I glanced out the viewport and saw a new beast emerging from the thick-packed vegetation in the background. I've seen some fairly strange creatures since I was assigned to the zoological department, but this one took the grand prize.

It was about the size of a giraffe, moving on long, wobbly legs and with a tiny head up at the end of a preposterous neck. Only it had six legs and a bunch of writhing snakelike tentacles as well, and its eyes, great violet globes, stood out nakedly on the ends of two thick stalks. It must have been twenty feet high. It moved with exaggerated grace through the swarm of beasts surrounding our ship, pushed its way smoothly toward the vessel, and peered gravely in at the viewport. One purple eye stared directly at me, the other at Davison. Oddly, it seemed to me as if it were trying to tell us something.

"Big one, isn't it?" Davison said finally.

"I'll bet you'd like to bring one back, too."

"Maybe we can fit a young one aboard," Davison said. "If we can find a young one." He turned to Holdreth. "How's the air analysis coming? I'd like to get out there and start collecting. God, that's a crazy-looking beast!"

The animal outside had apparently finished its inspection of us, for it pulled its head away and, gathering its legs under itself, squatted near the ship. A small doglike creature with stiff spines running along its back began to bark at the big creature, which took no notice. The other animals, which came in all shapes and sizes, continued to mill around the ship, evidently very curious about the newcomer to their world. I could see Davidson's eyes thirsty with the desire to take the whole kit and caboodle back to Earth with him. I knew what was running through his mind. He was dreaming of the umpteen thousand species of extraterrestrial wild-life roaming around out there, and to each one he was attaching a neat little tag: *Something-or-other davisoni*.

"The air's fine," Holdreth announced abruptly, looking up from his test tubes. "Get your butterfly nets and let's see what we can catch."

There was something I didn't like about the place. It was just too good to be true, and I learned long ago that nothing ever is. There's always a catch someplace.

Only this seemed to be on the level. The planet was a bonanza for zoologists, and Davison and Holdreth were having the time of their lives, hipdeep in obliging specimens.

"I've never seen anything like it," Davison said for at least the fiftieth time, as he scooped up a small purplish squirrel-like creature and examined it curiously. The squirrel stared back, examining Davison just as curiously.

"Let's take some of these," Davison said. "I like them."

"Carry 'em on in, then," I said shrugging. I didn't care which specimens they chose, so long as they filled up the storage hold quickly and let me blast off on schedule. I watched as Davison grabbed a pair of the squirrels and brought them into the ship.

Holdreth came over to me. He was carrying a sort of a dog with insect-faceted eyes and gleaming furless skin. "How's this one, Gus?"

"Fine," I said bleakly. "Wonderful."

He put the animal down—it didn't scamper away, just sat there smiling at us—and looked at me. He ran a hand through his fast-vanishing hair. "Listen, Gus, you've been gloomy all day. What's eating you?"

"I don't like this place," I said.

"Why? Just on general principles?"

"It's too *easy*, Clyde. Much too easy. These animals just flock around here waiting to be picked up."

Holdreth chuckled. "And you're used to a struggle, aren't you? You're just angry at us because we have it so simple here!"

"When I think of the trouble we went through just to get a pair of miserable vile-smelling anteaters, and—"

"Come off it, Gus. We'll load up in a hurry, if you like. But this place is a zoological gold mine!"

I shook my head. "I don't like it, Clyde. Not at all."

Holdreth laughed again and picked up his faceted-eyed dog. "Say, know where I can find another of these, Gus?"

"Right over there," I said, pointing. "By that tree. With its tongue hanging out. It's just waiting to be carried away."

Holdreth looked and smiled. "What do you know about that!" He snared his specimen and carried both of them inside.

I walked away to survey the grounds. The planet was too flatly incredible for me to accept on face value, without at least a look-see, despite the blithe way my two companions were snapping up specimens.

For one thing, animals just don't exist this way—in big miscellaneous quantities, living all together happily.

I hadn't noticed more than a few of each kind, and there must have been five hundred different species, each one stranger looking than the next. Nature doesn't work that way.

For another, they all seemed to be on friendly terms with one another, though they acknowledged the unofficial leadership of the giraffe-like creature. Nature doesn't work *that* way, either. I hadn't seen one quarrel between the animals yet. That argued that they were all herbivores, which didn't make sense ecologically.

I shrugged my shoulders and walked on.

Half an hour later, I knew a little more about the geography of our bonanza. We were on either an immense island or a peninsula of some sort, because I could see a huge body of water bordering the land some ten miles off. Our vicinity was fairly flat, except for a good-sized hill from which I could see the terrain.

There was a thick, heavily wooded jungle not too far from the ship. The forest spread out all the way toward the water in one direction, but ended abruptly in the other. We had brought the ship down right at the edge of the clearing. Apparently most of the animals we saw lived in the jungle.

On the other side of our clearing was a low, broad plain that seemed to trail away into a desert in the distance; I could see an uninviting stretch of barren sand that contrasted strangely with the fertile jungle to my left. There was a small lake to the side. It was, I saw, the sort of country likely to attract a varied fauna, since there seemed to be every sort of habitat within a small area.

And the fauna! Although I'm a zoologist only by osmosis, picking up both my interest and my knowledge second-hand from Holdreth and Davison, I couldn't help but be astonished by the wealth of strange animals. They came in all different shapes and sizes, colors and odors, and the only thing they all had in common was their friendliness. During the course of my afternoon's wanderings a hundred animals must have come marching boldly right up to me, given me the once-over, and walked away. This included half a dozen kinds that I hadn't seen before, plus one of the eye-stalked, intelligent-looking giraffes and a furless dog. Again, I had the feeling that the giraffe seemed to be trying to communicate.

I didn't like it. I didn't like it at all.

I returned to our clearing, and saw Holdreth and Davison still buzzing madly around, trying to cram as many animals as they could into our hold.

"How's it going?" I asked.

"Hold's all full," Davison said. "We're busy making our alternate selections now." I saw him carrying out Holdreth's two furless dogs and picking up instead a pair of eight-legged penguinish things that uncomplainingly allowed themselves to be carried in. Holdreth was frowning unhappily.

"What do you want *those* for, Lee? Those dog-like ones seem much more interesting, don't you think?"

"No," Davison said. "I'd rather bring along these two. They're curious beasts, aren't they? Look at the muscular network that connects the—"

"Hold it, fellows," I said. I peered at the animal in Davison's hands and glanced up. "This *is* a curious beast," I said. "It's got eight legs."

"You becoming a zoologist?" Holdreth asked, amused.

"No—but I am getting puzzled. Why should this one have eight legs, some of the others have six, and some of the others only four?"

They looked at me blankly, with the scorn of professionals.

"I mean, there ought to be some sort of logic to evolution here, shouldn't there? On Earth we've developed a four-legged pattern of animal life; on Venus, they usually run to six legs. But have you ever seen an evolutionary hodgepodge like this place before?"

"There are stranger setups," Holdreth said. "The symbiotes on Sirius Three, the burrowers of Mizar—but you're right, Gus. This *is* a peculiar evolutionary dispersal. I think we ought to stay and investigate it fully."

Instantly I knew from the bright expression on Davison's face that I had blundered, and made things worse than ever. I decided to take a new tack.

"I don't agree," I said. "I think we ought to leave with what we've got, and come back with a larger expedition later."

Davison chuckled. "Come on, Gus, don't be silly! This is a chance of a lifetime for us—why should we call in the whole zoological department on it?"

I didn't want to tell them I was afraid of staying longer. I crossed my arms. "Lee, I'm the pilot of this ship, and you'll have to listen to me. The schedule calls for a brief stopover here, and we have to leave. Don't tell me I'm being silly."

"But you are, man! You're standing blindly in the path of scientific investigation, of—"

"Listen to me, Lee. Our food is calculated on a pretty narrow margin, to allow you fellows more room for storage. And this is strictly a collecting team. There's no provision for extended stays on any one planet. Unless you want to wind up eating your own specimens, I suggest you allow us to get out of here."

They were silent for a moment. Then Holdreth said, "I guess we can't argue with that, Lee. Let's listen to Gus and go back now. There's plenty of time to investigate this place later when we can take longer."

"But—oh, all right," Davison said reluctantly. He picked up the eight-legged penguins. "Let me stash these things in the hold, and we can leave." He looked strangely at me, as if I had done something criminal.

As he started into the ship, I called to him.

"What is it, Gus?"

"Look here, Lee. I don't *want* to pull you away from

here. It's simply a matter of food," I lied, masking my nebulous suspicions.

"I know how it is, Gus." He turned and entered the ship.

I stood there thinking about nothing at all for a moment, then went inside myself to begin setting up the blastoff orbit.

I got as far as calculating the fuel expenditure when I noticed something. Feedwires were dangling crazily down from the control cabinet. Somebody had wrecked our drive mechanism, but thoroughly.

For a long moment, I stared stiffly at the sabotaged drive. Then I turned and headed into the storage hold.

"Davison?"

"What is it, Gus?"

"Come out here a second, will you?"

I waited, and a few minutes later he appeared, frowning impatiently. "What do you want, Gus? I'm busy and I—" His mouth dropped open. *Look at the drive!*

"You look at it," I snapped. "I'm sick. Go get Holdreth, on the double."

While he was gone I tinkered with the shattered mechanism. Once I had the cabinet panel off and could see the inside, I felt a little better; the drive wasn't damaged beyond repair, though it had been pretty well scrambled. Three or four days of hard work with a screwdriver and solderbeam might get the ship back into functioning order.

But that didn't make me any less angry. I heard Holdreth and Davison entering behind me, and I whirled to face them.

"All right, you idiots. Which one of you did this?"

They opened their mouths in protesting squawks at the same instant. I listened to them for a while, then said, "One at a time!"

"If you're implying that one of us deliberately sabotaged the ship," Hodlreth said, "I want you to know—"

"I'm not implying anything. But the way it looks to

me, you two decided you'd like to stay here a while
longer to continue your investigations, and figured the
easiest way of getting me to agree was to wreck the
drive." I glared hotly at them. "Well, I've got news for
you. I can fix this, and I can fix it in a couple of days. So
go on—get about your business! Get all the zoologizing
you can in, while you still have time. I—"

Davison laid a hand gently on my arm. "Gus," he
said quietly, *"we didn't do it.* Neither of us."

Suddenly all the anger drained out of me and was
replaced by raw fear. I could see that Davison meant it.

"If you didn't do it, and Holdreth didn't do it, and *I*
didn't do it—then who did?"

Davison shrugged.

"Maybe it's one of us who doesn't know he's doing
it," I suggested. "Maybe—" I stopped. "Oh, that's nonsense. Hand me that tool-kit, will you, Lee?"

They left to tend to the animals, and I set to work on
the repair job, dismissing all further speculations and
suspicions from my mind, concentrating solely on joining Lead A to Input A and Transistor F to Potentiome-
ter K, as indicated. It was slow, nerve-harrowing work,
and by the mealtime I had accomplished only the barest preliminaries. My fingers were starting to quiver
from the strain of small-scale work, and I decided to
give up the job for the day and get back to it tomorrow.

I slept uneasily, my nightmares punctuated by the
moaning of the accursed anteaters and the occasional
squeals, chuckles, bleats, and hisses of the various other
creatures in the hold. It must have been four in the
morning before I dropped off into a really sound sleep,
and what was left of the night passed swiftly. The next
thing I knew, hands were shaking me and I was looking
up into the pale, tense faces of Holdreth and Davison.

I pushed my sleep-stuck eyes open and blinked. "Huh?
What's going on?"

Holdreth leaned down and shook me savagely. "Get
up, Gus!"

I struggled to my feet slowly. "Hell of a thing to do, wake a fellow up in the middle of the—"

I found myself being propelled from my cabin and led down the corridor to the control room. Blearily, I followed where Holdreth pointed, and then I woke up in a hurry.

The drive was battered again. Someone—or *something*—had completely undone my repair job of the night before.

If there had been bickering among us, it stopped. This was past the category of a joke now; it couldn't be laughed off, and we found ourselves working together as a tight unit again, trying desperately to solve the puzzle before it was too late.

"Let's review the situation," Holdreth said, pacing nervously up and down the control cabin. "The drive has been sabotaged twice. None of us knows who did it, and on a conscious level each of us is convinced *he* didn't do it."

He paused. "That leaves us with two possibilities. Either, as Gus suggested, one of us is doing it unaware of it even himself, or someone else is doing it while we're not looking. Neither possibility is a very cheerful one."

"We can stay on guard, though," I said. "Here's what I propose: first, have one of us awake at all times—sleep in shifts, that is, with somebody guarding the drive until I get it fixed. Two—jettison all the animals aboard ship."

"*What?*"

"He's right," Davison said. "We don't know what we may have brought aboard. They don't seem to be intelligent, but we can't be sure. That purple-eyed baby giraffe, for instance—suppose he's been hypnotizing us into damaging the drive ourselves? How can we tell?"

"Oh, but—" Holdreth started to protest, then stopped and frowned soberly. "I suppose we'll have to admit the possibility," he said, obviously unhappy about the prospect of freeing our captives. "We'll empty out the hold, and you see if you can get the drive fixed. Maybe later we'll recapture them all, if nothing further develops."

We agreed to that, and Holdreth and Davison cleared the ship of its animal cargo while I set to work determinedly at the drive mechanism. By nightfall, I had managed to accomplish as much as I had the day before.

I sat up as watch the first shift, aboard the strangely quiet ship. I paced around the drive cabin, fighting the great temptation to doze off, and managed to last through until the time Holdreth arrived to relieve me.

Only—when he showed up, he gasped and pointed at the drive. It had been ripped apart a third time.

Now we had no excuse, no explanation. The expedition had turned into a nightmare.

I could only protest that I had remained awake my entire spell on duty, and that I had seen no one and nothing approach the drive panel. But that was hardly a satisfactory explanation, since it either cast guilt on me as the saboteur or implied that some unseen external power was repeatedly wrecking the drive. Neither hypothesis made sense, at least to me.

By now we had spent four days on the planet, and food was getting to be a major problem. My carefully budgeted flight schedule called for us to be two days out on our return journey to Earth by now. But we still were no closer to departure than we had been four days ago.

The animals continued to wander around outside, nosing up against the ship, examining it, almost fondling it, with those damned pseudo-giraffes staring soulfully at us always. The beasts were as friendly as ever, little knowing how the tension was growing within the hull. The three of us walked around like zombies, eyes bright and lips clamped. We were scared—all of us.

Something was keeping us from fixing the drive.

Something didn't want us to leave this planet.

I looked at the bland face of the purple-eyed giraffe staring through the viewport, and it stared mildly back at me. Around it was grouped the rest of the local fauna, the same incredible hodgepodge of improbable genera and species.

That night, the three of us stood guard in the control room together. The drive was smashed anyway. The wires were soldered in so many places by now that the control panel was a mass of shining alloy, and I knew that a few more such sabotagings and it would be impossible to patch it together anymore—if it wasn't so already.

The next night, I just didn't knock off. I continued soldering right on after dinner (and a pretty skimpy dinner it was, now that we were on close rations) and far on into the night.

By morning, it was as if I hadn't done a thing.

"I give up," I announced, surveying the damage. "I don't see any sense in ruining my nerves trying to fix a thing that won't stay fixed."

Holdreth nodded. He looked terribly pale. "We'll have to find some new approach."

"Yeah. Some new approach."

I yanked open the food closet and examined our stock. Even figuring in the synthetics we would have fed to the animals if we hadn't released them, we were low on food. We had overstayed even the safety margin. It would be a hungry trip back—if we ever did get back.

I clambered through the hatch and sprawled down on a big rock near the ship. One of the furless dogs came over and nuzzled in my shirt. Davison stepped to the hatch and called down to me.

"What are you doing out there, Gus?"

"Just getting a little fresh air. I'm sick of living aboard that ship." I scratched the dog behind his pointed ears, and looked around.

The animals had lost most of their curiosity about us,

and didn't congregate the way they used to. They were meandering all over the plain, nibbling at little deposits of a white doughy substance. It precipitated every night. "Manna," we called it. All the animals seemed to live on it.

I folded my arms and leaned back.

We were getting to look awfully lean by the eighth day. I wasn't even trying to fix the ship anymore; the hunger was starting to get me. But I saw Davison puttering around with my solderbeam.

"What are you doing?"

"I'm going to repair the drive," he said. "You don't want to, but we can't just sit around, you know." His nose was deep in my repair guide, and he was fumbling with the release on the solderbeam.

I shrugged. "Go ahead, if you want to." I didn't care what he did. All I cared about was the gaping emptiness in my stomach, and about the dimly grasped fact that somehow we were stuck here for good.

"Gus?"

"Yeah?"

"I think it's time I told you something. I've been eating the manna for four days. It's good. It's nourishing stuff."

"You've been eating—the manna? Something that grows on an alien world? You crazy?"

"What else can we do? Starve?"

I smiled feebly, admitting that he was right. From somewhere in the back of the ship came the sounds of Holdreth moving around. Holdreth had taken this thing worse than any of us. He had a family back on Earth, and he was beginning to realize that he wasn't ever going to see them again.

"Why don't you get Holdreth?" Davison suggested. "Go out there and stuff yourselves with manna. You've got to eat something."

"Yeah. What can I lose?" Moving like a mechanical

man, I headed toward Holdreth's cabin. We could go
out and eat the manna and cease being hungry, one
way or another.

"Clyde?" I called. "Clyde?"

I entered his cabin. He was sitting at his desk, shaking convulsively, staring at the two streams of blood
that trickled in red spurts from his slashed wrists.

"Clyde!"

He made no protest as I dragged him toward the
infirmary cabin and got tourniquets around his arms,
cutting off the bleeding. He just stared dully ahead,
sobbing.

I slapped him and he came around. He shook his
head dizzily, as if he didn't know where he was.

"I—I—"

"Easy, Clyde. Everything's all right."

"It's *not* all right," he said hollowly. "I'm still alive.
Why didn't you let me die? Why didn't you—"

Davison entered the cabin. "What's been happening,
Gus?"

"It's Clyde. The pressure's getting him. He tried to
kill himself, but I think he's all right now. Get him
something to eat, will you?"

We had Holdreth straightened around by evening.
Davison gathered as much of the manna as he could
find, and we held a feast.

"I wish we had nerve enough to kill some of the local
fauna," Davison said. "Then we'd have a feast—steaks
and everything!"

"The bacteria," Holdreth pointed out quietly. "We
don't dare."

"I know. But it's a thought."

"No more thoughts," I said sharply. "Tomorrow morning we start work on the drive panel again. Maybe with
some food in our bellies we'll be able to keep awake
and see what's happening here."

Holdreth smiled. "Good. I can't wait to get out of

this ship and back to a normal existence. God, I just can't wait!"

"Let's get some sleep," I said. "Tomorrow we'll give it another try. We'll get back," I said with a confidence I didn't feel.

The following morning I rose early and got my toolkit. My head was clear, and I was trying to put the pieces together without much luck. I started toward the control cabin.

And stopped.

And looked out the viewport.

I went back and awoke Holdreth and Davison. "Take a look out the port," I said hoarsely.

They looked. They gaped.

"It looks just like my house," Holdreth said. "My house on Earth."

"With all the comforts of home inside, I'll bet." I walked forward uneasily and lowered myself through the hatch. "Let's go look at it."

We approached it, while the animals frolicked around us. The big giraffe came near and shook its head gravely. The house stood in the middle of the clearing, small and neat and freshly painted.

I saw it now. During the night, invisible hands had put it there. Had assembled and built a cozy little Earth-type house and dropped it next to our ship for us to live in.

"Just like my house," Holdreth repeated in wonderment.

"It should be," I said. "They grabbed the model from your mind, as soon as they found out we couldn't live on the ship indefinitely."

Holdreth and Davison asked as one, "What do you mean?"

"You mean you haven't figured this place out yet?" I licked my lips, getting myself used to the fact that I was going to spend the rest of my life here. "You mean you don't realize what this house is intended to be?"

They shook their heads, baffled. I glanced around,

from the house to the useless ship to the jungle to the plain to the little pond. It all made sense now.

"They want to keep us happy," I said. "They knew we weren't thriving aboard the ship, so they—they built us something a little more like home."

"*They?* The giraffes?"

"Forget the giraffes. They tried to warn us, but it's too late. They're intelligent beings, but they're prisoners just like us. I'm talking about the ones who run this place. The super-aliens who make us sabotage our own ship and not even know we're doing it, who stand someplace up there and gape at us. The ones who dredged together this motley assortment of beasts from all over the galaxy. Now we've been collected too. This whole damned place is just a zoo—a zoo for aliens so far ahead of us we don't dare dream what they're like."

I looked up at the shimmering blue-green sky, where invisible bars seemed to restrain us, and sank down dismally on the porch of our new home. I was resigned. There wasn't any sense in struggling against *them*.

I could see the neat little placard now:

EARTHMEN. Native Nabitat, Sol III.

Harlan Ellison got his start as a writer in the hardboiled mystery and science fiction digests of the 1950s. My reading was almost entirely limited to science fiction for some years after they let me have a card to the adult section of the public library in 1958. Reasonably I should have run into Harlan's work immediately.

I didn't. The only decent newsstand in town was nowhere near either my home or school. I didn't start reading the SF magazines until about 1960, and Harlan didn't have any hardcover books available until the late '60s. My first contact with Harlan's fiction was through my American Literature class when I was a junior in high school.

Through, not in. The Iowa school systems have a deservedly fine reputation. At the time I lived there, Iowa had the highest literacy rate and the highest average level of education in the United States. (I have no reason to believe that has changed; I just don't have the figures before me to check.)

While Iowans take education seriously, they're a conservative lot. Farmers who take chances go bankrupt even faster than farmers who try to play it safe; and that's saying a lot. Clinton High School was privileged to have on its faculty a young English teacher, Eugene Olsen, who was a professional writer on the side. The school board was aware of the situation and approved, to the extent of renting him a writing office downtown in order to keep him from leaving.

But they expected Mr. Olsen to avoid making waves that would embarrass them; and he was very careful to keep his end of the bargain.

There's nothing you can write that won't be offensive to somebody, generally for reasons that would never occur to the writer. (I was once attacked for maligning mastiffs.) Mr. Olsen's writing, fiction and non-fiction both, was done under a pseudonym. He kept it secret from all but the three or four students he most trusted not to start a scandal.

201

It was to the same not-handful of us in 1961 that he loaned the tremendous discovery he'd made, a book of mainstream stories titled Gentleman Junkie—*by Harlan Ellison, a young writer who also wrote SF.*

It was a stunning volume. I read it only once before returning it, and I've never seen another copy; but not only did the general impact stay with me, two of the individual stories are still bright in my mind. I immediately bought all the Ellison I could find.

My initial contact with Harlan's work had a funny side-effect, though: it almost didn't occur to me that he was a natural for this volume. This is a science fiction anthology—and I don't think of Harlan as a science fiction writer.

"Blind Lightning" certainly is SF; is an excellent story; and isn't quite what you might expect of an Ellison piece, either.

But if I weren't keeping this book pretty close to genre, I'd sure have used "No Game for Children" instead. . . .

BLIND LIGHTNING

Harlan Ellison

When Kettridge bent over to pick up the scurrying red lizard, the thing that had been waiting, struck.

Thought: *this is the prelude to the Time of Fast. In bulk this strangely-formed will equal many cat-litters. It is warm and does not lose the essence. When the Essence-Stealer screams from the heavens, this strangely-formed will be many feastings for me. Safety and assured essence are mine. O boon at last granted! To the Lord of the Heaven I turn all thought! Lad-nar's essence is yours at ending!*

The thing rose nine feet on powerfully-muscled legs; it had a sheened, glistening fur. It resembled a gorilla and a Brahma bull and a Kodiak bear and a number of other Terran animals, but it was none of them. The comparison was as inaccurate and brief as the moment Kettridge half-turned. He saw one of the thing's huge paws crashing toward him. The brief moment ended and Kettridge lay unconscious.

The huge beast bent from the waist and scooped up the man in the form-fitting metallic suit, brushing

in annoyance at the belt of tools around the human's
waist.

Lad-nar looked over one massive shoulder at the sky.

Even as he watched, the roiling dark clouds split and
a forked brilliance stabbed down at the jungle. Lad-nar
squinted his eyes, unconsciously lowering the thin secondary lids over them, filtering out the worst of the
light.

He shivered as the roar screamed across the sky.

Off to his left another blast of lightning fingered down,
struck a towering blue plant with a shower of sparks
and a dazzling flash. Thunder bubbled after it. The
jungle smoked.

Thought: *many risings and settings of the great
warmer it has taken this Time of Fast to build. Now it
will last for many more. The great warmer will be
hidden and the cold will settle across the land. Lad-nar
must find his way to the Place of Fasting. This strangely-
formed will be many feastings.*

He shoved the man under one furry arm, clasping his
unconcious burden tightly. Lad-nar's eyes were frightened. He knew the time of death and forbidden walking was at hand.

He loped off toward the mountains.

The first thing Kettridge saw when he awoke was the
head of the beast. It was hanging suspended in the light
from the storm. The roar of the rain pelting down in
driving sheets, the brilliant white light of the lightning,
all served as background for the huge beast's head.
That wide, blunt nose, three flaring nostrils. The massive double-lidded eyes—light from the fires outside blazing up in them like twin flickering comets. The high,
hairy brow. The deep-black half-moons under the
cheekbones.

The mouth of ripping, pointed teeth.

Kettridge was a man past the high tide of youth. He

was not a strong man. At the beast's snort, the white-haired Earthman fainted.

It was a short stretch of unconsciousness. Kettridge blinked several times and tried to push himself up on elbows alarmingly weak. The sight that greeted him was substantially the same as before.

Lad-nar was still sitting, powerfully muscled legs crossed, inside the mouth of the small cave, staring at him. Only the monstrous, frightening head, with pointed ears aprick, hanging there immobile.

"What—what—*are* you? We weren't expecting anything this large. The—the—survey said—" Kettridge quavered into silence.

Thought: *what is this? This strangely-formed speaks in my head! This is not one with the cat-litters. They cannot speak! Is this a symbol, an omen, from the Lord of the Heaven?*

What is it you ask, strangely-formed?

Kettridge felt the surge of thoughts in his mind. Felt it smash up against one nerve after another, sliding down and down in his head as the thoughts reverberated like an echo from far away. Over and over again.

"My God, the thing's telepathic!"

Old Kettridge knew it at once. He knew it because he had never experienced it before, and there was no doubting it. There had been a first time for everything for him. He knew the first time he had touched fire. He had known instantly it was fire, it would always be fire, and he must not touch it again.

He had known the first time love spoke to him. That had been once and never again. But he had known it the once it did speak.

There are those things which Man senses but once, and knows them—under whatever names he has assigned them—for what they are.

"You're telepathic!" he said again, hardly daring to believe it was true.

Thought: *what is that? What do you speak of, strangely-formed? What is it that you say, that I hear as reading of the essence? How is it you speak? Are you from the Lord of the Heaven?*

Lad-nar's thick, leathery lips had not moved. The fanged mouth had not twisted in speech. To Kettridge it seemed there was a third being in the cave. The hideous beast before him, himself . . . and a third. A speaker who roared in his mind, in a voice sharp and alert.

Thought: *there is no one else here. This is the Place of Fasting. Lad-nar has cleansed this place of all previous fasting ones. You do not answer. There is fear mixed into your essence, like the cat-litters. Yet you are not one with them. Speak! Are you an omen?*

Kettridge's lips began to tremble. He looked intently at the great hulk across from him. The Earthman had suddenly realized that the being was not only telepathic, but two-way receptive. It could not only direct its thoughts into Kettridge's mind, it could just as easily pluck the ideas from the Earthman's head.

This was no animal.

This was no beast.

This was sentient life. If not of a high cultural level, at least of fantastic mental abilities.

"I—I am from Earth," ventured Kettridge, sliding up against the warm stone wall of the cave.

Thought: *the Heaven home! I know, I know! O thankings! The Lord of the Heaven has sent you to me as many feastings.*

In the space of a few short seconds, as Lad-nar spoke in thoughts, Kettridge received a complete picture of the being's life. He knew there was a race on Blestone—many more like Lad-nar. All in a barbaric hiding state. The preliminary survey had not indicated any life of this sort. Obviously Lad-nar's race was dying off.

Kettridge tried to blank his thoughts. He had to wait.

Thought: *you can not hide the speaking in my head*.

Kettridge became frantic. He knew what the thing planned for him. He received a sharp, cold mental image of the being crouched over his body, ripping an arm loose from its socket. The picture was *too* clear. He became ill, and the being's thoughts in his head reverberated a dislike of the Earthman's powers of imagination.

Thought: *you have seen the feasting. Yet you are not like the cat-litters that squeal fear, fear, fear all the time that I feast on them. If you are not to eat, omen from the Heaven Lord—what are you?*

Kettridge felt his throat muscles tighten. His hands inside the heat-resistant gloves clenched. He felt his age settle around him as though it was a heavy mantle. "I'm an alien ecologist," he said, knowing it would do no good.

Thought: *this has no meaning for me*.

"I'm from Earth. I'm from one of those—" Then he stopped, drawing breath in quickly, pulling the resilient hood of the suit against his mouth with the effort. The being could not possibly know about "one of *those* out there." It could not see the stars. Only occasionally could it see the sun. Only when the clouds parted. The dense cloud blanket of Blestone hid space forever from the eyes of this monstrous being.

Thought: *Urth! The Heaven home! I know! I know!*

There was a jubilation, a happiness in the thoughts. Something incongruous and terrifying when the old man put them into the head of that great thing illuminated by the storm.

Yet there was a humanness, a warmth, also.

Thought: *now I will sleep. Later I will feast*.

With the single-minded simplicity of the aborigine the great beast put from its mind this revelation of its religion, and obeyed the commands of its body. Tired from hunting, Lad-nar began to sleep.

The thoughts dimmed and faded out of Kettridge's mind like smoke wraiths as the huge animal slipped onto its side, effectively blocking the open mouth of the cave. In a moment, they were gone entirely from Kettridge's suddenly throbbing head. The beast known as Lad-nar was asleep.

Kettridge felt for the service revolver at his belt. The charges in there were enough to stop a good-sized animal.

Then he looked at the nine feet of corded muscle and thick hide that lay there. He looked at the narrow confines of the cave. There was no chance to kill that beast before he could rip the Earthman to shreds.

. . . and did he really *want* to kill Lad-nar?

The thought bothered him. He knew he had to kill the beast—or be killed himself.

. . . and yet . . .

Outside the lightning boiled and crashed all around the cave. The long storm had begun.

Through the thin slit between the rocks and the beast, Kettridge could see the sky darkening and darkening as the storm grew. Every moment there was a new cataclysm of light and flash as streamers of fire flung themselves through the air. The night shattered itself against the rank jungle and howled in frenzy!

Kettridge rubbed his leathery, wrinkled cheek. The metal-plastic hood of the suit rubbed against the skin. "I'd have been blistered and boiled," he muttered, looking at the sleeping Lad-nar.

Blestone's atmosphere was an uncomfortable-to-humans 140–150° Fahrenheit. That would make the beast's body heat somewhere near 130°. Which would have effectively ruined the aging career of Benjamin Kettridge, had not the Earthman's insulated suit protected him.

The old man hunched up small against the wall, feeling the rough stone through the suit. It somehow reassured him.

He knew the beam from the *Jeremy Bentham* was

tuned to the suit-sensitive, but they wouldn't come to
pick him up till his search time was finished, and that
was a good six hours away. He wasn't the only ecologist
from the study-ship on Blestone, but they were a low-
pay outfit and they got the most for their money by
leaving the searchers in solitude for the full time.

The full time had another six hours to run.

More than enough time for Lad-nar to get hungry.

He ran the whole thing through his mind, sifting the
facts, gauging the information, calculating the outcome.
It didn't look good.

He knew more about Lad-nar than the beast could
have told him, though. That was a factor in his favor.
He knew about its religion, its taboos, its—and here he
felt his throat dry out again—eating habits, its level of
intelligence and culture. The beast had thought it, had
thought it all, and Kettridge had received it all.

Not quite what you signed up for, is it, Ben? he
thought. Startled first at the muddiness of his own
mental speech, he answered himself wearily, *No, not at
all.*

Kettridge wondered what Lad-nar would think were
he to tell the creature he wasn't the blue plate special,
but a washed-out, run-down representative of a civilization that didn't give one hoot in Hell about Lad-nar or
his religion. That didn't even care if his race died away.

He'd probably chew me up and swallow me, thought
Kettridge. Then he added, *which is exactly what he'll
do anyhow.*

It seemed so strange. Two days ago he had been
aboard the *Jeremy Bentham,* study-ship one year out of
Cap City, and here he was today, main course at a
Blestonian aborigine's feast.

The laughter wouldn't come.

It wouldn't come because Kettridge was old, and
tired, and he knew how right it was that he die here, in
this way. It was a fit end. It was somehow right in a

Greater Scheme of Things. Lad-nar was doing all he knew. He was protecting himself. He was surviving.

Which is more than you've been doing for the last ten years, Ben, he told himself. Benjamin Kettridge had long ago stopped surviving. He knew it as clearly as he knew he would die here on this hot and steaming world far from the sight of Earth. *I'm glad I'm dying out of sight of that Sun.*

Think about it, Ben. Think it over. Now that it's all finished and you tumble out of things at fifty-six years of age. Think about it. Think about the waste, and the crying and the bit of conviction that could have saved you. Think about it all.

Then the story unfurled on a fleeting banner. It rolled out for Ben Kettridge there in a twilight universe. In a matter of a few minutes he had found life in that shadowy mind-world preferable to his outside existence.

He saw himself as a prominent scientist, engaged with others of his kind on a project of consequence to mankind. He saw his own worry and nagging anxiousness at the danger in the experiment.

He heard again the talk with Fenimore. He heard it more clearly than the blast and rush of the thunder outside.

"Charles, I don't think we should do it this way. If something were to happen . . ."

"Ben, you old bug, you! Nothing whatever can possibly happen—except what we want to happen. The Compound is as safe as breast milk, and you know it. There's no reason why everyone should know about it before we use it, though. That damned government has a way of pooh-poohing every major development, corrupting it, putting it off, worrying over it.

"First we demonstrate its applicability—*then* we let the dunderheads scream about it. After they know its worth, they'll build monuments to us!"

"But don't you understand, Fenimore? There are too many random factors in the formulae. There's a fundamental flaw in there—if I could—only—figure it out."

"Get this, Ben. I don't mean to pull seniority on you, but you force me. I'm not a harsh man, but this is a dream I've had for twenty years, and no piddling pen-scratching on your part is going to put it off. We test the Compound Thursday!"

It had been a dream for Fenimore. A dream that had overnight turned into a nightmare of twenty-five thousand dead, and hospitals stacked eight deep with screaming, intestine-twisted patients, howling for death rather than the suffering.

The nightmare had reached out clammy, thready tentacles and dragged in Kettridge, too. In a matter of days a reputation built of years of privation and sweat was reduced to rubble. Kettridge had barely escaped the mass lynchings. But he did not escape the inquests. What little reputation he had left had saved him—and a few others—from the gas chambers. But Life . . .

Life was at an end for him.

Ten years of struggling to eat, barely keeping alive—for no one would hire one of the men who had caused the Mass Death—had sunk Kettridge lower and lower. There was still a common decency about him that prevented a slump into some gutter, just as there was an inner desire to continue living. Even Life as it was to him then. Kettridge never became—as the others who escaped—a flophouse rummy or a suicide. He just became anonymous.

Lower and lower. Till there was nothing lower except slashed wrists or the bottle.

Kettridge had been too old, by then, for either.

And always there had been the knowledge that he could have stopped the project, had he voiced his doubts, instead of brooding in silence.

Finally the study-ship post had come. Ben Kettridge,

with another name, had signed on. Three years, out to the stars, the cramp and squalor of shipboard, studying and cataloguing. It hadn't been good, but it was a way to keep going.

Besides, how could he face the sun of Earth many more days—with *that* on his conscience?

So Ben Kettridge had become an alien ecologist. One year out from Cap City, and *this*!

He wanted to scream. He wanted to scream very badly. His throat muscles drew up and tightened inside the wrinkled neck. His mouth, inside the flexible hood, opened wide, till the corners stretched in pain.

The pictures had stopped. He had withdrawn in terror from the shadowed mind-world, and he was back in a stone prison with a hungry aborigine for keeper.

His mind was a shrieking torrent of horror and futility and self-hatred. It was all a vortex, drawing his brain down into a black chasm. Oh, if he could only scream!

Lad-nar stirred.

The huge furred body twisted, snorted softly, and sank back into sleep. Kettridge wondered momentarily if the strength of his thoughts had disturbed the beast.

What a fantastic creature, thought Kettridge. *He lives on a world where the heat will fry a human and shivers in fear at lightning storms*.

A strange compassion came over Kettridge. How very much like a native of Earth this creature was. Governed by its stomach and a will to survive. A religion founded in fear and nurtured on terror. Lightning: the beast thought of it as a Screamer From the Skies. The occasionally glimpsed sun: The Great Warmer.

Kettridge pondered on the simplicity and common sense of Lad-nar's religion.

When the storms gathered, finally building up enough charge to begin the lightning and thunder, Lad-nar knew the cold would set in. Cold was anathema to him. He knew the cold sapped him of strength, the lightning struck him down. So he stole a cat-litter and hid for the weeks it would take the gigantic storms to abate. The high body heat of the creature dictated that it have much food to keep it alive when the temperature went down. When a cat-litter wasn't handy, why then just *kill and eat an alien ecologist*. Kettridge found the last thought standing out in his mind.

This was no stupid beast, Kettridge reminded himself.

His religion was a sound combination of animal wisdom and native observation. The lightning killed: don't go abroad in the storms. The storms brought cold: get food and stay alive.

It was so simple to analyze the situation. Simple, yes, but impossible to get himself out of it!

Not that I care, Kettridge mused.

I stopped caring long ago. The urge to survive? He laughed aloud. To his mind came the picture of himself. Thin, weary-looking. As though a world of agony had seeped like sand into his bones. His face was a lined and broken thing. It was tired. From the gray hair to the cleft chin. From the broken bridge of the aquiline nose to the thinned, parched lips. *I'm older than fifty-six*, he thought. There were men at fifty-six, he knew, who were still following the trails of the young.

I'm too sorry for myself.

It seemed strange. He had never churned these thoughts around in just this manner before. He had been prepared, almost eager, to let himself be beaten down, to be trampled under feet of sadness and self-pity. He was waiting for the creature to waken, then it would be at an end . . .

It was indeed strange how an odd situation could bring a man to a realization of himself.

Here is a chance, he thought. The words came unbidden.

In just these words. Here is a chance. Here was a chance not only to survive—something he had long since stopped doing consciously—but a chance to reinstate himself. If only in his own mind. Here was an aborigine, member of a dying race, a cowering beast of the caves, afraid to walk in the storms, in fear of the lightning, shackled by a primitive religion. Doomed forever to the land, never to see the sky.

In that split moment Ben Kettridge devised a plan to save his soul.

There are times when men sum up their lives. Take accounting and find themselves wanting. This was one of those times. So hopeless did it seem, that Ben Kettridge told himself, *This is a chance*.

Lad-nar suddenly became a symbol of all the people who had been lost in the Mass Death. In the mind of an old and tired man, many things are possible.

I must get out of here! Ben Kettridge told himself, over and over, almost as an incantation.

But more than that he knew he must save the poor hulk before him. And in saving the animal, he would save himself. Lad-nar had no idea what a star was. Well, Ben Kettridge would tell him. Here was a chance! Here was a chance!

The old man slid up flat against the wall. His back was strained with the effort to sink into the stone. Watching the alien beast come to wakefulness was almost the epitome of horror.

The huge body tossed and heaved, then rose. Directly. It sat erect from the thin, pinched waist, raising the massive wedge-shaped chest, the hideous head, the powerful neck and arms. A thin trickle of sleep-spittle dripped from a corner of its fanged mouth. It sat up and

Thought: *Lad-nar hungers*.

"Oh, God in Heaven, please let me have time! Please allow me this—this—*little* thing! I beg you!"

Kettridge found himself with hands clasped on his chest, face raised to the roof of the cave. For the first time in his life he felt tears of appeal on his cheeks.

He spoke to God with the tongue of a man who has

never known a God. Science had been his deity—and that God had turned against him. He spoke from a heart so long full of misery and wandering it never knew it *could* speak to a God.

Thought: *you speak to the Lord of the Heaven.* Lad-nar seemed awed. It watched, its huge brilliant eyes suddenly unslitted and wide.

Kettridge thought at the beast.

Lad-nar! I come from the Lord of the Heaven. I am a Lord greater than the Lord of the Heaven! I can show you how to walk in the storms! I can show you how to—

The creature's roar deafened Kettridge. Along with it came the mental scream! The old man felt himself lifted off the floor by the force of that blow to the mind, and hurled against the rocks. His body burned and ached from the pounding, but he knew it had been his own reflexes that had done it.

The aborigine leaped to his feet, threw his taloned hands upward and bellowed his rage.

Thought: *you speak that which is forbidden! You say that which is untrue and unclean! No human walks when the Essence-Stealer speaks in the night! You are a fearful thing! Lad-nar is afraid!*

"Heresy. I've spoken heresy!" Kettridge wanted to rip off the metal-plastic hood and tear his tongue from his own mouth. This was the way he had begun his own salvation! Heresy!

Thought: *yes, you have spoken that which is unclean and untrue!*

Kettridge cowered in fear. The beast was enraged. How could it be afraid, when it stood there so powerful and so massive?

Thought: *yes, Lad-nar is afraid! Afraid!*

Then the waves of fear hit him. Kettridge felt his head begin to throb. The tender fiber of his mind was being twisted and seared and buffeted. Washed and burned and scarred forever with the terrible all-consuming fear the animal had coursing through itself.

Stop, stop, Lad-nar! I speak truth! I speak truth!

He spoke, then. Softly, winningly, trying to convince a being that had never known any God but one that howled and slashed in streamers of electricity. He spoke of himself. He spoke of his powers. He spoke of them as though he believed he had them. To himself he thought the things he was saying. He built himself a glory on two levels.

Slowly, Lad-nar calmed, and the waves of fear diminished to ripples. The awe and trembling remained, but there was a sliver of belief.

Kettridge knew he must work on that.

All too easily, down somewhere in his own mind, came back the picture of that huge creature, ripping and eating, ripping and eating . . .

"I come from the Heaven-Home, Lad-nar. I speak in the words of a God, for I *am* a God. A stronger God than the puny Essence-Stealer you fear!" As if to punctuate his words, a flash of lightning struck just outside the cave, filling the hollow with fury and light.

Kettridge continued, spilling the words faster and faster. "I can walk abroad in the storm, and the Essence-Stealer will not harm me. Let me go out and I will show you, Lad-nar." He was playing a dangerous hand; at any moment the beast might leap. It might dare to venture that leap hoping Kettridge was speaking falsely, rather than incur the wrath of a God he *knew* was dangerous.

Kettridge continued talking.

"Let me out, Lad-nar. Let me walk from this cave. I will show you." He edged toward the cave's mouth, his hands in their metal-plastic gloves flat to the wall.

He knew the insulated suit would protect him from the viciousness outside.

Thought: *stop!*

"Why, Lad-nar? I can show you. I can show you how

to walk in the night when the Essence-Stealer screams, and you can scream back at him and laugh at him, Lad-nar." He didn't know why he was talking, he could have thought it just as well, but there was a reassurance in the sound of his voice in the cave.

The old man felt the weariness seeping through his body. *Oh, if I were a younger man. If it weren't so late!*

Thought: *Lad-nar does not know what less age means, but why should I let you go? You may have been sent by the Lord of the Heaven to see if I should lose my essence. The Lord of the Heaven may be trying to take you back from me because I listened to your unclean and untrue sayings. Then I will have no feastings! Then I will lose my essence!*

Kettridge reminded himself that the beast was indeed clever. Not only did it fear the wrath of the Lord of the Heaven and his screaming death, but Lad-nar knew if he let the man go he would have nothing to eat during the coming cold days.

"Let me go, Lad-nar. I will bring you back a cat-litter for your feasting. I will show you that I can walk in the night and I will bring you food. I will bring back a cat-litter, Lad-nar!" He prayed, silently, it would work.

Thought: *if you are a God, why do you speak to the Lord of the Heaven?*

Kettridge bit his lip. He kept forgetting . . .

He stopped thinking. He blocked it off. He willed himself to stop thinking. He must let his instincts answer for him.

"Because I want the Lord of the Heaven to know that I am as great as he and not afraid of him and that my prayers to him are only to show that I am as great as he." It was gibberish, but it was a deep gibberish, and if he kept talking, the beast would shuck off the thoughts rather than try to fathom them.

The Earthman knew he had one factor in his favor: Lad-nar had never heard anyone speak against the Gods, and so one who did it and did not get blasted *must* be a God.

Kettridge hit him with the appeal again, before the animal had time to wonder.

"I'll get you a cat-litter, Lad-nar. Let me go! Let me show you! Let me show you that you can walk in the storms as I do! I, too, am a great God!" There was so much at stake here, so little time, so deep a hell waiting.

Thought: *you will go away*.

There was a petulance, a little child sound, to the objection, and Kettridge knew the first step had been achieved.

"No, Lad-nar. Here is a rope." He drew a thin cord of tough metal-plastic from his utility belt. His hand jiggled against the service revolver on his tool belt and he laughed deep inside once more as he thought of how useless it was.

Useless. Only in his wits was there salvation.

He would not have used the gun in any case. There was more at stake here than just his life.

"Here is a rope," he repeated, extending the coiled cord. "I will tie it about myself, like this . . . and . . . now! You take this end. Hold it tightly so that I can't escape. It is long enough so that I may go out and seek a cat-litter and show you I can walk abroad."

At first the native refused, eyeing the glistening, silvery cord with fear in his deeply-pooled eyes. But Kettridge spoke on two levels, and spoke, and spoke, and soon the beast touched the cord.

It drew back its seven-taloned hand quickly.

The third time it grasped the cord.

You have just lost your religion, Kettridge thought.

Lad-nar had "smelled" with his mind. He had sensed a cat-litter fairly close to the cave. But he did not know where.

Kettridge stepped out of the dark mouth of the cave, into the roaring maelstrom of a Blestonian electrical storm.

The sky was a tumult of heavy black clouds, steel and ebony and ripped dirty cloth. The clouds tumbled over themselves and died split apart as a bolt crashed through. The very air was charged, and blast after blast of lightning sheared away the atmosphere in zig-zagged streamers.

Kettridge stood with legs apart, body tilted forward against the pull of the cord, hands shading his eyes against the glare, the almost continuous glare, of lightning eruptions.

He was a small, thin man, and had it not been for the cord, he might easily have been swept away by the winds and rain that sandpapered the rocky ledge.

Streamers, branches, forks—the illumination of the arcing bolts was something magnificent and terrible. The old man stood there with the pelting rain washing over him, obscuring his vision through the hood, leaving only the glare of the storm for him.

He took a step, two, three.

The bolt slashed at him through a rift in the mountains. It roared over the precipice and streaked at him. It materialized out of nowhere and everywhere, splintering the stones at his feet. The rock flew up in planed, smoothed slivers, shooting in every direction. Kettridge fell flat and the crack of thunder rolled in on him. He realized it had come with the lightning, that he had been listening to it for almost a minute, before he realized what it was.

The effect on his body was sudden.

Immediately he went deaf. His skin began to prickle with the feel of a million tiny threads pushing into the flesh. His legs and hips were numb, his eyes reflected coruscating pinwheels of brilliance. He could see nothing but light on light inside light over light light light light . . .

There was a paralysis of his bladder.

Thought: *God! You are no God! The Essence-Stealer has screamed and you have fallen!*

The rope tightened and Kettridge felt himself being dragged back into the cave.

"No!" he screamed hurriedly. The pressure eased. "No, Lad-nar. That was the Essence-Stealer's scream. Now I shall have mine. I *am* a God, I tell you! Let me show you, Lad-nar!"

Then he seized on the lightning blast for his own purpose. "See, Lad-nar! The Essence-Stealer has struck me, but I am still whole. I will rise and walk again. You will see!"

Everywhere the lightning burned and crashed. The whole world was filled with the noise of frothing air and ripping jungle and screaming elements.

He clawed himself to his knees. His legs were weak and numb. The prickling was still there, but lessened. His eyes were starting to unglare and focus again. He still could hear nothing. He half-rose, sank back to one knee, rose again.

His head felt terribly heavy and unanchored.

Then he stood erect.

And he walked.

The storm raged about him. Lightning struck and struck again. Near him, to the side of him, behind him. One bolt sizzled down and struck him directly. The metal insulating suit served its purpose a second time. The bolt slashed, hit, and side-flashed off, exploding a small, wizened tree growing up through a crack in the rocks. The tree flew into the air, one whole side charred and burned, the other unscarred.

It fell with a crash directly across Kettridge's path.

The symptoms of lightning-stroke were multiplied many times in Kettridge, but there was no answering thought of scorn from Lad-nar. Obviously the beast had withdrawn from his mind, in fear.

And he walked.

Soon he came back to the cave.

Thought: *you are a God! This I believe. But the Lord of the Heaven has sent his Essence-Stealers. They, too,*

*are mighty, and Lad-nar will lose his essence if he
walks there.*

"No, Lad-nar. I will show you how to protect yourself." The old man was sweating and white from his
walk, and the numbness extended through his body.
He could hear nothing, but the words came clearly to
him.

He began to unseal the form-fitting suit.

The storm had already lowered the temperature
enough so that he knew he would not fry.

In a few minutes he had the suit off, and it had
shrunk back to a pocket-sized replica of the full-sized
garment.

Kettridge felt ill. He felt old and tired and used. It
was time to go home, time to quit. It was all over. He
had won.

"Lad-nar, take this. Here, give me your hand."

The beast looked at him with huge, uncomprehending
eyes. The old man felt closer, somehow, to this strange
creature than to anyone he had ever known. Kettridge
pulled his glove on tighter and reached for Lad-nar's
seven-taloned hand. He pulled at the arm of the form-
fit suit, and it elastically expanded.

After much stretching and fitting, the beast was encased in the insulating metal-plastic.

Kettridge wanted to laugh at the bunched fur and
awkward stance of the massive animal. But again, the
laughter would not come.

"Now, Lad-nar, put on the gloves. Never take them
off, except when the storms are gone. Always put this
God-suit on when the Essence-Stealers scream, and
you will be safe."

Thought: *now I can walk in the night?*

"Yes. Come." He moved toward the cave's mouth.
"Now you can get a cat-litter for yourself. I did not
bring one because I knew you would believe me and
get your own. Come, Lad-nar." He motioned to the
beast to follow him out onto the rocks.

Thought: *how will you walk without the God-suit?*

Kettridge ran a seamed hand through his white hair. He was glad Lad-nar had thought the question. The multiple flashes of a many-stroked blast filled the air with glare and noise.

Kettridge could not hear the noise.

"I have God-brothers who wait for me in the great house from across the skies that will take me back to the Heaven Home. They will hurry to me and they will protect me."

He did not bother to tell the great beast that his search time was almost up and that the *Jeremy Bentham*'s flitter would home in on his suit beam. It would have been useless homing, had he not secured time.

"Go! Walk, Lad-nar!" he said, throwing his arms out as he felt a God would. "And tell your brothers you have screamed at the Essence-Stealers!"

Thought: *I have done this*.

The great animal stepped cautiously toward the rocky ledge, fearful and hesitant. Then it bunched its huge muscles and leaped out into the full agony of the storm which crashed in futility about his massive form.

"One day Man will come and make friends with you, Lad-nar," said the old man, softly. "One day they will come down out of the sky and show you how to live on this world of yours so that you don't have to hide."

Kettridge sank down against the inner wall of the cave, suddenly too exhausted to stand.

He had won. He had redeemed himself. If only in his own mind. He had helped take some life from a race, yet he had given life to another race.

He closed his eyes peacefully. Even the great blasts of blind lightning did not bother him as he rested. He knew Lad-nar had told his brothers.

He knew the ship was coming for him.

Lad-nar came up the incline and saw the flitter streaking down, lightning playing along its sides in phosphorescent glimmers.

Thought: *God! God! Your God-brothers come for you!*

He bounded across the scarred and seared rocks, toward the cave.

Kettridge rose and stepped out into the rain and wind.

He ran a few steps, waving his arms in signal. The flitter altered course and headed for the old man.

The lightning struck.

It seemed as though the bolt knew its target. It raced the flitter, sizzling and burning as it came. In a roar of light and dark and screamings it tore at the old man, lifting him high into the air, charring and burning and ripping.

The body landed just outside the cave, blistered and bleeding. The old man was still alive . . .

Thought: *God! God! You have fallen! Rise, rise, rise! The Essence-Stealers . . .*

The thoughts were hysterical, tearful, torn and wanting. Had the beast been able to shed tears, Kettridge knew it would have done so. The old man lay sightless, eyes gone, senses altogether torn from him. The Essence ebbed.

He thought:

Lad-nar. There will come other Gods. They will come to you and you must think to them. You must think these words, Lad-nar. Think to them, Show me a star. *Do you hear me, Lad-nar? Do you . . .*

Even as the great beast watched, the essence flickered and died. In the animal's mind there was a lack, a space of emptiness. Yet there was a contentment. A peace, and Lad-nar knew the essence of the God who walked in the light was soft and unafraid at ending.

The aborigine stood on the rocks below the cave and watched the flitter sink to the stone ledge. He watched as the other Gods from the skies emerged and ran to the charred hulk lying on the stones.

Through his head, like the blind lightning, streaking

everywhere, lightning, the words remained, and re-
peated . . .
Thought:
Show me a star.

This is the first published story of James H. Schmitz. His second story wouldn't appear for another six years.

Most of Schmitz's fiction—I won't claim to have seen all of it, but I've certainly read a decent sample—involves interstellar shenanigans of one sort or another. The events are always viewed from the aspect of a likeable character with enough flaws to make him—or very often her—perfectly believable, even against a background of gaudy space-opera.

"Greenface" contains the same careful, caring, descriptions of the people, but—uniquely for Schmitz— the action is set in the here-and-now. The story harks back to an earlier day, when the world had its unexplored corners and there might be more horrors than bilharzia and schistosomiasis lurking in them. Not that "Greenface" is a naive story. Quite the contrary.

I like Schmitz's space operas, with their psychic powers, blasters and interstellar spies.

But I like "Greenface" very much indeed.

GREENFACE

James H. Schmitz

"What I don't like," the fat sport—his name was Freddie Something—said firmly, "is snakes! That was a whopping mean-looking snake that went across the path there, and I ain't going another step nearer the icehouse!"

Hogan Masters, boss and owner of Masters Fishing Camp on Thursday Lake, made no effort to conceal his indignation.

"What you don't like," he said, his voice a trifle thick, "is work! That little garter snake wasn't more than six inches long. What you want is for me to carry all the fish up there alone, while you go off to the cabin and take it easy—"

Freddie already was on his way to the cabin. "I'm on vacation!" he bellowed back happily. "Gotta save my strength! Gotta 'cuperate!"

Hogan glared after him, opened his mouth and shut it again. Then he picked up the day's catch of bass and walleyes and swayed on toward the icehouse. Usually a sober young man, he'd been guiding a party of fishermen from one of his light-housekeeping cabins over the lake's trolling grounds since early morning. It was hot work in June weather and now, at three in the afternoon, Hogan was tanked to the gills with iced beer.

He dropped the fish between chunks of ice under the sawdust, covered them up and started back to what he called the lodge—an old two-story log structure reserved for himself and a few campers too lazy even to do their own cooking.

When he came to the spot where the garter snake had given Freddie his excuse to quit, he saw it wriggling about spasmodically at the edge of a clump of weeds, as if something hidden in there had caught hold of it.

Hogan watched the tiny reptile's struggles for a moment, then squatted down carefully and spread the weeds apart. There was a sharp buzzing like the ghost of a rattler's challenge, and something slapped moistly across the back of his hand, leaving a stinging sensation as if he had reached into a cluster of nettles. At the same moment, the snake disappeared with a jerk under the plants.

The buzzing continued. It was hardly a real sound at all—more like a thin, quivering vibration inside his head, and decidedly unpleasant. Hogan shut his eyes tight and shook his head to drive it away. He opened his eyes again, and found himself looking at Greenface.

Nothing even faintly resembling Greenface had ever appeared before in any of Hogan's weed patches, but at the moment he wasn't greatly surprised. It hadn't, he decided at once, any real face. It was a shiny, dark-green lump, the size and shape of a goose egg standing on end among the weeds; it was pulsing regularly like a human heart; and across it ran a network of thin, dark lines that seemed to form two tightly shut eyes and a closed, faintly smiling mouth.

Like a fat little smiling idol in green jade—Greenface it became for Hogan then and there. . . . With alcoholic detachment, he made a mental note of the cluster of fuzzy strands like hair roots about and below the thing. Then—somewhere underneath and blurred as though seen through milky glass—he discovered the snake, coiled up in a spiral and still turning with labored writhing motions as if trying to swim in a mass of gelatin.

Hogan put out his hand to investigate this phenomenon, and one of the rootlets lifted as if to ward off his touch. He hesitated, and it flicked down, withdrawing immediately and leaving another red line of nettle-burn across the back of his hand.

In a moment, Hogan was on his feet, several yards away. A belated sense of horrified outrage overcame him—he scooped up a handful of stones and hurled them wildly at the impossible little monstrosity. One thumped down near it; and with that, the buzzing sensation in his brain stopped.

Greenface began to slide slowly away through the weeds, all its rootlets wriggling about it, with an air of moving sideways and watching Hogan over a nonexistent shoulder. He found a chunk of wood in his hand and leaped in pursuit—and it promptly vanished.

He spent another minute or two poking around in the vegetation with his club raised, ready to finish it off wherever he found it lurking. Instead, he discovered the snake among the weeds and picked it up.

It was still moving, though quite dead, the scales peeling away from the wrinkled flabby body. Hogan stared at it, wondering. He held it by the head; and at the pressure of his finger and thumb, the skull within gave softly, like leather. It became suddenly horrible to feel—and then the complete inexplicability of the grotesque affair broke in on him.

He flung the dead snake away with a wide sweep of his arm, went back to the icehouse and was briefly but thoroughly sick.

Julia Allison was leaning on her elbows over the kitchen table studying a mail-order catalogue when Hogan walked unsteadily into the lodge. Julia had dark-brown hair, calm gray eyes, and a wicked figure. She and Hogan had been engaged for half a year. Hogan didn't want to get married until he was sure he could make a success of Masters Fishing Camp, which was still in its first season.

Julia glanced up smiling. The smile became a stare. She closed the catalogue.

"Hogan," she stated, in the exact tone of her pa, Whitey Allison, refusing a last one to a customer in Whitey's bar and liquor store in town, "you're plain drunk! Don't shake your head—it'll slop out your ears."

"Julia—" Hogan began excitedly.

She stepped up to him and sniffed, wrinkling her nose. *"Pfaah!* Beer! Yes, darling?"

"Julia, I just saw something—a sort of crazy little green spook—"

Julia blinked twice.

"Look, infant," she said soothingly, "that's how people get talked about! Sit down and relax while I make up coffee, black. There's a couple came in this morning, and I put them in the end cabin. They want the stove tanked with kerosene, ice in the icebox, and coal for a barbecue—I fixed them up with linen."

"Julia," Hogan inquired hoarsely, "are you going to listen to me or not?"

Her smile vanished. "Now you're yelling!"

"I'm *not* yelling. And I don't need coffee. I'm trying to tell you—"

"Then do it without shouting!" Julia replaced the coffee can with a whack that showed her true state of mind, and gave Hogan an abused look which left him speechless.

"If you want to stand there and sulk," she continued immediately, "I might as well run along—I got to help Pa in the store tonight." That meant he wasn't to call her up.

She was gone before Hogan, struggling with a sudden desire to shake his Julia up and down like a cocktail for some time, could come to a decision. So he went instead to see to the couple in the end cabin. Afterwards he lay down bitterly and slept it off.

When he woke up, Greenface seemed no more than a vague and very uncertain memory, an unaccountable scrap of afternoon nightmare. Due to the heat, no doubt. *Not* to the beer—on that point Hogan and Julia remained in disagreement, however completely they became reconciled otherwise. Since neither wanted to bring the subject up again, it didn't really matter.

The next time Greenface was seen, it wasn't Hogan who saw it.

In mid-season, on the twenty-fifth of June, the success of Masters Fishing Camp looked pretty well assured. Whitey Allison was hinting he'd be willing to advance money to have the old lodge rebuilt, as a wedding present. When Hogan came into camp for lunch, everything seemed peaceful and quiet; but before he got to the lodge steps, a series of piercing feminine shrieks from the direction of the north end cabin swung him around, running.

Charging up to the cabin with a number of startled camp guests strung out behind him, Hogan heard a babble of excited talk shushed suddenly and emphatically within. The man who was vacationing there with his wife appeared at the door.

"Old lady thinks she's seen a ghost, or something!" he apologized with an embarrassed laugh. "Nothing you can do. I . . . . I'll quiet her down, I guesss. . . ."

Hogan waved the others back, then ducked around behind the cabin, and listened shamelessly. Suddenly the babbling began again. He could hear every word.

"I did so see it! It was sort of blue and green and wet—and it had a green face, and it s-s-smiled at me! It f-floated up a tree and disappeared! Oh—G-G-Georgie!"

Georgie continued to make soothing sounds. But

before nightfall, he came into the lodge to pay his
bill.

"Sorry, old man," he said. He still seemed more
embarrassed than upset. "I can't imagine what the little
woman saw, but she's got her mind made up, and we
gotta go home. You know how it is. I sure hate to leave,
myself!"

Hogan saw them off with a sickly smile. Uppermost
among his feelings was a sort of numbed vindication. A
ghost that was blue and green and wet and floated up
trees and disappeared was a far from exact description
of the little monstrosity he'd persuaded himself he *hadn't*
seen—but still too near it to be a coincidence. Julia,
driving out from town to see him next day, didn't think
it was a coincidence, either.

"You couldn't possibly have told that hysterical old
goose about the funny little green thing you thought
you saw? She got confidential in the liquor store last
night, and her hubby couldn't hush her. Everybody
was listening. That sort of stuff won't do the camp any
good, Hogan!"

Hogan looked helpless. If he told her about the camp
haunt again, she wouldn't believe him, anyhow. And if
she did believe him, it might scare her silly.

"Well?" she urged suspiciously.

Hogan sighed. "Never spoke more than a dozen
words with the woman. . . ."

Julia seemed doubtful, but puzzled. There was a
peculiar oily hothouse smell in the air when Hogan
walked up to the road with her and watched her start
back to town in her ancient car; but with a nearly
sleepless night behind him, he wasn't as alert as he
might have been. He was recrossing the long, narrow
meadow between the road and the camp before the
extraordinary quality of that odor struck him. And then,
for the second time, he found himself looking at
Greenface—at a bigger Greenface, and not a better
one.

About sixty feet away, up in the birches at the end of the meadow, it was almost completely concealed: a vague oval of darker vegetable green in the foliage. Its markings were obscured by the leaf shadows among which it lay motionless except for that sluggish pulsing.

Hogan stared at it for long seconds while his scalp crawled and his heart hammered a thudding alarm into every fiber of his body. What scared him was its size—that oval was as big as a football! It had been growing at a crazy rate since he saw it last.

Swallowing hard, he mopped sweat off his forehead and walked on stiffly towards the lodge, careful to give no sign of being in a hurry. He didn't want to scare the thing away. There was an automatic shotgun slung above the kitchen door for emergencies; and a dose of No. 2 shot would turn this particular emergency into a museum specimen. . . .

Around the corner of the lodge he went up the entrance steps four at a time. A few seconds later, with the gun in his hand and reaching for a box of shells, he shook his head to drive a queer soundless buzzing out of his ears. Instantly, he remembered where he'd experienced that sensation before, and wheeled towards the screened kitchen window.

The big birch trembled slightly as if horrified to see a huge spider with jade-green body and blurred cluster of threadlike legs flow down along its trunk. Twelve feet from the ground, it let go of the tree and dropped, the long bunched threads stretched straight down before it. Hogan grunted and blinked.

It had happened before his eyes: at the instant the bunched tips hit the ground, Greenface was jarred into what could only be called a higher stage of visibility. There was no change in the head, but the legs abruptly became flat, faintly greenish ribbons, flexible and semi-transparent. Each about six inches wide and perhaps six feet long, they seemed attached in a thick fringe all around the lower part of the head, like a Hawaiian dancer's grass skirt. They showed a bluish gloss wherever the sun struck them, but Greenface didn't wait for a closer inspection.

Off it went, swaying and gliding swiftly on the ends of those foot ribbons into the woods beyond the meadow. And for all the world, it *did* look almost like a conventional ghost, the ribbons glistening in a luxurious winding sheet around the area where a body should have been, but wasn't! No wonder that poor woman—

Hogan found himself giggling helplessly. He laid the gun on the kitchen table, then tried to control the shaking of his hands long enough to get a cigarette going.

Long before the middle of July, every last tourist had left Masters Fishing Camp. Vaguely, Hogan sensed it was unfortunate that two of his attempts to dispose of Greenface had been observed while his quarry remained unseen. Of course, it wasn't his fault if the creature chose to exercise an uncanny ability to become almost completely invisible at will—nothing more than a tall glassy blur which flickered off through the woods and was gone. And it wasn't until he drove into town one evening that he realized just how unfortunate that little trick was, nevertheless, for him.

Whitey Allison's greeting was brief and chilly. Then Julia delayed putting in an appearance for almost half an hour. Hogan waited patiently enough.

"You might pour me a Scotch," he suggested at last.

Whitey passed him a significant look.

"Better lay off the stuff," he advised heavily. Hogan flushed.

"What do you mean by that?"

"There's plenty of funny stories going around about you right now!" Whitey told him, blinking belligerently. Then he looked past Hogan, and Hogan knew Julia had come into the store behind him; but he was too angry to drop the matter there.

"What do you expect me to do about them?" he demanded.

"That's no way to talk to Pa!"

Julia's voice was sharper than Hogan had ever heard it—he swallowed hard and tramped out of the store without looking at her. Down the street he had a couple of drinks; and coming past the store again on the way to his car, he saw Julia behind the bar counter, laughing and chatting with a group of summer residents. She seemed to be having a grand time; her gray eyes sparkled and there was a fine high color in her cheeks.

Hogan snarled out the worst word he knew and went on home. It was true he'd grown accustomed to an impressive dose of whiskey at night, to put him to sleep. At night, Greenface wasn't abroad, and there was no sense in lying awake to wonder and worry about it. On warm clear days around noon was the time to be alert; twice Hogan caught it basking in the treetops in full sunlight and each time took a long shot at it, which had no effect beyond scaring it into complete visibility. It dropped out of the tree like a rotten fruit and scudded off into the bushes, its foot ribbons weaving and flapping all about it.

Well, it all added up. Was it surprising if he seemed constantly on the watch for something nobody else could see? When the camp cabins emptied one by one and stayed empty, Hogan told himself that he preferred it that way. Now he could devote all his time to tracking down that smiling haunt and finishing it off. Afterwards would have to be early enough to repair the damage it had done his good name and bank balance.

He tried to keep Julia out of these calculations. Julia hadn't been out to the camp for several weeks; and under the circumstances he didn't see how he could do anything at present to patch up their misunderstanding.

After being shot at the second time, Greenface stayed out of sight for so many days that Hogan almost gave up hunting for it. He was morosely cleaning out the lodge cellar one afternoon; and as he shook out a box he was going to convert to kindling, a small odd-looking object tumbled out to the floor. Hogan stared at the object a moment, then frowned and picked it up.

It was the mummified tiny body of a hummingbird, some tropical species with a long curved beak and long ornamental tail feathers. Except for beak and feathers, it would have been unrecognizable; bones, flesh, and skin were shriveled together into a small lump of doubtful consistency, like dried gum. Hogan, remembering the dead snake from which he had driven Greenface near the icehouse, turned it around in fingers that trembled a little, studying it carefully.

The origin of the camp spook seemed suddenly explained. Some two months ago, he'd carried the box in which the hummingbird's body had been lying into the lodge cellar. In it at the time had been a big cluster of green bananas he'd got from the wholesale grocer in town. . . .

Greenface, of course, was carnivorous, in some weird, out-of-the-ordinary fashion. Small game had become rare around the camp in recent weeks; even birds now seemed to avoid the area. When that banana cluster was shipped in from Brazil or some island in the Caribbean, Greenface—a seedling Greenface, very much smaller even than when Hogan first saw it—had come along concealed in it, clinging to its hummingbird prey.

And then something—perhaps simply the touch of the colder North—had acted to cancel the natural limits on its growth; for each time he'd seen it, it had been obvious that it still was growing rapidly. And though it apparently lacked solid parts that might resist decomposition after death, creatures of its present size, which conformed to no recognizable pattern of either the vegetable or the animal kingdom, couldn't very well exist anywhere without drawing human attention to themselves. While if they grew normally to be only a foot or

two high, they seemed intelligent and alert enough to
escape observation in some luxuriant tropical forest—
even discounting that inexplicable knack of turning transparent from one second to the next.

His problem, meanwhile, was a purely practical one.
The next time he grew aware of the elusive hothouse
smell near the camp, he had a plan ready laid. His
nearest neighbor, Pete Jeffries, who provided Hogan
with most of his provisions from a farm two miles down
the road to town, owned a hound by the name of Old
Battler—a large, surly brute with a strong strain of
Airedale in its make-up, and reputedly the best trailing
nose in the county.

Hogan's excuse for borrowing Old Battler was a fat
buck who'd made his headquarters in the marshy ground
across the bay. Pete had no objection to out-of-season
hunting; he and Old Battler were the slickest pair of
poachers for a hundred miles around. He whistled the
hound in and handed him over to Hogan with a parting
admonition to keep an eye peeled for snooping game
wardens.

The oily fragrance under the birches was so distinct
that Hogan almost could have followed it himself. Un-
fortunately, it didn't mean a thing to the dog. Panting
and rumbling as Hogan, cradling the shotgun, brought
him up on a leash, Old Battler was ready for any type of
quarry from rabbits to a pig-stealing bear; but he simply
wouldn't or couldn't accept that he was to track that
bloodless vegetable odor to its source. He walked off a
few yards in the direction the thing had gone, nosing
the grass; then, ignoring Hogan's commands, he returned to the birch, sniffed carefully around its base
and paused to demonstrate in unmistakable fashion what
he thought of the scent. Finally he sat on his haunches
and regarded Hogan with a baleful, puzzled eye.

There was nothing to do but take him back and tell
Pete Jeffries the poaching excursion was off because a
warden had put in an appearance in the area. When

Hogan got back to the lodge, he heard the telephone ringing above the cellar stairs and hurried towards it with an eagerness that surprised himself.

"Hello?" he said into the mouthpiece. "Hello? Julia? That you?"

There was no answer from the other end. Hogan listening, heard voices, several of them, people laughing and talking. Then a door slammed faintly and someone called out: "Hi, Whitey! How's the old man?" She had phoned from the liquor store, perhaps just to see what he was doing. He thought he could even hear the faint fluttering of her breath.

"Julia," Hogan said softly, scared by the silence. "What's the matter, darling? Why don't you say something?"

Now he did hear her take a quick, deep breath. Then the receiver clicked down, and the line was dead.

The rest of the afternoon he managed to keep busy cleaning out the cabins which had been occupied. Counting back to the day the last of them had been vacated, he decided the reason nobody had arrived since was that a hostile Whitey Allison, in his strategic position at the town bus stop, was directing all tourist traffic to other camps. Not—Hogan assured himself again—that he wanted anyone around until he had solved his problem; it would only make matters more difficult.

But why had Julia called up? What did it mean?

That night, the moon was full. Near ten o'clock, with no more work to do, Hogan settled down wearily on the lodge steps. Presently he lit a cigarette. His intention was to think matters out to some conclusion in the quiet night air, but all he seemed able to do was to keep telling himself uselessly that there must be some way of trapping that elusive green horror.

He pulled the sides of his face down slowly with his fingertips. "I've got to do something!"—the futile whisper seemed to have been running through his head all day: "Got to *do* something! Got to . . ." He'd be having a mental breakdown if he didn't watch out.

The rumbling barks of Jeffries' Old Battler began to churn up the night to the east—and suddenly Hogan caught the characteristic tinny stutter of Julia's little car as it turned down into the road from Jeffries' farm and came on in the direction of the camp.

The thrill that swung him to his feet was tempered at once by fresh doubts. Even if Julia was coming to tell him she'd forgiven him, he'd be expected to explain what was making him act like this. And there was no way of explaining it. She'd think he was crazy or lying. No, he couldn't do it, Hogan decided despairingly. He'd have to send her away again. . . .

He took the big flashlight from its hook beside the door and started off forlornly to meet her when she would bring the car bumping along the path from the road. Then he realized that the car, still half a mile or so from the lodge, had stopped.

He waited, puzzled. From a distance he heard the creaky shift of its gears, a brief puttering of the motor— another shift and putter. Then silence. Old Battler was also quiet, probably listening suspiciously, though he, too, knew the sound of Julia's car. There was no one else to hear it. Jeffries had gone to the city with his wife that afternoon, and they wouldn't be back till late next morning.

Hogan frowned, flashing the light on and off against the moonlit side of the lodge. In the quiet, three or four whippoorwills were crying to each other with insane rapidity up and down the lake front. There was a subdued shrilling of crickets everywhere, and occasionally the threefold soft call of an owl dropped across the bay. He started reluctantly up the path towards the road.

The headlights were out, or he would have been able to see them from here. But the moon rode high, and the road was a narrow silver ribbon running straight down through the pines towards Jeffries' farmhouse.

Quite suddenly he discovered the car, pulled up beside the road and turned back towards town. It was Julia's car all right; and it was empty. Hogan walked slowly towards it, peering right and left, then jerked around with a start to a sudden crashing noise among the pines a hundred yards or so down off the road—a scrambling animal rush which seemed to be moving toward the lake. An instant later, Old Battler's angry roar told him the hound was running loose and had prowled into something it disapproved of down there.

He was still listening, trying to analyze the commotion, when a girl in a dark sweater and skirt stepped out quietly from the shadow of the roadside pines beyond him. Hogan didn't see her until she crossed the ditch to the road in a beautiful reaching leap. Then she was running like a rabbit for the car.

He shouted: "Julia!"

For just an instant, Julia looked back at him, her face a pale scared blur in the moonlight. Then the car door slammed shut behind her, and with a shiver and groan the old machine lurched into action. Hogan made no further attempt to stop her. Confused and unhappy, he watched the headlights sweep down the road until they swung out of sight around a bend.

Now what the devil had she been poking about here for?

Hogan sighed, shook his head and turned back to the camp. Old Battler's vicious snarling had stopped; the woods were quiet once more. Presently a draft of cool air came flowing up from the lake across the road, and Hogan's nostrils wrinkled. Some taint in the breeze—

He checked abruptly. Greenface! Greenface was down there among the pines somewhere. The hound had stirred it up, discovered it was alive and worth worrying, but lost it again, and was now casting about silently to find its hiding place.

Hogan crossed the ditch in a leap that bettered Julia's, blundered into the wood and ducked just in time to avoid being speared in the eye by a jagged branch of aspen. More cautiously, he worked his way in among the trees, went sliding down a moldy incline, swore in exasperation as he tripped over a rotten trunk and was reminded thereby of the flashlight in his hand. He walked slowly across a moonlit clearing, listening, then found himself confronted by a dense cluster of evergreens and switched on the light.

It stabbed into a dark-green oval, more than twice the size of a human head, fifteen feet away.

He stared in fascination at the thing, expecting it to vanish. But Greenface made no move beyond a slow writhing among the velvety foot ribbons that supported it. It had shot up again since he'd seen it last, stood taller than he now and was stooping slightly towards him. The lines on its pulsing head formed two tightly shut eyes and a wide, thin-lipped, insanely smiling mouth.

Gradually it was borne in on Hogan that the thing was asleep. Or had been asleep . . . for now he became aware of a change in the situation through something like the buzzing escape of steam, a sound just too high to be audible that throbbed through his head. Then he noticed that Greenface, swaying slowly, quietly, had come a foot or two closer, and he saw the tips of the foot ribbons grow dim and transparent as they slid over the moss toward him. A sudden horror of this stealthy approach seized him. Without thinking of what he did, he switched off the light.

Almost instantly, the buzzing sensation died away, and before Hogan had backed off to the edge of the moonlit clearing, he realized that Greenface had stopped its advance. Suddenly he understood.

Unsteadily, he threw the beam on again and directed it full on the smiling face. For a moment, there was no result; then the faint buzzing began once more in his brain, and the foot ribbons writhed and dimmed as Greenface came sliding forward. He snapped it off; and the thing grew still, solidifying.

Hogan began to laugh in silent hysteria. He'd caught it now! Light brought Greenface alive, let it act, move, enabled it to pull off its unearthly vanishing stunt. At high noon, it was as vital as a cat or hawk. Lack of light made it still, dulled, though perhaps able to react automatically.

Greenface was trapped.

He began to play with it, savagely savoring his power over the horror, switching the light off and on. Perhaps it wouldn't even be necessary to kill the thing now. Its near-paralysis in darkness might make it possible to capture it, cage it securely alive, as a stunning justification of everything that had occurred these past weeks. He watched it come gliding toward him again, and seemed to sense a dim rising anger in the soundless buzzing. Confidently, he turned off the light. But this time Greenface didn't stop.

In an instant, Hogan realized he had permitted it to reach the edge of the little clearing. Under the full glare of the moon, it was still advancing on him, though slowly. Its outlines grew altogether blurred. Even the head started to fade.

He leaped back, with a new rush of the instinctive horror with which he had first detected it coming toward him. But he retreated only into the shadows on the other side of the clearing.

The ghostly outline of Greenface came rolling on, its nebulous leering head swaying slowly from side to side like the head of a hanged and half-rotted thing. It reached the fringe of shadows and stopped, while the foot ribbons darkened as they touched the darkness and writhed back. Dimly, it seemed to be debating this new situation.

Hogan swallowed hard. He had noticed a blurred shapeless something which churned about slowly within the jellylike shroud beneath the head; and he had a sudden conviction that he knew the reason for Old

Battler's silence. . . . Greenface had become as dangerous as a tiger!

But he had no intention of leaving it in the moonlight's releasing spell. He threw the beam on the dim
oval mask again, and slowly, stupidly, moving along
that rope of light, Greenface entered the shadows; and
the light flicked out, and it was trapped once more.

Trembling and breathless after his half-mile run, Hogan stumbled into the lodge kitchen and began stuffing
his pockets with as many shells as they would take.
Then he took down the shotgun and started back toward
the spot where he had left the thing, keeping his pace
down to a fast walk. If he made no blunders now, his
troubles would be over. But if he did blunder . . .
Hogan shivered. He hadn't quite realized before that
the time was bound to come when Greenface would be
big enough to lose its fear of him. His notion of trying
to capture it alive was out—he might wind up inside it
with Old Battler. . . .

Pushing down through the ditch and into the woods,
he flashed the light ahead of him. In a few more minutes, he reached the place where he had left Greenface.
And it wasn't there.

Hogan glared about, wondering wildly whether he
had missed the right spot and knowing he hadn't. He
looked up and saw the tops of the jack pines swaying
against the pale blur of the sky; and as he stared at
them, a ray of moonlight flickered through the broken
canopy and touched him and was gone again, and then
he understood. Greenface had crept up along such in-
termittent threads of light into the trees.

One of the pine tips appeared blurred and top-heavy.
Hogan studied it carefully; then he depressed the safety
button on the shotgun, cradled the weapon, and put
the flashlight beam dead-center on that blur. In a moment, he felt the familiar mental irritation as the blur
began to flow down through the branches toward him.

Remembering that Greenface didn't mind a long drop to the ground, he switched off the light and watched it take shape among the shadows, and then begin a slow retreat toward the treetops and the moon.

Hogan took a deep breath and raised the gun.

The five reports came one on top of the other in a rolling roar, while the pine top jerked and splintered and flew. Greenface was plainly visible now, still clinging, twisting and lashing in spasms like a broken snake. Big branches, torn loose in those furious convulsions, crashed ponderously down toward Hogan. He backed off hurriedly, flicked in five new shells and raised the gun again.

And again.

And again. . .

Greenface and what seemed to be the whole top of the tree came down together. Dropping the gun, Hogan covered his head with his arms. He heard the sodden, splashy thump with which Greenface landed on the forest mold half a dozen yards away. Then something hard and solid slammed down across his shoulders and the back of his skull.

There was a brief sensation of diving headlong through a fire-streaked darkness. For many hours thereafter, no sort of sensation reached Hogan's mind at all.

"Haven't seen you around in a long time!" bellowed Pete Jeffries across the fifty feet of water between his boat and Hogan's. He pulled a flapping whitefish out of the illegal gill net he was emptying, plunked it down on the pile before him. "What you do with yourself—sleep up in the woods?"

"Times I do," Hogan admitted.

"Used to myself, your age. Out with a gun alla time!" Pete's face drew itself into mournful folds. "Not much fun now anymore . . . not since them damn game wardens got Old Battler."

Hogan shivered imperceptibly, remembering the

ghastly thing he'd buried that July morning six weeks back, when he awoke, thinking his skull was caved in, and found Greenface had dragged itself away, with what should have been enough shot in it to lay out half a township. At least, it had felt sick enough to disgorge what was left of Old Battler, and to refrain from harming Hogan. And perhaps it had died later of its injuries. But he didn't really believe it was dead. . . .

"Think the storm will hit before evening?" he asked out of his thoughts, not caring particularly whether it stormed or not. But Pete was sitting there, looking at him, and it was something to say.

"Hit the lake in half an hour," Pete replied matter-of-factly. "I know two guys who are going to get awful wet."

"Yeah?"

Pete jerked his head over his shoulder. "That little bay back where the Indian outfit used to live. Two of the drunkest mugs I seen on Thursday Lake this summer—fishing from off a little duck boat. . . . They come from across the lake somewhere."

"Maybe we should warn them."

"Not me!" Jeffries said emphatically. "They made some smart cracks at me when I passed there. Like to have rammed them!" He grunted, studied Hogan with an air of puzzled reflection. "Seems there was something I was going to tell you . . . well, guess it was a lie." He sighed. "How's the walleyes hitting?"

"Pretty good." Hogan had picked up a stringerful trolling along the lake bars.

"Got it now!" Pete exclaimed. "Whitey told me last night. Julia got herself engaged with a guy in the city—place she's working at. Getting married next month."

Hogan bent over the side of his boat and began to unknot the fish stringer. He hadn't seen Julia since the night he last met Greenface. A week or so later he heard she'd left town and taken a job in the city.

"Seemed to me I ought to tell you," Pete continued

with remorseless neighborliness. "Didn't you and she used to go around some?"

"Yeah, some," Hogan agreed. He held up the wall-eyes. "Want to take these home for the missis, Pete? I was just fishing for the fun of it."

"Sure will!" Pete was delighted. "Nothing beats wall-eyes for eating, 'less it's whitefish. But I'm going to smoke these. Say, how about me bringing you a ham of buck, smoked, for the walleyes? Fair enough?"

"Fair enough," Hogan smiled.

"Can't be immediate. I went shooting the north side of the lake three nights back, and there wasn't a deer around. Something's scared 'em all out over there."

"Okay," Hogan said, not listening at all. He got the motor going, and cut away from Pete with a wave of his hand. "Be seeing you, Pete!"

Two miles down the lake, he got his mind off Julia long enough to find a possible significance in Pete's last words.

He cut the motor to idling speed, and then shut it off entirely, trying to get his thoughts into some kind of order. Since that chunk of pine slugged him in the head and robbed him of his chance of finishing off Greenface, he'd seen no more of the thing and heard nothing to justify his suspicion that it was still alive somewhere, perhaps still growing. But from Thursday Lake north-ward to the border of Canada stretched two hundred miles of bush—trees and water, with only the barest scattering of farms and tiny towns. Hogan sometimes pictured Greenface prowling about back there, safe from human detection, and a ghastly new enemy for the harried small life of the bush, while it nourished its hatred for the man who had so nearly killed it.

It wasn't a pretty picture. It made him take the signs indicating Masters Fishing Camp from the roads, and made him turn away the occasional would-be guest who still found his way to the camp in spite of Whitey Allison's unrelenting vigilance in town. It also made it impossible for him even to try to get in touch with Julia and explain what couldn't have been explained, anyway.

A rumbling of thunder broke through his thoughts. The sky in the east hung black with clouds now; and the boat was drifting in steadily toward shore with the wind and waves behind it. Hogan started the motor and came around in a curve to take a direct line toward camp. As he did so, a pale object rose sluggishly on the waves not a hundred yards ahead of him. With a start, he realized it was the upturned bottom of a small boat, and remembered the two fishermen he'd intended warning against the approach of the storm.

The little bay Pete Jeffries had mentioned lay half a mile behind; in his preoccupation he'd passed it without becoming conscious of the fact. There was no immediate reason to assume the drunks had met with an accident; more likely they'd landed and neglected to draw the boat high enough out of the water, so that it drifted off into the lake again on the first eddy of wind. Circling the derelict to make sure it was what it appeared to be, Hogan turned back to pick up the stranded sportsmen and take them to his camp until the storm was over.

When he reached the relatively smooth water of the tree-ringed bay, he throttled the motor and moved in slowly because the bay was shallow and choked with pickerel grass and reeds. There was surprisingly little breeze here; the air seemed almost oppressively hot and still after the free race of wind across the lake. Hogan realized it was darkening rapidly.

He stood up in the boat and stared along the shoreline over the tops of the reeds, wondering where the two had gone—and whether they mightn't have been in their boat anyway when it overturned.

"Anyone around?" he yelled uncertainly.

His voice echoed back out of the creaking shore pines. From somewhere near the end of the bay sounded a series of splashes—probably a big fish flopping about in the reeds. When that stopped, the stillness turned almost tangible; and Hogan drew a quick, deep breath, as if he found breathing difficult here.

Again the splashing in the shallows—closer now. Hogan faced the sound, frowning. The frown became a puzzled stare. That certainly was no fish, but some large animal—a deer, a bear, possibly a moose. The odd thing was that it should be coming *toward* him. . . . Craning his neck, he saw the reed tops bend and shake about a hundred yards away, as if a slow, heavy wave of air were passing through them in his direction. There was nothing else to be seen.

Then the truth flashed on him—a rush of horrified comprehension.

Hogan tumbled back into the stern and threw the motor on, full power. As the boat surged forwards, he swung it around to avoid an impenetrable wall of reeds ahead, and straightened out toward the mouth of the bay. Over the roar of the motor and the rush and hissing of water, he was aware of one other sensation: that shrilling vibration of the nerves, too high to be a sound, which had haunted him in memory all summer. Then there was a great splash behind the boat, shockingly close; another, a third. How near the thing actually came to catching him as he raced through the weedy traps of the bay, he never knew. Only after he was past the first broad patch of open water, did he risk darting a glance back over his shoulder—

He heard someone screaming. Raw, hoarse yells of animal terror. Abruptly, he realized it was himself.

He was in no immediate danger at the time. Greenface had given up the pursuit. It stood, fully visible among the reeds, a hundred yards or so back. The smiling jade-green face was turned toward Hogan, lit up by strange reflections from the stormy sky, and mottled with red streaks and patches he didn't remember seeing there before. The glistening, flowing mass beneath it writhed like a cloak of translucent pythons. It towered in the bay, dwarfing even the trees behind it in its unearthly menace.

It *had* grown again. It stood all of thirty feet tall. . . .

The storm broke before Hogan reached camp and raged on through the night and throughout the next day. Since he would never be able to find the thing in that torrential downpour, he didn't have to decide whether he must try to hunt Greenface down or not. In any case, he told himself, staring out of the lodge windows at the tormented chaos of water and wind, he wouldn't have to go looking for it. It had come back for him, and presently it was going to find its way to the familiar neighborhood of the camp.

There seemed to be a certain justice in that. He'd been the nemesis of the monster as much as it had been his. It had become time finally for the matter to end in one way or another.

Someone had told him—now he thought of it, it must have been Pete Jeffries, plodding up faithfully through the continuing storm one morning with supplies for Hogan—that the two lost sportsmen were considered drowned. Their boat had been discovered; and as soon as the weather made it possible, a search would be made for their bodies. Hogan nodded, saying nothing. Pete studied him as he talked, his broad face growing increasingly worried.

"You shouldn't drink so much, Hogan!" he blurted out suddenly. "It ain't doing you no good! The missis told me you were really keen on Julia. I should've kept my trap shut . . . but you'd have found out, anyhow."

"Sure I would," Hogan said promptly. It hadn't occurred to him that Pete believed he'd shut himself up here to mourn for his lost Julia.

"Me, I didn't marry the girl I was after, neither," Pete told him confidentially. "Course the missis don't know that. Hit me just about like it's hit you. You just gotta snap outta it, see?"

Something moved, off in the grass back of the machine shed. Hogan watched it from the corner of his eye through the window until he was sure it was only a big bush shaking itself in the sleety wind.

"Eh?" he said. "Oh, sure! I'll snap out of it, Pete. Don't you worry."

"Okay." Pete sounded hearty but not quite convinced. "And drive over and see us one of these evenings. It don't do a guy no good to be sitting off here by himself all the time."

Hogan gave his promise. He might, in fact, have been thinking about Julia a good deal. But mostly his mind remained preoccupied with Greenface—and he wasn't touching his store of whiskey these nights. The crisis might come at any time; when it did, he intended to be as ready for it as he could be. Shotgun and deer rifle were loaded and close at hand. The road to town was swamped and impassable now, but as soon as he could use it again, he was going to lay in a stock of dynamite.

Meanwhile, the storm continued day and night, with only occasional brief lulls. Hogan couldn't quite remember finally how long it had been going on; he slept fitfully at night, and a growing bone-deep fatigue gradually blurred the days. But it certainly was as long and bad a wet blow as he'd ever got stuck in. The lake water rolled over the main dock with every wave, and the small dock down near the end cabins had been taken clean away. Trees were down within the confines of the camp, and the ground everywhere was littered with branches.

While this lasted, he didn't expect Greenface to put in an appearance. It, too, was weathering the storm, concealed somewhere in the dense forests along the lake front, in as much shelter as a thing of that size could find, its great head nodding and pulsing slowly as it waited.

*　　*　　*

By the eighth morning, the storm was ebbing out. In mid-afternoon the wind veered around to the south; shortly before sunset the cloud banks began to dissolve while mists streamed from the lake surface. A few hours earlier, Hogan had worked the car out on the road to see if he could make it to town. After a quarter of a mile, he turned back. The farther stretches of the road were a morass of mud, barricaded here and there by fallen trees. It would be days before anyone could get through.

Near sunset, he went out with an ax and hauled in a number of dead birches from a windfall over the hill to the south of the lodge. He felt chilled and heavy all through, unwilling to exert himself; but his firewood was running low and had to be replenished. As he came back to the lodge dragging the last of the birches, he was startled into a burst of sweat by a pale, featureless face that stared at him out of the evening sky between the trees. The moon had grown nearly full in the week it was hidden from sight; and Hogan remembered then that Greenface was able to walk in the light of the full moon.

He cast an anxious look overhead. The clouds were melting toward the horizon in every direction; it probably would be an exceptionally clear night. He stacked the birch logs to dry in the cellar and piled the wood he had on hand beside the fireplace in the lodge's main room. Then he brewed up the last of his coffee and drank it black. A degree of alertness returned to him.

Afterwards he went about, closing the shutters over every window except those facing the south meadow. The tall cottonwoods on the other three sides of the house should afford a protective screen, but the meadow would be flooded with moonlight. He tried to calculate the time the moon should set, and decided it didn't matter—he'd watch till it had set and then sleep.

He pulled an armchair up to an open window, from where, across the sill, he controlled the whole expanse of the open ground over which Greenface could approach. The rifle lay on the table beside him; the shotgun, in which he had more faith, lay across his knees. Open shell boxes and the flashlight were within reach on the table.

With the coming of night, all but the brightest of stars were dimmed in the gray gleaming sky. The moon itself stood out of Hogan's sight above the lodge roof, but he could look across the meadow as far as the machine shed and the icehouse.

He got up twice to replenish the fire which made a warm, reassuring glow on his left side. The second time, he considered replacing the armchair with something less comfortable. The effect of the coffee had begun to wear off; he was becoming thoroughly drowsy. Occasionally, a ripple of apprehension brought him bolt upright, pulses hammering; but the meadow always appeared quiet and unchanged and the night alive only with familiar, heartening sounds: the crickets, a single whippoorwill, and now and then the dark wail of a loon from the outer lake.

Each time, fear wore itself out again; and then, even thinking of Julia, it was hard to stay awake. She was in his mind tonight with almost physical vividness, sitting opposite him at the kitchen table, raking back her unruly hair while she leafed through the mail-order catalogues; or diving off the float he'd anchored beyond the dock, a bathing cap tight around her head and the chin strap framing her beautiful stubborn little face like a picture.

Beautiful but terribly stubborn, Hogan thought, nodding drowsily. Like one evening, when they'd quarreled again and she hid among the empty cabins at the north end of the camp. She wouldn't answer when Hogan began looking for her, and by the time he discovered her, he was worried and angry. So he came walking through the half-dark toward her without a word; and that was one time Julia got a little scared of him. "Now, wait, Hogan!" she cried breathlessly. "Listen, Hogan—"

He sat up with a jerky start, her voice still ringing in his mind.

The empty moonlit meadow lay like a great silver carpet before him, infinitely peaceful; even the shrilling of the tireless crickets was withdrawn in the distance. He must have slept for some while, for the shadow of the house formed an inky black square on the ground immediately below the window. The moon was sinking.

Hogan sighed, shifted the gun on his knees, and immediately grew still again. There'd been something . . . and then he heard it clearly: a faint scratching on the outside of the bolted door behind him, and afterwards a long, breathless whimper like the gasp of a creature that has no strength to cry out.

Hogan moistened his lips and sat very quiet. In the next instant, the hair at the back of his neck rose, hideously of its own accord.

"Hogan . . . Hogan . . . oh, please! Hogan!"

The toneless cry might have come out of the shadowy room behind him, or over miles of space, but there was no mistaking that voice. Hogan tried to say something, and his lips wouldn't move. His hands lay cold and paralyzed on the shotgun.

"Hogan . . . *please!* Hogan—"

He heard the chair go over with a dim crash behind him. He was moving toward the door in a blundering, dreamlike rush, and then struggling with numb fingers against the stubborn resistance of the bolt.

"That awful thing! That awful thing! Standing there in the meadow! I thought it was a . . . *tree!* I'm not *crazy,* am I, Hogan?"

The jerky, panicky whispering went on and on, until he stopped it with his mouth on hers and felt her relax in his arms. He'd bolted the door behind them, picked

Julia up and carried her to the fireplace couch. But when he tried to put her on it, she clung to him hard, and he settled down with her, instead.

"Easy! Easy!" He murmured the words. "You're not crazy . . . and we'd better not make much noise. How'd you get here? The road's—"

"By boat. I had to find out." Her voice was steadier. She stared up at his face, eyes huge and dark, jerked her head very slightly in the direction of the door. "Was that what—"

"Yes, the same thing. It's a lot bigger now." Greenface must be standing somewhere near the edge of the cottonwoods if she'd seen it in the meadow as she came up from the dock. He went on talking quickly, quietly, explaining it all. Now Julia was here, there was no question of trying to stop the thing with buckshot or rifle slugs. That idea had been some kind of suicidal craziness. But they could get away from it, if they were careful to keep to the shadows.

The look of nightmare grew again in Julia's eyes as she listened, fingers digging painfully into his shoulder. "Hogan," she interrupted, "it's so big—big as the trees, a lot of them!"

He frowned at her uncomprehendingly a moment. Then, as she watched him, Julia's expression changed. He knew it mirrored the change in his own face.

She whispered: "It could come right through the trees!"

Hogan swallowed.

"It could be right outside the house!" Julia's voice wasn't a whisper any more; and he put his hand over her mouth.

"Don't you smell it?" he murmured close to her ear.

It was Greenface, all right; the familiar oily odor was seeping into the air they breathed, growing stronger moment by moment, until it became the smell of some foul tropical swamp, a wet, rank rottenness. Hogan eased Julia off his knees.

"The cellar," he whispered. "Dark—completely dark. No moonlight; nothing. Understand? Get going, but quietly!"

"What are you—"

"I'm putting the fire out first."

"I'll help you!" All Julia's stubbornness seemed concentrated in the three words, and Hogan clenched his teeth against an impulse to slap her face hard. Like a magnified echo of that impulse was the vast soggy blow which smashed at the outer lodge wall above the entrance door.

They stared, motionless. The whole house had shaken. The log walls were strong, but a prolonged tinkling of glass announced that each of the shuttered windows on that side had broken simultaneously. The damn thing, Hogan thought. It's really come for me! If it hits the door—

The ability to move returned to them together. They left the couch in a clumsy, frenzied scramble and reached the head of the cellar stairs not a step apart. A second shattering crash—the telephone leaped from its stand beside Hogan. He checked, hand on the stair railing, looking back.

He couldn't see the entry door from there. The fire roared and danced in the hearth, as if it enjoyed being shaken up so roughly. The head of the eight-point buck had bounced from the wall and lay beside the fire, glass eyes fixed in a red baleful glare on Hogan. Nothing else seemed changed.

"Hogan!" Julia cried from the darkness at the bottom of the stone stairs. He heard her start up again, turned to tell her to wait there.

Then Greenface hit the door.

Wood, glass, metal flew inward together with an indescribable explosive sound. Minor noises followed; then there was stillness again. Hogan heard Julia's choked breathing from the foot of the stairs. Nothing else seemed to stir.

But a cool draft of air was flowing past his face. And now there came heavy scraping noises, a renewed shattering of glass.

"Hogan!" Julia sobbed. "Come down! It'll get in!"

"It can't!" Hogan breathed.

As if in answer, the lodge's foundation seemed to tremble beneath him. Wood splintered ponderously; there was the screech of parting timbers. The shaking continued and spread through the entire building. Just beyond the corner of the wall which shut off Hogan's view of the entry door, something smacked heavily and wetly against the floor. Laboriously, like a floundering whale, Greenface was coming into the lodge.

At the bottom of the stairs, Hogan caught his foot in a roll of wires, and nearly went headlong over Julia. She clung to him, shaking.

"Did you see it?"

"Just a glimpse of its head!" Hogan was steering her by the arm along the dark cellar passage, then around a corner. "Stay there. . . ." He began fumbling with the lock of the cellar exit.

"What will we do?" she asked.

Timbers creaked and groaned overhead, cutting off his reply. For seconds, they stared up through the dark in frozen expectation, each sensing the other's thoughts. Then Julia gave a low, nervous giggle.

"Good thing the floor's double strength!"

"That's the fireplace right above us," Hogan said. I wonder—" He opened the door an inch or two, peered out. "Look over there!"

The dim, shifting light of the fireplace outlined the torn front of the lodge. As they stared, a shadow, huge and formless, blotted out the light. They shrank back.

"Oh, Hogan! It's horrible!"

"All of that," he agreed, with dry lips. "You feel something funny?"

"Feel what?"

He put his fingertips to her temples. "Up there! Sort of buzzing? Like something you can almost hear."

"Oh! Yes, I do! What is it?"

"Something the thing does. But the feeling's usually stronger. It's been out in the cold and rain all week. No sun at all. I should have remembered. It *likes* that fire up there. And it's getting livelier now—that's why we feel the buzz."

"Let's run for it, Hogan! I'm scared to death here! We can make it to the boat."

"We might," Hogan said. "But it won't let us get far. If it hears the outboard start, it can cut us off easily before we're out of the bay."

"Oh, no!" she said, shocked. She hesitated. "But then what can we *do*?"

Hogan said, "Right now it's busy soaking up heat. That gives us a little time. I have an idea. Julia, will you promise that—just once—you'll stay here, keep quiet, and not call after me or do anything else you shouldn't?"

"Why? Where are you going?"

"I won't leave the cellar," Hogan said soothingly. "Look, darling, there's no time to argue. That thing upstairs may decide at any moment to start looking around for us—and going by what it did to the front wall, it can pull the whole lodge apart. . . . Do you promise, or do I lay you out cold?"

"I promise," she said, after a sort of frosty gasp.

Hogan remained busy in the central areas of the cellar for several minutes. When he returned, Julia was still standing beside the exit door where he'd left her, looking out cautiously.

"The thing hasn't moved much," she reported, her tone somewhat subdued. She looked at him in the gloom. "What were you doing?"

"Letting out the kerosene tank—spreading it around."

"I smelled the kerosene." She was silent a moment. "Where are *we* going to be?"

Hogan opened the door a trifle wider, indicated the cabin immediately behind the cottonwood stand. "Over there. If the thing can tell we're around, and I think it can, we should be able to go that far without starting it after us."

Julia didn't answer; and he moved off into the dark again. Presently she saw a pale flare light up the chalked brick wall at the end of the passage, and realized Hogan was holding a match to papers. Kerosene fumes went off with a dim BOO-ROOM! and a flare of yellow light. Other muffled explosions followed in quick succession in various sections of the cellar. Then Hogan stepped out of a door on the passage, closed the door and turned toward her.

"Going up like pine shavings!" he said. "I guess we'd better leave quietly. . . ."

"It looks almost like a man in there, doesn't it, Hogan? Like a huge, sick, horrible old man!"

Julia's whisper was thin and shaky, and Hogan tightened his arms reassuringly about her shoulders. The buzzing sensation in his brain was stronger, rising and falling, as if the energies of the thing that produced it were gathering and ebbing in waves. From the corner of the cabin window, past the trees, they could see the front of the lodge. The frame of the big entry door had been ripped out and timbers above twisted aside, so that a good part of the main room was visible in the dim glow of the fireplace. Greenface filled almost all of that space, a great hunched dark bulk, big head bending and nodding slowly at the fire. In that attitude, there was in fact something vaguely human about it, a nightmarish caricature.

But most of Hogan's attention was fixed on the two cellar windows of the lodge which he could see. Both were alight with the flickering glare of the fires he had set; and smoke curled up beyond the cottonwoods, rising from the far side of the lodge, where he had opened other windows to give draft to the flames. The fire had a voice, a soft growing roar, mingled in his mind with the soundless rasping that told of Greenface's returning vitality.

It was like a race between the two: whether the fire, so carefully placed beneath the supporting sections of the lodge floor, would trap the thing before the heat kindled by the fire increased its alertness to the point where it sensed the danger and escaped. If it did escape—

It happened then, with blinding suddenness.

The thing swung its head around from the fireplace and lunged hugely backward. In a flash, it turned nearly transparent. Julia gave a choked cry. Hogan had told her about that disconcerting ability; but seeing it was another matter.

And as Greenface blurred, the flooring of the main lodge room sagged, splintered, and broke through into the cellar, and the released flames leaped bellowing upwards. For seconds, the vibration in Hogan's mind became a ragged, piercing shriek—became pain, brief and intolerable.

They were out of the cabin by that time, running and stumbling down toward the lake.

A boat from the ranger station at the south end of Thursday Lake chugged into the bay forty minutes later, with fire-fighting equipment. Pete Jeffries, tramping through the muddy woods on foot, arrived at about the same time to find out what was happening at Hogan's camp. However, there wasn't really much to be done. The lodge was a raging bonfire, beyond salvage. Hogan pointed out that it wasn't insured, and that he'd intended to have it pulled down and replaced in the near future, anyway. Everything else in the vicinity of the camp was too sodden after a week of rain to be in the least endangered by flying sparks. The fire fighters stood about until the flames settled down to a sullen

glow. Then they smothered the glow, and the boat and
Pete left. Hogan and Julia had been unable to explain
how the fire got started; but, under the circumstances,
it hardly seemed to matter. If anybody had been surprised to find Julia Allison here, they didn't mention it.
However, there undoubtedly would be a good many
comments made in town.

"Your Pa isn't going to like it," Hogan observed, as
the sounds of the boat engine faded away on the lake.

"Pa will have to learn to like it!" Julia replied, perhaps a trifle grimly. She studied Hogan a moment. "I
thought I was through with you, Hogan!" she said. "But
then I had to come back to find out."

"Find out whether I was batty? Can't blame you.
There were times these weeks when I wondered myself."

Julia shook her head.

"Whether you were batty or not didn't seem the
most important point," she said.

"Then what was?"

She smiled, moved into his arms, snuggled close.
There was a lengthy pause.

"What about your engagement in the city?" Hogan
asked finally.

Julia looked up at him. "I broke it when I knew I was
coming back."

It was still about an hour before dawn. They walked
back to the blackened, twisted mess that had been the
lodge building, and stood staring at it in silence.
Greenface's funeral pyre had been worthy of a Titan.

"Think there might be anything left of it?" Julia asked,
in a low voice.

"After that? I doubt it. Anyway, we won't build again
till spring. By then, there'll be nothing around we
might have to explain, that's for sure. We can winter in
town, if you like."

"One of the cabins here will do fine."

Hogan grinned. "Suits me!" He looked at the ruin
again. "There was nothing very solid about it, you

know. Just a big poisonous mass of jelly from the tropics. Winter would have killed it, anyway. Those red spots I saw on it—it was already beginning to rot. It never really had a chance here."

She glanced at him. "You aren't feeling sorry for the thing?"

"Well, in a way." Hogan kicked a cindered two-by-four apart, and stood there frowning. "It was just a big crazy freak, shooting up all alone in a world where it didn't fit in, and where it could only blunder around and do a lot of damage and die. I wonder how smart it really was and whether it ever understood the fix it was in."

"Quit worrying about it!" Julia ordered.

Hogan grinned down at her. "Okay," he said.

"And kiss me," said Julia.

I'm generally a happy sort of person. I whistle as I walk down the sidewalk. I take pleasure in television sitcoms. I have a great sense of humor.

Well, an enthusiastic sense of humor, at least. Under the right stimulus, I will literally fall off my chair with laughter and roll on the floor. This has happened with some regularity ever since I started watching a TV show called "Topper" when I was eight years old. (At home this isn't a major problem, but it became awkward when I sank out of my theater seat during the opening credits of Monty Python and the Holy Grail.*)*

I mention this, because it isn't a conclusion often drawn by those who've never met me but have read my fiction (of which the story included in this volume is a not-atypical example).

Bob Sheckley became one of my favorite writers as soon as I started buying paperbacks and chanced into his early collections. Not just for his sense of humor. Bob didn't forget he was telling a story, so the characters and their interactions had to be believable even though they were told in a very brief compass. (For example, his first collection, Untouched by Human Hands, *packs thirteen stories into 170 pages.)*

Another facet of early Sheckley humor was that you could never be sure the amusing folks you were reading about would survive the story. Bob was willing to follow the story's logic no matter where it led, and no matter how shocking it was to somebody who'd thought he was reading a different sort of story. Remember the first time you ran into "The Seventh Victim"?

But sometimes that logic led to a very different sort of climax. . . .

HUNTING PROBLEM

Robert Sheckley

It was the last troop meeting before the big Scouter Jamboree, and all the patrols had turned out. Patrol 22—the Soaring Falcon Patrol—was camped in a shady hollow, holding a tentacle pull. The Brave Bison Patrol, number 31, was moving around a little stream. The Bisons were practicing their skill at drinking liquids, and laughing excitedly at the odd sensation.

And the Charging Mirash Patrol, number 19, was waiting for Scouter Drog, who was late as usual.

Drog hurtled down from the ten-thousand-foot level, went solid, and hastily crawled into the circle of scouters. "Gee," he said, "I'm sorry. I didn't realize what time—"

The Patrol Leader glared at him. "You're out of uniform, Drog."

"Sorry, sir," Drog said, hastily extruding a tentacle he had forgotten.

The others giggled. Drog blushed a dim orange. He wished he were invisible.

But it wouldn't be proper right now.

"I will open our meeting with the Scouter Creed," the Patrol Leader said. He cleared his throat. "We, the Young Scouters of planet Elbonai, pledge to perpetuate the skills and virtues of our pioneering ancestors. For that purpose, we Scouters adopt the shape our fore-bears were born to when they conquered the virgin wilderness of Elbonai. We hereby resolve—"

Scouter Drog adjusted his hearing receptors to am-plify the Leader's soft voice. The Creed always thrilled him. It was hard to believe that his ancestors had once been earthbound. Today the Elbonai were aerial beings, maintaining only the minimum of body, fueling by cos-mic radiation at the twenty-thousand-foot level, sensing by direct perception, coming down for sentimental or sacramental purposes. They had come a long way since the Age of Pioneering. The modern world had begun with the Age of Submolecular Control, which was fol-lowed by the present age of Direct Control.

". . . honesty and fair play," the Leader was saying. "And we further resolve to drink liquids, as they did, and to eat solid food, and to increase our skill in their tools and methods."

The invocation completed, the youngsters scattered around the plain. The Patrol Leader came to up to Drog.

"This is the last meeting before the Jamboree," the Leader said.

"I know," Drog said.

"And you are the only second class scouter in the Charging Mirash Patrol. All the others are first class, or at least Junior Pioneers. What will people think about our patrol?"

Drog squirmed uncomfortably. "It isn't entirely my fault," he said. "I know I failed the tests in swimming and bomb making, but those just aren't my skills. It isn't fair to expect me to know everything. Even among the pioneers there were specialists. No one was ex-pected to know all—"

"And just what are your skills?" the Leader interrupted.

"Forest and Mountain Lore," Drog answered eagerly. "Tracking and hunting."

The Leader studied him for a moment. Then he said slowly, "Drog, how would you like one last chance to make first class and win an achievement badge as well?"

"I'd do anything!" Drog cried.

"Very well," the Patrol Leader said. "What is the name of our patrol?"

"The Charging Mirash Patrol."

"And what is a Mirash?"

"A large and ferocious animal," Drog answered promptly. "Once they inhabited large parts of Elbonai, and our ancestors fought many savage battles with them. Now they are extinct."

"Not quite," the Leader said. "A scouter was exploring the woods five hundred miles north of here, coordinates S-233 by 482-W, and he came upon a pride of three Mirash, all bulls, and therefore huntable. I want you, Drog, to track them down, to stalk them, using Forest and Mountain Lore. Then, utilizing only pioneering tools and methods, I want you to bring back the pelt of one Mirash. Do you think you can do it?"

"I know I can, sir!"

"Go at once," the Leader said. "We will fasten the pelt to our flagstaff. We will undoubtedly be commended at the Jamboree."

"Yes, *sir!*" Drog hastily gathered up his equipment, filled his canteen with liquid, packed a lunch of solid food, and set out.

A few minutes later, he had levitated himself to the general area of S-233 by 482-W. It was a wild and romantic country of jagged rocks and scrubby trees, thick underbrush in the valleys, snow on the peaks. Drog looked around, somewhat troubled.

He had told the Patrol Leader a slight untruth.

The fact of the matter was, he wasn't particularly

skilled in Forest and Mountain Lore, hunting or tracking. He wasn't particularly skilled in anything except
dreaming away long hours among the clouds at the
five-thousand-foot level. What if he failed to find a
Mirash? What if the Mirash found him first?

But that couldn't happen, he assured himself. In a
pinch, he could always gestibulize. Who would ever
know?

In another moment he picked up a faint trace of
Mirash scent. And then he saw a slight movement
about twenty yards away, near a curious T-shaped formation of rock.

Was it really going to be this easy? How nice! Quietly
he adopted an appropriate camouflage and edged forward.

The mountain trail became steeper and the sun beat
harshly down. Paxton was sweating, even in his air-
conditioned coverall. And he was heartily sick of being
a good sport.

"Just when are we leaving this place?" he asked.

Herrera slapped him genially on the shoulder. "Don't
you wanna get rich?"

"We're rich already," Paxton said.

"But not rich enough," Herrera told him, his long
brown face creasing into a brilliant grin.

Stellman came up, puffing under the weight of his
testing equipment. He set it carefully on the path and
sat down. "You gentlemen interested in a short breather?"
he asked.

"Why not?" Herrera said. "All the time in the world."
He sat down with his back against a T-shaped formation
of rock.

Stellman lighted a pipe and Herrera found a cigar in
the zippered pocket of his coverall. Paxton watched
them for a while. Then he asked, "Well, when are we
getting off this planet? Or do we set up permanent
residence?"

Herrera just grinned and scratched a light for his cigar.

"Well, how about it?" Paxton shouted.

"Relax, you're outvoted," Stellman said. "We formed this company as three equal partners."

"All using *my* money," Paxton said.

"Of course. That's why we took you in. Herrera had the practical mining experience. I had the theoretical knowledge and a pilot's license. You had the money."

"But we've got plenty of stuff on board now," Paxton said. "The storage compartments are completely filled. Why can't we go to some civilized place now and start spending?"

"Herrera and I don't have your aristocratic attitude toward wealth," Stellman said with exaggerated patience. "Herrera and I have the childish desire to fill every nook and cranny with treasure. Gold nuggets in the fuel tanks, emeralds in the flour cans, diamonds a foot deep on desk. And this is just the place for it. All manner of costly baubles are lying around just begging to be picked up. We want to be disgustingly, abysmally rich, Paxton."

Paxton hadn't been listening. He was staring intently at a point near the edge of the trail. In a low voice, he said, "That tree just moved."

Herrera burst into laughter. "Monsters, I suppose," he sneered.

"Be calm," Stellman said mournfully. "My boy, I am a middle-aged man, overweight and easily frightened. Do you think I'd stay here if there were the slightest danger?"

"There! It moved again!"

"We surveyed this planet three months ago," Stellman said. "We found no intelligent beings, no dangerous animals, no poisonous plants, remember? All we found were woods and mountains and gold and lakes and emeralds and rivers and diamonds. If there were something here, wouldn't it have attacked us long before?"

"I'm telling you I saw it move," Paxton insisted.

Herrera stood up. "This tree?" he asked Paxton.

"Yes. See, it doesn't even look like the others. Different texture—"

In a single synchronized movement, Herrera pulled a Mark II blaster from a side holster and fired three charges into the tree. The tree and all underbrush for ten yards around burst into flame and crumpled.

"All gone now," Herrera said.

Paxton rubbed his jaw. "I heard it scream when you shot it."

"Sure. But it's dead now," Herrera said soothingly. "If anything else moves, you just tell me, I shoot it. Now we find some more little emeralds, huh?"

Paxton and Stellman lifted their packs and followed Herrera up the trail. Stellman said in a low, amused voice, "Direct sort of fellow, isn't he?"

Slowly Drog returned to consciousness. The Mirash's flaming weapon had caught him in camouflage, almost completely unshielded. He still couldn't understand how it had happened. There had been no premonitory fear-scent, no snorting, no snarling, no warning whatsoever. The Mirash had attacked with blind suddenness, without waiting to see if he were friend or foe.

At last Drog understood the nature of the beast he was up against.

He waited until the hoofbeats of the three bull Mirash had faded into the distance. Then, painfully, he tried to extrude a visual receptor. Nothing happened. He had a moment of utter panic. If his central nervous system was damaged, this was the end.

He tried again. This time, a piece of rock slid off him, and he was able to reconstruct.

Quickly he performed an internal scansion. He sighed with relief. It had been a close thing. Instinctively he had quondicated at the flash moment and it had saved his life.

He tried to think of another course of action, but the

shock of that sudden, vicious, unpremeditated assault had driven all Hunting Lore out of his mind. He found that he had absolutely no desire to encounter the savage Mirash again.

Suppose he returned without the stupid hide? He could tell the Patrol Leader that the Mirash were all females, and therefore unhuntable. A Young Scouter's word was honored, so no one would question him, or even check up.

But that would never do. How could he even consider it?

Well, he told himself gloomily, he could resign from the Scouters, put an end to the whole ridiculous business; the campfires, the singing, the games, the comradeship . . .

This would never do, Drog decided, taking himself firmly in hand. He was acting as though the Mirash were antagonists capable of planning against him. But the Mirash were not even intelligent beings. No creature without tentacles had ever developed true intelligence. That was Etlib's Law, and it had never been disputed.

In a battle between intelligence and instinctive cunning, intelligence always won. It had to. All he had to do was figure out how.

Drog began to track the Mirash again, following their odor. What colonial weapon should he use? A small atomic bomb? No, that would more than likely ruin the hide.

He stopped suddenly and laughed. It was really very simple, when one applied oneself. Why should he come into direct and dangerous contact with the Mirash? The time had come to use his brain, his understanding of animal psychology, his knowledge of Lures and Snares.

Instead of tracking the Mirash, he would go to their den.

And there he would set a trap.

*   *   *

Their temporary camp was in a cave, and by the time they arrived there it was sunset. Every crag and pinnacle of rock threw a precise and sharp-edged shadow. The ship lay five miles below them on the valley floor, its metallic hide glistening red and silver. In their packs were a dozen emeralds, small, but of an excellent color.

At an hour like this, Paxton thought of a small Ohio town, a soda fountain, a girl with bright hair. Herrera smiled to himself, contemplating certain gaudy ways of spending a million dollars before settling down to the serious business of ranching. And Stellman was already phrasing his Ph.D. thesis on extraterrestrial mineral deposits.

They were all in a pleasant, relaxed mood. Paxton had recovered completely from his earlier attack of nerves. Now he wished an alien monster *would* show up—a green one, by preference—chasing a lovely, scantily clad woman.

"Home again," Stellman said as they approached the entrance of the cave. "Want beef stew tonight?" It was his turn to cook.

"With onions," Paxton said, starting into the cave. He jumped back abruptly. "What's that?"

A few feet from the mouth of the cave was a small roast beef, still steaming hot, four large diamonds, and a bottle of whiskey.

"That's odd," Stellman said. "And a trifle unnerving."

Paxton bent down to examine a diamond. Herrera pulled him back.

"Might be booby-trapped."

"There aren't any wires," Paxton said.

Herrera stared at the roast beef, the diamonds, the bottle of whiskey. He looked very unhappy.

"I don't trust this," he said.

"Maybe there are natives here," Stellman said. "Very timid ones. This might be their goodwill offering."

"Sure," Herrera said. "They sent to Terra for a bottle of Old Space Ranger just for us."

"What are we going to do?" Paxton asked.

"Stand clear," Herrera said. "Move 'way back." He broke off a long branch from a nearby tree and poked gingerly at the diamonds.

"Nothing's happening," Paxton said.

The long grass Herrera was standing on whipped tightly around his ankles. The ground beneath him surged, broke into a neat disc fifteen feet in diameter and, trailing root-ends, began to lift itself into the air. Herrera tried to jump free, but the grass held him like a thousand green tentacles.

"Hang on!" Paxton yelled idiotically, rushed forward and grabbed a corner of the rising disc of earth. It dipped steeply, stopped for a moment, and began to rise again. By then Herrera had his knife out, and was slashing the grass around his ankles. Stellman came unfrozen when he saw Paxton rising past his head.

Stellman seized him by the ankles, arresting the flight of the disc once more. Herrera wrenched one foot free and threw himself over the edge. The other ankle was held for a moment, then the tough grass parted under his weight. He dropped head-first to the ground, at the last moment ducking his head and landing on his shoulders. Paxton let go of the disc and fell, landing on Stellman's stomach.

The disc of earth, with its cargo of roast beef, whiskey and diamonds, continued to rise until it was out of sight.

The sun had set. Without speaking, the three men entered their cave, blasters drawn. They built a roaring fire at the mouth and moved back into the cave's interior.

"We'll guard in shifts tonight," Herrera said.

Paxton and Stellman nodded.

Herrera said, "I think you're right, Paxton. We've stayed here long enough."

"Too long," Paxton said.

Herrera shrugged his shoulders. "As soon as it's light, we return to the ship and get out of here."

"If," Stellman said, "we are able to reach the ship."

*   *   *

Drog was quite discouraged.

With a winking heart he had watched the premature springing of his trap, the struggle, and the escape of the Mirash. It had been such a splendid Mirash, too. The biggest of the three!

He knew now what he had done wrong. In his eagerness, he had overbaited his trap. Just the minerals would have been sufficient, for Mirash were notoriously mineral-tropic. But no, he had to improve on pioneer methods, he had to use food stimuli as well. No wonder they had reacted suspiciously, with their senses so overburdened.

Now they were enraged, alert, and decidedly dangerous.

And a thoroughly aroused Mirash was one of the most fearsome sights in the Galaxy.

Drog felt very much alone as Elbonai's twin moons rose in the western sky. He could see the Mirash campfire blazing in the mouth of their cave. And by direct perception he could see the Mirash crouched within, every sense alert, weapons ready.

Was a Mirash hide really worth all this trouble?

Drog decided that he would much rather be floating at the five-thousand-foot level, sculpturing cloud formations and dreaming. He wanted to sop up radiation instead of eating nasty old solid food. And what use was all this hunting and trapping, anyhow? Worthless skills that his people had outgrown.

For a moment he almost had himself convinced. And then, in a flash of pure perception, he understood what it was all about.

True, the Elbonaians had outgrown their competition, developed past all danger of competition. But the Universe was wide, and capable of many surprises. Who could foresee what would come, what new dangers the race might have to face? And how could they meet them if the hunting instinct was lost?

No, the old ways had to be preserved, to serve as

patterns; as reminders that peaceable, intelligent life was an unstable entity in an unfriendly Universe.

He was going to get that Mirash hide, or die trying!

The most important thing was to get them out of that cave. Now his hunting knowledge had returned to him.

Quickly, skillfully, he shaped a Mirash horn.

"Did you hear that?" Paxton asked.

"I thought I heard something," Stellman said, and they all listened intently.

The sound came again. It was a voice crying. "Oh, help, help me!"

"It's a girl!" Paxton jumped to his feet.

"It *sounds* like a girl," Stellman said.

"Please, help me," the girl's voice wailed. "I can't hold out much longer. Is there anyone who can help me?"

Blood rushed to Paxton's face. In a flash he saw her, small, exquisite, standing beside her wrecked sportsspacer (what a fool-hardy trip it had been!) with monsters, green and slimy, closing in on her. And then *he* arrived, a foul alien beast.

Paxton picked up a spare blaster. "I'm going out there," he said coolly.

"Sit down, you moron!" Herrera ordered.

"But you heard her, didn't you?"

"That can't be a girl," Herrera said. "What would a girl be doing on this planet?"

"I'm going to find out," Paxton said, brandishing two blasters. "Maybe a spaceliner crashed, or she could have been out joyriding, and—"

"Siddown!" Herrera yelled.

"He's right," Stellman tried to reason with Paxton. "Even if a girl *is* out there, which I doubt, there's nothing we can do."

"Oh, help, help, it's coming after me!" the girl's voice screamed.

"Get out of my way," Paxton said, his voice low and dangerous.

"You're really going?" Herrera asked incredulously.

"Yes! Are you going to stop me?"

"Go ahead." Herrera gestured at the entrance of the cave.

"We can't let him!" Stellman gasped.

"Why not? His funeral," Herrera said lazily.

"Don't worry about me," Paxton said. "I'll be back in fifteen minutes—with her!" He turned on his heel and started toward the entrance. Herrera leaned forward and, with considerable precision, clubbed Paxton behind the ear with a stick of firewood. Stellman caught him as he fell.

They stretched Paxton out in the rear of the cave and returned to their vigil. The lady in distress moaned and pleaded for the next five hours. Much too long, as Paxton had to agree, even for a movie serial.

A gloomy, rain-splattered daybreak found Drog still camped a hundred yards from the cave. He saw the Mirash emerge in a tight group, weapons ready, eyes watching warily for any movement.

Why had the Mirash horn failed? The Scouter Manual said it was an infallible means of attracting the bull Mirash. But perhaps this wasn't mating season.

They were moving in the direction of a metallic ovoid which Drog recognized as a primitive spatial conveyance. It was crude, but once inside it the Mirash were safe from him.

He could simply trevest them, and that would end it. But it wouldn't be very humane. Above all, the ancient Elbonaians had been gentle and merciful, and a Young Scouter tried to be like them. Besides, trevestment wasn't a true pioneering method.

That left ilitrocy. It was the oldest trick in the book, and he'd have to get close to work it. But he had nothing to lose.

And luckily, climatic conditions were perfect for it.

* * *

It started as a thin groundmist. But, as the watery sun climbed the gray sky, fog began forming.

Herrera cursed angrily as it grew more dense. "Keep close together now. Of all the luck!"

Soon they were walking with their hands on each others' shoulders, blasters ready, peering into the impenetrable fog.

"Herrera?"

"Yeah?"

"Are you sure we're going in the right direction?"

"Sure. I took a compass course before the fog closed in."

"Suppose your compass is off?"

"Don't even think about it."

They walked on, picking their way carefully over the rockstrewn ground.

"I think I see the ship," Paxton said.

"No, not yet," Herrera said.

Stellman stumbled over a rock, dropped his blaster, picked it up again and fumbled around for Herrera's shoulder. He found it and walked on.

"I think we're almost there," Herrera said.

"I sure hope so," Paxton said. "I've had enough."

"Think your girl friend's waiting for you at the ship?"

"Don't rub it in."

"Okay," Herrera said. "Hey, Stellman, you better grab hold of my shoulder again. No sense getting separated."

"I am holding your shoulder," Stellman said.

"You're not."

"I am, I tell you!"

"Look, I guess I know if someone's holding my shoulder or not."

"Am I holding your shoulder, Paxton?"

"No," Paxton said.

"That's bad," Stellman said, very slowly. "That's bad, indeed."

"Why?"

"Because I'm definitely holding *some*one's shoulder."

Herrera yelled, "Get down, get down quick, give me room to shoot!" But it was too late. A sweet-sour odor was in the air. Stellman and Paxton smelled it and collapsed. Herrera ran forward blindly, trying to hold his breath. He stumbled and fell over a rock, tried to get back on his feet—

And everything went black.

The fog lifted suddenly and Drog was standing alone, smiling triumphantly. He pulled out a long-bladed skinning knife and bent over the nearest Mirash.

The spaceship hurtled toward Terra at a velocity which threatened momentarily to burn out the overdrive. Herrera, hunched over the controls, finally regained his self-control and cut the speed down to normal. His usually tan face was still ashen, and his hands shook on the instruments.

Stellman came in from the bunkroom and flopped wearily in the co-pilot's seat.

"How's Paxton?" Herrera asked.

"I dosed him with Drona-3," Stellman said. "He's going to be all right."

"He's a good kid," Herrera said.

"It's just shock, for the most part," Stellman said. "When he comes to, I'm going to put him to work counting diamonds. Counting diamonds is the best of therapies, I understand."

Herrera grinned, and his face began to regain its normal color. "I feel like doing a little diamond-counting myself, now that it's all turned out okay." Then his long face became serious. "But I ask you, Stellman, who could figure it? I still don't understand!"

The Scouter Jamboree was a glorious spectacle. The Soaring Falcon Patrol, number 22, gave a short pantomime showing the clearing of the land on Elbonai.

The Brave Bisons, number 31, were in full pioneer dress.

And at the head of Patrol 19, the Charging Mirash Patrol, was Drog, a first-class Scouter now, wearing a glittering achievement badge. He was carrying the Patrol flag—the position of honor—and everyone cheered to see it.

Because waving proudly from the flagpole was the firm, fine-textured, characteristic skin of an adult Mirash, its zippers, tubes, gauges, buttons and holsters flashing merrily in the sunshine.

I was in Viet-Nam—more precisely, Viet-Nam and Cambodia—for less than a year. I'm not a hero, and nothing bad happened to me.

After I got back to the World and had a chance to think about things, I decided that the closest I'd come to dying in Nam had nothing to do with enemy action. We were on a Medcap. I have no idea what the acronym actually means, but medical and civil affairs patrol adequately describes what was involved.

Basically, a few armored vehicles from the squadron's headquarters troop drove into a friendly village. They carried the unit medic; the civil affairs officer (S-5, for those of you who care); and a couple of interrogators like me to talk informally with the villagers about the local situation while the medic dispensed pills and changed dressings.

I don't know that Medcaps did an enormous amount of good, either in the military sense (bringing first warning of planned enemy attacks, say) or for the villagers with real medical problems. It bothers me to remember the man with elephantiasis of the scrotum, waiting patiently in line for what help the medic could give him.

But the Medcaps weren't a bad thing. We didn't cause his elephantiasis, and maybe the changed dressings showed a few of the villagers that at least our intentions were good.

They had enough evidence of problems with our results. A conversation with a village headman sticks in my mind, though I couldn't tell you whether it occurred that afternoon or another one. We were supposed to get an idea of the community's economic base, so I asked what crops his village grew.

"Peanuts," he said. "All peanuts."

I don't know exactly what I'd expected, but it wasn't peanuts. "Why do you grow peanuts?" I asked.

"Well, three years ago the planes came over and sprayed all the rubber trees. They died, so we put

281

in peanuts because it takes too long to grow rubber trees."

We left the village and drove back toward the fire-base. We'd waited too long; it started to rain long before we got to the road. Big drops, then a real cloudburst. The dust was powdery and white when we started, but it turned into glistening, charcoal-gray mud within a minute.

Lightning started to hit all around us.

I was riding on a Zippo, an armored personnel carrier converted into a mechanized flame-thrower. The driver's hatch was in front. Behind him was the track commander's cupola, mounting a machinegun and the short, broad nozzle of the flame-thrower. I sat on the back deck, over the two hundred gallons of napalm filling the vehicle's cargo compartment. Ten feet over my head waved the whip antennas for the radios.

We moved onto the dike between two paddies. It was raining as hard as I've ever seen it come down. Across the field to the left was a line of low trees, probably on another dike. They were barely visible through the downpour. Lightning struck one of the trees, blasting it in a sizzling yellow flash.

Because of the antennas and the height of the Zippo itself, we were taller than any of those trees in the near distance. I expected to die any moment. If the lightning didn't do the job directly, the explosion of two hundred gallons of gasoline and plasticizer certainly would.

It didn't happen, of course. The edge of the storm moved off; the lightning bolts grew more distant. I'd gotten wet and spattered with mud thrown up by the tracks. Don't mean nothin'.

It didn't seem like a big thing afterwards, either, but it was only very recently that I figured out why.

Every waking minute of my tour in Nam, I expected to die. You can't live like that and stay sane. I wasn't sane. I did the jobs they told me to do, and I got back to the World. That one particular moment, I really was very near death, but I'd been living in that moment for months already and for months to come.

Don't mean nothin'.

The character in "The Hunting Ground" isn't me. He lives in the house in Durham where we rented an apartment after I got back. The stump in the yard is the one I sat on, and the hydrangeas are the ones that grew beside the house next door; but Lorne isn't me.

I wouldn't say there was nothing of me in him, though.

THE HUNTING GROUND

David Drake

The patrol car's tires hissed on the warm asphalt as it pulled to the curb beside Lorne. "What you up to, snake?" asked the square-bodied policeman. The car's rumbling idle and the whirr of its air conditioner through the open window filled the evening.

Lorne smiled and nodded the lighted tip of his cigarette. "Sitting on a stump in my yard, watching cops park on the wrong side of the street. What're you up to, Ben?"

Instead of answering, the policeman looked hard at his friend. They were both in their late twenties; the man in the car stocky and dark with a close-cropped moustache; Lorne slender, his hair sand-colored and falling across his neck brace. "Hurting, snake?" Ben asked softly.

"Shit, four years is enough to get used to anything," the thinner man said. Though Lorne's eyes were on the chime tower of the abandoned Baptist church a block down Rankin Street, his mind was lost in the far past. "You know, some nights I sit out here for a while instead of going to bed."

Three cars in quick succession threw waves of light and sound against the rows of aging houses. One blinked its high beams at the patrol car briefly, blindingly. "Bastard," Ben grumbled without real anger. "Well, back to the war against crime." His smile quirked. "Better than the last war they had us fighting, hey?"

Lorne finished his cigarette with a long drag. "Hell, I don't know, sarge. How many jobs give you full pension after two years?"

"See you, snake."

"See you, sarge."

The big cruiser snarled as Ben pulled back into the traffic lane and turned at the first corner. The city was on a system of neighborhood police patrols, an attempt to avoid the anonymous patrolling that turned each car into a miniature search and destroy mission. The first night he sat on the stump beside his apartment, Lorne had sworn in surprise to see that the face peering from the curious patrol car was that of Ben Gresham, his squad leader during the ten months and nineteen days he had carried an M60 in War Zone C.

And that was the only past remaining to Lorne.

The back door of Jenkins' house banged shut on its spring. A few moments later heavy boots began scratching up the gravel of the common drive. Lorne's seat was an oak stump, three feet in diameter. Instead of trying to turn his head, he shifted his whole body around on the wood. Jenkins, a plumpish, half-bald man in his late sixties, lifted a pair of canned Budweisers. "Must get thirsty out here, warm as it is."

"It's always thirsty enough to drink good beer," Lorne smiled. "I'll share my stump with you." They sipped for a time without speaking. Mrs. Purefoy, Jenkins' widowed sister and a matronly Baptist, kept house for him. Lorne gathered that while she did not forbid her brother to drink an occasional beer, neither did she provide an encouragingly social atmosphere.

"I've seen you out here at 3 A.M.," the older man said. "What'll you do when the weather turns cold?"

"Freeze my butt for a while," Lorne answered. He gestured his beer towards his dark apartment on the second floor of a house much like Jenkins'. "Sit up there with the light on. Hell, there's lots of VA hospitals, I've *been* in lots of them. If North Carolina isn't warm enough, maybe they'd find me one in Florida." He took another swallow and said, "I just sleep better in the daytime, is all. Too many ghosts around at night."

Jenkins turned quickly to make sure of the smile on the younger man's face. It flashed at his motion. "Not quite that sort of ghost," Lorne explained. "The ones I bring with me . . ." And he kept his smile despite the sizzle of faces in the white fire sudden in his mind. The noise of popping, boiling flesh faded and he went on, "There was something weird going on last night, though—" he glanced at his big Japanese wristwatch— "well, damn early this morning."

"A Hallowe'en ghost with a white sheet?" Jenkins suggested.

"Umm, no, down at the church," said Lorne, fumbling his cigarettes out. Jenkins shrugged refusal and the dart of butane flame ignited only one. "The tower there was—I don't know, I looked at it and it seemed to be vibrating. No sound, though, and then a big red flash without any sound either. I thought it'd caught fire, but it was just a flash and everything was back to normal. Funny. You know how you hold your fingers over a flashlight and it comes through, kind of? Well, the flash was like that, only through a stone wall."

"I never saw anything like that," Jenkins agreed. "Old church doesn't seem the worse for it, though. It'll be ready to fall down itself before the courts get all settled about who owns it, you know."

"Umm?"

"Fellowship Baptist built a new church half a mile north of here, more parking and anyhow, it was going to cost more to repair that old firetrap than it would to build a new one." Jenkins grinned. "Mable hasn't missed a Sunday in forty years, so I heard all about it. The city bought the old lot for a boys' club or some such fool thing—I want to spit every time I think of my property taxes, I do—but it turns out the Rankins, that's who the street's named after too, they'd given the land way back before the Kaiser's War. Damn if some of them weren't still around to sue to get the lot back if it wasn't going to be a church any more. So that was last year, and it's like to be a few more before anybody puts money into tearing the old place down."

"From the way it's boarded up and padlocked, I figured it must have been a reflection I saw," Lorne admitted. "But it looked funny enough," he added sheepishly, "that I took a walk down there last night."

Jenkins shrugged and stood up. He had the fisherman's trick of dropping the pull tab into his beer before drinking any. Now it rattled in the bottom. "Well," he said, picking up Lorne's can as well, "it's bedtime for me, I suppose. You better get yourself off soon or the bugs'll carry you away."

"Thanks for the beer and the company," Lorne said. "One of these nights I'll bring down an ice chest and we'll really tie one on."

Lorne's ears followed the old man back, the sound of his boots friendly and even in the warm April darkness. A touch of breeze caught the wisteria hedge across the street and spread its sweetness, diluted, over Lorne. He ground out his cigarette and sat quietly, letting the vines breathe on him. Jenkins' garbage can scrunched open and one of the empties echoed into it. The other did not fall. "What the hell?" Lorne wondered aloud. But there was something about the night, despite its urban innocence, that brought up memories from past years more strongly than ever before. In a little while Lorne began walking. He was still walking when dawn washed the fiery pictures from his mind and he returned to his apartment to find three police cars parked in the street.

The two other tenants stored their cars in the side yard of the apartment house. Lorne had stepped between them when he heard a woman scream, "That's him! Don't let him get away!"

Lorne turned. White-haired Mrs. Purefoy and a pair of uniformed policeman faced him from the porch of Jenkins' house. The younger man had his revolver half drawn. A third uniformed man, Ben, stepped quickly around from the back of the house. "I'm not going anywhere but to bed," Lorne said, spreading his empty hands. He began walking towards the others. "Look, what's the matter?"

The oldest, heaviest of the policemen took the porch steps in a leap and approached Lorne at a barely-restrained trot. He had major's pips on his shoulder straps. "Where have you been, snake?" Ben asked, but the major was between them instantly, growling, "I'll handle this, Gresham. Mr. Charles Lorne?"

"Yes," Lorne whispered. His body flashed hot, as though the fat policeman were a fire, a towering sheet of orange rippling with the speckles of tracers cooking off . . .

". . . and at any time during the questioning you may withdraw your consent and thereafter remain silent. Do you understand, Mr. Lorne?"

"Yes."

"Did you see Mr. Jenkins tonight?"

"Uh-huh. He came out—when did you leave me, Ben? 10:30?" Lorne paused to light another cigarette. His flame wavered like the blade of a kris. "We each drank a beer, shot the bull. That's all. What happened?"

"Where did you last see Mr. Jenkins?"

Lorne gestured. "I was on the stump. He walked around the back of the house—his house. I guess I could see him. Anyway, I heard him throw the cans in the trash and . . . that's all."

"Both cans?" Ben broke in despite his commander's scowl.

"No, you're right—just one. And I didn't hear the door close. It's got a spring that slams it like a one-oh-five going off, usually. Look, what happened?"

There was a pause. Ben tugged at a corner of his moustache. Low sunlight sprayed Lorne through the trees. Standing, he looked taller than his six feet, a knobbly staff of a man in wheat jeans and a green-dyed T-shirt. The shirt had begun to disintegrate in the years since it was issued to him on the way to the war zone. The brace was baby-flesh pink. It made him look incongruously bull-necked, alien.

"He could have changed clothes," suggested the young patrolman. He had holstered his weapon but continued to toy with the butt.

"He didn't," Ben snapped, the signs of his temper obvious to Lorne if not to the other policemen. "He's wearing now what he had on when I left him."

"We'll take him around back," the major suddenly decided. In convoy, Ben and the other, nervous, patrolman to either side of Lorne and the major bringing up the rear, they crossed into Jenkins' yard following the steep downslope. Mrs. Purefoy stared from the porch. Beneath her a hydrangea bush graded its blooms red on the left, blue on the right, with the carefully-tended acidity of the soil. It was a mirror for her face, ruddy towards the sun and grey with fear in shadow.

"What's the problem?" Lorne wondered aloud as he viewed the back of the house. The trash can was open but upright, its lid lying on the smooth lawn beside it. Nearby was one of the Budweiser empties. The other lay alone on the bottom of the trash can. There was no sign of Jenkins himself.

Ben's square hand indicated an arc of spatters six to eight feet high, black against the white siding. "They promised us a lab team but hell, it's blood, snake. You and me've seen enough to recognize it. Mrs. Purefoy got up at four, didn't find her brother. I saw this when I checked and . . ." He let his voice trail off.

"No body?" Lorne asked. He had lighted a fresh cigarette. The gushing flames surrounded him.

"No."

"And Jenkins weighs what? 220?" He laughed, a sound as thin as his wrists. "You'd play hell proving a man with a broken neck ran off with him, wouldn't you?"

"Broke? Sure, we'll believe that!" gibed the nervous patrolman.

"You'll believe *me*, meatball!" Ben snarled. "He broke it and he carried me out of a fucking burning shithook while our ammo cooked off. And by God—"

"Easy, sarge," Lorne said quietly. "If anybody needs shooting, I'll borrow a gun and do it myself."

The major flashed his scowl from one man to the other. His sudden uncertainty was as obvious as the flag pin in his lapel: Lorne was now a veteran, not an aging hippie.

"I'm an outpatient at the VA hospital," Lorne said, seeing his chance to damp the fire. "Something's fucking up some nerves and they're trying to do something about it there. Wish to hell they'd do it soon."

"Gresham," the major said, motioning Ben aside for a low-voiced exchange. The third policeman had gone red when Ben snapped at him. Now he was white, realizing his mortality for the first time in his twenty-two years.

Lorne grinned at him. "Hang loose, turtle. Neither Ben or me ever killed anybody who didn't need it worse than you do."

The boy began to tremble.

"Mr. Lorne," the major said, his tone judicious but not hostile, "we'll be getting in touch with you later. And if you recall anything, anything at all that may have bearing on Mr. Jenkins' disappearance, call us at once."

Lorne's hands nodded agreement. Ben winked as the lab van arrived, then turned away with the others.

Lorne's pain was less than usual, but his dreams awakened him in a sweat each time he dropped off to sleep. When at last he switched on the radio, the headline news was that three people besides Jenkins had disappeared during the night, all of them within five blocks of Lorne's apartment.

The air was very close, muffling the brilliance of the stars. It was Friday night and the roar of southbound traffic sounded from Donovan Avenue a block to the east. The three north-bound lanes of Jones Street, the next one west of Rankin, were not yet as clotted with cars as they would be later at night, but headlights there were nervously darting through the houses and trees whenever Lorne turned on his stump to look. Rankin Street lay quietly between, lighted at alternate blocks by blue globes of mercury vapor. It was narrow, so that cars could not pass those parked along the curb without slowing, easing; a placid island surrounded by modern pressures.

But no one had disappeared to the east of Donovan or the west of Jones.

Lorne stubbed out his cigarette in the punky wood of the stump. It was riddled with termites and sometimes he pictured them, scrabbling through the darkness. He hated insects, hated especially the grubs and hidden things, the corpse-white termites . . . but he sat on the stump above them. A perversely objective part of Lorne's mind knew that if he could have sat in the heart of a furnace like the companions of Daniel, he would have done so.

From the blocky shade of the porch next door came the creak of springs: Mrs. Purefoy, shifting her weight on the cushions of the wing-back chair. In the early evening Lorne had caught her face staring at a parlor window, her muscles flat as wax. As the deeper darkness blurred and pooled, she had slipped out into its cover. Lorne felt her burning eyes, knowing that she would never forgive him for her brother's disappearance, not if it were proven that Jenkins had left by his own decision. Lorne had always been a sinner to her. Innocence would not change that.

Another cigarette. Someone was watching. A passing car threw Lorne's angled shadow forward and across Jenkins' house. Lorne's guts clenched and his fingers crushed the unlit cigarette. *Light. Twelve men in a rice paddy when the captured flare bursts above them. The pop-pop-pop of a gun far off, and the splashes columning around Lt. Burnes—*

"Christ!" Lorne shouted, standing with an immediacy that laced pain through his body. Something was terribly wrong in the night. The lights brought back memories, but they quenched the real threat that hid in the darkness. Lorne knew what he was feeling, *knew* that any instant a brown face would peer out of a spider hole behind at AK-47 or a mine would rip steel pellets down the trail . . .

He stopped, forcing himself to sit down again. If it was his time, there was nothing he could do about it. A fresh cigarette fitted between his lips automatically and the needle-bright lighter focused his eyes.

And the watcher was gone.

Something had poised to kill Lorne, and had then passed on without striking. It was as unnatural as if a wall collapsing on him had separated in mid-air to leave him unharmed. Lorne's arms were trembling, his cigarette tip an orange blur. When Ben's cruiser pulled in beside him, Lorne was at first unable to answer the other man's, "Hey, snake."

"Jesus, sarge," Lorne whispered, smoke spurting from his mouth and nostrils. "There's somebody out here and he's a *bad* fucker."

Carrier noise blatted before the car radio rapped a series of numbers and street names. Ben knuckled his moustache until he was sure his own cruiser was not mentioned. "Yeah, he's a bad one. Another one gone tonight, a little girl from three blocks down. Went to the store to trade six empties and a dime on a Coke. Christ, I *saw* her two hours ago, snake. The bottles we found, the kid we didn't . . . Seen any little girls?"

There was an upright shadow in front of Ben's radio: a riot gun, clipped to the dashboard. "Haven't seen anything but cars, sarge. Lots of police cars."

"They've got an extra ten men on," Ben agreed with a nod. "We went over the old Baptist church a few minutes ago. Great TAC Squad work. Nothing. Damn locks were rusted shut."

"Think the Baptists've taken up with baby sacrifice?" Lorne chuckled.

"Shit, there's five bodies somewhere. If the bastard's loading them in the back of a truck, you'd think he'd spread his pickups over a bit more of an area, wouldn't you?"

"Look, baby, anybody who packed Jenkins around on his back—I sure don't want to meet him."

"Don't guess Jenkins did either," Ben grunted. "Or the others."

"PD to D-5," the radio interrupted.

Ben keyed his microphone. "Go ahead."

"10-25 Lt. Cooper at Rankin and Duke."

"10-4,10-76," Ben replied, starting to return the mike to its holder.

"D-5, acknowledge," the receiver ordered testily.

"Goddam fucker!" Ben snarled, banging the instrument down. "Sends just about half the fucking time!"

"Keep a low profile, sarge," Lorne murmured, but even had he screamed his words would have been lost in the boom of exhaust as Ben cramped the car around in the street, the left wheels bumping over the far curb. Then the accelerator flattened and the big car shot towards the rendezvous.

In Vietnam, Lorne had kept his death wish under control during shelling by digging in and keeping his head down. Now he stood and went inside to his room.

After a time, he slept. If his dreams were bright and tortured, then they always were . . .

"Sure, you knew Jackson," Ben explained, the poom-poom-poom of his engine a living thing in the night. "He's the blond shit who . . . didn't believe you'd broken your neck. Yesterday morning."

"Small loss, then," Lorne grinned. "But you watch your own ass, hear? If there's nobody out but cops, there's going to be more cops than just Jackson disappearing."

"Cops and damned fools," Ben grumbled. "When I didn't see you out here on my first pass, I thought maybe you'd gotten sense enough to stay inside."

"I was going to. Decided . . . oh, hell. What's the box score now?"

"Seven gone. Seven for sure," the patrolman corrected himself. "One got grabbed in the time he took to walk from his girl's front porch back to his car. That bastard's lucky, but he's crazy as hell if he thinks he'll stay that lucky."

"He's crazy as hell," Lorne agreed. A spring whispered from Jenkins' porch and Lorne bobbed the tip of his cigarette at the noise. "She's not doing so good either. All last night she was staring at me, and now she's at it again."

"Christ," Ben muttered. "Yeah, Major Hooseman talked to her this morning. You're about the baddest man ever, leading po' George into smoking and drinking and late hours before you killed him."

"Never did get him to smoke," Lorne said, lighting Ben's cigarette and another for himself. "Say, did Jackson smoke?"

"Huh? No." Ben frowned, staring at the closed passenger-side windows and their reflections of his instruments. "Yeah, come to think, he did. But never in uniform, he had some sort of thing about that."

"He sheered off last night when I lit a cigarette,"

Lorne said. "No, not Jackson—the other one. I just
wondered . . ."

"You saw him?" Ben's voice was suddenly sharp, the
hunter scenting prey.

Lorne shook his head. "I just felt him. But he was
there, baby."

"Just like before they shot us down," the policeman
said quietly. "You squeezing my arm and shouting over
the damn engines 'They're waiting for us, they're waiting for us!' And not a fucking thing I could do—I didn't
order the assault and the Captain sure wasn't going to
call it off because my machine-gunner said to. But you
were right, snake."

"The flames . . ." Lorne whispered, his eyes unfocused.

"And you're a dumb bastard to have done it, but you
carried me out of them. It never helped us a bit that
you knew when the shit was about to hit the fan. But
you're a damn good man to have along when it does."

Lorne's muscles trembled with memory. Then he
stood and laughed into the night. "You know, sarge, in
twenty-seven years I've only found one job I was any
good at. I didn't much like that one, and anyhow—the
world doesn't seem to need killers."

"They'll always need us, snake," Ben said quietly.
"Sometimes they won't admit it." Then, "Well, I think
I'll waste some more gas."

"Sarge—" The word hung in the empty darkness.
There was engine noise and the tires hissing in the near
distance and—nothing else. "Sarge, Mrs. Purefoy was
on her porch a minute ago and she didn't go inside. But
she's not there now."

Ben's five-cell flashlight slid its narrow beam across
the porch: the glider, the wing-back chair. On the far
railing, a row of potted violets with a gap for the one
now spilled on the boards as if by someone vaulting the
rail but dragging one heel . . .

"Didn't hear it fall," the policeman muttered, clack-
ing open the car door. The dome light spilled a startling

yellow pool across the two men. As it did so, white motion trembled half a block down Rankin Street.

"Fucker!" Ben said. "He couldn't jump across the street, he threw something so it flashed." Ben was back in the car.

Lorne squinted, furious at being blinded at the critical instant. "Sarge, I'll swear to God he headed for the church." Lorne strode stiffly around the front of the vehicle and got in on the passenger side.

"Mother-*fuck!*" the stocky policeman snarled, dropping the microphone that had three times failed to get him a response. He reached for the gear lever, looked suddenly at Lorne as the slender man unclipped the shotgun. "Where d'ye think *you're* going?"

"With you."

Ben slipped the transmission into drive and hung a shrieking U-turn in the empty street. "The first one's birdshot, the next four are double-ought buck," he said flatly.

Lorne jacked the slide twice, chambering the first round and then shucking it out the ejector. It gleamed palely in the instrument light. "Don't think we're going after birds," he explained.

Ben twisted across the street and bounced over the driveway cut. The car slammed to a halt in the small lot behind and shielded by the bulk of the old church. It was a high, narrow building with two levels of boarded windows the length of the east and west sides; the square tower stood at the south end. At some time after its construction, the church had been faced with artificial stone. It was dingy, a grey mass in the night with a darkness about it that the night alone did not explain.

Ben slid out of the car. His flash touched the small door to the right of the tower. "Nothing wrong with the padlock," Lorne said. It was a formidable one, set in a patinated hasp to close the church against vandals and derelicts.

"They were all locked tight yesterday, too," the patrolman said. "He could still be getting in one of those windows. We'll see." He turned to the trunk of the car and opened it, holding his flashlight in the crook of his arm so his right hand could be free for his drawn revolver.

Lorne's quick eyes scanned the wall above them. He bent back at the waist instead of tilting his head alone. "Got the key?" he asked.

The stocky man chuckled, raising a pair of folding shovels, army surplus entrenching tools. "Keep that corn-sheller ready," he directed, holstering his own weapon. He locked the blade of one shovel at 90° to the shaft and set it on top of the padlock. The other, still folded, cracked loudly against the head of the first and popped the lock open neatly. "Field expedients, snake," Ben laughed. "If we don't find anything, we can just shut the place up again and nobody will know the difference."

He tossed the shovels aside and swung open the door. The air that puffed out had the expected mustiness of a long-closed structure with a sweetish overtone that neither man could have identified. Lorne glanced around the outside once more, then followed the patrolman within. The flames in his mind were very close.

"Looks about like it did last night," Ben said.

"And last year, I'd guess." The wavering oval of the flashlight picked over the floor. The hardwood was warping, pocked at frequent intervals by holes.

"They unbolted the old pews when they moved," Ben explained. "Took the stained glass too, since the place was going to be torn down."

The nave was a single narrow room running from the chancel in the north to the tower which had held the organ pipes and, above, the chimes. The main entrance was by a side aisle, through double doors in the middle of the west wall. The interior looked a gutted ruin.

"You checked the whole building?" Lorne asked. The pulpit had been ripped away. The chancel rail remained though half-splintered, apparently to pass the organ and altar. Fragments of wood, crumpled boxes, and glass littered the big room.

"The main part. We didn't have the key to the tower and the major didn't want to bust in." Ben took another step into the nave and kicked at a stack of old bulletins.

White heat, white fire— "Ben, did you check the ceiling when you were here last night?"

"Huh?" The narrow Gothic vault was blackness forty feet above the ground. Ben's flashlight knifed upward across painted plaster to the ribbed and paneled ceiling that sloped to the main beam. And— "Jesus"

A large cocoon was tight against the roof peak. It shimmered palely azure, but the powerful light thrust through to the human outline within. Long shadows quivered on the wood, magnifying the trembling of the policeman's wrist as the beam moved from the cocoon to another beside it, to the third—

"Seven of the fuckers!" Ben cried, taking another step and slashing the light to the near end of the room where the south wall closed the inverted V of the ceiling. Above the door to the tower was the baize screen of the pipe loft. The cloth fluttered behind Mrs. Purefoy, who stood stiffly upright twenty feet in the air. Her face was locked in horror, framed by her tousled white hair. Both arms were slightly extended but were stone-rigid within the lace-fringed sleeves of her dress.

"She—" Lorne began, but as he spoke and Ben's hand fell to the butt of his revolver, Mrs. Purefoy began to fall, tilting a little in a rustle of skirts. Beneath the crumpled edge of the baize curtain, spiked on the beam of Ben's flashlight, gleamed the head and foreclaws of what had been clutching the woman.

The eyes glared like six-inch opals, fierce and hot in a dead white exoskeleton. The foreclaws clicked sideways. As though they had cocked a spring, the whole flat torso shot down at Ben.

An inch long and scuttling under a rock it might have

passed for a scorpion, but this lunging monster was six feet long without counting the length of the tail arced back across its body. Flashing legs, flashing body armor, and the fluid-jewelled sting that winked as Lorne's finger twitched in its killer's reflex—

Lorne's body screamed at the recoil of the heavy charge. The creature spun as if kicked in mid-air, smashing into the floor a yard from Ben instead of on top of the policeman. The revolver blasted, a huge yellow bottle-shape flaring from the muzzle. The bullet ripped away a window shutter because a six-inch pincer had locked Ben's wrist. The creature reared onto the back two pairs of its eight jointed legs. Lorne stepped sideways for a clear shot, the slide of his weapon slick-snacking another round into the chamber. On the creature's white belly was a smeared, multibrancate star—the load of buckshot had ricocheted off, leaving a trail like wax on glass.

Ben clubbed his flashlight. It cracked harmlessly between the glowing eyes and sprang from his hand. The other claw flashed to Ben's face and trapped it, not crushingly but hard enough to immobilize and start blood-trails down both cheeks. The blades of the pincer ran from nose to hairline on each side.

Lorne thrust his shotgun over Ben's right shoulder and fired point blank. The creature rocked back, jerking a scream from the policeman as the claws tightened. The lead struck the huge left eye and splashed away, dulling the opal shine. The flashlight still glaring from the floor behind the creature silhouetted its sectioned tail as it arched above the policeman's head. The armed tip plunged into the base of his neck. Ben stiffened.

Lorne shouted and emptied his shotgun. The second dense red bloom caught like a strobe light the dotted line of blood droplets joining Ben's neck to the withdrawn injector. A claw seized Lorne's waist in the rolling echo of the shotgun blasts. His gunbutt cracked on the creature's armor, steel sparking as it slid off. The extending pincer brushed the shotgun aside and clamped over Lorne's face, half-shielding from him the sight of the rising sting.

Then it smashed on Lorne's neck brace, and darkness exploded over him in a flare of coruscant pain.

The oozing ruin of Mrs. Purefoy's face stared at Lorne through its remaining eye when he awoke. Everything swam in blue darkness except for one bright blur. He blinked and the blur suddenly resolved into a street-light glaring up through a shattered board. Lorne's lungs burned and his stiffness seemed more than even unconsciousness and the pain skidding through his nerve paths could explain. He moved his arm and something clung to its surface; the world quivered.

Lorne was hanging from the roof of the church in a thin, transparent sheath. Mrs. Purefoy was a yard away, multiple wrappings shrouding her corpse more completely. With a strength not far from panic, Lorne forced his right fist into the bubble around him. The material, extruded in broad swathes by the creature rather than as a loom of threads, sagged but did not tear. The clear azure turned milky under stress and sucked in around Lorne's wrist.

He withdrew his hand. The membrane passed some oxygen but not enough for an active man. Lorne's hands patted the outside of his pockets finding, as he had expected, nothing with a sharp edge. He had not recently bitten off his thumbnails. Thrusting against the fire in his chest, he brought his left hand in front of his body. With a fold of the cocoon between each thumb and index finger, he thrust his hands apart. A rip started in the white opacity beneath his right thumb. Air, clean and cool, jetted in.

"Oh, Jesus," Lorne muttered, even the pain in his body forgotten as he widened the tear upwards to his face. The cocoon was bobbing on a short lead, rotating as the rip changed its balance. Lorne could see that he had become ninth in the line of hanging bodies, saved from their paralysis by the chance of his neck brace. Ben, his face blurred by the membrane holding him next to Lorne, had been less fortunate.

Ten yards from where Lorne hung and twenty feet below the roof beam, the baize curtain of the pipe loft twitched. Lorne froze in fearful immobility.

The creature had been able to leap the width of a street carrying the weight of an adult; its strength must be as awesome as was the rigidity of its armor. Whether or not it could drive its sting through Lorne's brace, it could assuredly rip him to collops if it realized he was awake.

The curtain moved again, the narrow ivory tip of a pincer lifting it slightly. The creature was watching Lorne.

Ben carried three armor-piercing rounds in his .357 magnum for punching through car doors. Lorne tried to remember whether the revolver had remained in Ben's hand as he fell. There was no image of that in Lorne's mind, only the torch-like muzzle blasts of his own shotgun. Slim as it was, his only hope was that the jacketed bullets would penetrate the creature's exoskeleton though the soft buckshot had not.

Lorne twisted his upper torso out of the hole for a closer look at Ben, making his own cocoon rock angrily. The baize lifted further. The streetlight lay across it in a pale band. Why didn't the creature scuttle out to finish the business?

Brief motion waked a flash of scintillant color from the pipe loft. The curtain flapped closed as if a volley of shots had ripped through it. Lorne recognized the reflex: the panic of a spider when a stick thrusts through its web. Not an object, though; the light itself, weak as it was, had not stopped it when necessity drove, but the monster must have felt pain at human levels of illumination. Its eyes were adapted to starlight or the glow of a sun immeasurably fainter than that of Earth.

"Where did you come from, you bastard?" Lorne whispered.

Light. It gave him an idea and he fumbled out his butane lighter, adjusting it to a maximum flame. The sheathes were relatively thin over the victims' faces to aid transpiration. At the waist, though, where a bulge showed Ben's arm locked to his torso, the membrane was thick enough to be opaque in the dim light. Lorne bent dangerously over, cursing the stiffness of his neck brace. Holding the inch-high jet close, he tried to peer through Ben's cocoon. Unexpectedly the fabric gave a little and Lorne bobbed forward, bringing the flame in contact with the material sheathing Ben.

The membrane sputtered, kissing Lorne's hand painfully. He jerked back and the lighter flicked away. It dropped, cold and silent until it cracked on the floor forty feet below. Despite the pattern of light over it, the curtain to the loft was shifting again. Lorne cursed in terror.

A line of green fire sizzled up the side of Ben's cocoon from the point at which the flame had touched it. The material across his face flared. The policeman gave no sign of feeling his skin curl away. The revolver in his hand winked green.

Lorne screamed. His own flexible prison lurched and sagged like heated polyethylene. Ben was wrapped in a cancerous hell that roared and heaved against the roof-beams as a live thing. Green tongues licked yellow-orange flames from the dry wood as well. Lorne's cocoon and that to the other side of Ben were deforming in the furnace heat. Another lurch and Lorne had slipped twenty feet, still gripped around the waist in a sack of blue membrane. He was gyrating like a top. The loft curtain had twitched higher each time it spun past his vision.

The bottom of Ben's cocoon burned away and he plunged past Lorne, face upward and still afire. Bone crunched as he hit. The body rebounded a few inches to fall again on its face. The roar of the flames muffled Lorne's wail of rage. His own elongated capsule began to flow. Flames grasped at Lorne's support. Before they could touch the sheathing, the membrane pulled a last few inches and snapped like an overstretched rubber band. The impact of the floor smashed Lorne's jaw against his neck brace, grinding each tortured vertebra against the next. He did not lose consciousness, but the shock paralyzed him momentarily as thoroughly as the creature's sting could have done.

Bathed in green light and the orange of the blazing roof panels, the scorpion thing thrust its thorax into the nave. Its walking legs gripped the flat surface, dimpling the plaster. The creature turned upward towards the fire, three more cocoons alight and their hungry flames lapping across the beams. Then, parti-colored by the illumination, its legs shifted and the opal eyes trained on Lorne. The light must be torture to it, muffling in indecision its responses, but it was about to act.

A small form wrapped in a flaming shroud dropped to thump the floor beside Lorne. His arms would move again. He used them to strip the remaining sheathing from his legs. It clung as the heat of the burning corpse began to melt the material. Something writhed from a crackling tumor on the child's neck. The thing was finger-long and seemed to paw the air with a score of tiny legs; its opalescent eyes proved its parentage. The creature brought more than paralysis to its victims: it was a gravid female.

Green flame touched the larva. It burst in a pustulant smear.

The adult went mad. Its legs shot it almost the length of the nave to rebound from a sidewall in a cloud of plaster. The creature's horizontally-flattened tail ruddered it instinctively short of the fire as it leapt upward to the roof peak. It clung there in pale horror against the wood, eyes on the advancing flames. Three more bodies fell, splashing like ginkgo fruits.

Lorne staggered upright. The fire hammered down at him without bringing pain. His body had no feeling whatever. Ben's hair had burned. His neck and scalp were black where skin remained, red where it had cracked open to the muscle beneath. The marbled background showed clearly the tiny, pallid hatchling trying to twist across it.

Lorne's toe brushed the larva onto the floor. His boot heel struck it, struck again and twisted. Purulent ichor spurted between the leather and the boards. Lorne knelt. In one motion he swung Ben across his shoulders and stood, just as he had after their helicopter had nosed into the trees and exploded. Logic had been burned out of Lorne's mind, leaving only a memory of friendship. He did not look up. As his mechanical steps took him and his burden through the door they had entered, a shadow wavered across them. The creature had sprung back into the loft.

Lorne stumbled to his knees in the parking lot. The church had been rotten and dry. Orange flames fluffed through the roof in several places, thrusting corkscrews of sparks into the night sky. Twelve feet of roof slates thundered into the nave. Flame spewed up like a secondary explosion. There were sirens in the night.

Without warning, the east façade of the tower collapsed into the parking lot. Head-sized chunks of Tennessee-stone smashed at the patrol car, one of them missing Lorne by inches. He looked up, blank-eyed, his hands lightly touching the corpse of his friend. Of its own volition, the right hand traced down Ben's shoulder to the raw flesh of his elbow. The tower stairs spiralled out of the dust and rubble, laid bare to the steel framework when the wall fell. On the sagging floor of the pipe loft rested a machine like no other thing on Earth, and the creature was inside it. Tubes of silvery metal rose cradleform from a base of similar metal. The interstices were not filled with anything material, but the atmosphere seemed to shiver, blurring the creature's outline.

And Lorne's hand was unwrapping Ben's stiff fingers from the grips of his revolver.

Lorne stood again, his left hand locking his right on the butt of the big magnum. He was familiar with the weapon: it was the one Ben had carried in Nam, the same tool he had used for five of his thirteen kills. It would kill again tonight.

Even in the soaring holocaust the sharp crack of Lorne's shot was audible. Lorne's forearms rocked up as a unit with the recoiling handgun. The creature lurched sideways to touch the shimmering construct around it. A red surface discharge rippled across the exoskeleton from the point of contact. Lorne fired again. He could see the armor dull at his point of aim in the center of the thorax. Again the creature jumped. Neither bullet had penetrated, but the splashing lead of the second cut an upright from the machine. The creature spun, extending previously-unglimpsed tendrils from the region of its mouth parts. They flickered over a control plate in the base. Machinery chimed in response.

The shivering quickened. The machine itself and the thing it enclosed seemed to fade. Lorne thumb-cocked the magnum, lowered the red vertical of the front sight until it was even with the rear notch; the creature was a white blur beyond them. The gun bucked back hard when he squeezed; the muzzle blast was sharper, flatter, than before. The first of the armor-piercing bullets hit the creature between the paired tendrils. The exoskeleton surrounding them shattered like safety glass struck by a brick.

The creature straightened in silent agony, rising onto its hind legs with its tail lying rigidly against its back. Its ovipositor was fully extended, thumb-thick and six inches long.

"Was it fun to kill them, bug?" Lorne screamed. "Was it as much fun as this is?" His fourth shot slammed, dimpling a belly plate which then burst outward in an ugly gush of fluids. The creature's members clamped tightly about its spasming thorax. The tail lashed the uprights in red spurts. The machine was fading and the torn paneling of the loft was beginning to show through the dying creature's body.

There was one shot left in the cylinder and Lorne steadied his sights on the control plate. He had already begun taking up the last pressure when he stopped and lowered the muzzle. No, let it go home, whatever place or time that might be. Let its fellows see that Earth was not their hunting ground alone. And if they came back anyway—*if they only would*!

There was a flash as penetrating as the first microsecond of a nuclear blast. The implosion dragged Lorne off his feet and sucked in the flames so suddenly that all sound seemed frozen. Then both sidewalls collapsed into the nave and the ruins of the tower twisted down on top of them. In the last instant, the pipe loft was empty of all but memory.

A fire truck picked its way through the rubble in the parking lot. Its headlights flooded across the figure of a sandy-haired man wearing scorched clothing and a neck brace. He was kneeling beside a body, and the tears were bright on his face.

Have You Missed?

DRAKE, DAVID
At Any Price
Hammer's Slammers are back—and Baen Books has them!
Now the 23rd-century armored division faces its deadliest
enemies ever: aliens who *teleport* into combat.
55978-8 $3.50

DRAKE, DAVID
Hammer's Slammers
A special *expanded* edition of the book that began the
legend of Colonel Alois Hammer. Now the toughest, mean-
est mercs who ever killed for a dollar or wrecked a world
for pay have come home—to Baen Books—and they've
brought a secret weapon: "The Tank Lords," a brand-new
short novel, included in this special Baen edition of *Hammer's Slammers*.
65632-5 $3.50

DRAKE, DAVID
Lacey and His Friends
In Jed Lacey's time the United States computers scan
every citizen, every hour of the day. When crime is detected, it's Lacey's turn. There are a few things worse than
having him come after you, but they're not survivable
either. But things aren't really that bad—not for Lacey and
his friends. By the author of *Hammer's Slammers* and *At
Any Price*.
65593-0 $3.50

**CARD, ORSON SCOTT; DRAKE, DAVID;
& BUJOLD, LOIS MCMASTER**
(edited by Elizabeth Mitchell)
Free Lancers (Alien Stars, Vol. IV)
Three short novels about mercenary soldiers—never be-
fore in print! Card's hero leads a ragtag group of scientific
refugees to sanctuary in Utah; Drake contributes a new
"Hammer's Slammers" story; Bujold tells a new tale of
Miles Vorkosigan, hero of *The Warrior's Apprentice*.
65352-0 $2.95

DRAKE, DAVID
Birds of Prey

The time: 262 A.D. The place: Imperial Rome. There had never been a greater empire, but now it is dying. Everywhere its armies are in retreat, and what had been civilization seethes with riots and bizarre cults. Against the imminent fall of the Long Night stands Aulus Perennius, an Imperial secret agent as tough and ruthless as the age in which he lives. But he stands alone—until a traveller from Earth's far future recruits him for a mission so strange it cannot be disclosed.

> 55912-5 (trade paper) $7.95
> 55909-5 (hardcover) $14.95

DRAKE, DAVID
Ranks of Bronze

Disguised alien traders bought captured Roman soldiers on the slave market because they needed troops who could win battles without high-tech weaponry. The leigionaires provided victories, smashing barbarian armies with the swords, javelins, and discipline that had won a world. But the worlds on which they now fought were strange ones, and the spoils of victory did not include freedom. If the legionaires went home, it would be through the use of the beam weapons and force screens of their ruthless alien owners. It's been 2000 years—and now they want to go home.
> 65568-X $3.50

DRAKE, DAVID, & WAGNER, KARL EDWARD
Killer

Vonones and Lycon capture wild animals to sell for bloodsport in ancient Rome. A vicious animal sold to them by a trader turns out to be more than they bargained for—it is the sole survivor of the crash of an alien spacecraft. Possessed of intelligence nearly human, it has two goals in life: to breed and to kill.

> 55931-1 $2.95

DAVID DRAKE

"Drake has distinguished himself as the master of the mercenary sf novel."—**Rave Reviews**

WILL *YOU* SURVIVE?

In addition to Dean Ing's powerful science fiction novels—*Systemic Shock, Wild Country, Blood of Eagles* and others—he has written cogently and inventively about the art of survival. **The Chernobyl Syndrome** is the result of his research into life after a possible nuclear exchange . . . because as our civilization gets bigger and better, we become more and more dependent on its products. What would *you* do if the machine stops—or blows up?

Some of the topics Dean Ing covers:
* How to *make* a getaway airplane
* Honing your "crisis skills"
* Fleeing the firestorm: escape tactics for city-dwellers
* How to build a homemade fallout meter
* Civil defense, American style
* "Microfarming"—survival in five acres
 And much, much more.

Also by Dean Ing, available through Baen Books:

ANASAZI
Why did the long-vanished Anasazi Indians retreat from their homes and gardens on the green mesa top to precarious cliffside cities? Were they afraid of someone—or something? "There's no evidence of warfare in the ruins of their earlier homes . . . but maybe the marauders they feared didn't wage war in the usual way," says Dean Ing. *Anasazi* postulates a race of alien beings who needed human bodies in order to survive on Earth—a race of aliens that *still* exists.

FIREFIGHT 2000
How do you integrate armies supplied with bayonets and ballistic missiles; citizens enjoying Volkswagens and Ferraris; cities drawing power from windmills and nuclear powerplants? Ing takes a look at these dichotomies, and more. This collection of fact and fiction serves as a metaphor for tomorrow: covering terror and hope, right guesses and wrong, high tech and thatched cottages.
